Merely Magic

PATRICIA RICE

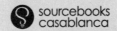

Published by Sourcebooks Casablanca, an imprint of Sourcebooks, Inc.
P.O. Box 4410, Naperville, Illinois 60567–4410
(630) 961–3900
FAX: (630) 961–2168
www.sourcebooks.com

Originally published in 2000 by Dutton Signet.

Library of Congress Cataloging-in-Publication Data

Rice, Patricia
  Merely magic / by Patricia Rice.
      p. cm.
  1. Witches--Fiction. 2. Northumberland (England)--Fiction. I. Title.
  PS3568.I2925M47 2011
  813'.54--dc22

                         2010043650

              Printed and bound in Canada.
              WC 10 9 8 7 6 5 4 3 2 1

*To Robin, who had the faith and courage
that I lacked, and the supreme self-confidence
to act on both.*

Prologue

"MAMA DIED."

"Because she did not listen to me, love." Smelling of rich evergreen and roses, the old woman pulled her ten-year-old granddaughter into her plump arms.

"Papa doesn't want me." Ninian tried not to snivel as she curled into the first welcoming embrace she could remember receiving.

"Because you are a Malcolm, and men fear what they do not understand. You'll see when you are older."

"Papa says I am a witch, Grandmama. I'm not a witch, am I?"

"You're a Malcolm, dear, and that's nearly the same. Witches can accomplish great good if they listen to their elders and do as they're told." The old woman set her away and straightened Ninian's shoulders. "Sit up here beside me, and I'll read you a story." She patted an ancient leather-bound book in her lap.

"My mama didn't want me to be a witch," Ninian whispered, suddenly frightened as she climbed onto the chair and sensed her grandmother's determination.

"Your mama denied what she was, love, and she died of it. Never deny who you are, and you'll live a long and happy life."

"Who I am?" she inquired, snuggling into her grandmother's powdery embrace, momentarily reassured by her promises.

"A Malcolm, my dear," the old lady repeated. "Be proud and grateful for your heritage. We can have anything we want, if we want it hard enough. We must just never deny who we are, as the story tells us. An Ives once tried to force his Malcolm lady to deny her heritage, and it nearly destroyed the village."

Ninian loved stories. Happy, she settled down to listen.

One

Northumberland, 1750

ALONE ON THE EDGE OF THE CLEARING, NINIAN MALCOLM Siddons sat on an overturned stone from the circle that had once dominated this hill and contemplated the bonfire and dancing couples laughing below. It was a very lonely business being a Malcolm. Tonight, she'd much rather dance and sing and shout for joy in the firelight like everyone else.

She wanted to scream and yell, "I'm here! Here! It's just me!"

But there was danger in achieving that kind of attention. She could not indulge her volatile nature and throw tantrums at the unfairness of life; it would only enhance the village's fear of her. As her grandmother had taught her, she must remember who she was, what she was, and be proud of it. She had a gift and a talent no other had been granted, and she must use them wisely. Making the villagers fear her was not wise.

She sighed and rolled her eyes in exasperation. "Gifts" and "talents" weren't quite as valuable or exciting as the magic in fairy tales. If only she possessed *real* magic, she could summon a lover to dance with her. She smiled as the fantasy formed in her mind. What kind of lover would she summon? Dark and passionate? Fair and loving? One who would give her fat, jolly babies?

One who would dance with her.

She'd never even considered sharing her life with anyone

until Granny died last winter. Given her circumstances, it didn't pay to consider it now. She must dedicate her life to the people of Wystan just as Granny had done—or deny her heritage and forfeit everything as her mother had.

The bonfire leapt higher into the starry May night as someone added new brush to the flames. With the aid of the moon above, the glade sparkled with the silvery glow of a thousand candles, filling the night with enchantment.

Beltane was a night to celebrate the earth's richness, to throw off the dark of winter's cold. She should exult in the promise of spring, not fret over what she could never have. It was time to shrug off her grief over her grandmother's death and go on with the business of living.

If only she knew precisely what that was. Tending her herbs, healing the sick, and delivering babes did not hold quite the promise she'd hoped now that she faced those tasks alone.

Eagerly, she sat up as an excess of hilarity and high spirits buffeted her with the approach of the dancers.

"Have you heard? Lord Ives is repairing the castle!" Tom, the wheelmaker's son, crowed as he and several others gathered to catch their breaths.

"We'll all be rich!" Alice, a farmer's daughter, expressed her excitement with glee.

"This time next year, we'll have fat pigs in our pens and geese on our tables." Son of a sheep farmer, Nate passed his cup of ale to the next person.

The return of an Ives to Wystan after all these years worried Ninian. She'd thought the legend in her grandmother's storybook little more than a fairy tale and had never feared it, until now, with the recent return of the mysterious nobleman.

According to the story, long, long ago, Ives and Malcolms had been the nobility of this land, building castles and protecting their people. But according to the legend, disaster destroyed their happy land upon the marriage of an Ives lord and a Malcolm lady. Prosperity had fled, the Ives lords moved away, and only Malcolms remained to care for the people as best as they could. As others left to seek riches elsewhere, the village shrank, and there was no need for more than one

Malcolm here. So even the Malcolms left. Ninian's aunts had followed their aristocratic husbands and moved on to better things. Ninian's particular gift fared better in the isolation of the village, so she had chosen to stay behind.

Why had a legend walked out of her storybook as soon as her grandmother died? And if this Lord Ives could make the village wealthy, would they need Ninian at all? Or would he bring the tragedy the storybook predicted?

Clamping down a frisson of fear and blocking out such silly superstition, Ninian watched the unaccompanied bachelors expectantly as the musicians struck up a new song.

Nate grabbed his companion's hand, and Gertrude giggled and ran off with him to join the dancers. As the other young men chose partners and laughing couples dashed toward the revelry, leaving Ninian behind—again—her dimples disappeared and her shoulders sagged with the weight of loneliness.

It shouldn't matter that they didn't ask her to dance. They were simple, uneducated village boys, and she was a Malcolm. Malcolms were not only witches, but nobility, educated far beyond the means of simple farmers. She understood. She really did. But the music was so lively and the moon so beautiful...

An old lady laughed as Gertrude slapped Nate's face and flounced off. "That one has aught but one thing on his mind," the old one said to her companion.

All the village girls knew about Nate's hot hands and sweet words. Still, even well plied with ale, he danced a fair step, and Ninian wouldn't have minded one whirl about the fire. Just one.

It wasn't as if she expected love.

❧

A pagan fertility rite, how appropriate.

Standing in the deepest shadows of the forest's edge, Drogo Ives, Earl of Ives and Wystan, crossed his arms and watched as the bonfire in the clearing blazed skyward. The hypnotic notes of flute and fiddle carried on the wind along with the sounds of laughter.

He'd come to this deserted outpost of northern England in hopes of studying the stars, not human behavior. Heaven only knew, he had sufficient specimens for study in London should he wish to take up the science of people, but he preferred the distance and mathematical precision of stars. At least stars were predictable.

The bonfire had aroused his curiosity when he'd seen it from his windows. He'd spent a long and grueling day over the estate accounts, correspondence, and decisions regarding his brothers' latest escapades, and inexplicably, he'd been drawn to the sight of the leaping flames.

A lone figure lurking in the half shadow between him and the convivial couples in the clearing captured his curiosity. He might not be from these parts, but he had sufficient knowledge of folklore to recognize the village's celebration of Beltane. As spring fertility rites went, this one was fairly tame. He even recognized the primitive urge within himself to procreate. The warmth of a new May eve, the hum of nature's nocturnal creatures seeking mates, the gravid fowls and burgeoning plant life of spring stirred even the most stoic of mankind into desiring to create replicas of themselves within a woman's womb.

Drogo clanged a steel door shut on that thought as he watched the solitary figure in the clearing.

Her pale hair glimmered with moonlight, curling in wild ringlets over her shoulders and halfway down her back, uncovered by cap or cloth. He had caught a glimpse of her face earlier as she exchanged words with some of the couples. She had a round face of ivory purity with mysterious light-colored eyes he could barely discern in the silver swath of moonlight.

And she had a figure men would kill for. He surveyed her ample bosom and trim waist with jaundiced gaze. Country beautiful, built for breeding. Why then was she not a part of one of the amorous couples cavorting around the fire? She should have men dancing attendance at her fingertips.

He had no intention of becoming so involved in village affairs that he might ask. He craved a solitude he couldn't achieve in London, and he didn't need another woman mucking up his life or his mind. He'd do better to return to his studies in the tower or to the tedious stacks of frantic messages from London.

The silver goddess turned just enough for him to perceive the yearning in her expression, a yearning that so matched his own, the loneliness of it nearly crippled him.

He *wouldn't* feel this way. He had no right. He had far more on his table than he could possibly consume as it was. Asking for the delicacy that wasn't his was obnoxious selfishness.

As if sensing his tumult, the moon maiden turned and gazed into the forest where he stood. His sudden fierce arousal at the sight of her starlit features decided the matter. He would not become his father, dancing heedlessly to temptation's call, following his cock like a tail.

Let her find another partner for this night of amour. He had nothing to offer.

∞

Thinking she saw a shadow slip into the darkness, Ninian shivered. Perhaps Satan walked on a night like this, as her grandmother warned, for only a soulless devil could escape her notice. Her gift for sensing human emotion might not include understanding what she felt, but it gave her the ability to discern someone's presence.

Granny had taught her how to deal with external devils, like dangerous men. Ninian wished she'd taught her how to deal with internal devils, like doubt and loneliness. Granny had thought everything easily cured by herbs and amulets, but as far as Ninian was concerned, amulets couldn't cure anything. Still, she would respect her grandmother's memory and keep an open mind. Granny had known a great deal more than Ninian could ever hope to learn.

The music changed, and laughing couples drifted from the fire. Instead of leaving as she ought, she lingered, hoping against foolish hope that at least one of the men would dare ask her to dance, now that they had more ale in them. She tried her best to smile naively as the other maids did.

"They say the earl has three wives." Nate laughed as he approached, his arm once more wrapped firmly around Gertrude's shoulders.

"They say all Ives are devils who only walk the night." Tom grinned as Alice shrieked in horror and cuddled closer under his arm.

Perhaps Ninian wasn't the only one who'd noticed a presence at the forest's edge. She glanced over her shoulder again, but the shadow had disappeared.

"You know what they say happened the last time an Ives walked this land," Nate whispered in the ominous tone of a man relating a ghost story. "He mated with a witch, and the entire valley flooded."

All heads turned in Ninian's direction.

Ninian's stomach soured as the attention. No matter how hard she tried to be one of them, the curse of her heritage always erected barriers. She didn't know why she had joined them tonight, except that sometimes, the cottage echoed with loneliness.

Harry, the shoemaker, shifted attention back to himself. "Since this Ives already has three wives, he's not likely to need more, is he?"

The lads guffawed. The women tittered.

Grateful for Harry's diversion, Ninian clung to her dimpled smile and watched the dancing as the conversation swirled on without her.

Even Harry, who'd defended her verbally since she'd set his broken finger, would never do more than nod his head in her direction. It would take a brave man, indeed, to court a Malcolm witch. She should be used to rejection by now.

The villagers' superstitions about her origins didn't cause her undue concern. England hadn't burned a witch in—oh, a hundred years or more. They hadn't hanged one in twenty or thirty. They had more civilized methods of destroying witches these days. A wrong word or look, and she'd see nothing but their cold backs. And with the poor harvest of these last years and after the bad winter—she couldn't blame them. Unlike Granny, she couldn't convince people to do what was good for them with amulets and promises. She could only heal the sick with her knowledge of herbs. Her gift for empathy was singularly useless and more nuisance than help.

She wished things could be different. Just once, she would like someone to accept her as she was, to hold her close and dance with her in the firelight, like normal people.

And she *was* normal, she told herself fiercely. She just knew a little more about herbs than most, had an unpredictable ability to sense what others felt, and the intelligence to apply both. She wasn't a witch. She was a Malcolm.

Yet in the minds of many, there was no difference.

With a wistful sigh, Ninian drifted from the glade into the forest, away from the celebrations, away from the sight of the others slipping pair by pair into the shadows of the grass and trees, there to create the bumper crop of babies she would deliver come winter. Babies she would never have. The ache at that thought was best excised with work.

Strolling among the trees, putting the bonfire and the amorous crowd far behind, Ninian sought the babbling burn where the herb she required grew. In the full light of the moon, the agrimony should contain all the power she needed for the morrow's work. She wished the stream ran through her grandmother's property so she needn't stray so far to obtain it, but no one had ever complained of her trespass on Ives' land. Of course, until recently, there had been none to do the complaining.

Lord Ives had certainly stirred a controversy by returning after generations of neglect, but Ninian didn't indulge in gossip. Surely, no man could legally have three wives. She knew enough of human temperament to doubt even his ability to have three mistresses under one roof, although contemplating the nature of such a man aroused dangerous fantasies.

Deliberately turning her thoughts to the herb and the best means of persuading Mary's little boy to drink an infusion of it to soothe his aching throat, Ninian didn't catch the presence following her until it was too late to hide.

She knew at once who it was and why. Nate. Even as she caught the strength of his arrogance, coupled with his muddled anger and a whiff of fear, he staggered into view from around a bend in the road.

Caught in the open with nowhere to run, she donned her best defense, the one she used to make children giggle. Blinking innocently, she wrapped a curl around her finger. Her dimpled features, blonde ringlets, and blue eyes could deceive any man into doubting legends. Weren't all witches dark and dangerous? "Why Nate, whatever are you doing here? Gertrude will be most disappointed without your company."

"Gertrude went off with that oaf, Harry. You're much prettier than she is. You shouldn't have left so soon." He sidled closer, eyeing her bosom.

She could smell the ale on him and sensed his reckless determination. Despite her short stature, Ninian knew she was strong, but Nate not only stood taller, he outweighed her by several stone.

"Why, Nate, how thoughtful of you to see me home," she replied airily, "but you needn't, really. Go back to the fun."

"Ives land is the long way around to your cottage," Nate said with suspicion.

"Oh, but I so wanted the watercress in the burn!" Ninian slipped away as he reached for her. If she wasn't good enough to dance with in front of one and all, she certainly didn't intend to dally with him in private. Lonely she might be, but crazy she was not. "I'll be fine. Do go."

"You know there's no other man in the village for you but me." He tried a cajoling tone as he stepped toward her. "My father has the most sheep and the most land. I'm strong. I can do the work of three men."

Ninian knew the kind of "work" he had in mind and suppressed a wry grimace at his vanity. "Why, Nate! You flatter me." She couldn't run fast enough to elude him, but she had five times the wit he possessed, especially when he was muddled with drink.

"I'll show you how good I can be." Apparently encouraged by her lack of coyness and a good dose of grog, Nate threw aside his fears and grabbed for her.

Prepared, Ninian sidestepped, thrust out her ill-shod foot,

and let him trip over it. In his alcohol-induced haze, he slipped in the mud, threw his arms up to steady himself, and splatted nicely in the icy stream. That should drown his over-heated ardor.

With behavior like this, Ninian supposed she deserved the epithets he spewed as he sat up, gasping.

"I'll get you for this, witch!" he howled, shaking his fist at her while water rivulets trickled down his forehead.

Well, so much for warding off ill will. She might as well throw sticks and stones while she was at it. "If I were truly witch, I'd rot your balls, you silly fool!" she shouted back. Granny would not have been happy with her. After all these years of taking the safe and narrow path, she was throwing it all away in a fit of spite. She knew better.

Cursing, Nate righted himself on the slippery rocks, splashed to his feet, and lunged for the bank and Ninian. Well, perhaps she hadn't completely forfeited her innocuous facade. He didn't fear her enough to run.

As he grabbed for her, a cool voice intruded from the dark-ness of the trees.

"Is there some problem?"

Startled by a voice from nowhere, Nate slid back down the bank and hit the water again. In the act of retreat, Ninian froze.

She hadn't *felt* any presence. How could that be? No one *ever* walked up on her like that without her extra sense picking up some warning. Wide-eyed, she swerved to stare in the direction from which the voice emerged.

Swiping water from his eyes, Nate shakily climbed to his feet again. "Who's out there?" he demanded.

Ninian suspected he was shivering with more than cold. Despite his boasts, Nate possessed the same ignorant super-stitions as most of the villagers. Right now, at the sound of that eerie disembodied voice, Ninian understood his fear of the unknown.

"We are having a disagreement over my ability to see myself home," she replied boldly, willing the stranger to show himself. The absence of any human emotion from the direction of the voice scared her as much as the absence of a physical presence.

To her relief, a solid shadow separated from the trees. Male, taller than Nate, with wide shoulders and a disturbingly graceful physique, the mysterious intruder hid his features by remaining out of the moon's light. "You're trespassing," he stated with the same lack of inflection as when he'd first spoken.

"Lord Ives!" Nate hastily backed out of the burn, scrambling up the bank on the far side. He cast Ninian a terrified glance. "He *is* the devil, and you're in league with him!"

Sighing at this inevitable conclusion, Ninian raised her arms, waved the ruffles of her long sleeves, and threw an eerie "Boo!" in Nate's direction. She laughed as Nate fled, screaming, into the forest.

"I'm glad that amused you," Lord Ives said from behind her, with what might have been a hint of dryness. "Would you care to explain what it meant?"

Of course, his lordship was new to the area. He didn't know the local folklore about Malcolm witches and Ives devils. Turning to judge his reaction, she had to look up much farther than she liked. Through slivers of moonlight, his silhouette was breathtakingly impressive and much too close.

Her grandmother had taught her about the temptations of dark forces to which witches were drawn. She should be wary.

"Welcome to Wystan, my lord." She curtsied as she'd been taught long ago. Straightening, she added wickedly, "I'm Ninian Malcolm Siddons, resident witch." Her grandmother had also sworn an imp lived inside her instead of sorcery.

Instead of laughing or stepping away in fear as would any normal man, Lord Ives cocked his head with interest. "Ninian? A saint's name?"

Not only fearless, but with a knowledge of ancient history. Interesting. Grandmother had said men didn't take well to learning. "My mother had a strange sense of humor," she admitted. How odd that he queried her name, but not her reputation.

"I see." The hint of dryness disappeared into cool tones again. "I don't think it safe for a young woman in these woods at night. I'll escort you home."

"Please pardon my trespass, my lord," she said belatedly, "but there are herbs I need along this stream. Do you mind?"

"Would it matter if I said 'yes'?"

Observant, also. She shook her head. "I might be very sorry to go against your wishes, but I would not leave young Matthew with a sore throat."

"Quite." He seemed to withdraw within himself, or perhaps the moon shifted behind a cloud. "Then let us be on with it. I take it you are an herbalist and not a witch?"

"I see you are a natural philosopher," she commented evasively as she scanned the burnside where the agrimony grew. She didn't care what he believed, and she refused to succumb to the temptation of too much Beltane fantasy.

Many men were tall and physically graceful, with voices that could command attention with just a whisper. Granny had told her the devil possessed such charms, while promising much and producing evil. If she pretended the earl was Satan, she could safely ignore the unusual pattering of her heart at his proximity. Just because she had wished for a lover didn't mean she would fall for the charms of any man who came along—and certainly not an Ives.

Frowning, she crouched down to better study the streambed. Perhaps the darkness concealed what she knew to be there.

He must have heard her muttered curse of frustration. He stepped closer, his long boot-clad legs halting near her hand. "What is it?"

"It's gone. It used to grow thick…" She pushed past the undergrowth, searching closer to the water. "The watercress is gone too, but that could be…" She prodded the moist soil at the edge with a stick. "Nothing kills violets," she muttered in puzzlement. "The sweet rushes are dead!" she exclaimed a moment later. "That's not possible!"

He crouched beside her and prodded his walking stick along the embankment. "I don't see much of anything but rocks. Are you sure you have the right place?"

The fine hairs on the back of her neck rose as his hand brushed near hers, but faced with a disaster of this proportion, she had no patience with her odd reaction. The burn provided a goodly portion of her remedies. If she couldn't heal, she had no place here at all. A cold chill iced her blood. Surely the legend of Malcolm and Ives bringing disaster couldn't already be coming true. Maybe it was Ives men alone who caused it.

Refusing to panic, she pushed farther upstream. "I *know* this is right," she muttered, mostly to herself. She wasn't accustomed to anyone accompanying her, and the black void that was her companion registered very strangely, enabling her to ignore him on a comfortable level. "Here's the path I made. This is where I added ashes and manure to sweeten the soil. I *know*…" She stopped and broke a branch of willow hanging over the embankment. "Dead," she whispered as the branch snapped.

"Trees die," he said from behind her. "In this cold damp, it's a wonder they live."

"No. No, it's not right…" Stepping carefully through the darkness, she broke a branch here, crouched to examine a tree root there. "I'll have to come back in daylight, follow the stream…" But fear licked along her veins. Without her remedies, she was less than nothing. She must discover—

"You'll do no such thing," he informed her. "In fact, it's time I saw you home."

Muttering to herself, she tucked the dried leaves and branches she'd gathered into her apron pocket and strode back to the path. According to her grandmother, in the scheme of things, men had only one purpose—the same services as the devil offered Eve. But the earl owned this property, and she had to at least pretend to listen to him.

Striding down the path, analyzing all the reasons the plants might have died, refusing to believe all was lost, Ninian jumped as strong fingers caught her elbow.

"You will break a leg walking so heedlessly."

Prickles crept along her skin where his fingers pressed her through her shift sleeve. The sensation unnerved her. Had her idle wishes for a lover summoned this man? She should have paid heed when Granny warned her about wishing for what she could not have, especially on a night of power, like Beltane.

"Witches see in the dark," she said blithely, giving his grasp a not-too-subtle tug.

The long fingers only clenched her tighter. "Unlike that lout, I'm not inclined to superstition and I mean you no harm. I will see you safely home."

Wisely, Ninian surrendered the fight, lest he grasp her tighter still. His touch unsettled her as much as his lack of emotional presence. Never had her awareness been centered only on the physical. And never had the physical been so deeply felt as with this man. She could not sense if he lied or laughed at her, but perversely, she trusted what he said. A wealthy aristocrat would have no interest in a village wench, or if he did, he would have offered her coin by now.

"Have you studied natural philosophy, my lord?" She would make the best of this enforced detour by picking his brain. Perhaps he would have a suggestion to chase away her fear about the absence of growth along the burn.

He hesitated before answering. "Somewhat," he reluctantly agreed.

"Do you know aught of the ways of water?"

"It's wet."

This time, she was certain she heard the dryness of his tone. He thought her a lackwit. So be it. She spoke aloud to hold back the uneasy awareness encompassing them.

"I know more of plants than water," she admitted. "I wonder if it's possible for water to become bad for plants as soil does when it goes sour."

Silence. Ninian fumed at this lack of response. She really needed someone who could discuss these things with her. Without Granny, she had no one with her level of knowledge.

"I have never noticed a stream without plant life at this time of year," he said reflectively.

She sighed in relief. "Not even after an unusually harsh winter?"

Again, the long thoughtful silence before his deep voice broke the night. "I am not overly familiar with these climes, but even in the Highlands, I have seen plant life along streams in May."

"That's what I thought." Satisfied at having a part of her theory confirmed, she mulled over the next hypothesis.

"Is your home very far from here?" he asked, breaking the lengthening silence.

Startled anew at thus being awakened from her reverie, Ninian blinked and glanced around. While she'd fretted, they had left the forest and now traversed the road from the village. "Not far."

She listened to the night around her, the soft hoot of an owl in a nearby field, the cheerful cries carried by the wind from those around the bonfire, and shivered at an all-too-familiar drunken anger she sensed nearby.

"Nate's hiding in the bushes outside my gate," she said calmly, nodding toward a picket fence covered in a thicket of overgrown roses. "By morning, he'll be convinced he saw you with horns and tail, riding the sky on my broomstick. You might wish to have a talk with him."

He shot her a sharp look and glanced at the bushes rustling outside the fence. "Talk seldom penetrates thick skulls." he replied.

Releasing her elbow, he strode determinedly toward the gate and jerked Nate from his hiding place.

In fascination, Ninian watched Lord Ives stride off, effortlessly hauling a struggling, protesting Nate without a single by-your-leave.

She thought she had every right to be afraid of a man like that.

Two

"WHAT THE DEVIL ARE YOU DOING HERE?" DROGO DEMANDED, returning from a dull day with his steward and irritated to discover that one of his brothers had tracked him to this desolate castle keep. Handsome enough to already have proved his Ives ability to procreate, Ewen crouched on the overgrown drive and attached a gear to what appeared to be a junk heap of scrap metal.

Drogo scraped at the mud on his boots as his brother reached for a wrench. His steward had insisted that he survey the bleak hills belonging to this barren estate, but unless they had coal under them, Drogo really wasn't interested. He needed to be back in London. Let the local sheepherders have the mud.

And let them keep the moonstruck little witch, too. She had haunted his sleep last night. How the devil had she known that rogue hid outside her gate? And why did he see her laughing eyes in every dark corner of this damned dungeon? She'd have him believing in witches at that rate. Could witches relieve him of disastrous siblings?

It would profit him to concentrate on the here and now, rather than the unattainable. He studied the tangle of wire and metal his brother was assembling.

"I could ask the same of you," Ewen replied as he threaded a pipe through a wheel, adjusted the gear, and sent the whole assembly wobbling down the drive. "I had to threaten to send Joseph up in my next balloon before he'd reveal your whereabouts. I didn't take you for the rural sort. I thought that was Dunstan's role."

A pity Ewen didn't possess their brother Dunstan's penchant for farming; Drogo could assign the neglected Wystan estate to this youngest of his legitimate brothers. But Ewen would sell the castle for wires and tin.

Eyeing the alarming contraption that couldn't possibly have been created in the few hours of his absence, Drogo assumed his most dour expression. "*I'm* establishing a coal mine and canal for transport and increasing our profits in the process. The question is, what are *you* doing besides building children's toys? Looking for handouts?" From London to Wystan was a damned long uncomfortable distance for Ewen to travel for a friendly visit.

From beneath an uncut hank of raven hair, Ewen didn't lose his cheerful grin. "I'm developing a better method of making iron more malleable that would require the heat generated by the coal in your mine. Don't you think that would be useful?"

It would, if Ewen had any chance of accomplishing one of his far-flung fancies. Drogo didn't see any hope of that, since Ewen inevitably lost interest in practical applications once he solved the theoretical problem. "And I suppose your creditors are threatening Newgate?"

"Actually, I just sold my capacitor and plans for an electrical circuit to a colonist." Ewen shrugged. "I can't see how he'll trigger the electricity or what he'll do with it if he does, but that's his problem. But malleable iron… That's something we can use."

"For less expensive swords." Drogo could see the value. He just knew Ewen's capricious mind would move on before he profited from it. Giving up on his muddy boots, Drogo climbed the castle's crumbling front steps. "So, what is it you want? My coins or my coal?"

"Both. I want to start a foundry." Leaving his contraption in the courtyard, Ewen eagerly followed. "No one would let me inside. What are you hiding in there?"

"Sarah's lost souls," Drogo said curtly, not expounding. "Come along then. I have a thousand things I need to do today, and you weren't among them."

"You need a woman, big brother," Ewen said cheerfully. "Do you never take time to look at a pretty girl or embrace the wind?"

"Keeping up with the lot of you is about as futile as embracing the wind," Drogo replied dryly. He didn't bother telling his rattlepated brother that he wasted his nights gazing at stars and admiring moon maidens. Someone in the family had to keep a sound head on their shoulders and their feet on the ground as an example of how normal, sane people lived. Their father, God rest his troubled soul, had never done so. As eldest, Drogo had been designated as the person in charge of responsibility.

Stargazing didn't fit the image he wished his brothers to emulate.

Ewen whistled as they crossed the enormous great room. "This place looks a hell of a lot better than your London place. Is that our stepsister's touch?"

"Probably." Drogo shrugged, indifferent to the polish the servants had been applying since their arrival.

At the sound of voices, Sarah appeared at the top of the stairs, her powdered hair immaculately curled, her brocade gown rustling as she glided downward. "Ewen! You have found us. I despaired of ever seeing civilization again."

Grinning, Ewen executed an exaggerated bow on her behalf. "Has Drogo kidnapped you and buried you alive out here?"

Sarah pouted prettily. "Mother threatened to dispossess me if I poisoned one more suitor, so I ran away. Only Drogo doesn't trust me to run by myself."

Impatiently, Drogo started up the stairs his stepsister had just descended. "You invited yourself, as I remember. Something about the planets being in the wrong house. I offered to send you to Brighton to find a husband instead."

"I don't want a husband," she called after him. "And we're all getting entirely too old for you to tell us what to do, Drogo Ives. What will you do when you don't have us to coddle any longer?"

"Watch after all the Ives bastards my brothers beget, I imagine." Ignoring Sarah's not-so-subtle jibe, Drogo led Ewen up the stairs into his tower study. He reached for the pen on his desk and glared at his brother. "How much?"

Along with an assortment of strings, coins, gears, and other mysterious objects, Ewen produced a scribbled list from his coat pocket and handed it over as he stubbornly pursued the more personal subject. "Even my bastards have mothers to coddle them. We're not all as irresponsible as our father. We can take care of any brats we produce."

"Fine then. The next time you produce one I won't increase your allowance." Sitting at his desk, Drogo scanned the list of supplies, sighed, and dipped his pen into the inkwell. It was a damned good thing he knew how to manage money better than his father had, or their continually growing family would all be starving in the street by now. Despite Ewen's fine protests, Drogo already supported two of his handsome brother's by-blows.

A shame none of his half-dozen younger brothers had learned the trick of high finance, or keeping their breeches buttoned.

❧

Frowning, Ninian shut her grandmother's storybook and left it on the front parlor table. She shouldn't have opened it. She should forget last night's encounter with Lord Ives and not be looking at a childhood tale embroidered by generations of Malcolm women. Malcolms had odd talents, but even her grandmother couldn't cause natural disasters. Of course, there was that time Aunt Hermione had soured all the milk...

Ridiculous. That was coincidence. Much of her grand-mother's power had been common manipulating, like telling Gertrude the lavender love charm would win Harry's heart, when all it did was instill confidence in a girl hampered by shyness.

Just because somewhere in the mists of time a Malcolm and an Ives had made an unhappy match did not mean she had to believe all Ives caused disasters. She still didn't have a right to think about a man with three wives.

This was an age of naturalism. Lord Ives wouldn't believe in legends, or witches.

Sighing, Ninian slipped from the cottage into the profusion of plants spilling over her garden. By starting seeds inside early, she had bay leaves big enough to harvest, mint thick around her ankles, columbine and foxglove blooming in glorious abundance in every nook and cranny. Plants, she knew how to handle. Men—it was best not to think of them.

⤜⤛

Ninian poured a spoonful of honeyed willow bark water down young Matthew's throat. It wasn't as effective as the agrimony, but she wasn't yet prepared to admit that the source of half her herbs had mysteriously gone bad. As soon as she left here, she needed to examine the stream in daylight.

"The earl grabbed Nate's jerkin and carried him off. I don't have any idea what he said to him." Ninian related the prior night's events to Matthew's mother, Mary, as she persuaded more medicine down the boy's throat.

"Good gracious," Mary exclaimed. "The earl must be a very strong man to drag Nate anywhere."

"Taller, but no heavier, I think. Nate was drunk." Making faces back at Matthew until he giggled, Ninian wiped his mouth and tucked his covers more securely around him, basking in the gratitude and love he radiated.

It seemed cruel that she could never have a family of her own when she had so much to offer. Her heart ached, but she told herself that God must have His reasons.

"You are not interested in the man, are you?" Mary asked with suspicion. "You know what the legend says about Malcolm and Ives destroying the land."

Ninian shrugged and tucked away her jar of medicine. "If he has three wives, he certainly has no interest in me. He'll be gone back to his city life soon enough."

"They say the castle once belonged to Malcolms," Mary said slyly.

"So? The cottage I have is much too big for me as it is. What would I do with an entire castle?"

"Have balls and servants," Mary dreamed aloud, apparently giving up her suspicion for the moment. "Dance all night and drink chocolate all day."

"And if I did that, who would make the willow bark for Matthew's throat?" Ninian asked pragmatically and finished packing her basket with the jars of salve and medicine.

"Well, there is that," Mary agreed. "Still, your mother must have had grand gowns and pretty lace and danced all night. You could have the same."

"Yes, and my mother died young." Covering the basket, Ninian stood and brushed down her old wool skirt, unadorned with so much as an inch of lace or a bit of embroidery. She preferred it that way.

She'd been only ten when her mother had died after the last of a series of miscarriages. Granny had warned that Malcolms could only bear their babes in Wystan, and Ninian's aunts had all dutifully done so. Not Ninian's mother. She'd birthed Ninian here, then gaily immersed herself in London's frivolities, denying her heritage and never returning to the place of her birth.

It was a tale Ninian had heard often, though she believed the reported "tradition" of returning to Wystan to give birth was her wily grandmother's way of controlling rich and powerful daughters who had strayed too far into the heathen life of London society.

Her grandmother's admonitions hadn't been necessary for Ninian. As curious as she might be of the roles of wives and mothers, as much as she loved children and wished for one of her own, she'd known for years that her place was in Wystan, where she was needed, where she was comfortable. As interesting as she found Lord Ives, he was still an Ives, and no temptation at all. Almost no temptation at all.

"Yes, but that doesn't mean you can't dress as pretty as Lord Ives's ladies," Mary said as she walked Ninian to the door. "Two of them visited Hattie's last week, and I've never seen anything so elegant."

"If they're reduced to buying Hattie's caps, they won't be elegant for long," Ninian observed. "She's nearly too blind to see the stitches these days. And it rained all last week. Surely they did not drag their best silks and laces through the mud?" Ninian retained fond memories of her mother's silk and laces, but it had been over a decade since she'd outgrown the last of hers. They were useless in this cold, damp climate, and she'd never considered buying more, although she could have all the silk she wanted, if she'd wanted it. Which she didn't.

"I suppose you're right, but did you never dream of other places, Ninian?"

As a child, she'd seen other places, and chosen Wystan, but Ninian didn't try to explain that to Mary. Granny had called Ninian an emotional weather vane, buffeted by whatever winds of passion brewed nearby. The explosive emotions of London's immense populace had often disoriented her and spun her like a whirligig. She preferred the isolation of Wystan, a quiet world that she knew and understood.

Saying her farewells, Ninian swept out of the cottage with every intention of exploring the mystery of the barren burn. If Lord Ives only walked the night, he wouldn't know if she trespassed during the day.

Two women with their silk-covered panniers flapping in the breeze stood in the village square, hanging on to their preposterously wide straw hats and arguing with Harry, the shoemaker. Ninian blinked in astonishment at the bewigged apparitions. They couldn't have been more out of place in this simple village had they rode in on elephants.

Glancing around, she wasn't certain whether to be relieved or disappointed that she saw no sign of Lord Ives. Perhaps he really did only appear at night.

Imagining the ladies' difficulty in explaining what they wanted to unimaginative Harry, Ninian smiled wider. She could not understand why the taciturn Lord Ives would want two magpies for wives, much less three, and she certainly wouldn't carry that thought as far as the others had. His sleeping arrangements weren't her concern. Remembering the odd warmth she'd felt in his lordship's proximity, she didn't pursue that avenue either.

As she hurried down the path into the woods, she didn't

worry about dirtying her practical leather shoes. Rural fashion appealed to her. The big pocket of her apron held all the herbs and plants she liked without need of tying pockets inside her homespun skirt, and her petticoat wouldn't carry her off in the wind like a giant kite as surely panniers and all that trailing silk would.

Musing on wires and silks and kites, she reached the burn much sooner than expected—and stopped short at the sight of Lord Ives a few feet away, poking his walking stick in the dead debris.

Amid the gray shadows of new leaves and clouds, he appeared nearly as formidable as he had last night. Tall, garbed in unfashionable black, and unsmiling, he frowned at Ninian's approach.

"The soil is coated with a malodorous slime," he said to her.

Shaken but undeterred by his presence, Ninian dipped down to examine the soil more closely. She rubbed her fingers in it, then sniffed them. "Sulfur?"

"Quite possibly."

She didn't sense his surprise at her knowledge so much as see it in the slight uplifting of dark brows. Lord Ives had most disconcertingly dark and piercing eyes, with thick eyebrows that curled upward at the ends. She couldn't call him a handsome man, so much as a compelling one. Her stomach lurched uncertainly at the intelligence staring back at her, intelligence she craved in a companion.

She hastily tested the soil again. "Sulfur, and something else." Thoughtfully, she wiped her fingers on her apron and gazed in dismay at the brown leaves and crumbling foliage that had once been a fairy garden of emerald hues. "It's as if it has been blasted by the devil," she murmured.

"More likely a type of acid, unless you prefer to search me for horn and tails."

His tone was as dry as the brittle leaves they walked upon, and Ninian warmed in appreciation of his humor. She glanced up, and her smile faltered beneath the impact of his intense stare. She didn't want to look away.

Taking a deep breath, she broke his spell. "I have already

explained to the villagers that horns and tails do not fit well under silks and wigs." Daringly, she lifted an eyebrow at his unadorned black hair. "Although surely they can see for themselves that you are hiding nothing in that department."

He shrugged and returned to poking at the rocks along the bank. "I shouldn't think sulfur a naturally occurring chemical in water."

Reminded of her place, Ninian pulled her cloak more tightly around her. "Then I must explore and see where this blight begins."

"So you can cast a spell upon it?"

"Or wave my magic wand," she replied airily, striking out upstream.

"I think not." He caught her elbow and drew her back.

The spring air warmed around her, and heat sang through her veins. She didn't know whether to respond with interest or panic, but heeding her grandmother's more practical warnings about men, she pulled away.

Unable to read the earl's thoughts or emotions, she studied his harsh features for answers. He had a sharp blade of a nose, a stiff, stern jaw, vestiges of laugh lines around his eyes, and a sensuous curve to his upper lip that particularly captivated her. Masculine interest flared in his eyes at her scrutiny.

Shaken, she returned to their argument. "You cannot stand guard over the entire stream, day and night."

"I will send someone better prepared to walk these woods alone." He glanced pointedly at her diminutive figure. "It's my property. When the source of the blight is found, I'll deal with it as I deem appropriate."

Anger simmering, she hid it behind disarming dimples. "Not with witch's incantations? How unspirited of you."

His dark brows drew into a V. "There is no such thing as magic."

"Of course, there isn't," she soothed. "I'm sure there's a purely natural reason for the stream to die and a thoroughly natural solution. I'll just consult a few trees, shall I?"

Her skirts swung tauntingly as she walked off. An unexpected beam of sunlight shot through the screen of clouds and leaves to catch on her golden ringlets, reminding the earl with a shock of her ability to recognize an intruder concealed by shrubbery.

Perhaps she just had uncanny eyesight.

Her challenge awoke an unholy curiosity in him that wasn't entirely intellectual but heated his blood far more than was good for either of them.

Three

STARING AT THE NIGHT SKY, DROGO ADJUSTED THE TELESCOPE on his desk, tried to jot a note, and cursing the dry quill, dipped it in an inkwell. He should hire a secretary.

He didn't want a secretary. These few moments he hoarded for himself were the only pure pleasure he possessed in a life of constant demands. People always asked too much of him, and secretaries were people. Besides, it was too late to hire anyone. His business with the coal mine was almost done, and he doubted if he would linger in the area another week.

Adjusting the telescope one final time, he grunted in satisfaction, and bending nearer the flickering candle, he noted the location and date of the celestial object he'd observed. He was almost certain he'd found a hitherto unknown planet. He needed better equipment. And more time for his studies.

He could buy the equipment. Time was more difficult to obtain.

After carefully sanding his notes and placing them in his leather folio, he looked up and caught a glimpse of another project he'd started out of curiosity stirred by a forest nymph. He didn't generally waste time listening to women, nymphs or not, but she'd engaged his intellect in the puzzle of the blighted stream.

Drogo wandered to the tower windows he'd had installed upon his arrival. This far north of London's smoke and fog the vista of starlit firmament spread out before him as far as heaven itself—as distant as the peace he craved.

Briefly, he wondered what it would be like without the responsibilities of his title, to come and go as he pleased, to act on impulse without thought to consequences. He might as well picture life without his half-dozen younger brothers. He didn't have the imagination for it. He did what was necessary and savored these rare moments of quiet when they appeared.

The moon was waning, but its silver light poured over the ancient forest below, returning his thoughts to the moon maiden. More than enchanting; she fascinated him—he supposed because of the night and the moon and his own curiosity.

Mostly, women were a mysterious other world to him, one of soft fragrances and whispery silks and incomprehensible giggles. He enjoyed the sensual pleasures when he visited their world, but he wasn't likely to linger among them. They weren't logical and didn't provide sufficient intellectual stimulus. The baffling moon maiden hadn't provided silks and giggles, but she'd stirred his interest. Odd.

He glanced down at the experiment the encounter had inspired. He'd set out pots of grass he'd dug from the yard. He'd watered half the pots with liquid from the dying burn and half with water from the castle well. All the grass looked seriously unhappy.

The witch would no doubt tell him his own malaise blighted the plants.

Grimacing at that illogical thought, Drogo watered the plants again. *Witches.* In this day and age. Silly, superstitious twits.

A corner of his mouth turned up as he remembered her flapping her sleeves and terrifying the bumpkin, Nate, into flight. He'd often wished he had that ability. Maybe he could hire her to stand on the tower stairs and terrify the castle inhabitants into leaving him alone.

Too late for tonight though. He heard the patter of feminine feet on the stone even as he thought it. He swore they knew the instant he rose from his desk. Maybe all women were witches. His limited experience would certainly indicate something decidedly hellish about them upon occasion.

"Drogo!" The door burst open on Sarah's usual breathless note. "Come quickly! I swear, the ghost is walking. Hurry!"

He did no such thing. He tilted his head, heard the sound of the wind picking up, and looked at his stepsister with disfavor. "The branches are rubbing the windows again. Don't be such a goose, Sarah."

"Don't be such a stubborn ass, Drogo!" Several years younger than he, but a widow now and far more worldly-wise than she ought to be, Sarah tossed her powdered head of curls. "There's moaning, and footsteps, and I swear, something crashed. Claudia is in hysterics, and Lydie could go into labor any minute out of sheer fright."

The thought of Lady Lydie in labor frightened Drogo more than any threat of haunts. Why the devil had he let them follow him here?

Because Sarah's mother had thought her daughter safer away from society's wagging tongues after she'd nearly poisoned her last suitor with one of her witch's brews. At the time, he hadn't anticipated his stepsister bringing along an unwed mother and an unhappy companion. The potential for trouble was enormous, which was one of the reasons why he'd sent Ewen away. Of course, his brother's invention of a "ghost-catcher" that had crashed through the ceiling in the middle of the night had speeded his departure.

Drogo was used to dealing with his brothers. He wasn't used to dealing with women and babies. Definitely not babies. He'd expected to be far gone before Lydie delivered.

Gritting his teeth, Drogo surrendered any idea of a peaceful evening reading the pamphlets on astronomy he'd received in the day's post. "There are no such things as ghosts," he reminded Sarah as he followed her down the stairs. "There may be squirrels in the attic or mice in the walls, but there are no ghosts."

"Well, you just come down out of your almighty tower and tell Lydie there are mice in the walls," Sarah answered tartly, lifting her wide skirts by the armful to negotiate the narrow stairs. "But I'd suggest you do it after you've called the midwife."

A midwife. By all the saints in heaven, he hadn't thought about midwives. Did the village even have one?

"Isn't it a little early for that?" he asked cautiously. His experience with Sarah as a child told him she was capricious, irresponsible, and capable of causing him grief just for amusement. She was supposed to be an adult now, but he still took anything she told him with an entire cellar of salt.

"It most certainly is, so I fervently hope you can trap your wretched mice. Or ghosts."

The dual screams echoing up the stairs from the rooms below warned the night's theatrics had only just begun.

Sarah flattened herself against the wall as Drogo pushed past and raced downward. In the candlelit darkness, he didn't see her smile of satisfaction.

༺ৡ༻

"It's all in the diary," Sarah said defensively, clutching a peeling leather volume to her chest in the face of her friends' dubious expressions. "It says so right here." She opened the frail, cracking pages and pointed out a paragraph. "All Malcolm women are witches, so it must have been a Malcolm witch who cursed the Ives."

"You don't really believe Drogo is cursed, do you?" Lydie asked, wrinkling her nose in confusion.

"*All* Ives are cursed!" Sarah declared grandly, slamming the book closed. "Just look at them. They all have miserably unhappy marriages and bear nothing but bastards. Boy bastards," she added in emphasis, as if that were curse enough. "I have three of them for half brothers, so I ought to know."

"There wouldn't be any earls left if that were true," Claudia, Lady Twane, pointed out. "And if I remember correctly, Drogo has two younger brothers and neither of them are bastards."

Undaunted by this hole in her theory, Sarah smiled. "That's a matter of opinion. My point is, what are we going to do about it?"

"Do about it?" Lydie squeaked, her eyes growing wide as she realized Sarah was off on another of her schemes.

"If a Malcolm cursed an Ives, then a Malcolm could uncurse one, couldn't she?"

"But, Sarah…" two voices protested as one.

"It doesn't matter. The planets say the time is propitious for Drogo to marry and have a son, and we will do what we can to see that accomplished."

As Sarah triumphantly returned the tattered leather volume to the library shelf, her companions exchanged knowing looks.

"If Drogo has a wife and heir, he'll have his hands so full, he won't have time to see what Sarah is up to," Lady Twane translated.

Lydie rolled her eyes.

⁂

Drogo located the moon maiden dreamily gathering rosebuds from the rampant brambles along her picket fence. The bushes at the castle weren't blooming. Wasn't it a little early for roses?

Obviously not, if she was picking them. Sarah was the one who believed in ghosts and witches and impossible feats of magic. Rampant roses in early May were not magic.

He felt a fool for seeking out the little herbalist on such a pretext, but Sarah had insisted, and he'd seen no real alternative—not if he wanted any peace at all.

Ninian looked up at him as if he'd materialized from another world but said nothing as he explained Lydie's condition and the foolishness of the women's complaints.

"I will pay whatever it takes," he stated dispassionately when, seeming struck dumb by his appearance, she didn't reply to the ladies' absurd request that she come to rid the castle of ghosts. Captured by the enchantment of her cornflower blue eyes, he wondered how anyone in his rational mind could consider this golden-haired innocent a witch, providing anyone rational could believe in witches.

His gaze dropped to the swell of a generous bosom disguised beneath the folds of her muslin kerchief. Men might call her sorceress, but for her physical charms, not her magical ones.

Drogo lifted his gaze again to discover a mischievous

dimple peeking from its hiding place. Pouty pink lips parted in a teasing smile as if she knew precisely what he was thinking.

Which, of course, she did, because all men must look at her that way. "The women are hysterical," he repeated calmly, despite his sudden surge of lust. He wondered why she did not let him past the gate, invite him into the house. In his experience, women fell all over their feet to entertain the Earl of Ives, one of the many reasons he'd fled to Wystan's isolation. This female smiled enticingly, but twiddled with a rose like a simpleton. Perhaps he'd mistaken her intelligence. Anyone who called herself a witch probably had a cog or two missing in her brainworks.

Patiently, he tried again. "Lady Twane has a nervous condition, and Lady Lydie is expecting her first child shortly. I understand you're a midwife. You must know the delicacy—"

She shook her head. "Call for me when she goes into labor. That, I can help with. Ghosts are not within my realm of knowledge."

So, she could speak when she wanted, fluently and with the educated accents of London. Unusual. The golden ringlets hid a brain, even if it was slightly cracked.

Bewildered by her benign smile, and wondering what could possibly be racketing through that strange noggin of hers, Drogo refused to accept defeat. He merely changed tactics. He nodded complacently. "Of course, I perfectly understand. Ghosts are a figment of the imagination, and you cannot promise what is not possible. I respect your honesty. However—"

Again, she interrupted with a shake of her pretty curls. "Ghosts are real enough. But I believe they should be left alone. You're the intruders. Those ghosts could have been there for hundreds of years. Why should they leave their home because trespassers are annoyed with their presence?"

Exasperated by her lack of logic, Drogo gripped the pickets of the gate that separated him from her. He did not have a temper, he told himself. Given his excitable but generally scientific family, calm logic had always served him best. Silly females who believed in ghosts weren't rational. Fine, then he would be irrational.

"Then don't disturb the ghosts. I'm concerned about Lady Lydie. Examine her, if you will. However, I'd be much easier if you could convince these infernal women that you've tried all within your power so they'll leave me in peace. If they believe in ghosts, they'll believe in the power of witches too. Merely sprinkle smelly things about the place, mutter a few magical words, yell 'boo' for all I care. I'll have the men on the roof searching for loose slates on the morrow."

She slipped the tip of a small white finger between rosy lips and stared at him from behind crystal blue eyes as if they were the insurmountable dividing wall between his world and hers. She blinked once, frowned quizzically as she tilted her head and studied him, then her befuddled mind apparently reached some decision, and she nodded.

As if that were a signal for her to return from a trance, she straightened her shoulders and her apron and smiled beatifically. "I'll come tomorrow, shall I?"

Slightly mystified but satisfied with the result of his task, Drogo relaxed enough to notice the lush profusion of purple, pink, and white flower heads bouncing on thick stalks just over her shoulder. The castle kitchen garden had barely revealed a poor shoot or two the last time he'd looked. Perhaps he needed a new gardener.

Dismissing the flowers as irrelevant, he nodded at her acceptance and walked away. On a whim, he made the mistake of glancing back. The nymph waved at him from her bower of rose canes as if she really were the fairy queen of a flower realm. Ridiculous thought. He straightened his shoulders and returned to the reality of the road ahead.

As he strode away, Ninian admired the aristocratic line of the earl's fitted coat, the determined pace of his gait, and the way the sun glinted off his ebony hair. She knew the dull brown of his long-tailed coat was less elegant than those of the gentlemen in London, but it was far above the crude jerkins of the towns-people, and it not only exactly matched his cockaded hat, but revealed the silver hilt of a sword—a weapon not often seen in these parts. The rich leather of his riding boots and the ornate head of his walking stick spoke of the wealth his coat did not.

She could not fathom why a lord of the realm, a man with riches beyond imagination, would require her poor services, as witch or midwife or anything else. And because she did not understand him, she felt compelled to try, despite the legends. Seldom did she meet someone she could not read, particularly a man. Women often confused their emotions so badly that she couldn't sort one from the other, but men—men were usually simple.

Her grandmother would have been proud of her restraint. The legend had it that the last Ives man to cross a Malcolm threshold had carried off the lady against her will.

Well, she hadn't let him cross the threshold.

Four

REFUSING TO BELIEVE SHE COULD BE ENTRANCED BY AN
aristocrat wearing a fashionable coat and expensive high-
topped boots, Ninian firmly closed her portmanteau as she
prepared to leave for the castle the next morning. The image
of Lord Ives standing at her garden gate, hat in hand, raven
hair gleaming in the sun, had haunted her all night, but it
was his eyes that held her spellbound. Deep set, shadowed by
heavy black lashes, framed by those thick curling eyebrows,
his eyes opened fascinating new worlds.

Still, she thought it mainly curiosity that drove her to agree
to this visit. She wanted to know more about the blighted
stream and the castle ghosts and... Lord Ives.

She supposed she really ought to search Granny's library for
some source of the story about Malcolms and Ives before *she*
crossed *his* threshold, but recklessly, she chose to find out the
truth on her own. It was time she explored a wider world.

She wouldn't admit to the restlessness Beltane had stirred in
her. She just needed something new and exciting in her life.

Could she chase away ghosts? It didn't seem likely,
especially since she didn't like to try. But her grandmother
had assured her that Malcolms could do most anything they
applied their minds to. Ninian had no proof of that. She
couldn't make amulets work. She had packed her grandmother's ancient book of incantations, but it might as well be
a chemist's manual for all the good it was. Maybe one of her

aunts or cousins could work the spells, but she'd only found success in healing remedies. She'd discovered and tested any number of effective herbs on her own, but she'd never laid a ghost to rest, made a love potion, or bewitched a cow. Or a man.

Laughing at that thought, she set out for Wystan Castle.

Portmanteau in hand, her hooded cloak pulled firmly around her against the dew, she stepped through the garden gate and nearly walked straight into a two-wheeled cart.

"Mornin', miss." The driver touched his battered felt hat. "His lordship sent me to wait on you."

"How thoughtful." Surprised and pleased, she threw her bag into the back of the cart and with the help of the driver, clambered up. No one had ever been thoughtful enough to offer her transportation. Perhaps the road was longer than she'd thought. She had never traversed the woods as far as Wystan Castle because no villagers lived in that direction, and the forest was too dense there for her to waste time exploring it without reason. Castles didn't hold as much interest for her as plants did. "Is it very far?"

"Not so far as a bird flies, but people can't fly."

Ninian digested the truth behind this platitude some time later as the cart finally ambled off the pitted, rutted main road onto the narrow drive leading to the castle. After years of disuse, the lane had nearly reverted to its natural state. The forest and underbrush beyond the drive looked impenetrable.

"Will his lordship be clearing the grounds?" she asked casually, eyeing a marvelous clump of birch almost lost in brambles.

"His lordship has interest in naught but books," the driver grumbled. "Ain't natural." He peered at her from beneath the crumpled brim of his hat. "There's them that says—"

"Oh, look at the woodbine," Ninian exclaimed at the cascade of greening vine ahead, cutting off any descent into gossip. She didn't want to know what people said about Lord Ives any more than she wanted to hear what they said about her.

The driver lapsed into silence, and Ninian savored the trill of bird song and the fresh scents of evergreen. Too much of England's forest land had been stripped bare or landscaped into unnatural quadrangles of neatly trimmed hedges, straight paths, and tidy flower beds. She preferred Lord Ives's method of leaving the land alone.

Of course, she would prefer cultivating the more beneficial trees and plants to allowing this kind of impenetrable wilderness, but perhaps, given time...

The horse slowed, and Ninian glanced ahead. The formidable stone walls of Wystan Castle towered across the road. Fortified at a time when border wars ravaged the countryside, it had never been fully modernized. The main block of the house loomed through the trees, with high stone walls and narrow windows that would allow little light inside. The rocky ground on which it had been built would once have been cleared of brush and trees, but years of neglect had brought the forest nearly to its doors.

The clouds parted overhead, and a shaft of light illuminated glass in the upper reaches of the tower. How odd, Ninian thought as she scrambled from the cart. Lord Ives had installed windows in the unheated watchtower.

A housekeeper let her in, and Ninian followed her stout, black-clad figure through the great hall and up the steps to the private floor.

Little had been done to improve the ancient decor. Moldering tapestries had apparently been cleaned and patched, but nothing could restore them to their medieval grandeur. The covers on the furniture had been removed and the wood beneath dusted and polished. The towering carved walnuts and oaks of an earlier age looked foreign and uncomfortable.

An old-style upholstered bed draped heavily in crewel-embroidered linen with faded blue silk linings filled the center of the room to which the housekeeper led her. At first, Ninian assumed she'd been brought to the bedchamber of Lady Ives, but the servant opened Ninian's bag and began laying her drab homespun into a chest of drawers inlaid with carvings more elaborate than the embroidery.

"I'll do that," she said hurriedly, taking her best apron from the woman's hands. She didn't want anyone touching the herbs and book at the bottom of the bag.

The woman nodded. "The lady will call for you," she said, before ambling off.

With a sigh, Ninian scanned the enormous room. Since the age of ten she'd lived simply, with plain country furniture and lathe and mud daub walls. She hadn't seen wainscoting and ornate ceilings since London, and she'd never seen tapestries like these. The room would burst with color had age not grayed the threads.

She started to examine a cloth swarming with trees and white figures, but the carved step beside the downy thickness of the bed distracted her. A bed so tall that one needed a stair to climb into it warned of bitter drafts about the floor. The room had no fireplace. The purpose of the heavy hangings and the thick carpet was evident.

The image of Lord Ives appeared, imprinted over the reality of the ornate bed. She could see him like some medieval lord in shirtsleeves waiting for his woman to disrobe and join him. She'd never had such thoughts until she'd looked into the earl's haunting eyes.

Her gaze dropped to the soft bed, and the air warmed around her. The perfume of roses tickled her senses, returning the image of the earl's dark gaze. Her breasts tingled as if he'd touched them.

She'd never possessed a sensual awareness of a man's masculinity until she'd met Lord Ives. Intellectually, she knew how men viewed women and what they did to them when they could. Emotionally and physically, she'd never quite understood why a woman would invite what seemed to her as rather awkward indignities. Now, understanding rippled just beneath her skin.

She hadn't come here out of curiosity about ghosts or blighted streams. She'd come to test her powers as a woman and a witch.

Uncomfortable with that self-discovery since Lord Ives was beyond her limits and she really didn't think she could chase ghosts, Ninian escaped the scent of roses by slipping into the hall. Arrow slits illuminated the far ends of the corridor, revealing only a row of doors and a worn carpet adorned with miscellaneous tables along the wall. She wondered if the other doors belonged to the women of the household. Perhaps the earl really did keep a seraglio.

She took the stairs down to the public rooms. The original great hall had evidently been added on to in a helter-skelter pattern she couldn't discern. She peeked in on a library and a gentleman's study with billiard table and a ladies' parlor and a small breakfast room. But the earthier scents of plants and soil drew her onward.

She halted at the sound of voices from behind a partially open door. Perhaps the hope of female companionship had drawn her here as much as anything else. The earl, she must remember, wanted her abilities as a witch, not a woman. Spirits dropping, she would have hurried past, but one cheerfully ribald feminine voice rang out clearly.

"Well, it's a pity I'm in an 'interesting condition' or I'd volunteer. Drogo is surely a more thoughtful lover than Charles, although admittedly, he's not very sympathetic to you, Sarah."

Another woman twittered. "When he looks at me from beneath those dark brows of his, I'm fair to fainting. But I fear I am barren," she finished sadly.

"And a good thing too. You're a married woman and could only bear him bastards," the younger first voice declared firmly.

"Now, girls, this discussion has grown quite old. We all owe Drogo more than we can repay in the usual way."

"If we disappeared tomorrow, Sarah, he wouldn't notice," the sad voice replied.

"Well, we know why that is, don't we?" the bossy voice— presumably Sarah's—continued. "But the planets say we have a chance to correct that. I've brought the herbs from London, and if we're in agreement that it's up to us to correct the…"

Ninian hurried away as the voice came closer and the parlor door closed firmly. Heart pounding, she nearly fell through the door at the far end of the hall.

It didn't sound as if any of the women were married to Lord Ives, but it certainly sounded as if they knew him as a lover.

She couldn't imagine the enormity of such a thing. She'd read tales of Oriental harems, but Lord Ives was *English*. And the one lady was *married*. Was the other bearing his child? Three mistresses rather than wives. She couldn't comprehend it all.

Uneasiness skittered across her skin, but she ignored it as she discovered the room to which she'd been drawn.

On the other side of the threshold, the frames for enormous windows ran along the entire length of the back wing of the castle. Tile floors still held the remnants of broken glass. Small oak saplings struggled to survive amid the debris of many autumns, protected by the warm stone of the outer wall.

A conservatory. The castle once had a conservatory. How very, very odd.

With her foot, Ninian brushed aside years of dead leaves, exploring the unfurling frond of a fern, the probing stems of valerian. Valerian! Ninian stooped to clear away pot shards and leaves to examine the root. No one willingly grew a plant that smelled so bad unless they meant to use it for sleep disorders or magic rituals.

Exploring farther, she uncovered evidence of old clay pots and disintegrating wooden planters. A few straggling herbs, ones hardy to the region, still survived exposure to the elements. Whatever else had grown here had long since died.

Mary had said the castle once belonged to a Malcolm. The Malcolm women were all purported to be witches.

Ninian cleared aside glass to uncover designs in the tile. She recognized the symbols for sun and moon and stars. This had been the heart of the Malcolm castle then—a wonderful conservatory of healing plants and a tribute to the earth that produced them.

It saddened her to see the soul of the house broken and neglected like this. Maybe this—and not Lord Ives—was why she'd been drawn here.

Even as she dared to think it, the object of her thoughts intruded upon her reverie.

"I should have known I'd find you here."

Ninian dropped a sprig of mint and swirled to meet the master of the household.

He wore a black traveling cloak and looked as if he'd just come in from a ride. As usual, he wore no wig, and his somber hair was drawn back in a ribboned club. The beginnings of a beard darkened his jaw, and his craggy brows shadowed his eyes as he gazed upon her. Ninian shivered. She had remembered him as an imposing presence, but on her own territory, she had not feared him. She was in his territory now, with nowhere to run should she need to. And he was everything masculine she'd ever dreamed about. The earthy scents of soil and plants surrounding them seemed somehow fitting, and intoxicating.

"It is a pity this room was lost." She gestured at the rotted frames, seeking solid ground as her senses reeled from the impact of his proximity. Was that the scent of male musk mixing with her own oil of roses?

The earl gave the structure a look of disinterest and shrugged. "I had the fallen tree removed, but there's little worth saving here. No furniture, only a few broken tables."

In his knee-high boots and billowing cloak, with those piercing eyes beneath curled eyebrows, he could have been Satan declaring the Earth beyond redemption. Bravely, Ninian stooped to retrieve the mint, crushing it to fill the air with freshness. "This was the heart of your house," she said quietly.

Dark eyebrows raised. "Not to me. It's the tower that I prefer."

Male and female, earth and sun, the distance between both was so great it was a wonder plants grew or children were born. Looking up from her crouched position at the length of the earl's booted calves and the shiny silver buttons on his breeches-clad thighs, she blinked and looked away again when her gaze traveled a smidgen too far.

His cloak had fallen back from his hips to reveal the tight cut of his breeches. Lord Ives was a very big man. Even the fresh smell of mint couldn't distract her from a vivid awareness of his masculinity.

"May I see the tower sometime?" Visiting his lair seemed suddenly important to her understanding of this man.

He quirked one eyebrow as he gazed down on her uncovered curls. She'd forgotten her cap. Hastily, brushing off her hands, she stood up. His gaze didn't rise with her, but now rested on her bodice.

"Only if you have need of me," he replied enigmatically.

With a swirl of his cloak, he stalked out, leaving Ninian feeling as if she'd just been stripped naked, examined, and found wanting.

Five

"WHAT ON EARTH ARE YOU DOING?" THE LOVELY WOMAN in the doorway exclaimed, peering from the conservatory threshold but not setting a silk-shod foot beyond.

Ninian halted her sweeping. She'd found enough dried grass on the grounds to fashion a decent broom and had uncovered a large portion of the tiles in the decimated conservatory. "I'm not accustomed to sitting still," she replied mildly.

"Obviously." The woman glanced at the little garden of plants Ninian had repotted in an old bucket. "I'm Drogo's stepsister, Sarah. Let me provide you with more..." She didn't complete the sentence but turned to leave, gesturing for Ninian to follow.

Stepsister! Not wife. Curious, Ninian wondered if a step-sister could be mistress.

"I will need to wash." Having never been a servant, she didn't follow orders well. Setting aside her broom, Ninian stepped over the threshold into the house. She felt inadequate enough in the lady's stylish presence; she didn't need to feel dirty, too.

Sarah schooled her obvious impatience and nodded toward another doorway. "The kitchen is through there. They'll have..." She waved her hand vaguely.

Well, she was accustomed to washing in kitchens. She and her grandmother had practically lived in the service room during the winter to keep from lighting more than one fire. Not that they couldn't have afforded more fires, but Grandmother had always been tightfisted, and Ninian had more important things to tend than fires.

She brushed herself off, washed as best as possible, and returned to the hall to find Sarah still waiting.

The elegantly slim lady looked her up and down, sighed faintly, then straightening her shoulders, marched toward the hall and the stairs.

Well, she'd always known she wasn't cut out to be a graceful swan of society, Ninian thought ruefully as she followed Sarah up the stairs. She had a sturdy peasant's build she couldn't change with any amount of magic. And no need to change, she reminded herself. She did not look out of place in her own home.

Sarah led her to a bedchamber in a different wing than where Ninian was situated. This wing looked slightly newer and more recently refurbished. She had time to glimpse gleaming mahogany and a brilliantly patterned carpet before her escort pushed open a door and introduced her into a room full of sunlight and exotically garbed women.

Including Sarah, three exotically garbed women, to be precise. Ninian quickly reduced the sensory bombardment to count her escort in blue silk and powdered coiffeur; a hugely pregnant lady in layers of flowing emerald and a frilled cap of dainty lawn; and a thin, timid woman hiding in the shadows.

"Ladies, meet Ninian Siddons. Miss Siddons, Lady Twane, and Lady Lydie, good friends of mine. And Drogo's, of course."

The pregnant girl giggled. Ninian noted the flash of vivacious dark eyes and surmised that Lady Lydie had hair as dark as the earl's beneath her cap. She was younger than the others, scarcely old enough to be carrying a child. Under Ninian's study, she smiled. "I thought midwives were old, gnarled creatures," she stated disingenuously.

"You are referring to my grandmother." Ninian smiled to relieve the effect of her bluntness. "Her hands were arthritic, so I acted as her hands. I've learned all she knew, which is more than most London physicians know." The sarcasm was instinctive. It was in the hands of London physicians that her mother had lost five infants.

"We've inquired, and you come highly recommended," Sarah replied soothingly. "We have no doubt that you're the best person for Lydie's lying-in. But it's the…" She fluttered her hands helplessly and looked to the others. "I feel so foolish saying this…"

"The ghost," Lady Twane stated firmly, still staring at Ninian. "We want you to send the ghost away. It is most distressing to be woken in the middle of the night by invisible temper tantrums."

Ninian didn't think there was a thing she could do about the spirits haunting Wystan Castle, but these women would never believe her until they saw for themselves. They were born of wealth and privilege and thought all their wishes could be carried out on command. They wouldn't understand that some things were not of this earth and could not be commanded.

"As I told Lord Ives, I am an herbalist, not a ghost-chaser. For that, you will need a priest. But if you wish, I will try talking to the spirits. I make no promises."

"Priests wear fancy robes and silk scarves and carry incense and candles," Lady Lydie said thoughtfully, gazing with interest at Ninian's simple garb. "Perhaps ghosts would be more impressed with your power should you wear something more…"

"Fashionable," Lady Twane finished caustically.

"Rich and powerful!" Sarah exclaimed. "That is exactly it! We shall give you the power of the church by ornamenting you with…" She waved her hand in a manner Ninian was coming to recognize. "Lydie, you are much the same height as Miss Siddons. You are certain to have something…"

Although Lady Sarah failed to finish sentences, she scarcely seemed the type to fear ghosts. These women hid themselves well behind layers of powder and silk and feathers, but this particular scheme spoke of subterfuge. Ninian sensed it in the air. "I do not think this is at all necessary—"

"But it is!" Lydie intruded. "We are all so bored sitting out here in Drogo's hideaway with naught else to amuse ourselves. Dressing you like a fashion doll would be oh so amusing, and it's certain to impress any ghosts lingering in the walls. Say you will, please? Then we can go ghost-hunting after dinner."

Ninian considered telling them she wasn't poor and could afford her own silks if she had any desire to wear silk. But the trust fund Granny had left in her care wasn't anyone's business but her family's.

Sarah was already rifling through Lydie's trunks, searching for the perfect gown. Lady Twane picked at the discards with a disdainful finger, but even she seemed to be interested in the scheme. She radiated pain, Ninian thought. All that submerged anger and grief and pain would be sufficient to wake any ghost from hiding. She suspected removing Lady Twane from the premises would quiet the haunts faster than she could.

"The blue!" Lydie ordered from her reclining position on the upholstered daybed. "It never suited me, but it will be perfect for her fair hair and eyes."

Ninian thought she ought to remind them that she was several inches shorter than anyone in here, but then she remembered the wealth of undergarments holding up their fashionable material and, panicking, shook her head. "No, please, I cannot…"

"Never say you can't," Sarah called from the depths of the trunk. "Look, won't this cap look sweet if we dress her hair…"

Ninian's hand flew to her hair. "No! I won't have flour or pomade."

"Of course not." Lydie waved away the protest. "Your hair is much too fascinating as it is, and surely ghosts come from a time when hair wasn't dressed. The cap with the blue ribbons, Sarah. It's just a wisp of lace."

Sarah shook out layers of rich brocade. "Perfect. No panniers. We need a heavy underskirt, Lydie. I saw a white one with gold thread…"

Dazed and bewildered by this sudden barrage of beautiful silks and colors, Ninian allowed them to replace her coarse linen with a frail lawn chemise adorned with layers of lace at sleeve and neckline. She gasped as they tightened the whale-bone bodice until she could scarcely breathe, but her protests went unheard until she declared the ghost would never hear her should she faint from lack of air.

The beautiful sky-blue brocade slid over her shoulders and underskirt like a waterfall, and she surreptitiously smoothed the sensuous material as they nipped and tucked it into place. As expected, it fell past the tips of her toes, but they fashioned a sash of darker blue silk and hauled the excess material around her waist and tied it in place. She felt like a stuffed pig, but the ladies oohed and ahhed and praised their own work so highly, she couldn't be so rude as to say so. Besides, the silk felt wonderful, and decadent.

"I don't suppose you have knowledge of astrology?" Lady Lydie asked as the others arranged Ninian's attire. "The stars tell us such wonderful things. Sarah has found this astrologer—"

Sarah hastily cut her off. "Miss Siddons knows about herbs, Lydie, not planets. We need her to teach us how to rid this place of ghosts."

Covering her mouth with a giggle, Lydie said not another word. Ninian could sense the confusion of emotion surrounding her, but it was impossible to tell what came from whom and why. She just knew they were hiding some conspiratorial secret, and it didn't take much thought to figure it had to do with her.

They attacked Ninian's hair next, cutting a fringe of curls around her face and brushing out thick ringlets until they billowed over her shoulders and down her back. They pinned it all in place with the scrap of lace, then stepped back to admire their handiwork.

"The modesty bit isn't very modest," Claudia, Lady Twane, noted, just as a gong tolled from deep within the bowels of the castle.

Ninian leapt at the booms. The ladies looked unconcerned by the constant ringing.

"Well, she is a little more well-endowed than Lydie," Sarah agreed. "But we haven't time. Drogo will disappear into the woodwork if we—"

"Wait! I can't go." Ninian glanced down at the scrap of transparent cloth scarcely covering the valley between the swells of flesh pushed up by her bodice, but Sarah caught her arm and dragged her toward the door. Ninian had seen her mother wear less, but she'd never seen herself as her mother.

"Of course, you can, dear. It's just us, and you look marvelous. Lydie, dear, do you want your meal sent up or are you able to manage the stairs…?"

That instantly diverted Ninian's thoughts from herself. "No, she should not be walking those stairs at this stage! I will fetch a tray and bring it up for her."

Sarah laughed. "We have servants, Miss Siddons." She glanced over her shoulder at Lady Lydie, who didn't seem interested in stirring from her reclining position. "We'll tell you all about it later, Lydie."

"I want to be there for the ghost hunt!"

"No one comes with me…" Ninian started to protest, but no one was listening.

Laughing, Sarah drew her relentlessly toward the stairs to the public rooms where the earl awaited his dinner. Feeling as if she wore more clothes than she owned but still shivering from exposure, Ninian surrendered the useless fight. She would put on her show of ridding the place of ghosts and leave in the morning. If they wished to make a toy of her in the meantime, what harm could it do?

The instant she saw Lord Ives's dark gaze fasten on her, Ninian knew the harm it could do. Her breasts swelled beneath his stare, and her nipples puckered. Had she seen that look on Beltane beneath the moonlight, she would be a lost woman by now, like all the other foolish girls who surrendered their virtue in a moment of moon magic.

After what seemed a thousand eternities, the earl finally lifted his gaze to Sarah and her companion. "I see you found something to amuse you this day," he said mildly, before offering his arm to Ninian. "Witches should always wear blue." With that ambiguous statement, he led her into the dining room, leaving the other women to follow.

So nervous she didn't think she could eat, Ninian clasped and unclasped her hands in her lap as Lord Ives seated the other ladies, then returned to the seat at the head of the table, beside hers. She was uncomfortable with this new awareness of her body. It had served her fine as a place to hang clothes. Her arms were meant for sweeping floors, not looking bare and enticing beneath a fall of expensive lace. She had never thought to have babies so considered her breasts a nuisance, until Lord Ives glanced at the way they pushed above her bodice, and his look burned all the way down to the place between her thighs.

"And this is your idea of ghost-hunting clothes?" he inquired of the table in general as a footman passed around the tureen of soup.

"Of course, Drogo, the very latest…" Sarah gestured and laughed.

"Nay, my lord," Ninian said at the same time. "But the ladies insisted."

"The ladies are bored and amuse themselves at our expense. Do not let them make you do anything you do not wish to do." Lord Ives returned his attention to his soup.

"He never notices us," Lady Twane whispered in her ear. "It does him good to know other people exist."

"No whispering, Claudia," Sarah warned from across the table. "He will ignore us no matter what we say. He's already calculating arcs and angles in his mind, or pounds and pence, and doesn't hear a word. He thinks we're so far from trouble out here, he can forget our existence."

His lordship did seem particularly taken with his soup, which he ladled up without noticing if the spoon was full or not. Ninian watched as he finally discovered the bowl was empty, looked surprised, and blinked back to his surroundings.

The look in his eyes was irresistible. He had such warm, dark, vulnerable eyes, eyes that could stir—an imp of mischief.

"That was a delightful chowder, my lord," she said demurely.

"Yes, yes, it was." He looked a bit perplexed, then signaled for the next remove and lost himself in the fish as it appeared.

Oh dear. A flawless, powerful earl might leave her cold, but this one… This one was lost somehow inside his head. The soup had been a broth, not a chowder. Ninian raised a questioning eyebrow to Sarah.

"It is quite deliberate, I'm convinced," she replied with a

shrug. "He shuts us all out by counting stars or whatever on earth it is he does in his head while we chatter on. He has not even noticed that Lydie is not here."

Ninian didn't think the earl was quite as oblivious as the ladies liked to think, but she didn't express her opinion aloud. A lifetime of keeping her thoughts to herself served her well now. She didn't think she had imagined his reaction to her. The earl wasn't just shutting out chatter. For whatever reason, he was denying the existence of feminine company. She didn't like being denied the masculine attention she had craved for so long. Experimentally, she brushed her hand over the sleeve of his coat.

The earl jerked to instant awareness, his eyes blazing with something dark and powerful as he turned to her. She felt the heat of that look deep within her, in a place never stirred before.

A shriek pierced the air, echoing off the towering stone walls.

Into the silence that followed, Lydie could be heard shouting, "That wasn't me! It must be the ghost!"

Six

DROGO LEAPED TO HIS FEET. "STAY HERE!" HE ORDERED, STALKING toward the staircase. He'd had quite enough of these practical jokes, and he would end them now. Sarah's latest preoccupation with astrology and witches and the supernatural had gone beyond the realm of scientific inquiry into the ridiculous. She'd practically poisoned her last suitor with some concoction she'd claimed would make him more amorous. It was evident that she had made up the ghost nonsense just to lure the pretty herb-alist into the castle for amusement. Well, he was not amused.

To his annoyance but not to his surprise, Miss Siddons ignored his command and ran after him. Knowing the wicked humor of Sarah and her friends, he assumed she was as much a butt of this joke as he was, and not one of its perpetrators. That didn't relieve his irritation. He preferred people to obey his commands.

"You'll tumble down the stairs and break your silly neck in that gown," he said harshly as she caught up with him.

"No thanks to your ladies." Showing no umbrage at his insult, she lifted the skirt until he could see her stockinged ankles and ran lightly ahead of him.

She'd probably wrapped those ankles around half the sheepherders in the village, he grumbled to himself as he increased his pace to catch up with her. He hadn't missed the grunts and groans in the shrubbery during the bonfire the other night. Pagan rituals celebrating the earth's fertility inevitably resulted in a crop of wailing infants in nine months' time. Maybe he should have indulged that night. Even if the fertility gods didn't oblige, he wouldn't be looking lasciviously at the heels of the local witch now.

The eerie screams had halted the minute they'd leapt from the table, but his guest aimed unerringly for the room from which earlier disruptions had emanated. Maybe she was part of Sarah's plot, after all.

The door she halted at led into the sitting chamber of a suite of rooms. From the size and location, Drogo figured it had once been the master suite, but he preferred the privacy of his tower to this central location. No one currently occupied the suite, but the women had rooms nearby.

"Stay here," the little witch ordered, twisting the latch and peering into the darkness beyond.

Seriously annoyed at being the recipient of his own command, Drogo produced a candle and flint from the niche beside the door and lit the wick. Once he had a flame, he shoved against the solid panel, ignoring the female slipping in beside him.

The room was icy as hell and filled with shadows from the flickering candle, but nothing leapt out and screamed at them.

"I can't sense anything with you in here," his buxom companion complained. "Stand outside and let me listen."

Ignoring that foolishness, Drogo lifted the candle and began a careful search of the cobwebbed draperies and ancient furniture. Lydie had probably produced the inhuman screech. She would do anything Sarah told her.

Miss Siddons stood in the center of the carpet, apparently communing with the spirits. Remembering the massive bed through the next door, Drogo wondered if she might be seduced into staying the night, waiting for another emanation. All that soft blonde voluptuousness could easily entice him to spare a few hours from his watch of the stars.

He tested the latch to the bedroom. Locked. He'd have to do something about that.

Without his realizing it, Miss Siddons had abandoned her listening post. Her small hand took the latch he'd just released and—opened it.

Raising his eyebrows, Drogo followed her into the bedchamber. She didn't seem at all aware of his presence or the proximity of the enormous bed. The females he knew would be giggling self-consciously at being caught alone in a bedroom with him. Or, more likely, they would be throwing themselves into his arms in mock fright or open seduction. He'd swear the little witch knew he was here and just didn't think him worth noticing.

He'd used his Northumberland mining venture as an escape from a barrage of family demands as well as the ploys of marriage-minded females. He had no reason to be irritated because this female didn't require his attention like everyone else, but he was.

Annoyed that he was annoyed, Drogo continued his search while the lovely lackwit drifted to the fireplace and listened to the wind in the chimney. In his opinion, the wind occasionally caught some loose stone or tree branch to produce the earsplitting shrieks. He'd hire a chimney cleaner and a tree pruner in the morning.

"There's no one here but us," she informed him, dropping her long skirt and sweeping toward the exit. "I'll come back sometime when you haven't disturbed the spirits. Is this the only room where they dwell?"

"There's nothing here but moldering furniture, rats, and drafts cold enough to freeze our ars... toes," he amended. Despite appearances to the contrary, he'd assume she was a lady and protect her ears accordingly.

"And your cat." She bent to lift a bundle of fur into her arms.

In the flickering light, the gray cat seemed to shoot him a malevolent look from the haven of the lady's bosom. "I don't have a cat," he said coldly.

In response, her dimples appeared in a bewilderingly unreadable smile as she stroked the cat until it purred. "If you say so, my lord. This must be a ghost cat."

Flummoxed by the enchanting smile and irritated by the illogic of her answer, Drogo struggled for a rational reply. Resorting to the superiority of his position, he nodded condescendingly and steered her from the suite into the hall. "A stray accidentally locked in here while chasing mice. It must have been his yowls we heard."

"Of course, my lord," she answered meekly, but there was nothing meek about her dancing dimples.

He'd liked to kiss the mischief off her rosy lips. He shouldn't be looking at her lips. Stiffly, Drogo slammed the door.

Let the ladies have their fun. He had better things to do. From experience, he knew she'd end up in his bed sooner or later. They always did. He didn't believe it was because women found him so overwhelmingly attractive, but his wealth and title overcame any objection to his character or looks. And since Sarah had started that rumor about his wanting a child… He should have wrung her neck long ago.

Nodding curtly, Drogo released her elbow. "Give my excuses, but I've work to do. I'll see you later."

He strode off to the isolated recesses of his tower.

Ninian shook her head as she watched him go. The room they'd just left reeked of anguish and anger, but she didn't expect a believer in naturalism to notice.

Wondering what Lord Ives did in his lonely tower, Ninian descended the stairs patting the lovely cat. Her grandmother had never allowed her to have pets—no sense in arousing the village's superstitions more than necessary—but she loved animals.

The cat's rumbling purr almost made up for his lordship's rudeness.

❧

With bold ink strokes, Drogo completed his calculation, jotted down his observations, and reached for his smaller telescope.

Before he could lift the sight to his eye, he heard the unmistakable patter of feminine footsteps. At last, the little witch had decided to explore his chambers. That one certainly didn't possess a shy bone in her body. Intrigued despite himself, he actually laid down his telescope in antici-pation. Would she have some sorry story of a dying relative or a long-lost love? Or would she just boldly present herself for his approval? By now, Sarah had probably told half the

British Empire of his admission that he would marry any woman who carried his child. He should have thrown Sarah from the parapets long ago. The possibility of bedding and wedding an earl had provided irresistible temptation for every unattached female in the damned kingdom, when all he'd meant was that he refused to support a herd of bastards as his family traditionally did.

It was a good thing he didn't mind occasionally trading feminine machinations for the erotic delights of seductive smiles and satin skin. His normally all masculine household was sorely deprived of feminine delights, but he saw no need to suffer permanent leg shackles when women came to him readily, without his having to lift a finger. And he could be rid of them as easily.

He hid his disappointment as Sarah peered around the corner of his door. "Are the demons haunting your sleep already this evening?" he taunted, turning back to his telescope and lifting it to the north-facing window.

"I'm lonely." She pouted.

"I warned you," he replied without compunction.

"I had no choice. Mother threatened to disown me. Besides, Lydie needed a hideaway."

Flouncing her skirts, she arranged herself in the window seat below his telescope. She leaned forward to expose the tempting mounds of her breasts. "We're not blood kin, Drogo," she whispered. "I could be the wife you need."

Drogo closed his eyes and cursed under his breath. Sarah had done her best to be circumspect since her arrival. It looked as if the act had finally fallen flat.

"I'm perfectly aware of our relationship," he said without rancor. He'd been down this path too many times to take anything personally. "You were born well before my father brought your mother into his household. But you still grew up as my younger sister. I can remember pulling your hair and calling you names when you kicked me. Don't make me regret offering you shelter."

She leaned back against the pillows with a frown, once more the busybody sister and not the temptress. "It might work, Drogo. Why not try? It's better than both of us living out our lives in loneliness."

"I'm not lonely and you shouldn't be. You can have any man of your choosing."

"I don't want another man who holds the purse strings." Resting her head against the wall, she stared at the night sky beyond the window. "But I want children. They wouldn't be a nuisance, Drogo. You could…"

"No," he said firmly. "I don't need children when I have the lot of you to contend with. Haven't you learned anything from our parents' marriages?"

She shrugged her nearly bare shoulders. "What choices have we? We lead expensive lives and cannot support ourselves without land or money. Your mother is fortunate that the courts forced your father to pay for her house and expenses. And you are fortunate that he dropped dead and left you his wealth before you came of age. Life is a gamble. We can only choose which game of chance to place our money on."

"Very philosophical, my dear, but this game of chance is closed. Find another."

He assumed grimacing would have creased her powder, so she settled for a reflective gesture of finger to lips. Drogo appreciated the performance, but his patience was wearing thin. He had hoped for a more natural bundle of blonde curls and pink lips tonight.

Drogo hoped the little witch wasn't quite as mercenary as Sarah. Miss Siddons seemed as if she might have a trainable mind. That could prove just as interesting as her abundant charms.

"The family won't leave you alone," Sarah warned, rising from her seat with a rustle of petticoats. "You can hide out here as much as you like, but like it or not, you are the official head."

"And arms and hands," Drogo muttered, returning to his telescope.

"Beastly man." She kissed his cheek and floated from the room.

Her scent filled the tower long after her departure. Cursing at the distraction, Drogo stared at the night sky, wondering for the millionth time if he'd made the right decision when he'd decided not to marry.

It seemed the only rational decision he could make. He remembered only too well the shock and anguish of the day his father had thrown his weeping, hysterical mother from their home. His younger brothers had screamed day and night after her departure. His father had drunk himself into a stupor. He wouldn't wish that emotional devastation on his worst enemy.

In the years since then, observing other people, other marriages, he'd reached the conclusion that the only way a man and a woman could live together in any kind of harmony was if they shared common interests and intellect, avoided emotional scenes, and abided by clearly defined rules. In the world he inhabited, that was nigh on impossible.

For the sake of an heir, he'd been inclined to attempt the impossible, until two things had gradually dawned on him. As his brothers grew older and more mature, he realized they could accept their share of responsibility, and he'd begun to understand that he really didn't need a child for an heir. His brothers would suit that purpose nicely.

And since he had yet to produce any of the bastards for which his family was famous, it had become apparent he could never sire a child. The only good reason for marriage was to produce a legitimate heir.

Ergo, he didn't need to marry.

He couldn't help it if logic didn't erase a yearning for the child he could not have, the child he'd never been, the child he would never hold.

In all the years of providing for his siblings, he could not remember ever once holding one in his arms.

❧

"What are you doing?" Drogo demanded as he entered his tower chamber and daylight revealed an easily identifiable feminine silhouette near his windows. He'd wanted her last night, not today.

The little witch spun around. Back in her customary drab homespun and apron this morning, she appeared to be stroking a kitten. A kitten. A second glance located last night's gray cat perched on his chair, watching him with a calculating gaze.

"Your nonexistent cat has apparently had nonexistent kittens. I'm petting one," she explained this with kind sincerity, as if he were an idiot who couldn't see what was right beneath his prominent nose.

He didn't know whether he was more annoyed at her for treating him like an idiot instead of an earl, or with himself for being disappointed that she hadn't sought him out last night. "Did you have some purpose here?" Briskly, he strode to his desk to fetch the papers for his steward.

"Sarah sent me to look for a wrap she said she'd left here last night." Ninian thought she kept the accusation out of her voice quite nicely, but the earl's knowing look discounted that theory. She turned her back on him and examined the plants in the window. They definitely didn't look healthy. "What are these?"

"Grass." His curt answer came from just behind her shoulder.

She tried not to jump at his proximity, but she grimaced at his typical response. "Were you experimenting in drowning it?"

"No."

She thought he would end it there, but to her surprise, he lifted a watering pot. "I took this water from the burn, and I'm using it on these pots here." He pointed out the dying grass on one side of the window. "The other pots I'm watering from the well."

Excitement lit little fires along Ninian's skin as she recognized the import of his experiment. "So you can see if it's actually the burn water causing the blight?" She had only her grandmother's teachings to guide her, but this man had learning and knowledge well beyond hers, and she thirsted to acquire it.

"Yes, but they seem equally blighted." Indifference returned to his voice.

"No, just overwatered. They have no air or sun here, so cannot absorb much liquid. They would fare better in a conservatory, with more sunshine and windows that open."

She poked at the grass with the blighted water. "The soil in these pots is smellier."

"Perhaps I should carry the pots outside."

She thought she heard awakening interest in his voice this time. It was difficult interpreting the signs people gave off in word and gesture when she was accustomed to just feeling what they felt, but she was learning with this man.

"That, or water them less," she agreed.

"Would you like to see what I've done with your brook?" he asked abruptly, holding out his hand to her.

She looked at his hand as if it were the devil's cloven hoof, but gingerly accepted it.

"You have found the source of the problem?"

Her pulse pounded beneath his fingers, and Drogo refused to let go when she tried to pull away. Women seldom aroused his curiosity. This one did. He would hold her captive until he'd dissected the reason for that.

"No, but I thought if I filtered the water, we might stop whatever damage the acid is causing." Her cold fingers warmed inside his. Idly, as he led the way downstairs, Drogo wondered how much interference he would receive if he installed the little witch in the castle and took her for mistress while he was here. She hadn't offered herself to him yet, but perhaps she was distrustful of his rank.

"We'll have a storm tonight."

The irrelevant comment jerked Drogo's attention back to the present. They had traversed the hall and stood in the doorway overlooking his sadly bedraggled grounds. His companion studied the heavy clouds above as if they were the only thing of consequence in her surroundings. Perhaps she needed to be reassured of his interest. He had yet to meet an available woman not tempted by the promise of title and wealth.

"Are you afraid of storms?" he asked with what he hoped was sympathy, or understanding. "I've seen some magnificent ones from my tower." He tucked her hand into the crook of his elbow and led her down the path he'd had cleared to the brook. With the trees in leaf, no one could watch their progress.

"Storms have their purpose," she said enigmatically, kicking at last year's leaves. "The sky's passionate attraction to the earth can be a trifle unsettling though."

Drogo grinned to himself. Her mind might take a warped approach, but she knew what he was about.

Once inside the cover of the trees, he slid his arm around her back, and drew her to him. She was soft and malleable in all the right places as he brushed his lips lightly along hers, testing his welcome. Sparks ignited everywhere they touched.

She sighed with pleasure and melted against him, brushing exploratory fingers along his jaw, but before he could engage her more fully, she pressed a hand to his chest and shoved away. "The earth and the moon fight their attraction with violence, my lord. I would rather we not do the same."

She stepped away and disappeared so swiftly into the woods, it was as if she'd merged with the trees.

Drogo cursed under his breath and struggled to regain control. He wouldn't let lust rule his head. He simply needed to find the right pattern of behavior that would entice the wretched sprite into his bed.

It was just a matter of problem solving, like a mathematical equation.

Seven

As she fled down the path, Ninian covered her mouth to hold on to the texture of the earl's lips imprinted on hers. They'd been slightly rough, narrow but with a sensuous fullness as they softened, tasting vaguely of coffee and sugar. The heat of his breath and brush of his whisker stubble still burned on her cheeks.

No one had ever touched her so intimately.

If she tried very hard, she might recollect her father lifting her into his arms and pecking her cheek when she was quite small. Her mother had never offered such caresses, as if she feared the child she had borne. Granny had welcomed her with hugs when she was young, but nothing could have taught her to expect what she had just experienced in the arms of Lord Ives.

She couldn't believe how magical something so simple as a human kiss could be.

She heard him crunching through the leaves behind her. Why had he kissed her? He had three elegant ladies at his beck and call. Was he like Nate, needing to conquer every female who crossed his path?

She didn't like to think so. She wanted to believe he felt the pull of the moon and earth as she did.

She must leave this place. The legends were right. Ives men were dangerous.

His long strides caught up with her without haste. She was

intensely aware of his physical presence. He didn't even touch her, and yet a shiver raised bumps on her skin as he fell in beside her and adjusted his stride to hers.

"How does a filter work?" she inquired when he said nothing.

"I hope to catch the damaging particles so only clear water flows downstream."

He was very adept at hiding his feelings. His voice reflected nothing more than his intellectual interest in the experiment. One would think the moment back there had never happened, that for one point in time their hearts hadn't beat as one. Excitement prickled along her skin, and her pulse accelerated at just his proximity, but he appeared completely indifferent.

"What could catch something so tiny as a particle?" She could play the same game. She had a strong will and an inquiring mind. She didn't have to wonder what his kiss would have become if she'd allowed him to continue.

Was it only her own desire vibrating between them now? Or was that truly interest in his dark glance? It was very frustrating not knowing these things.

"I am experimenting with a number of materials. Rocks and sand are easiest." He spoke as if from a lectern. "Plants have been known to work occasionally, but I have found none that survive in the substances in the brook."

"You have studied filters?"

"Not thoroughly, no. It's not a problem with which I've been presented before. My library is inadequate. But there are certain basic conclusions one can reach given the available evidence."

Ninian halted as she sensed a horse and rider nearby. The burn babbled just beyond the next copse.

Lord Ives looked down at her with curiosity. "Is there a problem?"

"Someone is studying your filter." Unhurriedly, she continued walking. She sensed no danger in the newcomer.

"Payton!" Lord Ives shouted as they passed through the copse and the rider became visible. "What news have you?"

Ninian idled on the edge of the forest as Lord Ives walked ahead to converse with the rider. The stranger was a slightly built man of no more years than the earl. His coat was of sturdy quality, but not expensively elegant. His placid mare nosed the grass away from the stream, and Ninian noticed the rider didn't allow her to drink the water. A commonsensical sort of man, she concluded, one who did as told and did it well, but without ideas of his own.

He nodded to her as she approached, and Lord Ives introduced his steward.

Payton touched his cap politely. "Miss Siddons. I have heard the village folk speak of you."

She dimpled and curtsied. "And you do not fear being cast under my spell?" She really shouldn't say these things. It tempted fate. But she'd been so very, very good at resisting temptation, she had to do something naughty for balance.

Payton looked vaguely startled but smiled. "I'm certain all men must be caught by your charms, mistress."

Lord Ives snorted. "You speak of the witchery of all women. Miss Siddons specializes in healing, not seduction. Tell me what you have found upstream."

She had not thought the earl had noticed or cared about her preferences. Noblemen tended to have more important things on their mind than local superstitions. Perhaps she should be flattered, but she was more interested in what Mr. Payton had to say. She crouched to examine the odd dam of rocks crossing the stream as the newcomer spoke.

"Plant life is failing for miles upstream but recovers slowly the farther downstream I go. Your filter is too new to have evidence of its success yet."

"You still haven't found the source?" the earl asked sharply.

"No, not yet."

Ninian sensed an aura of uneasiness about the steward as his mare sidestepped nervously. She started to speak, but Lord Ives beat her to it.

"The stream divides?"

"And has numerous tributaries. This stretch seems to be slower moving than others, which could be part of the problem."

"There is evidence of damage along one of the tributaries?" Ninian prompted.

Both men stared at her as she rose from the stream bank. Perhaps they weren't used to women speaking. She rather liked the light of interest in the earl's eyes.

Payton formulated his reply carefully. "The tributaries are smaller, faster flowing. I have noticed... a lack of lushness... in one, many miles from here. I haven't had time to explore its length."

"But you have some idea what it flows through?" Ninian prodded. The man wasn't telling the whole story.

Payton shrugged. "It flows from the hills beyond this property. I can't say more."

She frowned, considered questioning him further, and decided against it. Men tended to become stubborn when pressed. She wished she had a horse of her own so she could explore farther, but she wasn't much good at riding. She returned to studying the intricacies of the filter the earl had constructed. He'd used lumps of coal among the rocks and layers of gravel. Mostly, he'd caught dead leaves and branches. He'd have a large pond when the rain broke.

She sensed the steward's departure and tried to distinguish the earl's emotional presence from his physical one as he approached. She couldn't. He vibrated with a masculinity she responded to as if he were her life's blood pounding through her veins.

"He doesn't tell the whole truth, my lord." Brushing off her hands, she stood up again. She was tired of him looming over her.

Dark eyes studied her from behind his emotionless mask. "How so?"

"He must suspect the origins of the tributary carrying the poison, but is reluctant to verify it."

"And you can tell all this because...?"

She turned around and started back up the path. "A little bird tells me." She didn't waste her breath explaining. She had told him what she knew. He could either act on it or not. That was his choice.

He didn't comment on her evasion. Instead, he returned to their original intent. "What do you think of the filter?"

"Very ingenious, my lord. It should be interesting to discover if rocks can stop poison. It should be even more interesting to see how tonight's storm affects it."

"I've thought of that, but without further experimentation, I cannot say. If it's a poison, as you call it, some are diluted and rendered useless by heavy quantities of fluid. Perhaps a good downpour will clear the poison out."

She nodded in admiration at this assessment. "An excellent thought, my lord. I hope you are right. The stream provides valuable resources I cannot replace." She didn't think it healthy for her life in the village if she could no longer make remedies either, but he wouldn't understand the precariousness of life on the thin edge of superstition.

"At least the damage is limited to my land. We can hope for the best."

Ninian accepted the earl's hand in assistance as she climbed over a fallen log. His hand was warm and hard and much stronger than hers as it clasped her fingers and held them. She could almost summon reassurance from that grip, and she was reluctant to withdraw from it once she reached the other side of the log. He didn't release her of his own accord either.

It was as if they communicated through contact. Struggling to shake the sensation, she concentrated on her reply.

"I must warn the villagers not to use your stream," she replied slowly, trying to adapt to the current of sensation flooding through her hand and up her arm. Was this how Ives men bewitched their women? Did the earl possess some power stronger than her own?

"I'd best take a look at the kitchen water," Lord Ives said thoughtfully, staring ahead as if he had only the burn's problem in mind.

She couldn't take the eerie physical bond anymore. Tugging her hand free and lifting her skirt, she fled down the path to safety.

❧

They returned to a house in an uproar.

Lady Twane stood in the great hall, clasping and unclasping her hands, moaning in terror as she gazed up the stone stairway.

Screams and a crashing clatter emanated from the haunted suite above.

Lady Lydie leaned on the upper banister, staring down the hall toward the suite, her hand protectively covering her prominent belly as she hesitated over descending the stairs. She screamed an obscenity at Sarah, who stood beside Claudia, alternately urging Lydie to hurry down and Claudia to shut up.

"Where are the damned servants?" Sarah shouted as glass smashed overhead.

The gray cat sat on the newel post, tail twitching, watching their antics.

Lord Ives muttered a profanity worse than Lydie's and rushed toward the stairs.

As he caught Lydie and helped her down, Ninian had to assume the lady's child was his, since he played the part of solicitous protector so well. She recognized a tug of jealousy, but the wails of the unhappy inhabitant of the upper suite demanded her more immediate attention.

Ninian raced past the earl and up the stairway. She had hung birch and rowan branches in there earlier and scattered the hearth with dill. Perhaps she should have chanted Granny's protective charm as well. She wished she had a flint to light her divination incense.

She shouldn't need divination incense if the ghost's presence was strong enough to demolish a room.

She burst into the darkened suite, expecting an onrush of icy drafts or a chair flying at her head.

All within was calm.

She halted to catch her breath and slow her pounding heart. The drawn draperies shrouded the room in darkness, and the growing gloom of the coming storm prevented even a crack of light. She wished for Lord Ives and his candle, but she inched cautiously inside, seeking the source of the violent anguish vibrating the air.

"At last, a Malcolm," a sigh whispered in her ear.

Startled, Ninian froze. Her Gift did not generally lend to reading minds or hearing ghosts.

"Where there is no heart, we die," the voice whispered mournfully.

"What do you want, Ghost?" Ninian whispered hesitantly.

She was aware of Lord Ives entering behind her, listening. She thought he had a candle and a weapon in his hand, but he did no more than stand guard behind her.

She could sense consternation and frustration as the window draperies blew outward and the chairs rattled. But she received no reply.

Unable to make either head or tail of this, Ninian wished she possessed her grandmother's wisdom. She crept farther into the room, seeking with her senses. Pain, heartbroken torment… These she could feel, but not the thought rendering them.

"What must I do?" she asked of the air around her.

Lord Ives edged to the fireplace, inspecting it with a poker, hitting on nothing but solid stone.

"How can I help? What will make you rest in peace?" *Do you intend evil, or good?* she wanted to ask, but feared the reply. Given her attraction to an Ives, the arrival of a ghost in conjunction seemed ominous, at best.

"A Malcolm must live in Malcolm Castle again. Without hearts, we lose all."

The frantic emotions grew faint, and Ninian sought harder for the source. Lord Ives poked at the drapery, apparently oblivious to the sensations.

"Don't go," she called, but she already sensed the presence had departed.

Lost, she waited, hoping the spirit would return, that she would be struck by a blinding insight into the quandary she'd been handed. All she sensed was Lord Ives losing interest in the draperies and coming to place a hand on her shoulder.

"Are you all right?"

The heat of his hand reassured her in a way she could not explain. Perhaps communicating with a world beyond the mortal one had consequences requiring a human touch. Whatever, she jerked as if he'd awakened her.

"I'm fine. I've never communed with a ghost before."

"Did the ghost talk back?" he asked with a trace of irony, steering her gently toward the doorway.

"Do you know aught of your family's history?" Perhaps the answer lay there. The ghost certainly wished to tell her something.

"Very little." He opened the door to discover all three women waiting anxiously outside. "Have the servants bring up lamps and clean up the glass," he ordered. "I think the walls must be shifting. I'll have a stone mason check them."

He not only didn't believe, he wasn't listening. Angry now, shaken by the unearthly experience, Ninian halted where she stood, refusing to be guided by his comforting hand. "She's in pain!" she cried. "She's trying to warn us. We must listen and try to understand."

Lord Ives lifted his quirked eyebrows.

She glared back. "Was this place once owned by Malcolms?"

Lord Ives shrugged. She could see the frown of concern creasing his brow, but he apparently had no interest in ancient history.

"The original land deeds call it Malcolm Castle," Sarah replied. She lifted her hands helplessly as everyone turned to stare at her. "I have nothing better to do with my time than poke through old papers."

"Then I would research the means by which the Malcolms were dispossessed and the Ives acquired their land," Ninian said coldly. "The ghost is very angry and unhappy. I cannot take responsibility if you will not listen."

Ninian thought to stalk back to her room, gather her things, and march out of their aristocratic lives, but a thunder clap overhead and a cacophonous downpour on the roof slates halted her.

Into the silence following the thunder, Lord Ives spoke. "If you think to take back what your ancestors lost, you are dealing with the wrong man."

The wind howled. Or maybe it was the ghost moaning.

Eight

"NO, YOU CANNOT LEAVE TONIGHT. WE WON'T HEAR OF IT."
Lady Sarah swept Ninian's bag from the bed, caught her arm,
and steered her down the hall to the ladies' wing of the house.
"We are all scared senseless. You must tell us what to do."

Ninian was just a little bit tired of being steered and guided
wherever these people wanted, but she no more desired to
go out in the storm than the ladies wanted her to leave. She
wished she could look on them as the friends she craved, but
she feared they thought of her more as a toy to be played with.

"There is naught I can tell you," she protested feebly.

"Tell us what the ghost said!" all the ladies commanded as
they closed the door on Lydie's room and turned to Ninian.

"Ghosts don't speak much." Ninian said with a sigh as
Claudia held a shimmering blue-green gown up to her shoulders. She really needed a nap more than another session as a
fashion doll. Dealing with ghosts was draining.

Sarah began unfastening Ninian's gown and said, "It's obvious
there is some tragic history in this castle that we must right."

Amazed that flighty Sarah had laid her finger on the
problem, suspecting she did so only out of a fondness for
sentimental fiction, Ninian didn't argue as they stripped off
her gown and draped her in pannier hoops. "Perhaps if you
have papers in your possession, my lady, you might research
the castle's history." She pushed the women in the right direction, though she didn't expect much as a result.

As they dropped the gown over her head, Ninian stroked the frail damask and ignored the excited chatter. She had her mother's love of fine fabrics, it seemed. The panniers held the layers of silk off the floor. She still felt like a fashion doll, but the cold draft blowing up her legs beneath the wiring told her she was made of flesh and blood. She didn't like the way the tickle of the wind reminded her that she was young and restless and a man stood ready to please her anytime she beckoned.

Where had that thought come from? She couldn't read the earl's emotions. She couldn't know his intent. Perhaps aristocrats bestowed kisses thoughtlessly. He certainly hadn't seemed as disturbed by their kiss as she had been.

But somehow, she knew Lord Ives was as aware of her as she was of him.

"There are journals and ledgers and stacks of dusty books and papers in the library." Sarah hooked the fastenings of the gown's bodice with precision while Claudia adjusted the back lacing to fit Ninian's slimmer waist and fuller bosom.

"Perhaps, after you've discovered the story…" Ninian suggested tentatively, gasping as the lacing pulled tight and the whalebone structure dug in, "you might call me back again. Perhaps then I can understand—"

"Nonsense." Sarah stepped back and dusted off her hands as she gazed at her handiwork with approval. "You must stay and give us advice as to where to look…" She waved her hand. "Drogo is likely to leave at anytime, so we must solve this mystery…" Abruptly, she turned to Lydie with a small frown. "Shall we leave the ringlets loose again, or try something more sophisticated?"

Ninian didn't know where to begin protesting. She held her hand protectively to her hair and backed away. "I cannot—"

"She needs jewelry," Lydie decided. "Her obvious charms draw attention without it, but a little extra adornment never hurt."

Ninian's gaze dropped to the exaggerated plumpness of her breasts above the very narrow square cut of the bodice. "A modesty piece will suffice—"

Lydie's laughter cut her off. "Not with that gown. It's French. Isn't it wicked? Turn, and let me see how the train falls."

Ninian was buried in enough silk to clothe a village, yet she was half naked. "Wicked" wasn't the half of it. "Obscene" might come close. She shook her head and tried to find the dozen tiny fastenings molding her into this monstrosity.

Sarah grabbed her hands. "Don't be silly. It's perfect, as if it was designed for you. Lydie, you have some paste...?"

"That's all I have," the young woman replied with bitterness. "In the top drawer, Claudia." She indicated her massive trunk. "I'd thought I'd at least have jewels to sell."

"Well, yours wouldn't be the first family to sell off the family gems," Sarah drawled. "Perhaps if they'd told you of their precarious financial situation, you wouldn't have been quite so foolish as to get yourself with child on a man with no wealth."

"Would it have been better if she married a man with wealth and had her virginity taken by a beast?" Claudia asked caustically. "At least she's had some pleasure of it."

Ninian's head spun so with the barrage of information, she forgot her protests as Sarah fastened a gaudy tangle of glittering glass around her neck. She didn't know the difference between diamond and crystal, but the necklace picked up the colors of the gown and reflected it in a breathtakingly iridescent sparkle.

More importantly, she tried to unscramble the clues of their conversation. Lydie's child was by a poor man? Not the earl?

"I should have come to you for the herbs you told me—" Lydie popped her hand over her mouth with an "oops" before Sarah had time to cut her off.

These women were up to something. Maybe she ought to leave.

The dinner bell gonged loudly, echoing through the high stone corridors. This time, Ninian didn't jerk with surprise. Numb from an overabundance of information, her thoughts spinning, she escaped the room under the guidance of both Sarah and Claudia.

Lord Ives awaited them at the bottom of the stairs. The

discreet embroidery of his black coat and gold waistcoat and the expensive quality of his lace cuffs spoke of generations of wealth and aristocracy. Coal-black hair caught in a ribbon gleamed in the lamplight, and even though he was freshly shaved, the shadow of his beard accentuated the stark masculine planes of his jaw. Dark eyes glittered as he studied the bejeweled rainbow descending the stairs.

"You play their games well, Miss Siddons." He bowed mockingly and took her hand on his arm as Sarah delicately pushed her in his direction.

"No, I don't," she muttered under her breath.

He cocked an eyebrow but didn't inquire further as they reached the linen-bedecked table. Candlelight glimmered against silver, casting light on the storm's gloom.

"We have decided to research your castle, Drogo," Sarah declared cheerfully. "Miss Siddons will interpret for us."

"I have no…" Ninian shut up as a footman materialized to pour the wine. Why argue? She'd simply leave before the ladies called for their chocolate in the morning. The rain pounding against the windows warned of the foolishness of leaving tonight.

"An interesting project, I'm sure." Lord Ives lifted his wine, sipped, and nodded his approval to the servant. "And if you find nothing of interest, are you prepared to argue with a ghost?"

He was mocking them, Ninian knew. A man of science, with a toplofty intellectual bent, wouldn't heed things of the spirit, things that must be taken on belief without material evidence of their existence. It didn't matter. She could see no answer to the conundrum the ghost presented. Likely, the lady had existed here for centuries. She could exist a few more, until someone wiser interpreted her unspoken plea.

As Ninian sipped the rich wine, she noticed the earl's gaze drawn to the immodest exposure of her bosom. A warm flush crept along her skin, and she swallowed a large gulp of the wine. She coughed as fire burned down her throat.

"Gently, Miss Siddons," he admonished. "Wine must be sipped, not guzzled. Have you come to any further conclusions about our ghost?"

She practiced sipping, just to show she knew how. The wine really did affect her body temperature, she noted. She no longer felt the room's chill. Or perhaps it was the heat of his gaze on her neckline while his finger traced the edge of his glass.

"Since you do not believe in the ghost's existence," she answered tartly, "I cannot think you have any interest in my opinion."

"Now, now, Miss Siddons, do not judge dear Drogo so harshly." Sarah leaned over and patted her hand where it rested on the tablecloth. "He must see to believe, admittedly, but I cannot think him beyond hope. He just needs someone who can make him see through different eyes."

Ninian withdrew her hand and clasped it around the crystal stem of her goblet. "I wish you well of that task, my lady."

Drogo chuckled. "She has you there, Sarah. I think you underestimate Miss Siddons' perspicacity."

The footmen refilled his glass as a maid removed the soup course and a third servant presented the vegetable course. Ninian noticed that his lordship was more interested in the quality of his wine than in the food on his plate. The creamed potatoes were rather overspiced, admittedly, but she ate rather than swim in wine.

It seemed odd that he didn't shut her from his thoughts as he had the previous night. Why was he staring at her like that? And was that perspiration forming on his forehead in this damp air? His grasp on the goblet seemed oddly tense.

"The jewels look like something Lydie would wear," Lord Ives observed as Claudia and Sarah chattered. "They are tantalizing, but they do not really suit you."

The husky rasp of his voice and the odd intensity of his gaze seeped through her flesh into her racing blood. Her own skin felt tight and feverish.

Since she did not believe jewels or this gown or this company suited her, Ninian refrained from replying, couldn't reply. Her head spun too uncertainly. She was increasingly aware of his attention, of the flickering candlelight, of the steady pour of rain against the roof and windows. Lightning crackled, illuminating the candelabra-adorned table with ghostly illusions, and she had to blink not to see other people and earlier times in this hall.

She had always been attuned to the world and its essence around her, more so than most people. Usually, she was on the outside, wistfully watching as if she were the audience and all others, actors on a stage.

Tonight, she felt as if she were actually a part of the performance, at one with the drafts and the flickering candles and the ghosts laughing and drinking at the far expanse of the table beyond the candlelight.

She tried not to include the imposing man at her side in the world she sensed, but he filled it with his every breath, every movement, as if, in some time or place, they had belonged together. An odd urgency to test that theory swelled within her, but she didn't know how to act on it.

Without looking, she knew the moment when the shock of awareness hit him—the moment when he recognized the flow of energy between them. Somehow, she knew he felt the same heated demands pounding through his blood when he set his empty wineglass down and cursed beneath his breath. She didn't have to turn to see the reason for his curses, because it raced through her own veins, desire dancing in its wake. She didn't know if she sent out these vibrations or if he did, but they were as real as if he'd touched her and spoken the words aloud.

"Sarah, I will make you pay for this," he intoned ominously as he shoved his chair away from the table.

Ninian stared at the way his long fingers clenched the linen, at the silky dark hairs nearly hidden by the starched white lace falling over his hand. He had strong, sensuous fingers that would appreciate the texture of a woman's skin, fingers that would instinctively seek the erotic places…

She blinked in surprise at the path of her thoughts. Never in her entire life had she—

"Come, Miss Siddons. Let us escape before they poison us further." The strong brown fingers locked over her helpless white ones.

Oblivious to the company, she stared at their joined hands. Once again, his heat soaked through her skin, and she watched in fascination, hoping to observe the miracle, as if their flesh might become transparent.

Amusement laced his voice. "Obviously, you're not a very good witch, Miss Siddons. Don't you know protective spells against other witches?"

Other witches? Knowing she looked an idiot for blinking again, Ninian followed the tug of his hand and rose from her seat, focusing on his face for enlightenment, ignoring the smug smiles of their companions. The sardonic curl of the earl's lip should have told her something, but she could never read this man as she did others.

"Sarah has a friend who deals in magic potions. Isn't that what witches do?"

She shook her head in denial but didn't have the words to explain. He didn't seem to require a response. His heated look said everything as he held her hand trapped in his.

"I think I like you like this, Miss Siddons," he observed as she followed him compliantly across the towering hall. "You are usually much too wrapped up in your herbs and ghosts and healing. Being an object of your intense study is a pleasant change."

She should be embarrassed that he'd noticed her fascination, but she wasn't. She didn't even flinch as his strong arm circled her waist to steady her ascent of the stairs. She had the strangest notion that he craved the closeness as much as she did.

"Am I drunk?" she inquired soberly.

He chuckled again, a deep, perversely pleasurable chuckle that rumbled up from his insides and into hers.

"Victim of your own sorcery, I suspect. Or do you not dispense aphrodisiacs?"

"Aphrodisiacs work only on the deluded…" she started to say scornfully, then blinked again. He would think she had eye spasms, but she kept seeing things from strange angles. "I'm not deluded," she said firmly, to reassure herself, though she'd been suffering delusions from the moment she'd met this man.

"Probably not," he agreed, steering her down the darkened hallway to her room. "Just feeling the old pull of the moon and the tides like the rest of us mortals."

Thunder rolled overhead, but Ninian gave it no notice as she pondered his words. "Are you saying Sarah put something...?" She stumbled over the question as he pushed open her bedroom door, brushing unnecessarily close as he did so. She looked down to see the white of her breasts pressed dangerously near the dark cloth of the earl's coat, close enough for the lace of his jabot to tickle.

"That, or alcohol and excess stimulation have released our inhibitions, freeing us to act on our rather fundamental attraction to each other."

Attraction. He was attracted to her. The knowledge shivered down her spine, but her mind was too muddled to define its true meaning. She didn't think it was alcohol or aphrodisiacs burning through them, but she didn't know enough to explain the uncanny bond, the seemingly natural need to be with him.

To just once feel close to a man, this man.

The hand at her waist slid higher, pressing her closer. She was aware of dark eyes piercing the privacy of her heart, pinning it as it thumped, but she couldn't look beyond the lace at his throat to verify her awareness. "I see," she murmured foolishly.

"Come, Miss Siddons, it is no more than the throbbing excitement of a night beneath the full moon in a lover's arms. We may choose to indulge or not, as we please. It's rather pleasant having one's inhibitions removed, is it not?"

Somehow, he had her beside the high bed, with the door closed behind them. Ninian refrained from blinking again as she realized someone had lit candles all around the room and drawn the window draperies open on the electrifying flashes of lightning outside. The bed hangings were drawn open, too, revealing a bed turned down in open invitation. She wasn't too drugged or stunned to understand the precipice she was walking now. She could feel the edge crumbling as clearly as she could feel the carpet beneath her feet.

She had been lured to this castle for a purpose.

The brief revelation dissipated the instant Ninian lifted her eyes to Lord Ives. The dark reflective pools she looked into revealed her future more clearly than a crystal ball, if she could believe what she saw staring back at her—raw hunger, heady passion, and the uncertainty of loneliness.

She required the breezes of human emotion to function. He had nothing but lust to offer.

"We do not have to do this, you know," he reminded her, even as his dark head bent and his lips whispered over her cheek. "We can thwart the ladies' joke, say good night, and you can be on your way in the morning."

She could, but she already knew she would not. Logic had fled her wits, but instinct poured through her fingertips. She caressed the rich satin of his waistcoat, felt the tense hardness of the muscles beneath as he held himself still. She'd yearned for this sort of closeness all her life. Yearned for it, imagined it, questioned its existence. She could not deny her need to know—to take one step beyond the narrow world she knew.

"I am not beautiful," she murmured senselessly.

"That is like saying the moon has no charm," he scoffed, threading his fingers through her hair.

Shivering, Ninian wrapped her arms around the earl's broad shoulders and basked in the warmth and power of his hunger as he caught her against him. She'd never known a man's dominance, never walked in a man's world. What could it hurt to try just once?

Her grandmother's warnings fled with her wits. As Lord Ives drew her into his embrace, his wool coat wrapped her cold flesh in heat.

The flick of his tongue against her innocent lips tumbled all remaining barriers, plunging her into the depths of paradise.

Nine

BRAIN FOGGED WITH SARAH'S DAMNED LIQUOR AND THE perfume of the moon maiden's roses, Drogo descended swiftly from the logic of his mind into the passions of his body. Lovemaking had become too clinical for him these last years. The joy and exuberance of youth had faded with the cynicism of experience. Ninian's innocent kiss welcomed him to the excitement of his first time again.

Ninian. A saint, not a witch. Smiling at the odd path of his muddled thoughts, he drove his fingers deep into her hair and drank joy and wonder from the melting of her lips. He experienced her excitement as well as his own, arousing his senses doubly, heightening his desire with unprecedented speed.

Urgently, he demanded more, until her mouth opened beneath his, taking his tongue as if it were a holy wafer and not the possessive claim it was. Perhaps she considered lovemaking as a religious experience. In this case, she could be right. The sweetness of her breath breathed life into his soul. He wanted to inhale her. His grip tightened at her waist, pressing her breasts into his coat, until his breathing matched hers, their hearts pounded together, and the clothing between them was unnatural.

For a brief moment, Drogo wished the harpies hadn't imprisoned the nymph in this tent of whalebone and wire. In her simple attire, he could have thrown up her skirts and joined her without the delay of hooks and laces and acres of silk. Instead, he lowered his hands to the hooks of her bodice.

Ninian's awe-filled gasp as he released her bodice and his knuckle brushed the underside of her breast repelled any urge to hurry. Despite the burning urgency of his body, his mind functioned clearly enough to want this to happen slowly, seductively, and for the rest of the night. He needed to fill his hands with her flesh, taste of her skin, revel in her softness.

In the flutter of light and scent of a dozen candles, with the nurturing pour of rain from the skies, he could almost convince himself this was the woman who could swell with his child.

His mind danced past that thought as shadows danced past the curtained bed. He wanted her, and she wanted him. For the first time in a long time, that was enough.

"I give you this last chance to say no," he warned, releasing her mouth to draw his finger inquisitively over a pouting pink nipple. It drew up tighter, and he smiled. Her body answered more clearly than her words, he noted in relief, since he didn't think he *could* stop. For the first time in memory, he acted on instinct alone—the instinct for survival. If he did not have her, he surely would not survive. He cupped the fullness of her breast and stroked again, feeling the tug in his groin that she must feel in her womb.

"It's not right…" she protested weakly. Her breasts flushed with color at his attention, and her fingers dug more firmly into his shoulders, giving the lie to her denial.

He located the tapes of her skirt and loosened them, knowing there were things he should be saying, yet unable to form the sentences logically. The wire baskets at her hips collapsed on the floor, taking the lengths of silk with them.

She froze as he removed the soft lawn of her chemise, and she stood naked before him. Light played against skin finer than cream, unmarred except by a beauty mark where thigh met hip. No hollows or planes or hard angles here, he observed with a connoisseur's satisfaction, only rounded curves and a pillowed softness a man could lose himself in. He slid his thumb along the curve of her breast and waist, down to her hip until it rested just above her mound. *His*, his muddled mind declared, focusing on the welcoming entrance between her legs.

She tried to cover herself with her hands, but he caught them and spread them wide to better observe her.

"Exquisite," he murmured. "You were meant for better than sheepherders."

"My grandmother would kill me," Ninian whispered in one final protest, though she felt the power of him drawing her in already and knew the futility of words. Thousands of protests jumbled through her mind, but she could voice none of them. A creature of instinct, she could only act.

"Your grandmother would not know unless you bear fruit, and then she would be the happiest grandmother in the kingdom." He released her wrists to throw off his coat. "Everyone knows Ives men only produce sons, so I would be honor bound to marry you."

His waistcoat fell to join his coat, and Ninian stared at Lord Ives in wonder as he loosed his jabot. In shirtsleeves, the earl stood tall and wide shouldered, muscles rippling beneath his fine linen. Every arrogant inch of him screamed nobility and privilege. Only a man accustomed to riding the swiftest horses, gracing the most elegant drawing rooms, indulging in the idle games of archery and fisticuffs, could develop the easy grace and power he possessed. Here was no studious scientist but a stallion in the prime of life, willing and able to service any mare he cornered.

But then his mocking comments regarding sons and marriage sobered her. If their joining produced a child, he would marry her, and a Malcolm would once again occupy Malcolm Castle. The ghost's appearance seemed strangely prophetic. Was the ghost warning her against mating with an Ives? Her grandmother had said to be true to herself and avoid all Ives. But right now, being true to herself meant forgetting everything and everyone but this Ives.

"Ready to try your luck at becoming a countess?" he taunted, dropping his shirt on the floor.

Ninian gaped at his chest in awe. "No, that's not what I want," she whispered. Unable to resist, she ran her fingers through soft dark curls, and pleasure surged through her at his sharp intake of air.

"Good, because it's not likely." Without warning, he grabbed her by the waist and dropped her on to the down-turned bed linens. She sank into the feathers and did not have time to struggle up before he fell beside her, pinning her with a leg still clad in breeches.

"Does your skin taste as rich as it looks?" he asked, tickling her ear lobe with his tongue. His hard, dark body leaned over her, trapping her until her breasts tightened and her flesh tingled with his nearness. But instead of touching what she wanted, nay, *needed* touched, he continued his exploratory kisses along her throat, to her nape.

Just when she thought to scream a protest at his teasing, the earl claimed her mouth again, and his tongue took another intoxicating foray that left her breathless.

"If not for the storm I would continue this in my tower, under the stars," he murmured as he released her lips and pressed a trail of kisses down her throat. His tongue lapped gently at a nipple so achingly hard with neglected need that Ninian practically launched off the bed in pleasured surprise. "But then, perhaps a storm is appropriate for this night."

His mouth fastened more fully over her breast, and Ninian uttered a primal cry of joy and deep, powerful desire. Moisture pooled in her womb, and her body readied itself for this act she'd never expected to know.

As if understanding the strength of the tug between breast and womb, Drogo slid his hand between her thighs and spread her until she cried and shuddered beneath him. "You are as eager for this as I am," he said with satisfaction, rubbing lightly with the heel of his hand. "It's good to know it's not just the promise of wealth and title you crave." The feverish gleam in his eyes belied his words, as if he struggled to separate mind and body—and his body was winning.

"I… never… wanted that." She gasped as pinwheels of light spun behind her eyelids, and she realized she had no control over her own limbs. They spread wider at his urging, recognizing only the demands of the earl's questing fingers.

"Ahhh, but you can have that, all for the price of a babe in your belly. Imagine that, will you? A simple thing, one any woman can do."

Somewhere in the recesses of her mind, Ninian knew the fallacy behind his seemingly casual comments, but she had no interest in his worldly temptations. She wanted only the joining that would seal her fate and put her forevermore under his mastery. She knew the fallacy of that, too, but no longer cared.

As his thumb deepened the pressure and stroked higher, her back arched, and her hips rose and twisted and sought what only he could provide, until she screamed a protest at his delay and drove into his hand. Only then did he lower his head to suckle at her breast and apply the strokes that released the tension throbbing in her loins, in her womb, in every thread and nerve of her body.

She cried as her world exploded, and through her sobs, Ninian heard his chuckle of satisfaction. She couldn't react. She floated somewhere outside herself, unable to sort right from wrong, reality from illusion. She only knew—it wasn't enough.

She muttered an objection as he took his hand away, and he brushed a kiss against her cheek in response. "A moment, greedy moonchild."

The bed shifted, but lethargy held her too firmly in its grasp for her to turn and see where he went. She felt empty, deprived in some manner, but too content to question. This wasn't the form in which her grandmother had warned devils staked their claim.

"My turn," he announced from somewhere above her.

With difficulty, Ninian opened her eyes and stared straight up—into the dark features of a completely naked Lord Ives. Through the open bed hangings, lightning still flashed in the windows framing him. Thunder roared, and rain poured. Candle flame glowed and billowed in the cold drafts from the walls. Shadows played across flesh darker than hers, flesh covered in a soft down of black hair, muscled flesh that rippled with tension as he kneeled between her spread legs.

He loomed enormous, his curled eyebrows drawn down in concentration as he studied her while she studied him.

Gulping, fighting a shiver of panic at the irrevocable claim he would make next, she lowered her gaze to the arrow of hair on his chest as he leaned over, trapping her between corded arms. In the dim light, she could see the gleaming jut of his man's part, and even as terror spread, she opened her legs wider and lifted her hips to welcome him, understanding the reason for the ache of emptiness there.

"Ah, you know your place well, moonchild." Kissing her lips, teasing her breast into readiness, he positioned himself. "Do you wish to chant a spell for good luck?"

He didn't give her time to answer. In one powerful stroke, he penetrated her moistened passage, ruptured the barrier, and planted himself deep beneath her belly.

A cry of mixed rapture and pain tore from Ninian's throat. Drogo hesitated.

Then, with a curse, he withdrew and pumped again, driven by the consuming hunger between them.

She was too narrow, and he was too big. Only a devil would split her asunder like so. Ninian dug her fingers into the strong arms trapping her, but she couldn't pull away any more than he could stop. Instead, she opened wider still and met his thrust.

Driven by the urgency of the madness they'd plunged into, he stroked deeper, filling her more completely, claiming her in the eyes of God and man.

She wanted to scream but couldn't. She wanted to cry, but only a whimper emerged as he plundered her body with a sureness she no longer thought to escape.

The wind picked up outside, dousing the candles one by one. The strain and determination on her lover's taut features didn't falter as he drove her harder, forcing her back to the glorious heights through sheer strength of will.

Her hips lifted, and he growled approval deep in his throat, thrusting so high he carried her with him. Once started, she couldn't stop. She matched him stroke for stroke, taking him deeper, accepting his domination, giving up some piece of her soul in trade for the changes he promised.

"Yes!" he sighed through his teeth. "Now!" he commanded, caressing her urgently with his thumb, using the trick he'd already taught her.

And well taught, Ninian exploded all over again, inside, outside, through every racing particle of blood as he penetrated the hollow beneath her belly and poured his life force deep inside. He shuddered and groaned with the power of his own release, and Ninian's muscles contracted to hold him tighter.

For one brief moment, his soul touched hers, and joy poured through her at that brief whisper of knowledge. She saw inside of him, felt him, like a flicker of warmth… and then, it was gone, leaving her bereft.

Moisture trickled down her thigh as she slipped from full consciousness. She was aware of the man leaning over and suckling at her breast—the devil, if the legends were to be believed. She'd succumbed to temptation, and now he'd only to beckon and she must obey. His teeth grazed her nipple, and the connection returned, the tug between breast and womb, the pointed reminder of what a woman's body was designed to do. She had no doubt he'd done it, she realized sleepily as his mouth released her but his spell did not. The moon was in its proper phase. Her body had been primed and ready, and Malcolm women were always fertile. Too fertile, her grand-mother had said. And they always bore witches.

What had she done?

Lord Ives—Drogo—rolled over beside her, letting his hand play sensuous games with her breasts.

She didn't know what to say. She couldn't seem to care what she'd done, what she would do again, given a chance. Perhaps he was right, and Sarah had actually found an herb that would act as aphrodisiac. She didn't think so though. This connection was more than just of the body. It burned through her soul, as if she were truly possessed.

"I apologize."

Startled, Ninian found the strength to turn her head. He didn't look remorseful. He looked remarkably pleased with himself as he rode his hand over her belly and examined the birthmark on her hip.

"For what?" she asked, for lack of better response.

"For not believing you a virgin." He collapsed back against the bed, forming a pillow with his hands as he stared up at the canopy. "I was a dolt."

"A drugged one," she suggested.

He shrugged, and she admired the play of muscle in his broad shoulder.

"Not unless I've been drugged for days. I generally avoid virgins, so I suppose I convinced myself you weren't one."

She smiled. The studious professor was returning. "I'm well past the usual age of bedding," she admitted. "And I'm not inclined toward virginal simpering."

"That's it. You obviously deluded me into making an ass of myself."

He leaned on his elbow over her. He didn't look angry or menacing, so she decided he was teasing. It was hard to tell with a man who wore his face like a mask.

But the play of his hands on her flesh conveyed a message she could not mistake, nor deny. She arched beckoningly beneath his touch.

"I've always wondered what it was like." She caressed his bristled cheek, sampling this male texture she'd never encountered in her all-female world. His jaw twitched, but he did not pull away. She smoothed the ribbon hanging loosely from his long dark hair as it fell over his shoulder. "It was a trifle difficult counseling young girls when I knew nothing."

He nodded. "Glad to be of service. Anytime you like, I'm at your command."

He had to be teasing. She stroked the moisture of his lower lip. "Now?"

He tensed, obviously struggling again in the battle between mind and body. This time, however, his strength of will won. "You're sore and still feeling the effects of Sarah's mischief-making. I'll not take advantage of you again." Reluctantly, he pulled the covers up around her. "I'll put out the candles."

When he swung his legs over the side of the bed, she could see he was fully aroused again. Yawning, she admired the pride of Lord Ives until the candles smoked out. He was a very big man, in more ways than one.

With the rain still pounding on the roof, she snuggled into her pillows and slept.

Drogo carried the last candle to the bed and looked dispassionately down on her golden curls. He'd given up thought of wife and child many years ago. Cynicism had arrived with the events of the past year. Women would do anything for a title. This one did not strike him as so conniving, or desperate, but then, neither had the last one.

It was simpler and more productive to immerse himself in the mathematics and astronomy he loved than to indulge in painful human relationships.

But just for one night, he'd known real passion again. He would thank her for that.

And in the course of things, when he left here, as he knew must, he would see her taken care of, as he took care of all the people in his life.

Ten

Ninian woke to a cold dark bed. The heavy draperies had been pulled around her to prevent drafts, so she could see naught, but she knew it was still night, and she was alone.

She lay still, contemplating her new status of fallen woman. She'd not been brought up to consider human mating more than a natural extension of the earth's fecundity. One plowed and planted in spring to bring forth fruit in fall. Society placed impediments on this natural cycle for good reason, she supposed. Human children needed years of care and protection before they could go out on their own, so society required a man to protect the woman and the fruit they produced.

But Malcolm women didn't need a man's protection. Malcolm women took care of their own.

Uneasiness stole over her. She didn't mourn the loss of her virginity. She'd never expected to marry, and she had enjoyed the lesson he'd taught her. But the thought of bearing the child of an Ives…

Pulling the heavy covers more tightly around her, Ninian tried to recall words they'd uttered through the veil of passion. Ives men always produced sons, he'd said. Yet he'd said he wasn't married, and Lydie had indicated her child wasn't his. Did that mean Sarah's children weren't his either? Did he have no children?

Although women were always called barren when children didn't arrive, her grandmother had explained that it was not

always the woman's fault. Perhaps Lord Ives had infertile seed.
That would be best for both of them. She could enjoy the
lessons he provided without the burden of worrying over her
cursed fertility. Her aunts had provided enough females for
the Malcolm legend to continue without her duplicating their
efforts. She really didn't need to be arguing with an earl about
heirs and titles and all those worldly concerns she'd rejected
when she'd chosen to stay here with her grandmother and
accept her responsibility as the Malcolm healer.

Shivering at the enormity of the problem, deciding she
couldn't worry over things that couldn't be undone, she sat up
and pulled a heavy blanket with her as she sought her chemise.

She had to depart in the morning. She didn't like wasting
what remained of the night.

⟡

Drogo didn't hear her enter. He looked up from his desk
to see her standing there in the moonlight, her golden curls
tangled around her face, only her thin chemise protecting
her bare shoulders above the blanket she'd wrapped around
herself. She looked the part of enchantress she claimed to be,
and he smiled.

She looked vaguely startled that he'd smiled. So innocent.
He wished he could believe that innocence would last, but
it really wasn't necessary. She'd given him what no other
woman had, and he was properly grateful.

"You'll freeze," he admonished, rising to throw a few more
coals on the brazier. Blood surged to his groin at just the sight
of her, and he knew damned well Sarah's silly potion had
worn off hours ago.

"I did not mean to disturb your studies," she said primly,
not flinching as he halted in front of her. He knew his size and
possibly his station intimidated her, but she seemed to have no
sense of vulnerability, even after the pain he'd inflicted on her.
She drew a deep breath and daringly met his eye. "Why did
you leave my bed?"

The demands began already, but he supposed he owed her
an explanation. "Because I no longer had the excuse of too

much drink should I ravish you again." She had such a bright and open expression that it blinded him. He couldn't tell what went on in the diverting byways of her mind.

She met his gaze steadily. "You wanted to ravish me again?"

"Repeatedly," he agreed grimly.

Drogo might have believed Sarah's potion responsible for the remarkable experience they shared, but he'd just spent hours in a cold tower with nothing but mathematical equations dancing through his head, and the instant Ninian walked in the room, he wanted her again. As he had since Beltane.

He'd never needed a woman as he hungered for this one, and he didn't like the knowledge. He preferred controlling his environment and not the reverse.

Pacing, he wrestled with the illogic of the situation. He hadn't thought himself so crass as to be aroused by the power of total possession. Even as he thought that, he turned to watch the vivid expressions fleeting across her face and wanted her more.

She didn't have the grace to look mollified at his admission but continued challenging him with wariness. "Do you fear bewitchment?"

Startled, Drogo choked on a laugh. Turning more fully to admire her, he dipped his gaze to the place where her blanket slipped and the moon's light illuminated the pearl of her breasts. "I'm not a superstitious man," he reminded her. "I only feared harming you further."

"I am not harmed."

To his astonishment and deep, abiding pleasure, she dropped the blanket and stepped from its folds, blessing him with the sight of firm curves draped only in candleglow.

"I will warn you, though, that you will get no heirs from me. Malcolm women only bear girls."

"Once, there must have been a Malcolm man to lend you his name." The spurious debate over his nonexistent children had no importance to him. He'd come to terms with that long ago. He had not had time to come to terms with the witch's charms. Drogo reached for her, dragging her from the cold floor so they saw eye to eye, glorying in her responsiveness. "Do not cry rape come morning," he warned.

She wrapped her rounded arms around his neck and pressed his lips with a kiss he'd taught her, then added a mischievous lick of her own. "So long as you do not," she agreed.

Laughing for the first time in months, Drogo carried her downstairs to his chamber, where he could plant himself between soft thighs, heedless of the consequences.

An ardent student, she responded with alacrity to his lessons. He taught her so well, he actually forgot the stars and slept.

⌀

Ninian woke to the sun blazing in the west window of a strange chamber. Groggy with more than the prior evening's heavy wine, she winced and covered her eyes. Other aches replaced the one in her head. Her cheeks and breasts burned with a fiery rash. Her nipples ached. She never noticed her nipples. She peeked from beneath her arm to stare down at them in amazement where they purled tight in the cool air, ready for plucking.

The soreness deep between her thighs jerked her more fully to consciousness. She had done it. She had mated with Lord Ives. It hadn't been a vivid dream after all.

How odd. Her hand drifted over her belly but hesitated before dipping lower. He'd taught her the temptation of Eve. She knew her Bible well. Granny had insisted on it. But couldn't he be Adam rather than Satan? Must witches always be cursed by devils?

Remembering the bright fire of passion in the earl's eyes, the shadows of a harsh jaw, the way raven hair fell forward as he pumped into her, she couldn't say yea or nay. If she'd been possessed by a demon, he was kindlier than most. He'd covered her thoroughly in his rich blankets and set a fire burning in the grate.

Of course, demons were experts on fire. She giggled as she gave into the ridiculousness of her superstition. She was as bad as the villagers. Lord Ives had blighted nothing but her virginity, and that was no loss.

Her head spun as she sat up, and she steadied herself against the mattress. The result of too much wine and whatever foolish aphrodisiac Sarah had introduced into both wine and food, she surmised. Whatever on earth had possessed the silly woman to push her into bed with his lordship?

Well, it didn't matter now. It wasn't the end of the earth if she carried his child. The Malcolm trust fund ensured that no Malcolm female ever need go hungry. She could easily raise a daughter in the same way she had been raised. Her father might rant and rave over the injustice of it, but Malcolm women took care of their own.

A daughter. She smiled at the thought. She'd never considered an infant of her own before. She'd best start thinking about it now.

The dizziness didn't entirely dissipate once she washed in the warm water simmering over the grate and dressed in the clothes someone had thoughtfully provided. Unlike the extravagant evening gowns and panniers the ladies had dressed her in, these garments were of a practical nature. She fingered the delicate lawn chemise and lovely soft blue wool. Lord Ives probably thought he was providing for the comfort of a mistress. He wouldn't be happy once she persuaded him otherwise.

She needed to return to the people for whom her Gift was intended, to the village, where she belonged.

Wishing for a good birch bark tea to ease her aches, Ninian traipsed down the tower stairs to gather her things. She wished she could dally, but she knew the joining of Ives and Malcolm would bear a high price. She dare not risk the suffering described in the legends.

That Drogo could easily torment her, she had no doubt.

She debated bidding him farewell but decided it best not to disturb his studies again. The women would tell him soon enough.

She descended the stairs carrying her bag, fully expecting an argument should anyone see her in the hall. But the day was fine, and she had strong legs. She could walk the distance home. She didn't need anyone's help.

She hadn't expected all three women to be sitting around the fire, waiting for her. Perhaps it was well past noon, but she didn't consider herself of such importance that anyone would expect her company. They all looked up and watched her with interest as she crossed the flagstones.

"You're not thinking of leaving, are you?" Lydie inquired brightly as Ninian approached. "We've only just begun to search the library."

"You should not be climbing stairs," Ninian reminded her sternly.

She laughed and held a hand to her bulging belly. "I expect to be delivered of him any day, and if climbing stairs brings him sooner, I'll not complain."

"He may not be in a proper position if you deliver him sooner. For the child's sake as well as your own, stay upstairs." Ninian nodded to Sarah and Lady Twane. "You must see she obeys. I am not always available when a child decides to arrive."

"Oh, but of course you will be," Claudia said with dismay. "You'll be right here. You can't go anywhere yet."

Patiently, Ninian tried to dispel that foolishness. "I have a mother about to deliver in the village. When Lydie's time comes, if you send the cart, I'll be here in time."

"Oh, don't worry about that," Sarah replied airily. "We've sent word to the village so they know where to find you."

A small shiver of fear shook Ninian's spine. Were all of London nobility this selfish? If so, how had her mother tolerated them? Remembering her grandmother's curses of her father and his friends, she wondered if she should have listened more closely. "It is not so simple as that," she explained cautiously. "I have my garden to tend, herbs to dry, things I cannot do here."

Claudia brightened. "We'll ask Drogo to rebuild that old conservatory you were working on. You could grow all sorts of marvelous plants there. It will be lovely having our own apothecary in residence."

The thought of that conservatory was tempting. She could grow tender plants she had only heard about, plants that could be very useful… Ninian shook her head as she recognized temptation when she saw it. Perhaps the ladies were the devil's handmaidens, rather than Drogo. "No, thank you very much, but I must go."

Sarah stood and hugged her. "I am sorry to hear that, dear, but you really cannot leave, you know. After that last foolish chit got herself pregnant by another man and declared the child Drogo's, we simply cannot put him through that again. We must prove to him that any child you carry is his, beyond any possibility of doubt. We cannot do that if you go into the village."

Stunned, Ninian thought she had not heard her rightly. She sifted her brain for the proper response for something she couldn't have heard.

"He's gone into the village to check on the storm damage," Claudia offered. "I'm sure he'll bring back any news."

Ninian didn't know what his lordship's relation was with these three women, but she didn't intend to be one of them. She didn't need the approval of a man who already had three wives. Or mistresses. Or whatever they were.

Smiling falsely, she nodded. "I'll wait for him then."

Accepting a scone and tea, she ate unhurriedly, then returned upstairs with her bag, leaving the ladies chattering of researching the library. Instead of dropping her bundle in her room, she slipped down the hall, found the servants' stairs, and descended to the kitchen, easily retracing her path to the conservatory. Within minutes, she was in the woods and on her way home.

Evidence of the storm's havoc surrounded her as she picked her way over fallen trees and trudged through mud and puddles large enough to be ponds. Perhaps the heavy rain would have cleared the stream, and vegetation could return again.

Hurrying to investigate the damage to the village, Ninian stepped off the beaten path into the overgrown jungle of the woods. She knew her directions well, and she didn't fear the fairies as the villagers did. If fairies were actually spirits waiting to be reborn, as her grandmother's tales said, they could scarcely harm a living person.

She'd welcome their guidance right now. She'd just given herself to a man she could never marry, a man whose odd company of women thought to hold her prisoner for his sake, or for the sake of his purely imaginary heir. Really! Sarah had been reading entirely too many medieval romances in that library. Ninian wasn't certain which of them had run mad—the ladies for dreaming up this scheme or herself for falling into it.

She wondered if Sarah might have found stories about Malcolm women in her library and if that might be why she'd sought Ninian out. Surely any legend would relate the disaster of Ives joined with Malcolm. Sarah couldn't be so meanspirited as to…

Ninian halted beneath a rowan tree on the edge of a glade she'd never crossed before. Sunlight danced on a fairy ring in the dew-laden grass, and sensing a presence she could not see, she hesitated, her fingers digging into the rowan's bark.

The instant her hand touched the bark, something moved inside her, just as Lord Ives had last night.

Gasping, she released the bark, and her hand flew to cover the space between her hips. Recalling how Lord Ives had kneeled above her last night, claiming her as his own, she murmured a hurried protective incantation. Surely they couldn't have created a child in one night. But if they had… Her grandmother had been right about the fairies. A spirit had just been reborn within her.

She looked down at the place her hand protected. A child? Mother of all that was holy…

A Malcolm, the wind whispered. As long as there were Malcolms in Wystan, there would be Malcolm witches.

Lord Ives would call it superstitious folly. He was probably right. These were modern times. Fairies didn't exist. But she felt what she felt, and alive with the knowledge, she skirted around the glade, pretending the quickening of her womb was no more than an aftereffect of the night's passion.

She had truly eaten of the fruit of folly.

Granny had said denying her instincts denied her power. But instinct was so hard to prove…

Detours around the debris scattered by the storm took more time than she'd anticipated, even with the shortcut. It was late afternoon before she arrived at the beloved picket fence of her garden. She frowned at the broken rose canes and the place where the old oak had lost a limb and smashed a fence post. Safe within solid stone walls, she hadn't realized the storm's severity. A broken oak was a bad omen.

Caught by a frantic wail on the wind, Ninian fled through the gate and into the cottage. All seemed quiet.

Her gaze fell on the storybook on the parlor table, its pages flipping lazily on an unseen current. As she watched, they fell open and lay still. She could have sworn she'd left it closed. In trepidation, she turned the book so she could read the page.

> *"The child is a girl, my lord."*
>
> *Lightning flashed through the mullioned window, illuminating the pallor of his lordship's face as he heard the news.*
>
> *"Nonsense," he said softly. "Ives only sire sons. You are mistaken."*
>
> *His wife lovingly held out the whimpering bundle of blankets. "A daughter, my lord. A bonnie wee girl."*
>
> *"Then it's not mine."*
>
> *"No-o-o-o," the wind howled as he turned and strode out, never to be seen again.*
>
> *And his wife wept tears so long and so hard that the waters rose and the valley filled and the lands lay fallow for many years to come.*

The burn rose in times of flood...

No longer denying instinct, suddenly frantic, Ninian raced toward town.

Eleven

WHAT HAD SHE DONE? THE LEGENDS WARNED OF THE DANGERS of Malcolms and Ives. They created havoc together—like the storm, she thought as she ran toward the village. She could see the damage all around her. The late-evening sun breaking through the overcast clouds didn't warm her. Broken tree limbs loomed, anxious to grab her. The washed-out road threw obstacles in her path. She shivered as she saw a dead cow in the field and heard the rush of fast waters in the usually bubbling burn.

A Malcolm and an Ives had mated and already, the blight spread and destroyed. She'd given into temptation, and the devil's reward was already at hand. Her grandmother had been right. What had seemed so beautiful by moonlight, revealed its ugly face at dawn. This time instinct told her to be afraid.

By the time she reached the village, Ninian wasn't surprised when Gertrude grabbed her sisters and shoved them inside at her appearance. Nate's father made the sign against the evil eye and slammed his door in her face.

It's too late.

Mary. Mary wouldn't turn her back on her. She'd taught Mary and her children their letters. Ninian had delivered her babies, nursed them in sickness, played with them in health. Mary couldn't hate her.

Cautiously, Ninian slipped around to the back. Mary's cow

nibbled at a muddy patch of grass amid the debris left by the swollen stream. A tall hedge hid her from prying eyes. Surely, if no one saw them...

Mary peered cautiously around the door at Ninian's knock. She almost slammed it before Ninian had the sense to shove her heavy shoe in the crack.

"Mary, for the love of God! Tell me what's wrong," she pleaded.

Hesitantly, Mary stood in the crack, blocking all access to her children. "You've been with Lord Ives, haven't you?" she demanded. "Don't you remember the legends?"

"I've been tending to a woman about to give birth! What are people saying about me?" But deep in her heart, she already knew. She'd always been one step away from their superstition.

Ninian had tried diligently to play the part of simple healer, but the people in the village weren't fools. While all was well and she helped the needy, they tolerated her. She could see with her own eyes that all was no longer well, and the dreaded word "witch," had risen with last night's wind.

"There is sickness all over town," Mary whispered harshly. "The stream turned into a river and washed out our livestock and our homes and tore down all that we've built. Don't tell me the legends aren't true!"

"Oh, my God, Mary! I'm sorry, I'm so sorry." Ninian scrubbed at her eyes, fighting terrified tears, but nothing could drive away the stabbing pain. She had done this. Somehow, she must make it right, but how? She still couldn't believe what she'd done was wrong or that the earl and his household had any knowledge of witchery. It just wasn't possible. She had no magic.

"I don't know what to do," she whispered, panicking. "The earl has nothing to do with any of this. You must believe that. It has to be the stream. I've warned you..."

Mary looked wary but didn't turn away. "We've used that water for generations. It's never turned on us before."

"I don't know why. I need time... Please, Mary, what can I do?"

"It's better if you go back to the earl and his women—to your own kind," Mary said, her earlier harshness softened.

Glancing in horror at the gray cat wrapping itself around Ninian's ankles, she slammed the door.

Ninian had never known true loneliness until it blew through her like a winter wind now. Picking up the cat that had apparently followed her, she faltered under the loss of her only friend. She'd always known she was an outsider. She hadn't arrived in Wystan until she was ten, but she'd thought the villagers had accepted her over the years because Malcolms had lived here since the dawn of time. The tenuousness of her acceptance was apparent. She didn't belong anywhere. The emptiness of her life echoed hollow as she stared at the future ahead of her.

Sobs jerking her breath, Ninian trudged back to the road, hugging the cat for comfort. It would take weeks to send for her aunts. She could go to the castle and see if the ladies would persuade some of the male servants to aid the village, but it would be tomorrow before she could walk there and back. And it had to be those same servants who had reported the castle happenings to the villagers. Everyone knew what she had done.

Guilt and shame flooded her as it hadn't before. It had all seemed so right with Lord Ives holding her. Somehow, he had blinded her to reality. Now, she could see it was all wrong. She had fallen to the devil's temptation, despite all her wariness and strength, and he'd destroyed all she knew and loved.

Even as she thought of him, she walked straight into his arms.

The earl caught and steadied her in the dying shadows of daylight. Even now, with her life crumbling in pieces under the weight of what she'd done, his arms provided a haven of security.

"You shouldn't be here."

"I live here," she whispered as the cat fled her arms and her head spun with uncertainty. She used to live here. The whole world had turned upside down, and she didn't know if she was falling off or climbing on. The earl's strong grip offered safety, just for this minute, just until she found the ground beneath her feet.

"I'll take you home."

She didn't even know which home he meant, his or hers. Ninian shook her head in denial. She had to get away from the earl, from the village, go back to the only real home she'd known—her grandmother's cottage. She didn't know what she would do once she got there. Tears spilled down her cheeks again.

He didn't hug her, probably didn't know how to offer hugs of sympathy. He merely glanced down at her tear-stained face and drew her deeper into the shadows, toward the cottage.

"I'll take care of it," he said in utter certainty.

And he did.

In a haze of grief, Ninian watched as the earl shouldered all responsibility and assumed command. He stalked from door to door, commandeering shovels, hoes, and men, sending them to bury dead animals, repair torn roofs, drain swollen ditches. He might lack the ability to connect with people on any personal level, but he knew how to make them jump.

As the villagers crept from their houses and the earl's steward arrived to take command, Drogo silently took Ninian's arm and steered her toward the cottage.

Sarah waited in the kitchen. "I've gathered her things," she told him. "As quaint and charming as I'm sure this place is, I have no wish to remain here. The ghost was weeping when I left. Claudia is frantic. And Lydie vows the baby will arrive any minute."

"You'll come home with us," the earl commanded Ninian, leaving it evident he expected no argument by steering her toward the door.

Ninian knew she should resist. Granny would want her to stay here, to tend the garden, to find some means of helping the village.

But Granny had left her here all alone.

For the moment, she couldn't summon the courage or spirit to fight. She'd always thought friendship worked both ways, but it seemed no one wanted her except when she was useful. She wasn't useful now. Not to the village. Maybe she never had been. Maybe her gifts were just products of Granny's imagination and her own pride. They certainly hadn't aided her in saving the village.

Silently, Ninian followed the earl and Sarah from the cottage. She was needed at the castle. Maybe in a few weeks, things would return to normal, and she could come home to her garden again.

Closing the cottage door behind her, not looking at the broken rose canes of her garden, Ninian walked out the picket gate to the cart waiting to take her to the castle of her ancestors and the future fate had in store for her.

❧

Drogo rubbed his weary eyes as the candle guttered in a puddle of wax. He'd thought Ninian would have come to him by now. He'd left her in Sarah's care, but he didn't expect Sarah to offer much in the way of commiseration. He'd seen that blank gaze of grief before and knew the little witch needed more than sympathy.

In his experience, the first thing a woman did when confronted with disaster was turn to a man. The second thing she did was look around to see if he was the best man to feather her nest. Since he was the only man on the horizon, he assumed Ninian would be up here sooner or later, looking for the promise of a title. He really couldn't blame her. A woman had to have strong survival instincts in this world.

He would gladly offer the comfort of his bed. Unfortunately, he wasn't prepared to offer more unless his price was met.

The sound of feminine feet on the stairs outside his observatory stirred his tired brain, and he smiled. Women were so predictable.

His smile faded as Sarah entered, wearing only a thin night robe.

"I couldn't sleep," she said with that false bright smile she used when nervous.

"The ghost still weeping?" he asked, returning his quill to the stand. He could bury his sympathy for Ninian in work, but he hadn't been able to quell his arousal at the anticipation of her arrival. Sarah's presence quickly doused his ardor.

"No, but you didn't seem to be sleeping either. I thought you might like company."

Drogo shuffled through a drawer and produced a fresh candle, lighting it with the dying flame of the first. "I have work to finish. I have to return to London in the morning." He knew what she wanted. She hoped to prove she wasn't barren in the same way he hoped to prove—what? That he could sire bastards as easily as his father? Stupid.

Her mouth turned down, but she watched him with more curiosity than disappointment. "Your guest is still awake. I heard her crying as I passed by."

"She knows where to find me if she needs me," he answered curtly, returning his attention to the page of numbers on his desk.

"What if she doesn't need you?" Sarah asked softly. "She didn't strike me as the dependent type, like the rest of us."

She walked out, but her words nagged in her absence. Drogo glared at the numbers on the page but couldn't make sense of them any longer. Everyone needed him for one thing or another. The little witch wasn't any exception, just more stubborn than most.

And more tempting.

He shoved back his chair, and picking up his candle, wandered down from the tower to the hall where Sarah had conveniently placed Ninian. Women always came to him, not the other way around. He'd never pursued a woman in his life. He wasn't pursuing this one. He just wanted to see if she was all right. He certainly didn't need to seek out any more leeches to suck his life's blood out of him.

He could hear her sobs as he stood outside her door. He had no experience in dealing with female hysterics, but he couldn't bear hearing her cry. She'd been so full of light and mischief yesterday, he hated to hear her pain now.

Last night, she'd invited him in. He could see no reason why he should stand on propriety tonight. He tested the latch and opened the door.

She gasped, as she almost always did when he appeared.

He wondered if he really was so terrifying to look upon, and only Ninian in her innocence was open enough to show it. She didn't seem terrified though. She grabbed her sheet and covered herself as she sat up, and she looked furious enough to spit nails. In the flickering light of his candle, he could see the streaks of moisture on her cheeks, but he was more interested in the tangle of golden curls falling over rounded breasts.

"What do you want, my lord?"

"I heard you crying," he said simply, having no other words to offer. He wasn't a particularly gentle or compassionate man. He vaguely understood her disillusion but knew no real solution other than time. Physical comfort, however, he knew how to give and would willingly offer, if it was acceptable.

"I cry when I'm unhappy. Don't you?"

He thought she was being sarcastic, but he considered her question anyway. Logic usually worked best in emotional situations. "No," he finally answered. Not in a long time, anyway, but he didn't need to explain that. "I waited for you to come to me."

In this light, he couldn't tell if her eyes widened with surprise or anger. At least he'd given her something to think about that stopped her crying.

"I refuse to be one of your coven," she announced stoutly. "You may strike me dead, if you like."

Not a moonchild, but a lunatic. Staring down into the vehemence of her expression, Drogo sighed in bewilderment and lowered the candle to the table. It was a good thing he was leaving in the morning. "I won't pretend to understand what that means. I'll leave you with this. Good night."

"You won't pretend to understand that you've brought death and destruction to Wystan?" she demanded.

He glanced at her over his shoulder, so beautiful with her translucent face illuminated in the candlelight, and her defiant chin tilted proudly. Pity the beauty hid a cracked brain. "The storm brought destruction," he answered carefully.

"The burn never flooded like that before. It never died before. Ask your steward what he hides from you. My grandmother was always right. An Ives has ruined us again."

If he lived to be a hundred, he would never forget the wonder and beauty of a golden-haired witch in candlelight, even if she was a lunatic.

As utterly befuddled by his own reaction as hers, Drogo nodded politely and escaped.

Twelve

AWAKENED BY DAYLIGHT POURING THROUGH THE WINDOWS, Ninian wondered if she'd dreamed the last few days or just last evening's strange encounter with Lord Ives. As she dragged herself from bed in search of food, she reluctantly accepted that she must decide what to do about the rest of her life.

She could return to the cottage, raise cats, and plant herbs no one would ever use, and grow into the witchy old lady the villagers expected of her. Alone.

Unable to accept that forlorn future quite yet, she located the ladies in the same place as the day before—or at least two of them waited there. Sarah had an immense dusty tome on the table before her, while Claudia embroidered the hem of an infant's nightshirt.

Sarah glanced up from her reading and gestured at the empty chair. "You've just missed Drogo. He's off to rescue my brother Joseph from Newgate. Have a scone. The jam is heavenly."

Not certain whether to be relieved or not at news of the earl's departure, Ninian took the chair indicated and accepted a cup of tea. "Joseph? He's an Ives?" The legends had said to beware of Ives. How many of them were there?

Sarah smiled. "An Ives from the wrong side of the blanket, but we all grew up together."

Ninian wasn't certain she was prepared for this much information about the upper echelons of society. She buttered a scone to keep from thinking too deeply about anything. Pain lay only a thought away.

"Might I ask how many of you there are?" Perhaps she could grasp enough facts to keep her grounded. Really, if she knew more about these people, maybe she wouldn't be so afraid of them. Remembering her tirade at the earl last night, she thought again. Maybe she should be afraid.

Sarah wrinkled her brow in thought. "Well, Drogo is the eldest of the legitimate Ives, of course, since he inherited his father's titles. Dunstan is the second eldest. He manages the family estate. Ewen is third. I believe it must have been at that point poor Lady Ives decided she could not bear a fourth boy and denied the late earl her bed. I'm not at all certain of cause and effect, you understand, since my mother was married to my father rather than Drogo's, and I was scarce more than a child at the time."

She pushed the plate of scones toward Ninian. "Have another, dear. You must keep your strength up if you are to be a Countess of Ives."

Sarah didn't even take a breath after that strange announcement but continued following the path of her own thoughts. "Ives men are infamous for their prolificacy. There is scarce two years between Drogo and each of his brothers, and my mother bore the earl three more boys once they set up housekeeping. All bastards, my brothers are, of course, but Drogo supports them. He could scarcely do less, since they grew up in the same household."

Battered by both the barrage of Sarah's words and the tension of repressing her emotions, Ninian sipped her tea and eyed her manic hostess with caution. "I see. Of course, you do realize I am a Malcolm?" The question made as much sense to her as Sarah's chattering apparently made to Sarah.

"Oh, yes, Drogo did mention that. I'm sure the Malcolm ghost will be gratified to know a Malcolm will once again reside in Malcolm Castle. Although…" She puckered her brow slightly. "Drogo will never be able to stay here for any length of time. I'm certain he will wish to introduce you to the family and take his place in society once he has a child of his own."

Ninian smiled and nibbled her scone, wondering if Claudia would join in the idiocy. "You don't seem to understand," Ninian replied demurely, wishing them both to the devil. "Malcolms only bear witches. Female witches," she clarified, not wanting there to be any doubt that she would never bear an Ives heir, wishful thinking or not.

Lady Twane chirped quietly at this announcement. Sarah only shrugged.

"Well, that should make for some enlightening entertainment nine months hence, but it's of no matter. Drogo will marry you once he ascertains you're with child. You see, he thinks he can't have children. Lydie chose that moment to shriek her pain and terror from the chambers above.

Ninian continued nibbling her scone. She recognized the onset of childbirth. There wasn't any immediate need for hurry.

With quiet realization, she accepted that now the earl had departed, she didn't have to leave just yet. She was needed here.

❧

Drogo leaned back in his desk chair and studied the coquettish young lady hiding behind her fan. Her hairdresser had styled her powdered hair in tight, white ringlets that emphasized her kohl-darkened eyes and matched her heavily powdered face. He thought the combination of black and white ludicrous, and remembering a natural blend of sun-brightened golden curls and thick brown lashes, frowned at his lack of concentration.

"I'm sorry, I cannot tell you where Lady Twane is. Perhaps you should consult Sarah," he added maliciously. The twit in front of his desk would have no more idea of where Sarah was than she did her own sister, but he owed Sarah a grievance. He would let the pests descend on Sarah's mother. That formidable ogre would make her pay.

"I am *so* worried about Claudia," the lady whispered, rattling her fan, and leaning forward entreatingly. "Could you not help us? Lord Twane is beside himself with grief."

"Lord Twane beat the lady within an inch of her life more than once and has expressed his remorse every time. Pardon me for not believing his protestations of grief." Impatient with his visitor's patently false display of concern, Drogo picked up his pen. If this baggage thought he'd fall for her charms, she should grow another brain. Claudia's parents had sold her to the highest bidder, buying her younger sister time to find a wealthy man on her own. They certainly shouldn't be so enamored of themselves that they thought he would serve in that capacity. Or had the lady got herself with child and needed a title to go with it? That seemed to be the common ploy these days.

"Oh, but my lord, he truly sees the error of his ways this time. It's just that he's been so disappointed that Claudia cannot bear him a child..."

She stopped just in time, stepping away from Drogo's dagger glare.

"Twane has bastards aplenty. Let him adopt a few," he replied gruffly. "Now go on. I've work to do."

"Please, my lord." She sidled closer. "We've all been so concerned. Could you tell us where to find Sarah?"

He hadn't stood up when she entered, or offered her a seat, a tactical error he regretted as she laid an entreating hand over his. She had long, narrow fingers, beringed and bejeweled, unlike the soft unadorned hand that he'd held last. Ninian's honest touch had rung bells of sincerity somewhere deep in his soul. This woman's touch rang nothing. Perhaps the little witch had moonbeams for brains, but he couldn't doubt her innocence. Maybe lunatics were preferable to the deceitful jades of society?

He leaned back in his chair again and drew the feather of his pen through his fingers. "What hold does Twane have over you? Has he refused your father his quarterly allowance unless Claudia returns? Or does he demand you warm his bed in her place?"

She paled beneath her already white face powder and drew back her hand. "Don't be absurd," she protested.

But he knew he had her. He knew Twane. The baron possessed an animal lust unassuaged by nightly visits to brothels even as a bachelor. Claudia had confessed some of her husband's perversions to Sarah, who had promptly regaled Drogo with them, demanding he defend her friend's honor. He couldn't, of course. He was no relation. Hell, he had problems enough with his own relations without taking on the problems of friends of relations. There were more needy people in this world than he had time or money to rescue.

"I suggest you accept the offer of the first man strong enough to protect you, and then get the hell out of Twane's clutches," he said roughly. "I can't help you."

Desperately, she clasped her hands over her waist. "He raped me," she whispered. "He'll do so again. Please, my lord, you must find my sister."

Drogo sighed and rubbed the knot between his eyes. "You prefer your sister suffer in your place? How charming." Still, her plea jarred him. He couldn't leave a helpless female unprotected. Curse his dratted conscience; he saw his mother's desperation in every damned woman whose path he crossed. "I'll send you to my brother and his wife. They won't let Twane near you. That's all I can offer."

She looked as if she might object. She no doubt hoped he would offer her marriage. She'd probably hoped she could wield her wiles, seduce him, and pass off any child Twane got on her as his. She was certainly young and attractive enough for most men to take on faith. But Drogo was no longer that naive, and she apparently interpreted the coldness of his expression correctly.

She backed away. "Thank you, my lord. I am more than grateful and will attempt not to place too heavy a burden on your family."

"My carriage will be waiting outside in half an hour. See if you can pack discreetly," he warned.

Head bowed, she nodded and departed.

Joseph bobbed out of the priest's hole as soon as the door closed. "Hell's gate, Ives. Dunstan will have you by the ballocks for that. Or more likely, his wife will."

To school his patience, Drogo drew a mental image of his castle tower, complete with velvet skies and twinkling stars and Ninian shining golden naked beneath them. Even if he couldn't visit paradise in truth, his thoughts served him better than reality, for in his head, Ninian could be as brilliant in mind as in form.

The thought relaxed him sufficiently not to follow his first impulse to throttle his half brother.

"Your stay in Newgate has certainly extended your vocabulary," he said dryly, giving up on the calculations on the desk in front of him. Propping his boots on the already scarred walnut desktop, he opened a drawer and produced a handful of sweetmeats, not rewarding Joseph with any. "Have you nothing better to do but eavesdrop?"

The boy shrugged and dropped into the nearest chair. Despite his youth, he already possessed the wide shoulders of an Ives, and he twitched them nervously against the seat back. "I thought I'd guard your virtue. I saw her coming."

Drogo rolled his eyes at this eldest of his bastard brothers. At the moment, Joseph had chosen to ape him by refusing hair powder and wigs and going about in unadorned plain frock coats. Convenient for the family budget, at least. Too bad the dark curls softened the effect.

"As my heir, it's time Dunstan shared some of the burden." Drogo popped a candy and dallied with the image of Ninian a little longer. Was she really superstitious enough to think him the devil? If he returned to Wystan, would she still be furious with him and refuse his bed? Or would her unpredictable humor have changed to prefer a try at becoming countess?

Joseph slumped deeper into his chair. "Our father should have stopped while he was ahead. There's too damned many of us and not enough to go around. I don't know why you let Dunstan have the estate."

"Because he loves farming, and he's my heir. His children will someday inherit it. Makes sense to me."

"How do you know I wouldn't be good at farming?" Joseph muttered rebelliously.

"Because you were raised in town and don't know one end of a sheep from the other. How do you know you wouldn't enjoy the military?"

"Why did Dunstan and Ewen stay with your mother in the country and you didn't?" he countered.

Drogo sighed. Joseph had been but a lad of five when their father died. Not overly inquisitive, he'd always accepted their erratic family ties without question. Drogo supposed it was time his young brother began to question. He threw Joseph a walnut kernel from the mix. He missed.

"That was the separation agreement the courts allowed. My father kept his heir, and my mother was allowed to raise Dunstan and Ewen. My mother was allowed one of the smaller farms as her residence if she did not come to London and interfere with my father and your mother. It happens all the time. Remember it when the time comes for you to consider marriage."

"Never!" Joseph replied vehemently. "I'll not let any hellcat sink her claws in me. I might not be book fodder like you, but I'm not addlepated enough to saddle myself with whining women and clinging brats and courts demanding every last penny I earn."

"You've not earned any," Drogo observed wryly. "Have you decided on the military or the priesthood?"

Joseph scowled. "Are those my only alternatives?"

"Well, we could apprentice you to a solicitor. Just think of all the blunt you could earn from us writing marriage settlements for a living."

"And separation agreements." Gloomily, Joseph sought the missed kernel in the folds of his coat. "I don't suppose there's money to be made in architecture."

"The family never builds houses, and you'll not get any other clients. You can't draw worth a damn."

Joseph sighed as he located the treat and popped it in his mouth. "Might as well try your route, then. I'd rather grow rich in boredom than be shot at by red Indians."

"Smart choice. I'll make the arrangements. Why don't you tell Jarvis to send 'round the carriage?"

"Damned good thing you never married, Ives," Joseph drawled, standing up. "A wife would either pitch us all out on our ears, or run home to her mother after she discovered you with one of your tarts begging at your knees."

"Heaven forbid," Drogo agreed fervently. "I have enough on my hands. Can you imagine what it would be like in the next generation if I had a brood of boys of my own plus whatever bastards the rest of you breed?"

At thus being acknowledged as adult enough to breed bastards, Joseph brightened. "Can you imagine what would happen if an Ives had a girl?"

"There's Sarah," Drogo was forced to point out.

"Yeah, she ain't even an Ives and look at what's happened to her."

As Joseph idled out, Drogo contemplated the truth of his younger brother's comment. Maybe the lad had a brain or two after all.

Maybe God hadn't given him children because he already had an entire family of them.

⤛⤜

Morosely, Ninian dug her fingers into the dead sludge of the burnside. No amount of manure or ashes had returned plant life to the part of the stream running near Wystan Castle. The banks were as barren and muddy as after the flood.

The storm had wiped out the earl's filter. It had been nearly two months, and he hadn't returned to rebuild it. What had she expected? That the devil would repair his cruelty?

Or that he'd be longing to see her again as much as she craved his presence?

Knowing better than to think such thoughts, she picked her way upstream, searching for the lichen she'd discovered along a faster flowing part of the water. There was sickness in the village, but she lacked many of the fresh plants she needed to treat it. The flood had even taken her garden. She'd hoped to have accomplished more by now, to have restored health to the village so she might return home. But she couldn't even restore health to the plants, and the villagers still turned their backs on her.

The constant companionship of at least one of the ladies every time she entered town didn't help. In the villagers' narrow minds, she had returned to her own kind.

She had, however, managed to save Lydie's baby, both from childbirth and from Sarah's plans to put her out for adoption.

In these last months she'd learned more of Sarah's controlling nature than she liked. Whatever foolishness Sarah might
believe, Ninian had no intention of providing the earl with an
heir by marrying him. And she certainly didn't need anyone
else dictating her future. Granny's well-meaning manipula-
tions had been sufficient for a lifetime.

But the conservatory slowly growing behind the castle
held her captive with expectation. Ninian used the excuse of
Lydie's infant to stay where she felt needed, and she let Sarah
spin her idle fantasies in return for a reprieve from loneliness.
She would no doubt pay for her laziness one day, but she
hoped it would be when she was stronger.

She turned down the path to her garden, knowing full well
it annoyed the woman accompanying her.

"You're doing Lydie no favor," Sarah scolded as Ninian
stopped to dig another plant from the forest floor.

"And you are a more meddling and manipulative witch
than my grandmother ever was." Ninian gently eased the root
from the ground and into her basket.

"I'm just trying to help," Sarah protested. "Lydie's family
can't take her back with a child. They're telling everybody
she's visiting friends in Scotland. In a few weeks, she can go
home and find a good husband."

"A wealthy one, you mean." Ninian lifted a kitten from the
hole she'd just dug and rubbed its furry face against her own.
The cats followed her as much as Sarah did. She loved their
easy acceptance. Selfish creatures, they only required feeding.
"That should be Lydie's decision, not yours."

"Lydie is sixteen, and too foolish to know what's good for her.
No man will take her with a bastard. She can keep the child and
starve on the streets, or she can give the child a good home and
start a new life for herself, a safe one, with a man who might come
to love her. She's very beautiful and quite lovable, you know."

Ninian sat back on her heels and wiped the dirt from her
hands. "Men are not the solution to everything. Does Lord
Ives threaten to throw her from the castle?"

Sarah shrugged. "Drogo never threatens. But her parents
can cause a scandal if they discover he's protecting her."

Ninian tilted her head to look up at her. "And you'll do anything to protect Drogo?"

Sarah looked annoyed. "You see entirely too much. Hurry up, now. Claudia may have found another volume of family history by now."

Illness still ravaged the village, the crops had failed, and Ninian was no closer to a solution for her problems. She was certainly a failure as a witch.

But lately, she had had reason to suspect she was far more successful at some things than others.

If she wanted to escape Sarah's tyranny, she had best do it soon.

Thirteen

August, 1750

NINIAN CLUNG DIZZILY TO THE POTTING BENCH AND BLOCKED out Lydie's chatter as she concentrated on remaining upright. Swimming in and out of consciousness, she forgot to clench her fingers and almost lost her grip. Her knees wobbled. She couldn't force her legs to move.

Lydie shoved a stool beneath her. "It hit me that way, too. I was afraid to stand up for a week."

Heart pounding erratically, Ninian sank on to the stool, not registering anything Lydie said. Three months, and the earl still hadn't returned. She couldn't wait any longer for him to help solve her problems. She'd have to do it on her own. She'd have to ignore Sarah's hysterics over leaving. The ladies had comforted her when she needed friends, but she knew her duty. It was time to return to it.

How could she possibly fix the burn by herself?

"I'll call Sarah," Lydie said breathlessly. "She wanted to know the instant you quickened. So many women lose their babes in the first months, you know."

As Lydie departed, Ninian rested her head on her knees, just as Granny had taught her. The dizziness faded, replaced by what she had tried to deny.

Lord Ives had possessed her and stolen everything she possessed in return, leaving her with something far more dangerous—his child.

She carried the child of an Ives, of an earl, of a man she barely knew. In begetting this child, she'd lost the respect of the village and the only life she'd ever wanted. Had the begetting of the innocent soul in her womb been the cause of the ruination of Wystan?

How would she raise a child who would be scorned by every person in the vicinity?

"Ninian, are you well?"

Sarah's question seemed to come from a distance, but Ninian managed to nod her head. Maybe she would create her own village of unwed mothers, take Lydie and her babe home with her so she wouldn't be alone.

Not a chance. Sarah had plans for everyone. She would have to escape before the web tightened. She wouldn't give up her child. Never, no matter what nonsense these London lunatics dreamed up.

Taking Sarah's arm, Ninian stood up. Her head still spun, but not badly. The morning sickness had taken much of her strength, but it shouldn't last much longer. She'd be fine enough to return to her cottage any day now. To her empty cottage.

But there was one thing she needed to know before she left. Turning to the young girl who had returned with Sarah, she asked, "You have heard nothing from your baby's father?"

"The father is a footman," Sarah said scornfully, adding to Ninian's small stockpile of information, relieving her more than she liked to admit. "The child belongs here among the peasants, despite her sentimental silliness."

"I want to keep her," Lydie protested feebly. "She's all I have that's truly mine."

Sarah shrugged. "Then good luck finding employment to support her." Her eyes narrowed as she turned to Ninian. "You're pale. Come inside where it's cool. I'll not have you losing Drogo's son."

At that blatant announcement of all she feared, Ninian stared in dismay at Sarah's bland features until her vision narrowed and almost disappeared altogether. Swaying, she accepted Lydie's guidance into the cool kitchen. How long had they known? They'd planned this. They'd as much as said so. Why? Did they wish to steal her child too?

"I've written Drogo," Sarah said placidly.

Ninian swayed beneath this new blow. She'd told the earl? Catching the table, she lowered herself into a chair.

As if she didn't explode still another cannonball, Sarah continued, "He should be here to fetch you in a day or two."

Fetch her? The earl? May The Lady preserve her!

Ninian's gasp finally caught Sarah's self-absorbed attention.

"You thought we hadn't noticed?" she asked incredulously. "You've not had a monthly since you arrived, and it's hard to disguise your retching. Besides, the stars said you would carry his son." Contentedly, she handed Ninian a teacup as she contemplated Drogo's arrival. "It's a pity he could not find someone with more town polish," she shrugged, "but you'll do to beget his heirs. Now, he can't call me a silly female any longer, and I can have my children back. Maybe he will give me an allowance so I won't have to live with Mother or marry anyone I don't wish to marry."

The rest of Sarah's chatter became a distant buzz in Ninian's ears. The earl knew. He would be here any day.

He couldn't take her away. She couldn't leave Wystan. Especially not now.

She thought she heard the ghost howl at the thought.

～⁕～

Was he reading this right? Could it possibly be true?

Drogo struggled through Sarah's illegible, cross-hatched letter again, threw it on his desk, and stalked to the window to stare out at London's nightly fog. He jammed his hands in his coat pockets and clenched them into fists. He gritted his teeth and wrestled with the wildness pounding at the jaded walls of his heart.

He had to have misread. Sarah would do anything to move out of her mother's house. Or she had thought of a new scheme to get even with him for unleashing her mother's rage. He and Sarah had a long history of seeking revenge on each other.

But he knew beneath the bombast, Sarah only sought his approval.

Terror slithered in through a hitherto unknown crack in his guard. He must have misread Sarah's chicken scratching. He needed to reread it, prevent another dashing of his hopes. He didn't think he could survive another fall from the cliffs.

Joseph wandered in, trailed by his younger brother, David—the eldest two of his biblical trio of half brothers. Drogo wished his stepmother, Ann, would keep a tighter rein on her sons, but she hadn't even insisted that they complete their schooling after they'd been heaved out countless times for frolics too inventive for their own good.

"There's a new orchestra at Vauxhall," David suggested hopefully.

Drogo couldn't pull himself out of his fog to reply. Sarah's letter seemed to grow larger and more demanding the longer he let it lie there.

"Could I have the colors Joseph doesn't want?"

David had never been as insouciant as Joseph. He'd always fought for attention in the tumultuous upheaval of the Ives household, and he'd learned to do it well. At eighteen, he was taller and broader than Joseph and faster to come to blows.

He'd have to leave his brothers on their own if he returned to Wystan.

The dread rising in Drogo's soul had naught to do with his brothers. He turned and picked up Sarah's letter.

"You can join the cavalry after you've completed your education," he answered absently, staring at the paper in his hand. Was that an "m" or an ink blot in front of "other"? "Ninian, mother"? Was she telling him Ninian had adopted Lydie's child?

"Ain't that Sarah's letter? Is she coming home yet?" Joseph wandered over and tried to look over Drogo's shoulder. "She never did learn how to spell."

Maybe that was it. Maybe she had misspelled something and it had come out "child." What could she be saying here? Chilled?

"There's no sense in going to Oxford if I take colors," David protested, pacing the study. "I just need to know how to sit a horse and point a musket."

"And look good in a uniform," Joseph added sarcastically, giving up on the letter and helping himself to the sweetmeats in Drogo's desk.

"You'll gain promotions faster if you can at least write a letter better than your sister," Drogo muttered, collapsing in his chair and muddling through another sentence. They'd done what? Held Ninian captive? That didn't make sense. He shuddered to think of it. What sounded like "captive"? Or looked like? Cap? Tiv? Tin. Captain. They held Ninian captain?

"Girls don't need to write," David declared disdainfully. "She ain't had any teaching. I could write better than that when I was in leading strings."

"You never were in leading strings." Joseph sprawled in a chair in the same fashion as Drogo. "You ran wild all the time."

"No more so than Paul," David objected. "He needed caning—"

"Shut up, both of you." Drogo slammed the letter down and stood up. "I'm bringing Sarah back from Wystan. We may have guests. Tell Jarvis to prepare rooms. Tell your damned mother I'll fund her visit to Scotland if she leaves by day after tomorrow." He strode toward the door.

"What about the nursery set?" Joseph yelled after him.

"Sarah will want her children here. Open the nursery."

Drogo's voice drifted through the darkened, empty halls of his London town house as he took the stairs two at a time.

Beneath nearly identical dark curls, David and Joseph exchanged surprised looks. As far as they were aware, Drogo had never entered the neglected attic nursery since it had been furnished. Sarah and her children always stayed with their mother in London.

A major Ives upheaval was afoot.

❦

Cursing his foolishness, cursing Sarah, cursing the lazy horses he'd hired at the last posting house and urging them faster, Drogo raced his carriage through the night.

His terrified coachman had long since retired to the interior with a flask of gin. The lurching and swaying of the lumbering coach had nearly unseated the man more than once.

Drogo didn't miss his company. His own jumbled thoughts provided entertainment enough.

He'd given up on Sarah's letter. The only way he could determine the truth to his satisfaction was to confront the women personally. He knew Sarah could look him in the eye and blithely tell him entire books of lies. He was hoping the little lunatic was less sophisticated.

He was hoping a damned lot more than that.

As the night wore on and weariness crept in, he couldn't believe he not only had the ability to still hope, but that he would be interested at all.

He'd meant what he'd told Joseph. Marriage wasn't for him. He'd given it considerable thought before Dunstan decided to marry. By that time, it had become morbidly apparent he hadn't sired a single bastard on any woman who'd crossed his bed. Marrying for any reason but heirs was of no purpose. The family he had was sufficient proof that Ives weren't meant for monogamy, love was nonexistent, and children were far overrated, or so he'd told himself, repeatedly.

He didn't need a wife. He didn't need an heir.

But what if he'd finally, after all these years, begot one?

❧

"Impossible!" he exploded as the three harpies all talked excitedly at once.

"Impossible!" he declared later as he cornered Ninian in the privacy of her chamber and stared at her still slim waist. An explosion of fern fronds in the window behind her blurred the lines of her silhouette. Fern fronds?

Instead of exploding with anger as she had every right to do—Sarah had actually locked her in to prevent her leaving—the golden-haired witch tapped her finger against her lips and eyed Drogo as if he were a particularly recalcitrant schoolboy. "Well, as a naturalist, you must know it's not *impossible*. What we did results in babies."

He threw up his arms in exasperation and stormed

through the room's shadows. She'd pulled back the draperies to allow the meager sun through mullioned windows, but there wasn't enough light in the world to enlighten this mess. And plants crowded what little light existed. "What we did is nothing I haven't done ten thousand times before, and *I've not made babies!*"

She remained curiously unperturbed by his belligerency.

"If you're saying it's impossible after just one night... Ten thousand?" she inquired, diverted by the calculation. "Well, you might be right that it's unusual after just one night, if the moon wasn't in its proper phase, but unfortunately, it was. Not that I expect you to believe that," she added blandly.

Drogo swung around. "How very convenient." He could swear the fern wrapped a frond around her shoulders to shelter her.

She ignored his acidity and continued ticking off her list. "I suppose I could have gone into the village and seduced every man there after you left, which might make the child unlikely to be yours, but still, I wouldn't call the child *impossible.*"

"I can't have children," he said adamantly. He knew this as a fact. He'd experimented for years, without result. Not the result he craved, anyway.

She showed no sympathy. "Well, since I haven't been with any man but you, and I'm definitely experiencing every symptom of pregnancy known to womankind, you've either been misinformed, misled, or haven't tried hard enough. *Ten thousand* times?" she repeated in wonder. Then shaking her head, continued, "Or would you prefer to believe I'm the victim of the second Immaculate Conception?"

He wanted to throttle her. He'd been through this before, let his hopes soar, swung high with reckless abandon on joyous rainbows, only to have the clouds pulled out from under him. This time, he couldn't see how she might have become pregnant by another. She'd been an innocent when he'd taken her, of that, he had no doubt. And from what he knew of her and the village and Sarah, she wouldn't have lain with any other man. There must be another trick.

"I've known women to claim they're with child and

then mysteriously lose it directly after they've gained what they wanted."

Offended, she drew herself rigid and glared. "I don't *want* anything. I'm not the one who wrote you. But if it's my word you doubt, I'll be happy to retch up the contents of my stomach on you as many mornings as it takes to convince you."

Buffeted by their conflicting logics, Drogo stood bewildered in the face of her certainty. He'd thought her a simpleton, a pleasantly innocent miss with unpredictable moods. She didn't seem quite so simple now, although her mood was definitely odd.

With some trepidation, he eyed her stomach. She hadn't dressed for the occasion, he noted wryly. She wore her usual apron stuffed with God-knew-what plants and dead leaves and a bulky homespun gown that revealed nothing. Perhaps her waist was a little thicker? Had her breasts always strained the seams of her bodice?

"I'll have a physician examine you when we reach London," he decided coldly. He could see no alternative. He would have to go along with Sarah's little farce until it played out. He couldn't foresee any real danger to anything but his already jaded cynicism.

Delicate, rounded eyebrows rose. "London? I think not, my lord. My child will be born here. Malcolms cannot bear safely anywhere else but Wystan."

"That's a lot of superstitious claptrap," he said scornfully, finally standing on firmer ground. "If you carry my child, as you claim, we'll be married in a church, in London, with friends and family as witness. The child will be an Ives, not a Malcolm."

"The father's name has no bearing on the matter." Now that she'd won her point, she clasped and unclasped her hands, then turned to the plant-bedecked window. "I promised my grandmother I would not leave Wystan, and I certainly won't marry an Ives."

Again, he wondered about her sanity. He'd just offered marriage, and he was quite certain she had just turned him down. Perhaps it was her way of driving a bargain.

He hadn't run herd on a pack of unruly siblings by losing his patience. Logic and reasoning always prevailed over emotional posturing. He took a deep breath and counted stars in his head.

In calming his temper, he noticed delicate purple blooms on the plants she stroked. What plants bloomed this time of year?

Shaking his head, he returned to the focus of his concentration. If there was any chance at all that Ninian carried his heir, he must have it verified immediately by a reputable physician. He'd do whatever it took to accomplish this.

"You cannot bear a child alone," he said, seeking an opening in her defenses. "Do you have other relations you can call on?" He supposed, if a marriage came of this, he ought to know who to invite. The idea of marrying a lunatic, possibly into a family of lunatics, gave him pause. But he'd vowed not to do as his father had done. Any child of his would have a name, regardless of the mother.

"My aunts," she replied carelessly. "But I don't need them. I'll be fine here. I have a family trust fund."

"If we marry, you'll have more than a trust fund," he wheedled mercilessly. "You can have all of Wystan Castle, and more. But you must come to London first."

"No," she replied quietly. "I cannot."

He'd driven himself without sleep for days, worn the ragged ends of hope and despair until they'd frayed through, and his patience slipped a notch at her stubbornness. "I cannot marry you here. There is no church."

"I don't need a husband," she said indifferently. "I suppose you needed to know you've sired a child." She hesitated, and with great reluctance added, "And I suppose I cannot argue if you insist on giving her a name, since it would be for her good. But it could not be a real marriage. If you must insist on this absurdity, it can be done across the border in Scotland. It's only a few miles away, and a church isn't needed." With a hint of irony, she added, "Not that Lord Ives needs any more wives."

He ignored her levity. "I'll not let the lawyers eat away the estates after I die while my brothers dispute the legitimacy of my son because of a heathen wedding. It's London and a church in front of all the witnesses of family, as befits an earl."

Her shoulders sagged. "It won't be a son. You're doomed to disappointment if that's your desire, my lord."

"I've been doomed to disappointment all my life. If we leave now, we can reach London by week's end."

She turned, and the desolation in her eyes nearly cracked Drogo's hard heart wide open. Suddenly, she seemed no longer a helpless child, but a woman who knew far too much of life's dark secrets.

"I am a witch, my lord. And not a very good one at that. Why would you take me for wife?"

Drogo thought it might be a test of some sort. He couldn't see any other logical reason for so illogical a question. He really didn't want to believe the brain behind the beauty was cracked. "You're a beautiful woman, and you carry my child," he offered.

"I'm far less beautiful than Sarah's ladies, and any woman can carry a child. Send your women to me, and I'll advise them of the proper phases of the moon. Or sleep with them every night without fail, and you'll be a father as often as you like."

Wondering if this pint-sized asp knew things he didn't, if possibly his hectic life with its constant interruptions that prevented his taking a regular mistress might possibly be the reason he'd never sired a child, Drogo struggled between her warped logic and his own determination. Determination won.

"I crave neither wife nor child," he assured her, although he lied about the child. He wanted this one desperately, or he'd never have broken his neck to get here. The wife part bloody well worried him, but he would do whatever it took to make it work. He'd build her a conservatory in London. "I would give the child my support. Come with me to London, and let the physicians verify your assumption, for the child's sake."

Those seemed to be the words she wanted to hear. She searched his face.

"I would like to see London again, but I cannot stay, and I will not marry you," she warned, apparently satisfied with what she found. "If you want what is best for this child, you will return me here within a month's time."

It was already August. A month's time would be September, before the first snow blew. Much later than that, and she risked herself and the child with the exigencies of travel.

It didn't matter. If she carried his child, he had no intention of returning her here unless he could come with her, which wouldn't happen until he could spare the time from his duties. That happened seldom, if at all.

But he'd won this round. He offered a little flattery in return. "That's time enough to become better acquainted with all your moods. I think I like the seductress best." Drogo brushed her fair cheek, loving the feel of her peach-warm skin. He could have her back in his bed again.

At his impudence, Ninian slapped his hand. "Then marry an actress, my lord," she said sweetly, "not a witch."

Her logic definitely escaped him.

Fourteen

"You are certain mother will let me have the children?" Sarah asked anxiously as the coach swayed through another rut.

"They're in my nursery as we speak."

Fighting the churning in her stomach, Ninian glanced at the man who had fathered the child within her. Lord Ives sprawled with apparent unconcern on the leather seat across from her, his arm behind his head as he leaned against the window, one booted foot on the spare cushion beside him. Lydie and Claudia had opted to stay in the safety of Wystan.

The earl didn't appear a man worried about his virility or considering marriage to a witch. He didn't even seem much concerned by his stepsister's children. But Ninian sensed Sarah's tension and her surprise at the word "nursery," and she thought possibly she was missing an undercurrent. Lord Ives's ability to conceal his emotions from her was a severe impediment to their ever understanding one another. Absently, she stroked the gray kitten that had hidden in their food basket and considered the problem.

If he had no children, why would he have a nursery? Without the perception of her gifts, she had to reason out the undercurrents. Had he furnished a nursery in expectation and been disappointed?

From their conversation earlier, she would assume so. A man did not set up a nursery for no reason. She would feel sympathy for him, if she could. Right now, all she could summon was stomach-churning terror.

The earl knew every road, village, and inn on this journey and could control precisely when and where they would arrive, barring any accident. With solicitude, he had told the coachman to halt whenever Ninian felt queasy, stopped early at the best inns so she could rest, placed no demands on her at all—not even that she share his bed. He'd scarcely looked at her in that way, although more than once she'd caught him watching her. She didn't think her condition showed yet, but he seemed determined to detect the signs—or lack thereof. His interest stirred wistful yearnings best left buried.

"Are we almost there?" Ninian murmured into a gap in the conversation. The sun had lowered in the western sky, casting long shadows over the road.

With indolent grace, Ives sat up and peered through the curtains. "It will be dark before we reach the house, but I think we're safe enough at this hour. Or are you growing weary? I know an inn…"

She shook her head. "I would be there, if you don't mind. The sooner we arrive, the sooner I can leave."

Sarah's sharp intake of breath warned she hadn't been informed of this part of their agreement, and Ninian lifted a quizzical eyebrow.

He shook his head slightly at her in warning. "London is not so bad as that," he answered blithely. "Society will be returning from their country houses. The Lords will be in session, and there will be a round of balls. Don't rush us until you've seen what we have to offer."

The conspiratorial intimacy of his look quaked her insides, but she bestowed a dark look on him and returned to watching the window. She didn't know why he protected Sarah from their arrangement, but surely it would be safe enough to visit London for a few weeks. She supposed she really ought to see her family—and her father.

Wrinkling her nose at the vision of that confrontation, she subsided into silence.

Drogo paced up and down the hallway outside the bedchamber he'd assigned to Ninian—the one adjacent to his own. With Sarah to gabble, he didn't have any secrets. He'd been chided and glared at and been the recipient of more jests than he'd care to acknowledge from the array of brothers straggling through the house already this morning. The younger ones had been at school through his earlier fiascoes. They'd never let Drogo live this one down.

He could hear the physician's low murmur through the door if he tried, but he was too nervous to try. Ninian had turned stony with rage at being told she would have to submit to the indignity of a man examining her. He'd thought he would have to hold her to the bed, but he'd promised her a tour of the pleasure gardens and a visit to the seamstress to order baby linens, and Sarah had whispered assurances until she'd finally capitulated. It was a damned good thing she didn't prefer gold and jewels, or he'd be bankrupt within weeks. He hated being at the mercy of this or any other unpredictable female.

He detected what was almost certainly Ninian's giggle from behind the door. He'd never heard her giggle. Hell, he'd never heard her laugh at all, but he already knew she had more moods than all his brothers combined. Just what he didn't need for a wife—an emotional arsenal.

For a wife. If all went well. Not wanting to face that hurdle yet, he returned to wearing out the carpet. Was it a good sign that she was giggling and not heaving things at the physician's head? He supposed it didn't really matter. He could handle any female idiosyncrasy, much as he controlled his brothers' machinations. People were people, he reassured himself. He'd find what made her happy, and she'd settle down to her own pursuits, and he could return to his. It would just be a minor upheaval considering others he'd endured in his lifetime.

If she was breeding.

Damning himself for hoping, not understanding why he hoped, Drogo stationed himself across from the door as he heard the sounds of impending departure. Leaning with one shoulder against the wall, his arms crossed, he sought an insouciant pose as the doctor stepped out, pulling the door closed after him.

The physician beamed. "Congratulations, my lord, you're about to become a father."

All the air left Drogo's lungs. His heart halted. His knees crumpled. The wall was all that held him up. He stared at the doctor's outstretched hand a moment too long before recovering and shaking it fervently, accepting the older man's all-too-familiar slap on the arm. The physician had overseen the delivery of his half brothers and probably thought himself a part of the family.

Glancing anxiously at the closed door, Drogo let the doctor find his own way out. Heart pounding so hard he thought it would break loose of his chest, he straightened his neckcloth, tugged his cuffs clear of his coat sleeves, and cautiously opened the door.

At sight of him, Ninian broke into a gale of laughter.

Obviously part of the conspiracy, Sarah joined in.

Disgruntled, Drogo glared at them both. Ninian wore only a flimsy nightshift borrowed from Sarah for the occasion. She wore her golden curls in a silken cascade over the linen, but there was nothing childish about the woman sitting up against the pillows. She represented every female seductress ever portrayed in art or literature. She had a knowing gaze that saw straight into a man's soul, and a seductive full-lipped smile that told him she could provide all his secret desires. At the same time, she had eyes so blue and innocent he could swear she'd never taken him into her bed or spread her legs for him.

He had a momentary vision of those shapely legs spread across his bed and almost passed out from the rush of blood to his groin.

"It seems you've accomplished what others could not," he said dryly, approaching the bed with wariness.

That produced another gale of laughter.

He stood at the bedside, gazing down at the mysterious woman who would become his wife despite her protestations otherwise, and wondered what the hell he'd done. "Am I allowed to hear the jest?"

Still giggling, Ninian bit her lip and shook her head as a signal that she couldn't speak just yet. Schooling his patience, Drogo sat on the edge of the immense bed. He'd have to wallow across the covers to strangle her, he surmised. It was easier to wait.

Sarah offered her a sip of water, and gratefully, Ninian took it. She hiccupped once, then regained her composure. Drogo thought almost any other woman in the world would be looking at him in terror about now. He knew his wasn't a pretty visage, one the ladies swooned over, unless it was in fear. His wretched eyebrows and dark coloring were sufficient to classify him as closer to Gypsy than earl. The sharp blade of his nose and the square angles of his jaw, not to mention his blasted height, presented a fearsome appearance. He'd used it quite successfully in terrifying his siblings into behaving.

His intended bride—not a frightened bone in her body—grinned hugely. "That was quite edifying, my lord."

Drogo shot a glare at Sarah, who hastily stood and brushed out her gown. "I'll be leaving the two of you alone now to… ahh, discuss the wedding." She hurried out, closing the door firmly behind her.

Drogo returned his glare to Ninian, intending his look to ask what he would not.

She sighed. "Do you never smile, my lord?"

"You have not yet met my brothers," he replied grimly. "Smiling is not the general reaction to events in this household." He waited.

She grimaced. "You really don't want to hear the reason for our laughter," she warned. "It will not make you in the least happy."

"Why does that not surprise me?" Relaxing, he leaned back against one hand. "I prefer knowledge to ignorance, however. Let me hear it."

She almost looked embarrassed. She rearranged the lacy coverlet near her breasts and looked down. "Ummm, your London physician just asked questions."

Drogo played with that for a moment but couldn't see the humor. "And?"

"That's it, my lord. You brought me all the way to London so your physician could ask questions about what you already know for yourself." At his impatient glare, she shrugged. "He asked if we'd had 'sexual congress' and how long ago. He asked for the last date of my…" she struggled for a polite word, "…woman's time. And so on. He then merrily declared me *enceinte* and offered his congratulations."

Temper shooting from nil to explosive in a matter of seconds, Drogo forced his tone into politeness. He didn't want to terrify her. "He did not examine you?"

"Didn't touch me," she replied cheerfully. "It seems that's not 'done' in polite circles."

"Sarah knew," Drogo replied through clenched teeth. "He's her physician."

Ninian grinned again. "That's why I agreed to your preposterous suggestion." Her smile slipped away. "I'm sorry, my lord. Sarah should never have written you. The only way you'll have any proof that I carry any child at all is to wait a month, until you can see for yourself. And that doesn't prove the child is yours. What would you prefer I do?"

Her only concern seemed to be for him. That struck Drogo as odd to the extreme, but the puzzle she presented demanded his attention more. He couldn't believe her wanton enough to have slept with any other man. He accepted that he was the only devil in her bed. But he definitely wanted to ascertain her pregnancy before he committed both of them to an institution that had never fared well for his family. Maybe she wasn't trying to trick him, but she could be mistaken. She might have some passing malady.

"Then we must wait a month," he decided reasonably.

Any other woman would be indignant. This one took his delay with indifference. "My only interest is in doing what is best for the child. I think it will be good for her to have a father who acknowledges her and will support her should anything happen to me. Beyond that, I merely ask that I be returned to Wystan as soon as possible."

She had as odd a notion of parenthood as his parents, it seemed. Drogo didn't intend to inform her that he kept what was his, and that included her as well as the child. If he'd impregnated a lunatic, so be it. He'd accept the responsibility and the burden.

Maybe in a month's time she would come to enjoy what the city had to offer and not have any interest in returning to the cold dreariness of the north. It would behoove him to work toward that goal.

He cast an interested gaze to the swelling curves above her bodice. "Would you care to take more chances at conception, as a precaution against disappointment?"

He watched as her nipples tightened and pushed against the thin cloth, until she hastily pulled the covers up to her chin. "Not a chance, my lord. If you can't trust my word, I'd spend the rest of my life locked up in this room."

Adjusting the suddenly too-tight press of his breeches, Drogo admitted the truth of that. He'd not only seen too many cases of marital infidelity, but he'd been victim of female treachery one too many times. He preferred the certainty of the stars in the heavens over the vagaries of human nature.

He nodded curtly and rose from the bed. "I'll have Sarah take you 'round to the dressmakers. You'll be entertaining for a few months, at least. Spend what you wish."

He strode out, leaving Ninian staring after his broad back long after he'd departed. Months? Had he said "months"? Surely, she was mistaken. Or it had been a slip of the tongue. The earl had much on his mind and hadn't paid attention to his words.

She smoothed the soft fabric taut across her slightly rounded belly. It was impossible to tell what was her and what was the infant. She just didn't doubt its existence in the least—unlike the poor babe's confused father.

If she'd been impregnated by the devil, he was a fascinating one, at least.

She had to quit thinking like a superstitious, ignorant villager. She was in London now. She sighed and collapsed against the mountain of lacy pillows. Maybe she shouldn't have refused his offer of another tumble in bed.

But the blasted man thought she *lied*. She'd have to teach him better than that.

Fifteen

GUT CHURNING IN FRUSTRATION AFTER LEAVING NINIAN'S chamber, Drogo eluded his brothers and bolted the door to his study. As a precaution, he checked the priest's hole. He wasn't in a humor to endure any nonsense from Joseph today.

To have the damned doctor grant all his hopes in one minute, and have them dashed by Ninian the next, was too much for his shattered nerves. Ten in the morning, and he needed a brandy.

He didn't pour one. He couldn't teach his brothers not to imbibe like drunkards if he did so himself. The mantle of responsibility was a damned nuisance. Just once, he'd like to get drunk, throw a tantrum, or in some way behave as monstrously as the rest of the family.

But then, who would rescue him when he got thrown in Old Bailey? Despite their generous allowances, not a one of them would have a farthing saved to bail him out.

Ignoring the mountain of ledgers from his various estates and enterprises—ledgers on which he'd cut his first mathematical teeth—Drogo picked up the sheet of calculations he'd begun in Wystan. If he was right, he could very well have discovered a new planet. That accomplishment was surely greater than producing a child. Anyone could produce a child. His father had proved that.

Sighing in exasperation at the path of his thoughts, Drogo whittled at his pen nib. He didn't want a wife, didn't need a

wife, but something very human in him would like to have a
son, even if he didn't need one.

So, there was his weakness. Everyone was entitled to at
least one. He wanted Ninian to be breeding. He wanted to
watch his child grow, dandle a babe on his knee, teach his son
to ride and search the night skies for stars. He wanted to show
all of London that he could produce an heir and a spare, just
as his father had.

Pride goeth before a fall, he muttered, applying his attention to his calculations.

A discreet knock at the door interrupted his concentration
only minutes later.

Drogo considered ignoring it, except he knew none of his
brothers would rap discreetly. They'd pound and yell. It had
to be Jarvis, who would never disturb him for anything less
than a crisis involving spurting jugulars.

The angry voice approaching down the hallway decided
the matter. One of the dolts must have experimented with
flying and broke his fall on a vegetable cart. It would be easier
if they'd just get drunk and gamble like normal people. Ives
males had never been known for normality.

Dropping his pen in the stand, Drogo unbolted the door.
A florid, dapper gentleman shoved past Jarvis, shouting something incomprehensible about "daughters" and "responsibility." Jarvis, straight-faced, merely bowed and shut the door,
leaving Drogo trapped with a raving lunatic. Lunatics seemed
to be popular these days. He wondered if it was an epidemic.

Since he had no daughters and couldn't remember dallying
irresponsibly lately, Drogo merely took his chair and waited
for the old fellow to rant it out. Of a decade-old fashion, his
caller's clothes had seen better days, now that he observed
more closely. Although impeccably pressed and cleaned, the
frock coat's gold buttons had gone missing at the top, and
his neckcloth linen was thin enough to read through. A
gentleman, but one fallen on hard times.

"If you do not do right by her, I'll call you out, sir!" the
gentleman shouted. "She's my only daughter, and I'll not see
her ruined by an unprincipled rake!"

Unprincipled rake? Drogo considered that unexpected and rather dashing image of himself. Perhaps the man referred to one of his brothers. Admittedly, he wasn't a monk, but these days he limited his attentions to courtesans and widows and other would-be countesses. He wasn't much inclined toward virgin… Ninian.

With a nasty taste in his mouth to add to the churning in his gut, Drogo rose from his chair. "Might I have the pleasure of your name, sir?" he asked icily, hoping for a madman, but preparing for the worst.

The stout gentleman drew himself to his full height—a good head shorter than Drogo's. "Viscount Siddons, sir, father of the child you've molested and hidden away in your house of horrors. I demand satisfaction, sir. I *demand* it, I say!"

Dumfounded at both the accusation and the knowledge that the little midwife had a father among the *ton*, Drogo sought a conciliatory reply. After all, he had done just as the viscount said, although calling this old tomb a house of horrors was pushing it a little far.

Before a sufficient reply came to mind, the study door silently slid open. In astonishment, Drogo watched as Ninian wafted in, just as if he'd called for her.

"Hello, Father." Self-consciously, she pulled at the billowing skirt Sarah had apparently dressed her in.

The pale yellow didn't suit her, Drogo decided, but the expanse of the panniers was very effective in distancing her from either of the room's occupants. She scarcely looked at him and didn't bother approaching her father with more than words.

The viscount looked stupefied at the vision of loveliness addressing him. Embarrassed, he stuttered a bit before remembering his purpose. He swung to face Drogo. "This is an outrage! You will marry her at once, I say."

Drogo detected a hint of amusement in Ninian's tone as she interrupted the tirade.

"How are you, Father? You look well. In case you're wondering, I am quite fine."

"I can see that," the old man said testily, returning his gaze to her. "Decked out in all the finery he's bought you. Well, no daughter of mine—"

"Grandmother died last winter," Ninian interrupted again, obviously pursuing her own goals. "I wrote and told you, and you didn't reply."

"The old witch left you plenty enough to live on, and you've got wealthier than me to call on, if she didn't." The viscount huffed and glared. "It's not as if you ever expressed any interest in living with your poor old father."

Drogo saw the sadness behind her smile, even if her father didn't. Perhaps he knew nothing of the mysterious little witch, but he'd learned a little about her. She had a heart, and it broke as easily as anyone else's.

"I had no interest in living in London," she corrected mildly. "And no interest in asking grandmother to support me without giving her anything in return."

The viscount harrumphed and reddened slightly, then swung back to face Drogo. "No matter, any of this. You've ruined her, and you'll pay the price."

Like a candle flame, Ninian brightened the darkness her father cast. Amusement again laced her voice. Never one hasty to speak, Drogo let her have her moment.

"No, he won't, Father. Grandmother's trust is mine. Even should we marry, Lord Ives cannot give it to you."

That was the first Drogo had heard of this. He wasn't certain he approved of a woman possessing her own funds—especially one with as befuddled a mind as hers. He wasn't even certain it would pass a court test, but he had blunt enough of his own. He didn't need her pennies. Let her flaunt them in her father's face if she wished. "I think, perhaps, my dear, your father merely wishes to ascertain that marriage is what I had in mind when I brought you here." Diplomacy seemed the best tactic.

She threw him a look of annoyance with nothing befuddled about it. "Not especially. My father is always short of funds, although I suppose I can give him credit for not actually trying to sell me."

"Ninian!" the viscount shouted, outraged all over again.

"Marriage among the aristocracy is a form of monetary exchange," Drogo clarified for her, pacifying the old man's temper. Ninian looked more amused than irritated at his generous interpretation. "Perhaps, my dear, if you'll excuse us, I can assure your father that I am an honorable man."

"It should be interesting to know how much I'm worth, my lord. Just remember while you're haggling that I can only bear daughters, and I have no intention of marrying." Placidly, as if she'd only quoted the price of a cow, she slipped away.

Drogo sank into his chair again. The viscount wiped his brow with a wide handkerchief. The faint scent of roses and pine lingered between them, along with the image of golden curls and female mockery. Drogo thought he had a better definition of "witch" now. The blasted woman could read minds.

"I wish you well of her, my lord," the viscount said heavily, sinking into a leather chair without invitation. "Her mother was a delight, a pure delight. The most beautiful woman, with the sweetest nature, you've ever met. But those harridans she calls family..." He shivered in remembrance.

"Ninian is an exceptional young woman." Drogo thought it wise to defend the potential mother of his child, even if she was as mad as her father. He also thought it wise to find out more. "She mentioned aunts...?"

Muttering, the viscount shoved his handkerchief back in his pocket and cursed as the pocket corner tore. "Persephone—my wife—was the youngest, so they didn't mind if she married a mere viscount," he explained disparagingly. "But Stella and Hermione..." He rolled his eyes. "Stella is the Duchess of Mainwaring. Hermione is the Marchioness of Hampton. And in case you're wondering, they both thoughtfully married widowers who already had heirs. They've got half a dozen girls or more between them, last I counted. All the babes my wife lost were girls too." He looked chagrined. "Couldn't be less than honest about that."

A marchioness and a duchess! Drogo collapsed against his

chair back and groaned mentally, all thoughts of keeping Ninian as mistress exploding like David's temper. He'd bedded a simpleton in peasant's clothes and acquired a family more powerful than his own. The little matters of an all-female family or even lunacy or witchcraft scarcely compared in importance to a duchess and a marchioness. His family's reputation was precarious, at its best. The condemnation of the upper echelons of society could easily destroy his mother and any chance his brothers had to make a place of their own in the world.

"What the hell was she doing living like a peasant in Wystan?" he demanded, for lack of anything more rational to say as he struggled with a world turned upside down.

The viscount shrugged. "She's a Malcolm, and the old besom's heir. Ask them."

Drogo groaned mentally and surrendered the struggle. He'd lost any choice in whether or not he would marry Ninian in a month's time. He'd ruined a flower of aristocracy, and he knew the penalty, even if his intended bride did not. He would worry about how to tell her later, when his head quit screaming. He bit down hard on a candy.

"I've already applied for the license." Drogo forced himself to speak calmly. "We'll be married in four weeks' time, so Ninian may prepare her bride clothes. I'll be happy to discuss the settlements."

Viscount Siddons brightened.

He might as well make peace with his prospective father-in-law. The viscount might be the only ally he'd find in a marriage with an unwilling bride from a matriarchy containing both a duchess and a marchioness.

❦

No wonder Siddons never had any money, Drogo concluded as he wandered the dark halls to his bedchamber later that night. The man didn't know a valuable when he saw one, and he couldn't drive a bargain to save his life. The viscount's only interest had been obtaining whatever amount he'd felt his mother-in-law had deprived him of by keeping it in trust rather than giving it to him upon his wife's death.

Since Drogo had no idea what funds Ninian possessed, he'd told the old man they'd have to wait until they'd located her solicitor. He'd seen how Ninian lived. She couldn't have much. Good thing the viscount didn't seem to realize Drogo would willingly pay half his fortune for a wife who carried his child. His brothers would strangle him did they know the depths of his obsession. Fortunately, it looked as if he'd acquired her cheaply.

But as things stood, he had no choice but to take Ninian for wife, even if she carried no child. He could feel his last chance of progeny seeping away, his only hope hanging by the bare thread of Ninian's honesty.

He didn't think he'd tell her of their impending marriage just yet. Let her formidable aunts break the news that they would wed, will they, nil they.

On impulse, he stopped at Ninian's chamber door. Sarah had taken her shopping, he knew. They'd probably run up his accounts in every shop in the city, most of it for Sarah. It was a game she liked to play, helping out with their brothers and helping herself at the same time. She knew he knew it. She knew he'd make her pay in other ways. He hadn't figured out how to make her pay for a disaster of this proportion.

Drogo knocked, and received a vague acknowledgment he assumed meant welcome. He'd never kept a woman in this house, not with his brothers appearing unexpectedly at inopportune times. He was trying to adjust to the idea of having a woman at his beck and call. He opened the door without further hesitation.

Bareheaded, hair curling in wild lengths over her linen chemise, Ninian stood on the cushions of the window seat, staring over the London rooftops. She didn't even turn to see who entered.

"The fog is like an unhealthy wraith stealing down the chimneys," she observed. "It's a wonder anyone survives the air. Are you ready to send me home yet, my lord?"

Drogo reached for an unlit candle. "If you'll climb down from there and pull the draperies, I'll light this, and you'll find no fog in here."

She crossed her arms and didn't move. "I don't need light to know what's here. Has my father convinced you that I am a ruined woman and you must marry me and turn over all my funds to him?"

"Your father couldn't convince a cat to drink milk," he observed wryly, as the kitten leaped from a chair to wrap around his ankles. "We've sent for your grandmother's solicitor to determine the legality of the trust. You needn't worry. The money will remain yours, no matter what they decide. I don't have need of it."

Gazing upon voluptuous curves silhouetted in the window, Drogo wanted her with an urgency so potent he almost crossed the room and dragged her from her perch. If he had to marry her anyway, what difference did it make if she carried a child or not?

Because he'd never trust her out of his sight until he knew her safely bearing his seed, and that could mean never.

Ninian climbed down from the seat of her own volition. He could barely discern her silhouette against the fading light of the moon, but she was round in all the places he craved, curved in all the places he wanted to hold. Like some pagan fertility goddess, she exuded sexuality, and he was drawn to her like a condemned man to freedom.

"I'm to trust your word as you trust mine?" she asked sweetly.

She had him there. He didn't light the candle but admired the shimmer of a golden curl. "We'll learn. I'm a patient man."

She laughed lightly, a fairy breeze more than human sound. "You're a stubborn man, my lord. I may not be able to read you as I read others, but I know that much."

She would be his wife. He didn't know what to expect of one. He certainly didn't know what to expect of one as fey as this. One moment, she glittered with moonlit seduction, the next, she teased like a child. He'd seen her tears and heard her laughter. Wary, he remained where he was. "I have found that I accomplish my goals better when I give up no ground," he admitted.

"It seems that you stubbornly kept trying until you found the right woman," she acknowledged. She stood within reach, tempting him. "You *will* be a father come the new year, I promise. But you must promise to return me to Wystan before the snow flies."

"One thing at a time, moonchild," he answered gravely, keeping his distance and promising nothing.

Sixteen

GIVEN THE FREEDOM OF DROGO'S ABSENCE WHILE HE CONFERRED with his men of business, Ninian spent the next morning exploring his world. Apparently the Ives family didn't believe in selling property just because it was no longer in a fashionable neighborhood. The old house rambled through dark rooms with narrow windows much as the old castle did, but without a woman's touch, this one harbored drafty fireplaces, soot-coated carpets, and doddering furniture.

The library contained not only books, but bridles, saddles, and a sadly worn pair of boots. She'd sought the room hoping to find a book on water or blights. There had to be a reason, and a solution, besides her superstitious legends, but after an hour of fruitless searching, she could find nothing.

Her eye caught on a faint light glimmering through the shabby draperies in a connecting room, illuminating entire villages of small wooden buildings scattered across the fading carpet. Drawn to investigate, she discovered each represented an architectural work of art. Some were of churches she recognized, some of solid buildings she assumed were the houses of Parliament or other official edifices. The ones she liked best were of lovely homes with gracefully arched windows and pediments and delicate porticoes.

"That's the house I want to build."

Startled, Ninian nearly dropped the model in her hand as she swung to face still another man without any discernible presence. She breathed easier as she realized this one was considerably younger than Drogo and not nearly as formidable. Still, the shock of midnight hair, planed jaw, and wide shoulders marked him as an Ives.

He shrugged diffidently as he sauntered into the room, but Ninian recognized his curiosity as his gaze swept her from head to foot. She guessed him to be younger than herself but still very much a forceful male animal.

She held out the model of a Palladian mansion. "It is quite lovely. Did you make it?"

He took the model and held it up to the spare light from the window. "They're easily done. Most of them are copies. I want to design buildings of my own, though." As if realizing his rudeness, he dropped the hand holding the model and looked at her again. "I'm Joseph, the eldest of the bastard brothers."

Ninian blinked in surprise at this introduction. She was beginning to believe the danger of Ives men was their power to turn Malcolm women into stunned puppets. Too many shocks and the nervous humors departed. She nodded tentatively in greeting. "I'm Ninian Siddons." She didn't dare introduce herself as a witch, although the shock value seemed relevant.

"I know. Sarah told us." He set the model on a table with half a dozen others. "Women don't last too long in this family. My mother refuses to live here. Drogo's mother left long ago."

Ninian's gesture swept the dismal room and included a dying palm. "I can't imagine why. I thought the harp with harpsichord keys very inventive, and I'm certain that contraption in the dining parlor has an excellent purpose."

Joseph fought the beginning of a grin as he glanced around at the chaos of toy models covering the sofas and chairs. "Ewen wanted more sound out of the harp, and William thought he could speed delivery of meals with the contraption. I prefer building things to tearing them apart."

She nodded as if she understood completely. "An excellent philosophy, I'm sure, given the state of things around here." She didn't remember Sarah mentioning a William, but if all the brothers were this imaginative, perhaps one of them could shed light on the dilemma of the fouled burn. "William?" she inquired.

Embarrassed, Joseph shrugged. "Ummm, our half brother by the dairy maid."

Ninian thought that was more than she needed to know and changed the subject. "Are there servants, or is someone building them also?"

"Drogo threatened to disown the next one of us who tried to make a better servant. Mostly, they stay out of our way. Do you play cards?"

∼

"Ninian! Ninian, where are you, dear?"

Looking up from her attempt to learn piquet from Joseph—who had an extraordinary method of counting cards she didn't think quite fair—Ninian tilted her head and listened to the forceful vibrations racing her aunt down the hall.

"So, does she always sound like a battle-ax dripping honey or does she reserve that voice for straying nieces?" Joseph asked, raking in his winnings. They were playing for Drogo's sweetmeats since neither of them had any coins.

"How do you know who she is?" Ninian demanded. The perceptiveness of Drogo's half brother left her wondering if he wasn't half witch, or warlock, himself.

Joseph grinned. "I spy."

She kicked his ankle under the table as the Duchess of Mainwaring sailed through the open parlor doors. In these last few days she'd met three of Drogo's half brothers, and she understood well his need to remain in London to keep the lot of them under lock and key. She was almost grateful she'd never had siblings of her own. Almost.

"There you are, Ninian, darling!"

Rising from the table, Ninian let herself be engulfed in her aunt's sweet-powdered, rustling silk as the duchess hugged her and kissed both cheeks. The eldest of the aunts, Stella had four living daughters and several grandchildren and had learned to hug and kiss through trial and error, Ninian surmised. The rest of her family wasn't quite so demonstrative.

"It's good to see you, Aunt Stella." She coughed as several pounds of powder wafted through the air between them. Apparently her aunt had decided to storm the bastions in full battle gear: powdered wig, powdered cheeks, and powdered silk, all reeking of expensive Malcolm perfumes. "How did you know to find me here?"

"A little birdie told me, of course." Her aunt trilled with false laughter, glared at Joseph, who sat taking it in with a huge grin, then tugged Ninian's elbow. "Come, let us have a little girl talk. Where is your sitting room?"

As if Ninian had always had sitting rooms. Sighing, she shrugged at Joseph and led the way down the hall to her chamber. She could hear laughter pouring from the attic nursery where Sarah entertained her children. Drogo was at the solicitor's with her father—again. She supposed Aunt Stella had used her "gifts" to time this visit for a moment when her niece had no defenders. Stella didn't precisely read minds. She just knew what everyone was doing and when. It was a distinction that eluded Ninian.

With the thoroughness of a general on a battlefield, Stella swept through the bed chamber Ninian had been assigned. She nodded approvingly at the small fire burning on the grate, raised an eyebrow at the gold satin hangings of the enormous bed, frowned at the two fireside chairs, and checked the adjoining door to both Ninian's dressing room and the one leading into the sitting room beyond.

"Why isn't there a fire in there?" she demanded, sweeping back from the luxuriously furnished sitting room. "And is that *his* room on the other side?"

"I don't need two fires," Ninian answered, unperturbed, "and I assume it's his lordship's dressing room on the other side, just as mine connects here."

"You *assume*? You mean you don't know? You're living here in the chambers assigned for mistress of the household, and you've never been inside his rooms?"

Ninian wasn't about to admit that. She'd assumed all the rooms up here had been taken and she was assigned the only one empty. She didn't see what difference it made. She was perfectly willing—nay, eager—to share Drogo's bed as soon as he believed her about the babe. Sharing a sitting room seemed rather insignificant in comparison.

"Aunt Stella, are you here for a reason? I know how busy you are, so I'm sure you'll want to return to the demands of your family as soon as possible. How may I help?"

"You sound just like my mother, may the goddess preserve her." Huffing, Stella flounced her silk and panniers into one of the fireside chairs. Her elegantly curled wig tilted slightly, and she shoved it indecorously back in place and glared at Ninian as if it were her fault. "Sit, child. I thought your letter said you preferred to stay in Wystan. Tell me why on earth you're here."

"Because I thought it would be nice to see my family again?" she asked disingenuously, using her best dimpled smile. "Because I was lonely all by myself?"

"Nonsense." Stella sat back so hard, she raised another cloud of powder. "You're breeding. Even I can tell that. I haven't seen a notice in the paper. Where the devil is your father? Ives may think he's above the rest of us, but by my faith, he'll…"

"And a good day, to you, too, Your Grace."

Gasping, Ninian swung around to find Drogo lounging in the doorway, his broad shoulder propped against the door-jamb, his curled eyebrows raised in devilment. She wanted to slap him for sneaking up on her like that. No one could ever sneak up on her as easily, not even his brothers. But he looked so imposing in his flared black coat and lace-frilled jabot, she couldn't help but admire the picture. He winked.

She definitely wanted to slap him.

"There you are, you young scapegrace! And what do you intend to do about my niece?"

"Make her my wife, of course." He strolled into the room and propped a proprietary hand on the chair behind Ninian. The lace of his cuff brushed her shoulders, and a shiver quaked deliciously across her skin. "What else does one do with the most beautiful, most talented woman in the world?"

Perhaps she would kill him. Slapping didn't seem quite

sufficient. A good sound curse to start with, then pins through his limbs…

"I'll hold you to that, Ives. Ninian is special, as you've obviously discovered if it's your child she's breeding. If I'd known she had any interest in mooncalves, I would have brought her out and you could have met her in the usual way."

Mooncalves? Ninian rolled her eyes. She'd hardly call the dastardly earl a mooncalf. Batting her lashes, she interrupted their mutual posturing. "I have no interest in calves, moon or otherwise, nor marriage either. Malcolms cannot marry Ives, and I cannot live in London, so the matter is quite decided."

Hidden beneath her hair, Drogo's fingers scratched gently at her nape. She hated the way just his touch sent gooseflesh up and down her arms. It had been well over three months since he'd taught her the pleasures of her body, and just that small touch reminded her of all that they'd done, of what they could do again, if her aunt would just leave.

"Nonsense," Drogo said quietly.

"Fustian!" Stella shouted. Then realizing what Drogo had said, she glared at him. "I take it the matter isn't quite decided?" she demanded.

"I have found the most beautiful, talented woman in the world, but she's also the most unpredictable, illogical, and thoroughly incomprehensible creature alive. You'll have to give me time to bring her around to our way of thinking." Drogo sounded almost apologetic.

Ninian would wager he didn't look in the least apologetic. She started to utter a scathing reply, but his fingers squeezed her neck warningly.

"Well." Stella threw her hands in her lap, and her panniers sailed upward. Oblivious, she focused on Ninian. "My mother has filled your head with foolishness, no doubt, but it's best you listen to me, young lady. It's a pity you won't be able to give Ives his heir, but he has brothers aplenty who will do their duty in time. Your duty is to that daughter you carry. Should anything happen to you, she will need the support of all the family she can get. She'd be lost with the rest of us, just as you were, but as an Ives, she will be treated like a queen. They don't get girls often."

The duchess looked up at Drogo. "I hope you've spoken to that worthless father of hers."

"We've reached an agreement," he said solemnly. "I have the license. You are all welcome to the ceremony and breakfast, once I persuade your niece to the proprieties."

Stella glared at Ninian. "Enough foolishness. Ives is a perfectly acceptable consort. All those legends are silly superstitions, and it's time we put a halt to them. Have your children in Wystan, but do not let my mother's grim prognostications stand in your way otherwise. She would have tied all of us to that uninhabitable countryside if she could have. Thank goodness our father wasn't so backward."

Ninian knit her fingers together. "I'm needed back there," she murmured, not expecting anyone to understand or even listen. Even Drogo appeared to have forgotten the problems in Wystan, and he and her aunt both seemed to consider the burn far less important than this legendary meeting of Malcolm and Ives. Regardless, she'd been batted around like a ball all her life. Granny had offered her the only stability she'd known. She couldn't just throw out everything Granny had taught her, or she would have nothing left of herself.

"Of course you are, dear." Stella leaned forward and patted her hand. "But you have a husband and child who need you more. Family comes first."

Stella exuded sincerity. She truly believed what she said. Ninian thought there might be some truth to it, but in that case, she should never have a child, because she knew the village needed her more. Confused, she didn't argue.

Stella bustled to her feet and focused her mighty forces on Drogo. "There, that's settled. I recommend St. John's. They've had experience with Malcolm ceremonies. I'll take care of that. If you're planning on having the breakfast here, you'd best find more servants. Your entry hall is a scandal, and the parlor not much better. Ninian has been raised for more important concerns than dealing with servants."

Ninian was beginning to recognize the dry humor of Drogo's brittle voice as he accepted Stella's orders. "I'll see that it's done, Your Grace. You need not worry about your niece."

Ninian didn't bother seeing her aunt out. With fingers still clenched tightly, she stared into the fire, waiting for Drogo to leave. He didn't.

After closing the door behind her aunt, he settled into the chair Stella had forsaken. His long legs sprawled across the space between them, shoving aside her full skirts as he leaned forward and tried to force her to look at him. She wouldn't.

"The child deserves a name." He took her hands and unwrapped them.

"You believe there is one, then?" She darted a look to his face, saw the thoughtful frown, and knew he didn't.

"It doesn't matter much, does it? If there is one, it will be provided for. I'd not meant to marry, so there is no harm done."

Scowling, Ninian jerked her hands from his. "And what if I'd not meant to marry? Does my opinion not matter?"

Now that he had her attention, he sat back and draped an arm over the chair back. "Who would you marry? Nasty Nate? I sent him to the coal mines to work. He needed something better to do with his time than tickle the lasses. Is marriage to me so appalling?"

"I want to go home," Ninian insisted. "There is sickness there, and the crops are failing, and someone must do something before people starve this winter."

Drogo sat perfectly still until his eyes compelled her to stare into them, and she couldn't look away.

"You cannot replace their crops or sheep. You can brew all the remedies you like, but you cannot force anyone to take them. I am providing work for any able-bodied man who needs it. I will find some way to fund supplies for those who have no means of support. Money can take care of the village's problems far better than anything you can do. Your responsibility is to your child."

She felt his words deep down inside her, in the places he'd explored and opened up and made his. She couldn't tear her gaze away. Could she trust him? She was accustomed to knowing enough of people to trust them implicitly or be wary. With Drogo, she was at a loss.

His eyes promised sincerity. Even if she dismissed superstition and instinct, she had no experience with men to draw on, not with a man like this one.

Shaken, confused, she didn't know what to do. She dug her fingers into her palms and stared into the fire. The legends had warned about Ives men, but she hadn't paid heed and the flood had followed. Her aunt dismissed the legends as superstitious nonsense. The unhappy ghost had said Malcolm must mix with Ives before peace could reign. Drogo promised to repair damage she couldn't possibly hope to fix. All she had to do was go against all she knew, as she had already done—with such disastrous results.

Perhaps if she traded herself for the village's welfare, the sacrifice would be repaid with Drogo's bounty. She could not sacrifice the child, however.

Not looking at him, she bowed her head in surrender. "I will hold you to your word, my lord, but if my responsibility is to the child, then you must return us to Wystan after the wedding. I cannot successfully bear children elsewhere."

He caught her hand and kissed it, and Ninian knew the thrill of physical excitement. They would be married, and she could share his bed again.

He still made no promises.

Seventeen

DROGO STORMED IN LATE ONE EVENING AFTER A PARTICULARLY argumentative session of Parliament, threw his hat toward the hall table, and watched blankly as it hit the floor. He was quite certain there had always been a table there to catch it before.

Shrugging, he left the hat where it fell and strode to his study where he kept a particularly potent decanter of brandy. A man was allowed a glass of brandy in the evening. It was practically a social requirement. He just didn't feel sociable right now.

Entering the study, he halted in amazement at the sight of Dunstan gazing into a potted plant that had miraculously begun shooting out new leaves these past weeks. Drogo wasn't even certain why the plant was in front of his window or who had first moved it there. It had served as the repository of cigar ashes and leftover brandy in a dark corner of the room for as long as he could remember.

"It's growing," Dunstan said in greeting, without turning to see who entered. Evidence that this brother didn't idle his time behind a desk rippled in the thick muscles of his broad back and shoulders.

Drogo dragged the decanter from its hiding place, noted it was two inches lower than it should be, and shrugged. "Get used to it," he answered curtly. "You're married. You know the routine. Give me some pointers."

Dunstan snorted impolitely as he turned and helped himself

to another glass. Unfashionably shaggy, his inky straight locks proved his connection to the legitimate side of the family. Their younger half brothers all possessed their mother, Ann's, curls. "I've been living with our mother. I'm a lot more used to it than you ever will be. But even Mother couldn't make plants grow in a dungeon like this."

Drogo dropped into his desk chair and sipped appreciatively of the liquor, eyeing his brother as he did so. Dunstan never came to London if he could avoid it. His brother had grown up with country manners and detested the false politeness of society. He lived for the estate and its sheep and cows and other annoying animal nuisances. "So, have you come to see if you're being disinherited?"

Dunstan's wide brow wrinkled in thought. "I could fight it in the courts, I suppose. You have only Sarah's word that the child is yours, and everyone knows Sarah is *non compos mentis*."

"Well, at least one of us got something out of his education." Drogo took a deeper sip and regarded the thriving plant with suspicion. "Sarah isn't a total lunatic. She got out from under her mother's heavy hands and has attached herself and her brats to me by shepherding Ninian."

"If you want to take her word for it." Dunstan dropped into a heavy leather chair and tossed back a swallow of brandy. "I'll still fight it."

Unperturbed, Drogo picked up a letter opener and tapped the desk with it. "I'll cut you off if you do." He'd learned at an early age how to control his unruly brothers. His financial acumen had served them well in more ways than one. "If there is a child—and that's a matter of some dispute still—it could very well be a daughter. Don't make a fool of yourself until it's necessary."

"There will be a child. Sooner or later, there's always a child. Women arrange these things." Glumly, Dunstan threw back the rest of his brandy and reached for the decanter.

Drogo slid it away from him. "Problem at home?"

Dunstan glowered. "None of your business. You've suffered female conniving before and emerged unscathed. This one must be more devious."

Drogo thought about it, bouncing the letter opener against the wood as he did so. "No. You'll have to meet her. Admittedly, she's not the simpleton she looks, but she's not devious. If anyone's the mastermind here, it's Sarah. Ninian…" He glanced over his shoulder at the plant. "Well, Ninian makes things grow."

Dunstan chuckled with a half-drunken hiccup. "In her belly, right?"

Calmly, Drogo threw the sharp steel blade of the letter opener into the shelf behind Dunstan's head. The handle thrummed with the force of the impact. Dunstan instantly sobered and held up a hand in surrender.

"I apologize. You're not making my life easier, though."

Tapping his fingers against the desk, Drogo sipped the brandy again. "The title doesn't mean anything to you, does it?"

Dunstan shrugged his rugged shoulders. "Hadn't thought about it. Maybe not to me, but to my wife, and to any children we have."

"Celia's expecting?"

Dunstan looked uncomfortable. "No." He glared at Drogo's lifted eyebrows. "It's Celia, not me. You know that."

He did. Drogo leaned back in his chair and propped his feet on the desk. Dunstan had been overly fond of one of the maids in his youth. He'd been supporting the results for years. Ives men had no problems creating sons. Most of their problem extended from creating legitimate ones.

"I can arrange for you to have the country estate for your lifetime," he conceded. "You can use your share of the profits to invest in land for your children."

"Celia would rather invest in a London town house," Dunstan replied gloomily. "You don't have any idea how wives can wreak hell with your peace. Yours will probably want the country estate plus a new town house and a wardrobe fit for a queen. There won't be anything left for the rest of us."

Drogo's lips curled reluctantly at that observation. "Ninian will want me to rebuild Wystan, reroute a river, and clothe half the countryside, but she'll not ask me for anything." He hadn't given this much thought until now, but he recognized the truth as he spoke it. Unlike the rest of his demanding family, Ninian asked for nothing. She expected to do it all herself. He wasn't entirely certain how to deal with that.

"You're fooling yourself if you think it will stay that way," Dunstan warned. "They're all sweetness and light before they get their hooks in you. Once you're trapped, they turn into demanding harridans."

Considering what he knew of the forceful powers of Ninian's aunts, Drogo could see that happening, but he couldn't quite believe it. He itched to go upstairs to Ninian's chamber now, listen to her naive description of the day's activities, and relax in the pleasure of her soothing voice. She could heal with that voice, he'd decided. She didn't need herbs and magic potions. He rather liked the quaintness that saw nothing wrong with his entering her chamber anytime he liked. And her observations on city life were not only astute, but from an entirely new perspective to him.

"In the past few weeks, Ninian has brought home three orphans, a one-legged beggar, a fifteen-year-old prostitute, and an abused monkey. I've had to forbid her to go out on the streets without me." Drogo grinned in memory of the chaos below stairs with each of Ninian's little "surprises." Even his lax staff, accustomed to the fits and starts of his brothers, had been in an uproar. "I don't think 'harridan' precisely suits her."

"Then she's probably as crackbrained as Sarah. Between the two of them, they'll have you jumping out windows."

Without surprise, Drogo noticed the door opening and knew who it was before she entered. Ninian had an odd habit of appearing whenever he thought of her. But then, he spent a lot of time thinking about her these days.

She wore a pretty lavender wool dress unlike anything he'd seen on ladies elsewhere, but considerably more alluring than the peasant costume she'd adopted in Wystan. He might question his sanity and hers in developing this relationship, but he didn't question his attraction to her at all. She looked like an angel straight down from heaven, but an angel with a lusty streak that cranked all his wheels.

"Hello, my dear. Come meet my heir, Dunstan. He thinks we're both crackbrained."

"All Ives men are crackbrained," she agreed solemnly, drifting into the room.

Drogo bit back a smile at her riposte, and a delicious heat shot through him as she touched his shoulder, melting the smile out of him. How the hell did she do that?

Apparently oblivious to her effect, she held out her hand to Dunstan. Drogo raised his eyebrows as his brother actually stood up and bowed over it. Dunstan could be rude, crude, and uncouth when he chose to be, but apparently, he wasn't drunk enough to insult the next Countess of Ives.

"You're not like Drogo," she said in wonderment. "You radiate pain and rage and…" She twisted up her nose and pondered. "Spurned love? Is that possible? This city vibrates with so many emotions, it's difficult to sort it all out."

Dunstan raised a questioning eyebrow at Drogo.

Drogo shrugged. "She's trying to convince me she's deranged so I'll send her home."

"A witch, not a lunatic," Ninian said gently, patting his shoulder but still watching Dunstan. "Drogo won't believe anything I tell him, so you needn't think I'll reveal your secrets. I'd like to meet your wife sometime. I have a feeling the few women in this family really ought to know each other better."

Dunstan remained standing since Ninian didn't take a seat. "She loves any excuse to come to town. I'll bring her for the wedding."

"Good." Apparently satisfied, she focused her regard on Drogo. "Offer your brother a room for the night. I'll have them send up a warm bath and food."

Drogo leaned back and held her gaze. He loved the way he could command her complete attention. "What happened to the table in the hall?"

"Aunt Stella said we must make the place presentable, so Sarah has ordered the old pieces hauled away. I thought it might be easier to clean before the new ones are brought in. Joseph has a keen eye for design, so he's picked out a few things."

"There was nothing wrong with the old table," he said

mildly, more curious than perturbed by this rearrangement of his living quarters. "And Joseph is quite likely to choose something with more arches and pediments and statues than Westminster."

"Actually, he recommended a housekeeper." Patting Drogo's shoulder again, Ninian curtseyed to Dunstan and drifted out.

Collapsing back in his chair, Dunstan looked as if he'd been hit by a brick. "A *witch*?" he muttered. "My God, she looks like Venus. Too bad she's got maggots in her attic." He stopped and thought about that a minute. "I suppose that's the only way a woman could survive this family."

Drogo tented his fingers and regarded his brother coolly. "I think you'd best find that room she offered. I would have thrown you in the street."

Dunstan let that run right off his back. "No, you wouldn't. You'd leave me here to drink myself under the desk. The food sounds more appealing now that I've met your lovely intended." He grinned his white flashing grin of old. "This marriage will be a pleasure to watch. I have a feeling the immovable object has just met an irresistible force."

Drogo slowly emptied his glass after his brother departed. He'd never doubted the intelligence of any of his brothers. Dunstan could very well be right. He'd not ever considered himself an immovable object before, but Ninian was definitely an irresistible force. He wanted her desperately. And she didn't need him at all.

Pain? Rage? *Spurned love*? What the hell had she been talking about?

He glared at the healthy, uplifted leaves of the plant, as if it could explain.

Eighteen

London, September, 1750

IDLY, DROGO STROKED HIS USELESS TELESCOPE AND GAZED OUT his bedchamber window. The moon was out there. Even the thick London smoke and fog couldn't conceal it. But the stars were out of his reach tonight.

As if one thought led to another, he turned his gaze to the closed door between his chamber and the room connected to Ninian's. Tomorrow was their wedding day. He wondered if his reluctant countess had decided to flee yet. After these past weeks of patiently enduring the constant quarreling of his fractious family, she may have decided even the barren countryside of Wystan would be preferable. He really couldn't blame her.

She might be alone and frightened. A young woman should be with her family on her wedding eve. He'd thought he would have to argue with them to keep her where he and his family could watch over her. Ninian must have said something to her aunt because he'd never heard a word of objection. Odd family. They seemed to think Ninian needed no support from anyone. He supposed she was far more independent than the females he knew, but that didn't mean she didn't get lonely like everyone else.

He wasn't entirely certain when he decided to visit her, or if he decided at all. Carrying his wedding gift, he rapped lightly on the door to her chamber, not bothering to wait for her reply. She had never denied him, nor had she ever invited him. She just seemed to exist in here, a possession provided for the sole purpose of his use. He would have to learn to deal with that. He'd not only never imagined having a wife, he'd never imagined having one who didn't want him for husband. It made things deucedly awkward.

Entering, he saw no candle or fire to light his way, but a silver light illuminated the chamber, revealing an untouched bed. Drogo squelched an instant's panic. Laying down the gift on a bedside table, he passed the curtained bed and checked the tall window.

She stood with arms outstretched, silhouetted in a square of moonlight on the carpet, her golden hair streaming in a cascade to her waist as she reached for the stars, swaying to a music only she could hear. Oblivious to his presence, she spun and danced and reflected the moon's light as her gossamer gown drifted and clung and revealed far more than it concealed.

With an avid hunger he couldn't deny, Drogo sought the high curves of her breasts, the hard points pushing at the frail lawn of her gown, then drew his gaze downward, to the definite curve of her abdomen between rounded hips. With the fecundity of the statues of Druidic earth goddesses he'd seen in museums, she burgeoned with new life—*his* child.

In five months time, he would hold a child of his own in his arms.

He couldn't separate the thrill and terror of that knowledge from the thrill of pure lust. Primitive instinct warred with civilized protectiveness. A woman in her condition should be cosseted, not ravished.

A golden-haired witch demanded ravishing.

He stepped into the circle of moonlight, and she danced into his arms as if she were the part of him that was missing, returning home.

"The child is mine," he said gruffly, not knowing whether he asked or commanded as her lips parted beneath his. He stroked the hard protruding curve of her belly, and something very like joy pried its way into the shriveled remains of his heart. He had planted his seed and unbeknownst to him, she had nourished it. Both humbled and terrified, he didn't know how to behave. This was a situation far beyond his control.

Her tongue stroked his, distracting his decidedly muddled thoughts. Her soft fingers parted his robe and flattened against his chest, nipping at sensitive points until he groaned against her mouth and forgot the child.

"Yours and mine and God's," she agreed, rubbing against him like a cat.

He could swear he heard her purr as he filled his palms with her breasts and pressed his kiss deeper. The damned cat must be in here. It didn't matter. He needed her too much to hesitate now that she'd given him direction. He untied her ribbons and pulled the bodice down until her bare flesh rubbed his own. He crushed her aroused nipples against his chest and bit at her lips until she parted them again. He had been starving for this for four long months.

Right now, possessing this elusive female seemed more important than anything else on earth.

He inhaled her breath and sampled her tongue and lifted her from the floor. "You'll not deny me now." He stated it as a matter of fact, a line read from the book of knowledge. She was wild and free and not wholly of this earth, but she was his now.

She carried his child. Elation swelled within him, as if he'd conquered the sun.

"I cannot deny you," she answered simply. "The bonds are too strong."

He didn't know what she was talking about. He'd question her in the morning. Right now, he only knew his arms were full of delectable woman, sweet-smelling, soft, and wholly desirable, and he had gone four months wanting her. He tugged her gown past her feet and dropped it to the floor as he carried her to the bed.

"Tonight, and every night," he vowed, to her, to himself, to the powers that be. He wouldn't lose this woman as his father had lost his. He wouldn't have his life split asunder ever again. Maybe she could teach him to be whole.

"Every night until I return to Wystan," she promised carefully.

He ignored her amendment. They had no need to return to Wystan any time soon, and he wouldn't let her go without him. He laid her half across the high bed and spread her legs so he could stand between them.

She looked up at him as if he were all the gods in the world. Aroused to the point of bursting by the power she granted him, Drogo offered her pleasure before he sought his, suckling her breasts until she writhed with need, stroking her when she arched into his hand, easing her past the first peak with his fingers until she convulsed with the pressure.

Only then did he open his robe and claim the exquisite pleasure of entering her.

Ninian cried out with the sudden strain. Her muscles constricted against his invasion, then melted beneath the liquid fire of penetration. Her body was no longer her own, but his, contracting upon his command, parting with his thrust, lifting spasmodically with his rhythm until she no longer was herself, but part of him. She felt not only the male part which possessed her, but all of him, the soul he hid from her, the heart that beat through his blood, the passion that drove him. Her soul sang with happiness at this mating, at this coming home, and she followed him to the highest peak and over without a qualm.

The free-fall sensation as she floated back to earth scared her, but Drogo held her close, wrapping her legs around his hips and straining to stay with her until she landed. He remained lodged within her, stirring again even as he leaned over to brush her cheek with kisses and tease her breasts with wanting.

"I think I'll keep you close, moonchild," he whispered so softly she almost didn't hear. "I will want you every hour of the day."

That sounded exceedingly pleasant. Too languorous to argue, she slid her arms around his neck. "Good thing we can make only one child at a time," she murmured as his magic hands created ripples of sensation from her breasts to her womb.

"Then I suppose we must make love instead. Tell our child to move over, I'm coming in."

And he did, with a swiftness that left her gasping and ready for more.

Later, she lay within his arms and wondered anew at what she had done. Once upon a time, she had been a free woman, innocent of anyone's dominion. Then she had experimented with temptation and fallen into this man's bonds, silken though they might be. Now she carried his child and agreed to carry his name. That was the natural way of things, she supposed, but she didn't understand his hold on her. Why was it that he need only touch her and she surrendered to his wishes? It seemed more magic than natural. She had not been jesting earlier, she could not deny him. It did not bode well for her escape should he forbid her to return home.

"I brought you a wedding gift," he murmured against her ear, his hand waking to tenderly stroke the place where their child grew.

"So I see," she replied lightly, moving against his growing arousal.

He chuckled, a strange sound she heard seldom. She liked the way it rumbled in his chest and throat.

"That's not what I meant, although you're welcome to it." He lifted himself on one elbow and reached for the night table. "It's not the same as jewels, but I thought you might like it more."

In surprise, she accepted a heavy, musty-smelling leather tome. She sneezed and wondered if her husband was as odd as the rest of his family as she rippled the page edges in the darkness.

"It's the diary of a Malcolm lady," he explained. "I found it on the shelves in the library the other day. The language is old and may need translating."

"I can read old English and Latin and Norman French," she answered, reverently stroking the binding now that she knew what it was. "Malcolms do not surrender their books lightly, and Grandmother taught me to read the few we have."

He was silent for a moment, then caught her by surprise again. "You are much more intelligent than you allow people to know. Why do you insist on believing in superstitious nonsense?"

She shrugged. "Sometimes, I do not. Other times... It's who I am. Without my gifts, I am no one and worth nothing."

"You will be my wife, Countess of Ives, mother of my child. Isn't that enough?"

"No. That's the same as saying I'm your table and chair. Being possessed is meaningless. I must be who I am, and I am the Malcolm healer, if naught else. If you cannot accept this, you had best reconsider our marriage before it is too late."

"It's already too late. Call yourself what you wish, but others will call you countess. It's not an easy position to fill." He removed the book and set it aside. "I'll do what I can to help, but as I've said, I wasn't prepared for a wife. We'll learn together."

As he kissed her into surrender one more time, Ninian remembered why she had fallen into this man's bondage. He not only possessed the temptations of the devil, but he possessed an open mind that did not exclude her as so many others did. She could accept that, for now, just as her body accepted his.

෴

In the carriage seat across from Ninian, her husband-to-be scowled at the small crowd forming at the foot of the church steps. Her bridegroom was not a handsome man, nor even what one might call dashing. She thought those words too close to "pretty" to describe the Earl of Ives. Drogo was much more striking and definitely more aristocratic than pretty, and his scowl was fierce enough to frighten the ravens from the Tower. It no longer had the power to cast her into terror, however. What she was about to do had already accomplished that.

"They're *all* here," he complained. "I never thought to see the entire lot of them under one roof."

"They're not exactly under a roof yet." Ninian leaned over to look out the window. The street seemed lined with carriages. Weddings weren't precisely fashionable. They were just legal procedures necessary to bind the complicated entanglements of families and fortunes. They'd sent announcements, but they hadn't anticipated this kind of audience. Several of the carriages had crests painted on the doors.

Her aunts. "Would you care to postpone this to another day?" she asked nervously.

He shot her his infamous scowl. "Not under penalty of death. Let's get this over, and then they'll leave us in peace."

Ninian had serious doubts about that as the footman opened the carriage door, and Drogo climbed down to help her out. The morning fog had scarcely lifted beneath the September sun, and a cool breeze tugged at her cloak. Her aunts and cousins had no doubt taken refuge inside the church.

"Perhaps I should warn you," she started to say, before a barrage of emotions slammed into her so forcefully, she almost staggered. That was one of the inconveniences of the city she hadn't learned to handle, but the tumult she suffered now was more potent than the scattered feelings of passersby. This was directed at her as much as anyone.

Clinging to Drogo's arm, she glanced up to meet the dark eyes of a man taller and older than Drogo. She'd not met him before. He nodded curtly at her look. At the back of the crowd, he merely stepped inside the church and disappeared once he'd seen her. With his brothers all shouting for his attention at once, Drogo probably hadn't noticed.

"To the devil with you!" Drogo shouted, swiping hands off his crushed coat sleeve. "Are you afraid to face the women and so stay out here? Go inside where you belong."

"Have you seen those women?" one of them asked. "They're all fair as your bride, with their noses stuck halfway to the ceiling."

Ninian giggled. She thought the one speaking was Drogo's youngest half brother, Paul. He couldn't be much more than sixteen and newly down from school. His head swiveled at the sight of any female. Her cousins would have him spinning in circles.

"Have you seen what they've done to the church?" Joseph shouted above the rest, his eyes dancing with curiosity and merriment. "They have trees!"

Ninian winced as all those dark eyes turned questioningly to her. She cleared her throat. "Malcolms usually marry in forests. My aunts have adapted for changing times."

"Is there aught else I should know before we go in there?" Drogo asked with that dispassionate tone she knew too well.

She probably should have warned him sooner, but they seldom spent much time talking. After last night, she assumed her place was in his bed and no more. He certainly didn't place much value on anything she said. Still, she felt a little guilty at not explaining her family more thoroughly.

"Is there anything that would change your mind about going through with this?" she asked with more cynicism than anxiety.

He didn't think about it for long. Keeping an eye on his brothers as they pushed and shoved their way into the church, he glanced back to where her simple white gown still disguised her growing belly. "No, I cannot think there is."

"Then there is little point in delaying the proceedings." Determinedly, she took the first step.

"Why are you the only one here who isn't terrified?" he muttered, gripping her arm tighter as they proceeded upward.

"Your brothers aren't terrified," she replied as she watched her new family race inside for the best seats. "They're angry and uncertain, a bit jealous, and all of them are excited, probably more by my cousins than our nuptials. Who was that tall man who stood in back?"

She met Drogo's completely blank gaze. For once, she thought he wasn't hiding from her. He really didn't know. "He was an Ives," she insisted. "He looks more like you than any of the others."

"Poor sod," Drogo muttered. "Hope he has lots of blunt to balance things out. Come on, let's get this over."

"This is all your idea," she reminded him as they continued upward. "I warned you. My grandmother said Ives and Malcolm never mix. You have no idea what kind of disaster we're creating."

"Your foolish ghost claims a Malcolm should live in Malcolm Castle," he countered. "I can match superstition for superstition as well as any other."

Ninian searched the shadows of the church as they entered, but blinded by the sun outside, she could only see restless figures divided by the aisle. On her side of the church, a flower garden of colorful silks and blond heads and powdered coifs abounded. On Drogo's side, a sea of dark faces, somber coats, and knowing dark eyes turned to stare.

Drogo choked, and diverted, Ninian glanced worriedly at him. He nodded to two stiff feminine backs on his side, both in the front pew, on far ends.

"My mother and stepmother, in the same room. Lightning will strike us next."

"Well," she said prosaically, "at least my uncles and their sons aren't here. They apparently consider this a purely Malcolm event, not worthy of their exalted attention." She wrinkled her nose. "But I do believe that is my father talking with the lady on the near end of the pew."

"My mother." Drogo clutched her hand tighter as a cluster of women wearing white cloaks bore down on them. "Your father and my mother. I don't want to even think of it. Let's get this done before all hell breaks loose."

Considering the rampant emotions bombarding her as they waited for her attendants, Ninian could see his point. They ran the scale from joy and satisfaction to dark fury and disappointment. She tried to concentrate on the happy ones, as her grandmother had taught her, but the anger blotted out all else like a black cloud hiding the sun.

Drogo was making someone very unhappy with his marriage. She was afraid to find out who. Or why.

Nineteen

DROGO WATCHED IMPASSIVELY AS NINIAN'S COUSINS—HE assumed they were cousins by the fairness of their hair—cloaked her in a white satin cape and settled a circlet of what appeared to be twigs on her unpowdered hair. The twigs were wound with purple and white flowers, although he couldn't have named them had he tried, which he didn't. He had little patience with ceremony of any sort. He just wanted this over before his brothers figured out how to swing from the enormous medieval chandelier overhead.

He scowled as one of the older women approached him with a dark cape to match Ninian's. Glancing up from watching the girls fasten a golden chain to the cloth, Ninian caught his look.

"They're symbols," she whispered. "They're all just symbols. Don't worry about it." Despite her words, she frowned at the gold band closing around her neck.

Over her shoulder, Drogo watched a sea of dark heads turning to watch and whisper. He'd never live this nonsense down. He tried to find the man Ninian had warned him about, but the chandelier wasn't lit and the foggy morning light didn't penetrate the church's gloom.

Whispers echoed loudly in the Gothic acoustics of the cathedral, but actual words weren't discernible. Stoically, Drogo accepted the cloak, ignoring the woman fastening the gold band. All Ninian's relatives seemed to be blond and fair. No wonder his brothers were all atwitter.

"Be thankful they won't make us jump the broom," she whispered as two young girls emerged from the shadows carrying baskets of flower petals.

Broom? What the hell kind of pagan ceremonies did these women attend? Since the flower girls seemed to indicate the proceedings had begun, Drogo didn't inquire. He frowned in puzzlement as they led the way down the right side of the church instead of the center aisle, but Ninian held his arm and followed them as if it were perfectly natural to approach the altar in a circle instead of a straight line.

Ninian. Drogo permitted himself the luxury of a feeling of well-being as he remembered the open welcome he'd found in her bed last night. Glancing down at her golden head with its circlet of flowers, he relaxed even more. She had taken him with as much pleasure as he'd received from her, and in so doing, she had taken his seed and nourished it as she nourished the plants around her. She would make a good mother, and an exciting bed partner. What more could a man ask of a wife?

As they approached the altar from the side, Ninian's graceful cousins in their flowing white capes formed a half circle at the center aisle, and Drogo could see the trees his brothers talked about. They'd imported a potted oak and what appeared to be a rowan. The clergyman didn't seem to mind. Garbed in the traditional robes of a good Church of England bishop, he waited calmly for the procession's end.

If that was all the ceremony involved, Drogo could handle it. The gold band at his throat was a nuisance, the cloak a ridiculous affectation, but so was all this churchly ceremony. Marriage could be reduced to a few lines on a sheet of paper, and he'd be content. But women, for whatever reason, needed appropriate pomp.

Counting heads, wondering if he'd provided enough champagne for the breakfast, and hoping he could spirit Ninian back to his chambers immediately after the toasts, Drogo didn't pay much attention to the prayers. He kneeled when Ninian did, stood when called upon, and admired the innocent translucence of his bride's complexion as the light from the rose window fell upon her.

She wasn't a classical beauty, he admitted, but there was a purity and innocence—and goodness—to her rounded cheeks and chin and sparkling eyes that appealed to him. Perhaps he should have sought a wife from among the less sophisticated sooner. This one wouldn't connive behind his back, deceive him with pretty words, or flutter her lashes at other men. He had complete confidence in that, even if he didn't have complete confidence in the odd workings of her mind.

Patting himself on the back for being logical enough to accept that a woman's mind didn't work like his, Drogo didn't catch the bishop's intonations until he heard the whispers rise behind them. Ninian's hand squeezed his, and he returned to the moment.

Now that he had Drogo's attention, the bishop repeated his question. "Do you vow to love, honor, and take this woman in equality, for so long as you both shall live?"

Equality? "Love and honor" were familiar meaningless phrases he'd heard all his life but *equality*? The word seemed to whisper ever louder through the church, echoing back and forth and rising to the soaring rafters. Equality!

Ninian didn't look at him. Her side of the church hushed expectantly. His side seemed in imminent danger of explosion. What the devil was this *equality* business?

The heavy brass doors at the front of the church slammed open with a violent clang.

Reacting instinctively, Drogo tugged Ninian behind him, placing her out of danger as he swung to face whoever had entered. He hadn't forgotten Ninian's warning of a stranger in their midst, but the man staggering down the aisle with a pistol in one hand and sword in the other wasn't a stranger.

"Twane!"

His brothers all surged to their feet as a party of large men followed Twane. Drogo gestured for his family to stand back. His mother and stepmother screamed, but for the most part, Ninian's family appeared to regard the newcomers as a dramatic performance, perhaps part of the ceremony with which they weren't familiar. Behind him, Ninian stiffened, and her wrist tried to twist free of his grip.

"I want my wife, Ives!"

"You're foxed, Twane. Go home to your doxie and sleep it off." Drogo couldn't tear his gaze from Twane's to see what his brothers were up to now, but they'd disappeared from his field of vision. He had to calculate his next move carefully. Twane's men looked uncomfortable and would no doubt leave peacefully given half a chance. He had no idea of the accuracy of the pistol aimed at him, but it had only one shot. The sword was a different matter. He hadn't worn his own into the church; Twane had probably counted on that. If he tried to leap aside to avoid attack and disarm the madman, he endangered Ninian and the bishop. If he released her, would Ninian have sense enough to remove the clergyman and herself from the line of fire?

He heard her muttering something under her breath, but he couldn't make out the words. Her aunts in the front row appeared to take up the chant, though, and a low prayer rose and fell in rhythm. On the other hand, the loud grumble on his side of the church grew angrier and more boisterous. Backed by the confidence of his men and his drunkenness, Twane didn't appear to notice.

"Let's take this outside where we can discuss it privately," Drogo suggested, reluctantly releasing Ninian and praying she had sense enough to duck.

"My wife, Ives!" Twane raised his pistol and took aim.

An explosion of gunpowder shattered the growing rumble of voices. Someone tackled Drogo by his knees. Off balance, he tumbled down the altar stairs. Falling, pelted with an odd hail but feeling no wound, he twisted as he hit the bottom. Discovering Ninian kneeling on the step above him, he grabbed her and pulled her down, rolling over and covering her with his body while all hell broke loose over their heads. He couldn't believe the damned woman had knocked him down instead of running for cover.

"You idiots, now look what you've done!" Dunstan's voice rang out in the annoyed tone he reserved for castigating their younger brothers.

A frenzy of feathers flapping overhead created a crescendo of disconcerted female screams.

Feathers?

One drifted down to tickle Drogo's nose.

"Devil take it, where did the damned pigeons come from?"

That had to be Ewen. Cautiously, Drogo peered over his shoulder—and dodged a flapping wing.

"My family must not have been able to find doves," Ninian whispered from beneath him.

"Get him! Get the devil!" a male voice shouted as someone grabbed Drogo's arm.

Well, hell. Drogo elbowed his assailant and forgot about pigeons. If he'd been hit, he didn't feel it. He bloody well intended to put a hole in the ass who'd disrupted his wedding though, and he'd be damned if he let anyone touch Ninian. Keeping her huddled beneath him, he grabbed his assailant's arm and twisted until the man screamed and stumbled. Then he rose to his knees and jerked Twane's legs out from under him.

Twane landed with a thump, and Drogo was on him in an instant.

Amid the confusion, Ninian sat up and gazed in wonder at the magnificent chaos erupting through the once-peaceful cathedral. The bishop had dropped to kneel and pray behind the protection of the pulpit. Scattered bits of grain still flew through the dusty air and covered the aisle and half the pews. She recognized the inventiveness of Drogo's brothers in the cannon shot of grain pellets and didn't even bother looking for the weapon. They'd evidently intended to shower the wedding procession in a less than traditional fashion. The birds that were always part of Malcolm ceremonies had settled down to peck through the chaff on the marble floor.

The humans, however, were doing nothing so peaceful.

While Drogo and Twane rolled about the center aisle, scattering pigeons in their wake, Drogo's brothers leaped to defend him from Twane's army. Ninian identified young David swinging repeatedly at one of the men who, trapped between two pews, cowered and covered his face. The youngest, Paul, had leaped on the back of an enormous man, dislodging his wig. Gripping the man's sparse hair with one hand, he pummeled him with the other. The giant's shrieks as he ran down the aisle filled the church.

Drogo's mother and stepmother had fled to the protection of Ninian's aunts, who had ordered their broods into a protective ring. Since no one challenged them, they chanted the incantation for safety while shooting dagger glares at the men disrupting the sacred ceremony.

Ninian would have giggled if not for the danger of the still loaded pistol Drogo had kicked toward the altar, and the sword he had yet to dislodge from Twane's fist. Still kneeling, she reached for the pistol when a large arm caught her by the waist and jerked her upward.

"I don't think a pretty little thing like you needs to be playing with a man's weapons," a deep voice admonished.

She'd felt the rage approaching, but had thought it all a part of the chaos around her. Sometimes, her Gift was not at all helpful. Defiantly, she met the grim expression of the man Drogo couldn't identify, the man who most certainly had to be an Ives.

"The damned earl really doesn't know what he has here, does he?" the man asked, with almost a thoughtful tone.

Ninian heard past his words to the suppressed fury of this man's soul. She wouldn't scream and distract Drogo from his fight. Malcolm women didn't scream. Generally, they didn't fight either. But Ninian had always been a malcontent, as her grandmother had told her often enough.

Taking a lesson from Drogo's brothers, she grabbed the man's lace jabot at the throat, jerked his head down, and fastened her teeth into his extremely prominent nose.

He yowled in both pain and surprise. He caught her hair and tried to rip her away.

Ninian bit harder and kicked his shins with as much strength as she could muster. Her pointed kid slippers weren't as useful as her heavy country clogs, but they did their job. Her attacker began leaping about to avoid the blows.

"Drop her, and she'll let go," a voice spoke steadily from behind her.

Drogo. Ninian sighed in relief as the heavy hand at her waist fell away, and she released her aching grip on the man's nose. Drogo caught her and gently pulled her back against him. He was breathing hard, but he didn't seem to be hurt. She didn't dare turn to see. Holding his injured nose, the stranger focused his attention above her head.

"You would do well to look further into the origins of the family you marry into," the man said flatly. "Equality!" he snorted. "I suppose you're getting what you deserve."

With that, the large stranger stalked down the altar steps and past the men hauling Twane from the center aisle. He skirted around the chanting women—several of whom stopped chanting to admire his masculine form—and removed the musket from the Ives brother hastily reloading it with buckshot from his pockets. With scarcely a hitch to his progress, he marched out the front door.

"Who *was* that?" Ninian murmured from the comfort and safety of Drogo's arms. She didn't think her knees would lock under her if he let go. She didn't question the ease with which she sought the security of his shelter or his swiftness in offering it.

"Devil if I know," Drogo answered, although his voice held a thoughtful note. "But I daresay he won't stick his nose in our business again."

Ninian almost certainly heard him chuckle—whether at his witticism or her handiwork, she couldn't tell. With the enemy in retreat, Aunt Stella broke up the ring of chanting cousins and sailed toward the altar. The bishop emerged from hiding, all but shaking his ruffled feathers. Dunstan had begun to round up his excited brothers who, now that the danger was over, were overly aware of the admiring feminine glances from the other side of the church. Before all the powers descended on them, Ninian turned and hastily searched her bridegroom for injury.

Drogo caught her hands between his and forced her to look up at him. "I'm not one of your patients yet," he said gently. "Twane was too drunk to be much of an opponent."

"That was Claudia's husband?" Her husband's world was a

strange one, much more violent than the cloistered one she'd grown up in. She could scarcely blame Claudia for escaping to the peace of Wystan. She just didn't understand how all these worlds connected. Or her place in them. Her jaw still ached from her unprecedented violence.

Dunstan, Stella, and the bishop converged on them all at once, but Ninian's aunt and the clergyman fell into a heated conversation, leaving Dunstan to examine his brother for damage.

Deciding Drogo was relatively unharmed, he turned a wary glance to Ninian. "Remind me never to put my nose in your vicinity."

Too caught up in the whirlwind of emotions swirling around her, Ninian didn't even have the grace to blush as she leaned into her bridegroom's embrace. "Just don't stick it in my business." She said pertly, although uncertainty held her in its grip. Would he call off their wedding now? Or would the bishop?

"I won't ask what Twane wanted, but who the hell was that your bride nearly maimed?" Dunstan demanded, turning to Drogo, apparently satisfied Ninian wouldn't leap out and snack on him.

"Damned if I know, but I mean to find out." Drogo lifted Ninian's chin and forced her attention back to the conversation. "What did he say to you?"

Beneath his dark gaze, she blinked. He was forever doing that to her. She'd never known that much heated attention, and she needed time to become used to it. "Nothing we don't both already know," she answered without thinking.

Drogo raised his eyebrows and waited.

Ninian grimaced and straightened, reaching to set her coronet straight. "If I may quote him directly, he said, 'The damned earl really doesn't know what he has here, does he?' But what that has to do with anything is beyond my understanding. I've not met an Ives yet who made any sense to me."

"Ives?" both Dunstan and Drogo said at once.

She glared at them impatiently. "Of course. Did you not look at him? He's every bit an Ives." She glanced at Dunstan. "And he's even angrier than you are."

Aunt Stella chose that moment to descend upon them. "We're to take the rest of the ceremony to the church steps. The fool won't risk his precious church on the lot of you any longer. Ives, if you don't keep better control of those young nuisances…"

While she scolded, Ninian met Drogo's gaze. Did he intend to go through with the ceremony or had he time to realize they were wedding chaos to calamity?

She watched him study her face, then drop his gaze to the place where their child rested. His jaw tightened, and with that grim look she was beginning to recognize, he clasped her arm over his elbow. The brawl had half torn his black cloak from his shoulder, but the gold band remained fastened around his neck. She thought he looked more dangerous than a medieval knight returning from the Crusades.

"Marrying on the church steps is much more to my liking," he declared, hauling her with him down the aisle and past their expectant audience. "Equality?" he whispered in her ear as they hurried forward. "What the hell does that mean?"

Twenty

WITH THE DOVES—PIGEONS—DISPERSED AND THE GRAIN ALREADY thrown, the rest of the wedding was anticlimactic. As Drogo grimly repeated his vows—including the one of equality— Ninian accepted the token ring binding her to him, and preening Ives males carved swathes through flirting Malcolm females.

As Drogo leaned over to seal his vows by kissing his bride, a sigh of happiness wafted from their feminine audience, and ribald laughter and shouts erupted among the males. Feeling like one of the beleaguered characters in the political cartoons posted in news shop windows, Drogo limited the kiss to a highly unsatisfactory nibble.

"Scotland would have been better," he muttered against her lips.

"Or not at all," she answered sweetly.

She might very well have the right of that. Warily watching the crowd for any sign of Twane or his men—or the mysterious man who was bloody lucky to still have a nose—Drogo eased Ninian through the cheering mob of well-wishers.

"You don't suppose they'll all follow us home?" he asked glumly as he assisted her into their waiting carriage. He'd left a footman and a driver standing guard while they were inside, but he ordered a final hasty inspection while Ninian took her seat. He didn't fear Twane, but his brothers were capable of unfastening carriage wheels or placing Chinese firecrackers under seats.

"I suppose they'll not only follow us," Ninian replied as he climbed in beside her, "but I also suppose my uncles and their sons will be waiting at the house to welcome you into their ranks. They do like a free meal."

"They're not Malcolms, are they?" It didn't look as if he would be bedding his new bride any time soon, Drogo concluded with disgruntlement.

"Of course not, but I'm sure they'll be happy to console you with all the trials and tribulations we bring. Were it not for the lack of available men, Malcolm women should never have left the forest."

He'd had enough warnings. He really needed to start paying closer attention to the annoying details now that he had what he wanted. As the carriage halted in the convoluted traffic of a narrow intersection, Drogo studied the bland, innocent features of his country wife. "Are you trying to tell me all Malcolm women are… witches?" He had difficulty even saying the preposterous word.

Ninian tugged at the gold band fastening her cape. "Of some degree. Of course." The band snapped open, and she sighed in relief before looking up at him quizzically. "Did you have some doubt?" She continued without waiting for an answer. "Actually, from studying what books I could find at the cottage, I'm theorizing we're descendants of Druids. Women played a very large part in that cult."

Drogo was used to facing the world and its caprices with impassivity, but even he was having difficulty swallowing a lump this large. "Druids? Tree worshippers?"

She shrugged. "Trees have their powers, just as herbs do." She touched the halo of twigs in her hair. "Aunt Stella will have laid an enchantment on this rowan, offering me protection. Actually, though, rowan seeds are poisonous and can be used to disable enemies. You should approve of the logic."

"We should have forced rowan berries down Twane's throat?" It was easy to slip past her superstitious silliness while watching Ninian's luscious lips press together in an inviting bow. If only they had time, he could slide his tongue between that sweetness and have her skirts up shortly thereafter.

He checked the jam of horses and carts outside the window. If they delayed much longer… The carriage lurched into motion. Damn.

"Why do you hide Claudia from her husband?"

Were she anyone but Ninian, he would hear suspicion or jealousy in her question, but this one sounded as innocent as the lips speaking it. "He beats her, badly. Among other things," he added reluctantly. He didn't want to introduce a new bride to the perversions of some members of his sex.

"Ahh, that accounts for it. I should have bitten *his* nose." She folded her hands in her lap without explaining.

It seemed to him that she left a lot of things without explanation. Drogo narrowed his eyes. "Accounts for what?"

"Claudia's pain and anger and sorrow. And lack of…" She screwed up her face in search of the right word. "Her lack of confidence in herself, I guess. She's a very unhappy person. I'm glad she's safe now."

Drogo wanted to relax at this perfectly sensible answer. Ninian had spent months in Claudia's company, and his bride was more perceptive than most. But she'd pulled this little trick of describing people's feelings one too many times and a little too recently for comfort. He needed further reassurance. "I suppose you know that the same way you know Dunstan suffers from spurned love and that the man with the sore nose is angry? Not that any man wouldn't be angry after being bitten." Mentally, he rubbed his own prominent beak.

"Of course." Complacently, she glanced out the window at the row of older town houses they passed.

Other women never stopped talking. He'd married one who didn't know when to start. Curbing his impatience, Drogo tried again. "I thought witches cast spells, not read minds."

She shrugged, but he noticed she clasped her hands a little tighter. "I don't read minds. I have a gift for empathy. People call us witches for lack of any better word. We don't cast spells on people, although the weather—" She halted that train of thought. "We just have… special talents."

She looked so perfectly sane and beautiful when she said

things like that. Her golden curls were a picture of angelic purity, her blue eyes reflected the openness of the sky—and then she hit him with lightning bolts of lunacy from out of nowhere.

Sighing, Drogo leaned back in his seat and tried to quench a hot surge of ardor. If there was any witchcraft at work here, it was in the way she bewitched him with lust. She already carried his child. He should be satisfied with that.

"Talents," he repeated flatly, desperately looking for a thread of rationality. "Not the painting, musical sort?"

"Well, Lucinda paints wonderful portraits." She didn't seem to think the topic irrelevant. "Unfortunately, they tend to reflect the subject's character a little too clearly. If you have any deep, dark perversions, don't sit for her."

Drogo rubbed his temple and wondered if he should have Ninian sit for her artistic cousin but decided he didn't want to know the secrets of her soul—or her cousin's talent—that well. "And your talent?"

"I'm a healer," she answered diffidently, clasping and unclasping her fingers. "I just seem to have made a bit of a mess of it."

A healer. Well, that almost made sense. Living in the rural countryside without proper medical care, many women learned healing arts. He couldn't imagine that any of them were very good at it, lacking scientific methods, but even trained physicians often relied on the efficacy of herbal medicine.

"Sarah said you delivered Lydie's baby safely and helped it to thrive."

"Any decent midwife can do that," she scoffed. "I should have understood how Lydie's unhappiness affected the child and treated her accordingly, but I didn't. I was too worried about myself."

That veered a little too far from the rational path. Taking a deep breath, Drogo built a safe bridge over his new wife's lack of logic. "Sarah says you were better than any London physician. Don't minimize your talents."

The look she gave him should have scalded. He didn't know what he'd said wrong. He'd intended a compliment.

Momentarily floundering, he grasped for a more stable topic, one that would satisfy the taunting questions of his family.

"Exactly what is the meaning of that vow of equality we took?" he asked bluntly. "What happened to the usual thing, the 'love, honor, and obey'?"

Obviously disgruntled, she bunched the white satin of her cape into a ball. "The Malcolm ceremony used to make the groom promise obedience, but the duke balked at that. Grandmother said they fought for six months before he and Aunt Stella reached a compromise. It's not a difficult concept to embrace, is it?"

"Women aren't equal to men." Already battered by the illogic of Druids and unnatural talents, Drogo refused to let the lunacy continue. The carriage drew up to the house, but he ignored the orderly line of servants waiting on the steps. He wanted to set this straight before his countess developed any more delusions. "Women can't sail ships, build buildings, learn law, or govern countries. I'd be surprised to find one who could explain how their funds generated income."

Sky blue eyes narrowed into hostile slits above apple-round cheeks. "Did my father succeed in gaining access to my trust fund?"

"Of course not. It's tied up tighter than the Crown Jewels."

"A Malcolm woman established that trust," she said warningly. "Malcolm women control it, and Malcolm women fund it for the use of Malcolm women. And I know precisely how it earns interest and where to invest it. Aunt Stella may be head of our family, but Grandmother made me the treasurer." She flung the wad of satin to the opposite seat, composed her features, and offered him one of her dimpled, innocent smiles. "Shall we go in?"

Not only bewildered, but stunned, Drogo closed his eyes and shook his head in denial. She knew precisely what she was worth.

The solicitor had refused to disclose the extent of her trust fund, but he had made it apparent that there were sufficient funds to support an entire army of Malcolms.

Ninian was not only wealthier than he was, but she *knew* it, and she had still married him and his unruly family. She didn't need him. She was doing *him* a favor.

He had no control over her at all.

～

"The earl does not look like a happy bridegroom," Stella commented as she nibbled on a petit four from the lavish buffet table and watched Drogo sipping morosely at champagne while the cluster of men around him laughed and pounded each other's backs. None of them pounded Drogo's.

"My husband is a serious man," Ninian replied demurely, passing up the delicacies in favor of a dry biscuit to settle her queasy stomach. She'd thought the morning sickness had passed. Perhaps the babe objected to the day's stresses.

"Do not play the witless fool for me, young lady," Stella snapped. "Did he blame that disaster of a ceremony on you?"

"Of course not." Ninian sipped a little tea in hopes it would stay down. "Drogo is a very rational, very patient man. He is an upright pillar of society, a man of genius, a man who dedicates his life to family, and friends, and friends of family, and…"

"Your sarcasm is no better." Her aunt sighed as if bearing the burdens of the world. "You young girls have entirely too many romantic notions. Lucinda weeps daily because her father insists she marry a man of stature instead of the wastrel beau who recites poetry. In my day, we knew our duty to family."

Ninian pointed her biscuit in the direction of her young cousin. "If it's a man of stature the duke wants, he'd better steer her clear of young Joseph. He cheats at cards and won all my sweetmeats."

"Then play him for hazelnuts next time." Stella frowned at the laughing pair. "It's time we take our leave. Drogo might be a fine catch, but that illegitimate lot of rapscallions he calls brothers are nothing but trouble." She patted Ninian's cheek. "You'll be fine once you learn not to expect romantic fantasies. He may be a little stiff and unbending, but he's a good man. He'll take care of you and the babe. Call on me if you need anything."

"You're returning to the country?" Ninian really didn't need to ask. Malcolms needed woods as roses needed rain. She just wanted the reassuring presence of the familiar a while longer while she adjusted to her new role.

"You know how to reach me. You should have sent for me sooner when Mother died." Chiding her softly, Stella patted her again, then hurried to rescue her daughter from the charms of a roguish Ives.

"We'll be going, too, dear." Hermione appeared from out of nowhere. Quiet and unassuming where Stella was bold and loud, Ninian's younger aunt was still a force to treat cautiously. "These Ives men are much too… how do I put this delicately… *virile* to tolerate easily. Despite what Stella says, I really do think it might be a mistake to bring our families together." She smiled prettily from a face unlined by her middle years. "I'm sure you'll fare well, dear. I don't mean to insult your young man. But…" She sighed, glancing toward Drogo, who now stood alone, "he is a bit of a thundercloud, isn't he? Perhaps if I—"

"No, Aunt Hermie," Ninian hastily interrupted. "He's having a little difficulty accepting us, is all. He'll be fine."

Hermione looked doubtful. "If you say so, dear. I do hope you're reading him rightly. He does look a bit like Old Nick, doesn't he? But you're the expert. I'll bow before your greater knowledge." She blew Ninian a kiss, and trailing bits of lace and ribbons, mother henned her chicks toward the door.

Of course, that was the problem, Ninian acknowledged. Her Gift didn't apply to Drogo. She understood nothing about him. He could be plotting her demise right now, and she wouldn't even know he was angry.

Still, she couldn't subject Drogo to Hermione and her erratic spells. Hermione was a genius with perfumes and possessed a gift for bringing out the best in everyone with her scents, but she simply couldn't accept she didn't possess any mystical, occult, or psychic powers. The last time she'd attempted one of the lesser spells in her chap book, heat had curdled all the milk in the dairy for a week.

Ninian smiled at the memory of her two aunts arguing over

that incident. Hermione was as gentle as Stella was arrogant, yet they'd quarreled without once hurting each other. Perhaps Malcolms were strange to others, but she thought they could teach the rest of the population a thing or two.

Noting the strain on Drogo's jaw as her aunts and cousins fluttered around him to say their farewells, Ninian swallowed her doubts and crossed the room to relieve him of his onerous task. If Drogo was anything like his brothers, the feminine bombardment of scents, voices, and touches would drive him to the brink, much as all those *virile* Ives men were distracting her cousins. She thought the families together might resemble multiple Adams and Eves after their apple-tasting orgy, but Drogo's house was no Garden of Eden.

He turned and reached for her before she could speak her presence. Although he often appeared totally self-absorbed, he always seemed to know when she was there. Odd, since she could never sense him.

"Now, if you could only chase away my brothers," he whispered in her ear as he shook the duke's hand and watched the last of the Malcolm females flutter out the door.

"Abracadabra," she murmured in return, feeling her own female flutter at the warmth of his breath near her ear. She was fortunate that only one Ives male could disturb her this way. She didn't like feeling so unsettled.

He didn't laugh at her jest but regarded her with suspicion. Ninian sighed. She liked him much better as a natural philosopher who thought her a silly twit and not the arrogant male who protected all under his roof. She could already see the disadvantage of being a wife.

Fear prickled across her skin at that thought. She was married. Her child had a name. Would her husband allow her to return to Wystan or was she a prisoner of her decision?

Drogo's hand raised from her shoulder to tease at a sensitive spot just below her ear. "If I leave them with the champagne, do you think we could disappear upstairs?"

She wanted to turn and head for the stairs right now. Just the husky suggestiveness of his voice aroused a tingle that danced along her skin. The memory and anticipation of his lovemaking had haunted the back of her mind throughout the day's chaos. Now that she knew the power of his touch, she craved it constantly. The bond between them was deeper than the physical now, blessed by church and family. There was no reason at all to deny what they both wanted.

Except an instinct far older than time.

"Will we leave for Wystan in the morning?" she asked innocently.

"The session is not over, moonchild. I cannot leave." He murmured the endearment seductively, as if no other words but that one mattered.

"I can travel alone," she suggested, but the queasiness in her stomach lurched in expectation of an answer she didn't want.

"When we travel, we travel together," he said firmly.

"Then pray we travel soon, before the heat consumes us." Donning her best dimpled smile, Ninian bobbed a curtsy and sailed off for a long chat with Dunstan's wife.

She no longer saw her husband as the fantasy devil of legend, but as a man. Devils wreaked havoc and ruin, then had the courtesy to disappear. Men lingered to cause trouble a lot longer.

Twenty-one

"SHE'S LOVELY, DROGO," LADY MARGARET IVES SAID STIFFLY. "And her family is exceptional. I congratulate you."

His mother had refused to attend the wedding breakfast to show her disdain for his father's by-blows, but she hadn't been able to resist stopping by to greet him privately. Drogo had been only six when his father had removed him from her house, and they'd never developed a proper relationship, but he respected the pain she must have endured.

"Thank you. Shall I call her in to meet you?" he asked out of politeness. His mother had refused to come to his house before this, and he refused to go to a house where his younger brothers were not welcome. Ninian had not questioned the arrangement. She seldom questioned anything. He'd once thought that convenient. Now, he was beginning to wonder about her lack of curiosity. She'd avoided him ever since what he suspected was a disagreement about traveling to Wystan. With Ninian, it wasn't always easy to tell.

His mother looked at him curiously. "I've already met her, dear. Dunstan brought her to call on me last week."

Drogo didn't know whether to hold that against Dunstan or Ninian. One of them should have mentioned it. He nodded knowingly. "Of course, I'd forgotten. I've been rather busy lately."

"You're always busy, just like your father. Now that you

have a young bride, you'd best find time for her or risk losing her," she warned.

Drogo tried not to wince. His brothers might not know, but his father had told him of the girl child Margaret had birthed, a child that had not been his father's and that had died at birth. What had gone wrong between his parents was a long time ago, but the repercussions still resounded to this day. He would do well to take her warning to heart. It might be fashionable for wives to take lovers after providing the required heir and spare, but it wasn't sane. And above all else, Drogo intended to approach marriage sanely.

"I'll do my best." He hesitated and sighed. It had been a long day, and where he'd hoped to be closer to his new wife by the end of it, it seemed they were more distant than ever. He had little in the way of female guidance to explain what he'd done wrong. "But I have little practice at it," he admitted.

"Think of her as one of those stars you prize," she said dryly, gathering up her gloves. "Study her as you do the night skies."

He was afraid of what he would discover if he did. Not liking that realization, he nodded politely and escorted her to the door.

The September sun had already disappeared into the fog banks over the river as his mother gathered her skirts and climbed into her coach. He'd see no evening star twinkling through the murk. His brothers had already departed to their own separate activities, expecting him to celebrate his wedding night with his bride.

He didn't know where the hell his bride was.

Returning inside, Drogo climbed the stairs to see if he could locate her in her chamber. She didn't seem to think it necessary to tell him where she was going or what she was doing, even on their wedding day. She'd lived like a creature of the forest most of her life and was more independent than most females of his acquaintance. He supposed he could adapt to that. He really didn't need another person to watch and worry over. He just couldn't help worrying about her naiveté—or her befuddled mind—in a city this size.

No candle lit Ninian's room. No fire warmed her grate. No graceful silhouette danced in the misty light from the windows. More disappointed than he was willing to admit, Drogo turned to his own room, but he had little hope of finding her there. Not once had she ever come to him.

Finding it empty, as expected, he ordered fires in both grates and set out in search of his straying wife. This was his wedding night. He'd had high expectations of this day, but as he'd told her before, he was used to disappointment. Still, he didn't give up. There was all the night ahead of them. He'd not understood how little joy he had in his life until he realized how much he was looking forward to nights in Ninian's bed.

All his life he'd been the responsible one, the one who had led his drunken father home, the one who returned his mischievous brothers to their tutors, the one who managed the account books and the solicitors and the matters of estate. His stolen moments he'd devoted to stargazing and the astronomical calculations that so fascinated him. He didn't have an imaginative mind, but he liked to think there might be life on other planets, or perhaps the Greek gods resided there, and that some day he would find proof. It was the only fantasy he allowed himself, outside the bone-deep desire for a child of his own.

He didn't even know why he wanted the child. He'd never held his brothers as babies or dandled them on his knee. He'd always considered them a constant source of interruption and little more. Perhaps it was his one arrogance to have what he thought he could not. He had little experience with women, seldom took them seriously, avoided them at all costs except in bed, but they possessed the one ability he could not duplicate—the ability to procreate. For that, he was willing to allow Ninian into his life. Somehow.

After searching the nursery, inquiring of Sarah, and checking all the public rooms, Drogo still hadn't found her. The house wasn't as extravagantly large as the castle. It had been his grandfather's, and Sarah's mother, Ann, had detested it. His father had built a more modern one for her in the suburbs of Hyde Park Corner. Once he'd come of age, Drogo had insisted on moving in to attain some privacy from his motley lot of brothers. That had lasted just long enough for the first one to be kicked out of school.

Unless Ninian had run away, there was only one place left to find her.

Taking the back door above the kitchens, Drogo lifted his lamp and searched the darkened garden. His heart caught in his throat as he saw her lonely figure seated below him, slumped on the damp ground, with the fog swirling around her cascade of hair. She never wore it up as other women did, and he was glad of it. He loved the wild abandon of her curls.

He stepped softly, not wanting to frighten her, but she must have seen the lamp light. She turned and looked up at him through the wet fog. She looked almost haunted, so pale were her cheeks, and his heart did another panicky leap. "Are you well?"

She regarded him soundlessly, then returned her gaze to the blighted garden. "The soul is gone out of this land."

She'd drifted off on another of her mental journeys. He very much feared he'd taken a madwoman to wife, but a gentle one, one that tugged at hitherto unknown heartstrings. He would take good care of her and the child she carried. "You must come in. You'll catch a chill."

"I don't, generally." Sitting cross-legged on the bare ground, wearing one of her old gowns, she sifted dirt between her fingers. "There are carriage wheels on your roses, and a burned-out kettle in the thyme. I believe even savage Indians take better care of their land than that."

Drogo took a seat on the garden bench above her. She might not mind the damp ground, but he did. "Savage Indians must eat off the land. We do not."

She twisted her head to look up at him. "I am of this earth. I must take care of it. I sometimes wonder if you are not of the sky, and if we will ever meet. I believe in things of the spirit, but you see only with your mind."

Perhaps she was not so much out of her mind as in another place besides the one he inhabited. "I don't claim to fully understand you," he admitted. "But we've made a child together and must now learn to live with what we've done. What would you suggest?"

He thought she smiled. In the gloom, it was difficult to tell. He wanted to pull her into his arms and warm her, but he suspected she would slip through his fingers like the fog should he try.

"I like the way your mind works." She leaned over, plucked a clover from the beaten grass, and handed it to him. "It has four leaves," she informed him. "You are a very lucky man. There is an entire patch of them here."

Drogo bit back a sigh of exasperation. He wanted logical advice. She handed him superstitious good luck charms. "We should go in."

"You may, if you like. I need to think, and I think better outside."

He shrugged off his coat and leaned over to place it around her shoulders. "All right, can I help you think so you will come in sooner?"

She shifted the coat more snugly around her. "Thank you. I cannot read you as I do others, but I think you are a very nice man, just a little too intellectually elevated above the rest of us, perhaps. I exist, you know."

He stared down at her golden head and wondered if it was completely empty or if it just rattled. "Of course you exist. I never thought otherwise."

"No, you think I'm a convenience, like the bench you sit upon. That's not the same thing. There is a Me inside of me. A person. You've never met me, and you don't seem much interested in knowing me, so I've tried not to get in your way. But that isn't going to work if we live together, is it?"

A hollow opened inside him, a gaping, echoing hollow he recognized from long ago nights as a young child in a strange bed, in a strange house, without the familiarity of his mother or brothers around him. He tried not to let that emptiness speak through him. Carefully, logically, he applied his mind to whatever she might be trying to say. "I'm not used to having a woman in the house, if that is what you mean."

"No, that isn't what I mean. You had Sarah and Claudia

and Lydie in your castle, but you didn't know they existed either. You shut them out. Sarah is here now, and you seldom speak with her except in passing, as you would speak to your valet when you want your boots shined. I'm different, and that bothers you, but you're still trying to reduce me to the position of bootblack or whatever." She stroked the grass at her fingertips. "I think..." she hesitated as she formulated the phrases, "I think you've confined me to the role of Wife. A wife sleeps with you when you want it. She buys things, and her bills end up on your desk. She occasionally speaks, and you try hard to listen, but you really don't hear. Your mind is elsewhere."

He waited for her to go on, and when she didn't, he figured he was supposed to say something. He had no idea what to say. He could stand in front of the Lords and speak for hours, but he couldn't talk to his bride. Men talked about subjects he could understand. Women talked of things beyond his comprehension.

"I'm sorry. I really don't understand. You're my wife now. Wives and husbands share a bed. That's the purpose of marriage. What would you have me say?"

"That you will send me back to Wystan because you know that is where I belong."

That panicky feeling returned, and Drogo hastened to quiet it. He wouldn't let her leave him. Couldn't. He had to explain. He hated explaining himself, but his mother had said he must work at this, and so he would.

"Come here," he ordered. If he was going to do this, he would do it on his terms.

She looked up at him again, and then unquestioningly, she stood up and settled beside him, curling her warm, soft fingers into his. She smelled of roses. Drogo laid his hand over her gently sloped belly and stroked. She was round and firm, and he could almost feel the life blooming there. He took a deep breath.

"You know my parents lived separately?"

She nodded. "Sarah explained."

"Sarah knows nothing." He sounded curt, even to himself.

He tried again. "My mother is from a modest family. Her brother is a vicar. Her father owns a small estate close to the Ives holdings. My father was an arrogant man, raised to be an earl, the eldest and most spoiled of several sons. He always did as he pleased."

She wriggled slightly beside him, and Drogo realized the bench was hard. This was no time for these unveilings, but he would have it done. He took his hand from hers and pulled her on his lap, where she settled gladly. Her breath whispered against his cheek, and he breathed easier as he wrapped his arms around her plump waist. He could do this.

"It pleased him to seduce my mother. It did not please him when her father went to his and demanded that he do the honorable thing, nor did it please him when my grandfather agreed. But threatened with disinheritance, he did what was right, and they had the three of us in the first few years of their marriage."

"You and Dunstan and Ewen," she recited, apparently confirming her memory.

"Yes. But my grandfather was still alive at the time, and he refused to give up the reins to his holdings. My father was bored and sought entertainment elsewhere, challenges which drew him to London, leaving my mother behind with us. He stayed away for a year or more. My mother retaliated by finding a man who would love her as my father did not. My father sought revenge by bedding every woman who consented. This tale becomes worse with the telling. Would you rather go inside?"

She snuggled closer and leaned against his shoulder. Drogo breathed the fresh scent of her, rested his chin upon the silken warmth of her hair, and tightened his arms around her and his child. Taking that for answer, he continued.

"I know of at least one bastard he created in his dalliance across the countryside. I have a half brother, William, by a dairy maid in the village. My father set her up with a small competence. At the same time, he filed a petition for separation with the courts and demanded my mother be removed from his home."

She sighed, and her breath warmed the chill in his chest. "How old were you?"

"Six." He gritted his teeth and continued. "You must know the rest. With the proof of my mother's adultery, the court granted his petition, with the provision that Dunstan and Ewen be left with my mother. My father met Sarah's widowed mother, Ann, about that time, and set her up as mistress. When she bore him a son, Joseph, he moved her into his home in my mother's place since the separation agreement does not allow for remarriage. I do not know what hold Ann had on him, but after that, my father was content to settle down. Perhaps the death of my grandfather gave him the challenge he needed, but I saw little of that. I was fourteen when he died, and the responsibility of the earldom fell on me."

"And why do you tell me this?" she asked softly.

Drogo gritted his teeth against impatience. "To explain why I will never leave my wife as my father did. A wife and husband must live together, work together, play together, become one as my father and Ann did. He never strayed after he took her into his home, and I like to think they were happy together. That's what I want."

He held his tongue even though she made no immediate reply. Neither of them were talkers by nature, it seemed. He could live with that. He could not live without her beside him. He needed her in his bed at night, to remind him of why they were together. He needed his child where he could see him, watch him grow, be part of his life—something his father had denied Dunstan and Ewen.

"Your father and Ann must have loved each other to have managed a life together, even under such terrible circumstances. They had some common bond, whereas your father and mother did not."

"They had three children together," he said grimly.

"Ives men are very…" she chuckled and added, "*virile*. And with her upbringing, your mother would have tried to please him. Children are easy to make."

He growled, and Ninian turned her head up and patted his cheek. Drogo imagined his bristles burned her soft palm, but he reveled in the touch. He'd reached deep down to a place he didn't like to relate this story. He didn't want to ever go through it again. He wanted her in his bed right now, and if they didn't go soon, he would take her here on the grass. He needed to be deep inside her, outside of himself.

"Children really are easy to make, if the circumstances are right," she assured him, "else there would not be so many in the world. Raising them is another matter. And making a relationship between two grown people is even more difficult, I expect. We really have gone about things in reverse."

"That's Sarah's fault."

"No, it's ours. We played with fire and got burned. I do not regret it. I want this child, but if you mean what you are saying, if you mean to keep me at your side and see this child grow, then we have a very difficult road ahead."

"I don't see how," he said grumpily. If she would just come to his bed, the road would smooth considerably. "I'm wealthy enough to support you comfortably. I will not beat you. I am trying very hard to listen to you because I know I'm not good at that sort of thing. I've even told you what no other but my mother knows so we might understand each other better. What more can I do?"

"Believe I'm a Malcolm witch," she answered firmly, wiggling out of his grasp and standing. "Until you understand who I am, we can never be happy. I will try very hard to show you who I am, but we have left this too late. The child will be born in five months, and she must be born in Wystan."

"There is nothing in Wystan," he argued. "The session won't end for months, and then the holidays are upon us, and my brothers are here. I assure you, my steward is looking after the village. There is no reason to return there until spring."

"And until you understand and believe me, we are at cross-purposes. Good night, my lord. I'll see you in the morning."

She walked away. Drogo stared after her in disbelief. He'd bared the secrets of his soul, and she'd walked away. On their wedding night.

He jumped up to follow but stumbled over a rusting water can. In a fit of unusual fury, he flung it as hard as he could.

It crashed into the assortment of carriage wheels leaning against the fence, and the clatter and bang did nothing more than cause his neighbors to open their windows and yell, and dogs to howl all across the city.

Maybe he'd go find Twane and pound him into the ground.

Twenty-two

DEVIL TAKE IT! HE'D NOT LET HER GET AWAY WITH THIS. THIS was his *wedding* night. A husband had rights.

With dogs still howling in the distance, Drogo stomped up the stairs. He'd had to reassure the servants that they wouldn't be murdered in their beds by a wild gang of tin can throwing thieves. He'd learned to be firm with his brothers. He saw no reason why a wife should be any different.

Prepared to batter down a locked door, he nearly fell in as it swung open. Righting himself, he glared at the candle-lit bed.

Ninian had removed her old gown and sat in a simple shift against her pillows, reading the book he'd given her. At his entrance, she glanced up with curiosity but no fear.

He felt like an ogre. He didn't lose his temper, damn it. He *never* lost his temper.

Sighing, he took another deep breath and plunged his hand through his hair. Unlike his half brothers', his hair was thick and straight instead of curly, and the ribbon fell out easily. He must look like a wild man.

"This is our wedding night," he reminded her.

"We've already had our wedding night," she corrected. "That's the problem. We did this backward."

Ninian watched her husband standing there in all his masculine confusion and almost backed down. Firelight flickered over the taut planes of his dark features, and she remembered the night they'd met when she'd thought him the devil.

She still thought it sometimes, but for better or worse, he was her devil. She admired the way he controlled his temper before speaking. She also liked the way one thick strand of hair pulled loose to hang beside his ear, an obvious sign that she'd disturbed his usually ordered life.

She craved his attention and affection, and the heat in his eyes nearly burned through her resolution. She wanted to throw down the book and open her arms to him.

She couldn't open her arms to him. The life of their child depended on it.

"Backward?" he repeated, obviously bewildered.

"We had our wedding night first, and now we must go through the period of courtship where a couple learns to know one another."

He seemed stunned. Her logical, sensible, very controlled husband had difficulty grasping her intuitive version of their problem.

Just his presence stirred unbidden responses that caused her to regret her decision. She'd never seen him in daylight with his shirt off. She wanted to see *all* of him, in the morning light, in her bed, before and after making love. She wanted to see his laughter.

She stroked the gray cat on the bed beside her and watched Drogo coolly. She hoped it was coolly.

"You want courtship?" he asked in astonishment.

"We've done the wedding night, then the wedding. It seems logical." She beamed in approval of her own thinking.

"Courtship." He staggered to one of her fireplace chairs and collapsing, stared at her in incredulity. "I'm sitting here in my wife's bed chamber, while she wears nothing but a shift—which, by the way, shows your beautiful breasts and the roundness of our child quite delectably—and you want *courtship*?"

Heat bubbled through her at his words. Now that he'd mentioned it, she could feel the taut points of her nipples rubbing against the thin linen, and she very much wanted them touched as he'd touched them last night. But her daughter's future depended on her resisting a moment's pleasure.

"Call it what you will, then, but you must see me as I am

before we can go forward." She held up her book and asked
brightly, "Shall I read to you?"

He glared daggers. She was gambling he was not a man
who took women against their will. That was a very large and
dangerous gamble. He could overpower her without even
trying, because she'd cave in at the first kiss.

"I think, wife, that you are as insane as I believed you to
be from the first. Do you wish to drive me to the arms of
other women?"

She looked at him with interest. "Have you had other
women since our wedding night?"

He scowled. "It wasn't a wedding night. It was a moment
of insanity." At her continued look of interest, he shrugged
uncomfortably. "I've been busy. And then I received Sarah's
wretched letter, and everything's been arse backward since."

Unexpectedly, that news thrilled her. He'd not had any
women but her since they met. She radiated confidence now.
"Well, in the interest of equality, should you take another
woman, I'm free to look at other men."

"*What*?" He almost shot out of his chair as he roared this,
but he gripped the arms as if they were her throat and sat
down again. "So that's what that equality vow is about?"

"Well, I'm not precisely certain, given I've never married
before, but it sounds applicable."

He looked at her shrewdly, finally getting her measure.
"You're making this up as you go. You're angry because I
won't take you to Wystan, and you want to get even."

"No, I want to teach you a lesson," she said earnestly. She
wasn't much of a teacher, but he was an excellent student. He
caught on quickly, much too quickly.

"If I come over there and kiss you now, you wouldn't
even put up a fight, would you?" Dark eyes studied her as his
temper seemed to cool at this discovery.

She couldn't be any less than honest. "I don't know. I'd
like to think I'd try. The future of our child rides on it."

His curled eyebrows almost straightened as he lifted them.
"The future of our child rides on our not making love?"

"On our not having… sexual congress." She used the

physician's words. "Making love is entirely different. We haven't done that yet."

She thought his eyebrows would fly straight off his head. Then his eyes narrowed, and he glared at her again.

"I suppose this is some female nonsense about love and romance. You raise your hopes too high if you expect that to happen. I'm willing to be patient and give you time to fit into my life but do not expect love songs and sonnets from me."

Disappointment rippled through her, but she knew it had to be so. All she could hope to earn was his respect. "No, I only want you to know I exist," she insisted.

"Oh, I know you exist, all right." He lifted his long frame from the chair and approached the bed. "But we can take some time to know each other better. Just do not dally too long," he warned as he stopped beside the bed.

She didn't have too long. The child needed to be in Wystan now. But if she wanted to make this marriage work, she would hold out for as long as she could.

"I am not good at sharing," she admitted as he hovered over her. He was so large and intimidating and... virile. She didn't giggle at her aunt's word now. She need only glance sideways—like so—to see he was thoroughly aroused and hungry for her. She hastily glanced back to her book. "But I will do what I can to hurry the process."

"Give me a report each night on that book you're reading," he suggested.

Then, without warning, he leaned over and kissed her forehead, straightened, and walked out.

The cat meowed in protest at thus being disturbed. Ninian scratched its head sympathetically. She'd never sleep now.

❧

"Oh, dear." Sarah set down her tea cup and stared aghast at the news sheet she was reading. "Twane has filed a crim con suit against Drogo."

"A what?" Startled more by the violence of Sarah's emotions than her words, Ninian glanced up with alarm from the thyme she was potting.

"Criminal conversation, although adultery is a civil and not a criminal matter and is scarcely about conversation," she explained, her fury at the article muting as her active mind took charge. "The coward. Any real man would have challenged him to a duel."

"A duel?" Ninian asked in horror. She didn't like it when Sarah's mind started churning. She understood the power of pure emotion, but the deviousness of Sarah's convoluted brain eluded her. At the moment, she didn't like any part of this conversation. "Drogo does not fight duels, does he? I thought him a man of nature, not violence."

Sarah sent her an amused look over the top of the news sheet. "He is an *Ives*, my dear. They fight like rabid dogs even when they aren't challenged. Which is why, of course, that coward Twane didn't challenge him." She uttered a low curse as she returned to perusing the paper.

It seemed she had as much to learn about her husband as he did about her. Firming the soil around the newly planted thyme, Ninian thought furiously. Duels and swords repulsed her. Adultery on the other hand...

What could she say? She'd known Drogo lived with three women when she met him. She'd known Claudia was married, even if unhappily. It scarcely made a difference under the laws of God or man if he'd taken Claudia to his bed out of sympathy or a need to prove his virility. That awful man who had interrupted their wedding was in the right.

She tried to smother an annoying cough.

"What happens now?" she asked of Sarah, who still glowered at the article.

"Twane must produce evidence if Drogo disputes the suit. If Twane wins, he can ask for damages that will bankrupt us all." She sighed and shoved her tea cup aside. "I suppose if Claudia returns home, Twane would drop the suit."

"But Lord Twane would kill her, wouldn't he?" Ninian could tell that from Sarah's fear and panic, although she did her best to conceal it behind her insouciant behavior.

Sarah tightened her lips and shot her a sharp look but didn't respond directly. "I'll have to consult Claudia's chart. The stars brought you and Drogo together. Perhaps they'll tell how to keep Claudia and her husband apart." She folded up the paper and rose. "You'd best take something for that cough."

Ninian watered her plant and worried at her lower lip after Sarah departed. She certainly couldn't discredit Sarah's talents, given the eccentricity of her own. But even knowing her own abilities and that of her family, she wouldn't rely on them to untangle this affair. If such a thing as true magic existed, she'd conjure Lord Twane into a distant ocean. As it was, she only had her wits and her observations to work with, and they told her Drogo was in serious trouble.

Odd, that despite all his complaints of his brothers' scrapes, it was Drogo who had created the biggest danger to his family and only because he'd offered shelter to a friend.

She bit her lip hard on that thought and snapped a twig of the thyme. The fragrance woke her to where she was and what she was doing. Carefully, she carried the pot to the back garden and set it in a sunny spot between one of Ewen's preposterous inventions and what was apparently an attempt by Joseph to create a large scale model of—as usual, she studied the weathered paint and wooden columns trying to decide—a Parthenon play house?

It wasn't her place to go to Drogo and ask him about his problems, but it wasn't in her nature to ignore danger either.

A healer in an Ives' household needed far more than herbal lore.

❧

"Your solicitor seems concerned about some large expenditures you have ordered." Drogo dropped into the man-size upholstered wing chair beside Ninian's bed, then glanced down to discover what the devil he was sitting on. He didn't remember a chair his size in the delicate boudoir he'd assigned to Ninian. These uncontrollable changes in his environment kept him perpetually off balance.

"How I spend my funds is of no concern to my solicitor or to you. If he continues appealing to you, I shall most certainly find another man of business."

Another woman might have sounded angry. Ninian merely stated facts. The idea of a woman controlling her own funds made Drogo decidedly uneasy, but the trust was drawn up so only Malcolm women had any authority over it. If whatever Ninian was doing had passed the scrutiny of the intimidating Duchess of Mainwaring, he couldn't question it.

"Why don't you and your aunts use the funds for Wystan?" he asked out of curiosity.

"We can't. The trust agreement specifically denies it. There's a legend in our storybook about a Malcolm who..."

He hastily waved away another of her involved wives' tales.

"I can recommend another solicitor if you prefer, or your aunts might wish to name one of their own. This one merely seeks to impress me with his conscientiousness. How are you coming with your translation of the diary?"

He hadn't come in here to argue over money. He didn't want to admit he'd entered Ninian's chambers to court his wife either, but he couldn't put any other face on it. He'd gone four damned months without a woman, then indulged in one of the most sensual nights of his life, and he damned well didn't like sleeping in a cold bed again. He would simply take a few nights to study the situation, develop a plan of action, and put it in motion when the time was right.

Knowing that instead of being repelled by his less than extraordinary looks, his wife enjoyed the same passionate attraction for him as he did for her, gave him patience to suffer a few nights longer. He certainly didn't have to worry that she wanted his money.

He need only worry about her sanity, he reminded himself grimly.

"The handwriting is more difficult to translate than the language," Ninian complained. "My ancestress had a penchant for loops and swirls and strange circles and did not always use the best of pen nibs."

"Rather like Sarah."

She shot him a questioning look, then apparently recognizing his humor, smiled tentatively. It seemed she had as much difficulty knowing what to make of him as he did of her. That reassured him. Stretching out his legs toward the fire and trying not to stare too hard at the tempting thrust of her breasts against the thin nightshift, Drogo crossed his arms across his chest and prepared to be entertained.

"I do not know my history very well, but I looked up this date and the diary apparently begins during Cromwell's reign." She gently turned a brittle page. "The signature in the frontispiece is that of a Ceridwen Malcolm Ives."

"Ceridwen? That's Welsh, isn't it?"

"Yes, but until recently, my family has always drawn on strong Celtic names. If I had more education, I could possibly understand the connections in some of our old books and trace them back through history, but I can only make assumptions based on general reading." She coughed and covered her mouth to smother it.

"I should think your family would wish their daughters formally educated." It certainly didn't seem as if any man had ever stopped them, Drogo reflected cynically. He frowned at the cough. It seemed to be lingering. Perhaps he should call a physician… Ninian would have none of it.

"Remember where we live." She cleared her throat before continuing. "Wystan has no teachers. The cottage has a limited library, and that contains mostly handwritten herbals and the miscellaneous scribblings of our ancestors. We're a family who learns best by trial and error. It's not as if anyone can teach us to deal with our talents."

There she went again. Drogo squeezed his fingers together to prevent scoffing at her idea of "talent." "You must have many gardening books then. You have a green thumb when it comes to plants."

Her eyes narrowed, and she ignored his observation. "Ceridwen apparently also had a talent with plants. In these first few pages, she seems very young, but she is talking about potting her kitchen herbs for the winter."

Drogo wrinkled his nose in distaste. "If that's all she has to write about, you'll not learn much from there. I'd thought I'd given you something more interesting."

"Her name is Malcolm *Ives*, and the Ives was added in

different ink, as if added at a later date. I should think it will be very interesting to know how a Malcolm and an Ives came to marry."

Drogo had an uneasy feeling it might be far better if she did not know how they fared, but it was too late to think of that now. He did not know of a single happy marriage on his family tree, including Dunstan's, from the looks of it. He watched her warily. "You will not try comparing what you learn in there to us, will you? I can assure you, I am nothing like my ancestors."

She closed the book, crossed her hands neatly on the cover, then finally lifted her eyes to his. She took his breath away when she looked at him like that. How had he thought her a simpleton? She delved straight into his soul with that look. And stirred far lower portions than his soul.

"Is that because you have no bastards or because you have not tried?" she asked.

Damn the woman. Every time he started to relax in her company, she hit him with another brickbat. He scowled and rose from the chair. "I would have no bastards because I would have had the decency to marry any woman who bore my child, as you are well aware. Heal that cough, or I shall call a physician, whether you like it or not."

Muttering, he slammed out of her cheery room into the cold damp of his own. Why the devil could women never leave well enough alone?

Twenty-three

"NINIAN, YOU ARE A SAINT!"

Grimacing at the irony of Sarah's declaration, Ninian tested the forehead of the child in her lap. The fever was almost gone, she decided, as Sarah's toddler snuggled closer. Just a cold, then.

The babe in her womb stirred, and Ninian basked in the love of the moment—a peaceful child sleeping in her arms, and a new one growing beneath her heart. The contentment they offered insulated her against the buffeting of Sarah's emotion. If it hadn't been for the man who'd put this child inside her, she would no doubt be quite happy.

But the desperate desire for her husband's acceptance left her with a constant hollow ache she saw no means of assuaging.

"I only gave her a little willow water and sang her to sleep," Ninian answered complacently. She could use herbs to heal. She wished she could use her Gift for sensing emotion for something equally useful.

"That's not what I'm talking about, although I must say you're a candidate for sainthood for nursing cranky children as well." She pulled a letter from the inside pocket of her gown. "Claudia writes that you have offered her and her sister passage to Paris and a home with some of your relatives. Why did you not tell me? It solves everything."

Ninian wrinkled her nose at this praise and gently returned her patient to her bed. The toddler stirred sleepily in protest, but she stroked her brow and whispered a few words, and the child slept again.

Fighting a cough that might wake the child, she rose and smoothed her wrinkled gown over the increasing bulge of her belly. It was well into October, the baby was due in early February, and she hadn't made any progress in convincing her husband she must return to Wystan, with or without him. She'd regaled him with tales from her ancestor's diary until she'd reached the part where Ceridwen had flooded the valley in an excess of zeal to please her new husband. Drogo had laughed at the foolishness of anyone believing they could control rain, and she'd diverted him with discussing means of clearing the burn rather than read him the part that came after.

Ceridwen had given birth to a girl, and her Ives husband had disavowed it, claiming no Ives had ever fathered a girl. He'd set her aside in the cottage Ninian assumed was the one her grandmother called home. She was afraid to read further. It definitely didn't sound like the kind of material that would sway Drogo's intent. And it verified at least one of the legends in her storybook.

"It solves little." She sighed and slipped away from the child's bed. "Claudia will never be able to marry. I'm not at all certain her sister will be able to, even should she desire it. Their family has no dowry to offer without Lord Twane's help."

"They're alive," Sarah said defiantly. "Twane cannot reach them. And even should he continue his suit against Drogo, it will not win him a right to Claudia. And he will have to hire liars as witnesses to prove his suit."

Ninian arched her eyebrows. "Would he?"

Sarah looked at her in surprise. "You do not really think Drogo bedded Claudia, do you? She practically threw herself at him, and he brushed her off like an annoying gnat. You are the only woman who's caught and held his attention in *years*."

Held his attention? Stirred his lust, mayhap, but not his attention.

"Even that simpleton last year who told him she carried his child didn't hold his interest, except for the possibility of the babe," Sarah continued. "Drogo built his hopes up enough to build a nursery, and then had them dashed when another man came forward and warned him of the treachery."

No wonder the poor man took everything he heard with a grain of salt. Shaking her head, Ninian left Sarah in the nursery. If she believed Sarah's assertion that Drogo hadn't bedded Claudia…

She gasped in surprise as her husband materialized before her. Drogo caught her arm and steadied her as she rocked backward. The concern in his deep-set eyes had the power to captivate. Somehow, she had to escape this bond between them. The life of their child depended on it.

"I must speak with you," he said gravely.

He seldom spoke with her during the day. The last time had been the day he'd taken her to the lecture on Naturalism in the Study of Our Waterways. The professor had proclaimed the Thames a travesty of filth and a danger to humanity and had never once named another river or waterway in all of England. It had been a serious disappointment, and neither of them had learned anything from it. Drogo had not invited her to attend any other lectures since, and she did not blame him—especially after her disappointment at the lack of information to aid the burn, she'd publicly declared the professor a fraud concerned only with obtaining money for his experiments.

Her heart pattered a little faster at her husband's seriousness as she followed him into the sitting room between their chambers. The fire was always lit now that the damp of autumn had set in.

"How is your cough?" he asked, easing her onto the settee before the fire. His gaze dropped to the burden she carried as it always did when they met.

"It will go away when I return to Wystan," Ninian assured him. She assumed her growing ungainliness had lessened his desire, but she had seen no evidence that he'd strayed elsewhere. With another man, she might have read his guilt. With this one, she had to rely on the confidence of his brothers. She thought she might feel their guilt or shame if they knew Drogo had taken up with other women.

"Then it will go away once we leave London for Ives," he said confidently.

"There is something wrong?" she asked when he did not immediately explain the reason for this attention. The other was an old argument, one she must win, but not this moment.

He paced before the fire, hands behind his back, hair neatly tied in a queue—an intimidating figure of a man, but one who had shown her kindness, even if of the absent-minded sort.

"Your aunts have invited Dunstan and his wife to a house party."

She waited, but he didn't seem to think further explanation necessary. She could find no reason why this should disturb him. No wonder Ives and Malcolms did not get along. They didn't know how to talk to each other. Their minds didn't work the same.

"My uncles enjoyed Dunstan's theories on farming. We were invited also, if you'll remember. I see nothing wrong in that."

He swung around and glared down on her. "Dunstan grew up on a very small farm. He never saw London or society until he entered Oxford after he came of age and my mother no longer had control of him. She wanted him to be a vicar, like her brother, and saw no reason he should learn the ways of aristocracy."

He didn't say more, as if he'd said enough. Ninian struggled to find the path of his logic. "Your mother doesn't want him to associate with dukes?" Everything to do with this mysterious man she called husband was a puzzle. She searched his expression to see if she'd guessed right.

He rubbed his wide brow and looked away. "Dunstan is more comfortable in barns than in mansions. If he accepts the invitation, it is for the sake of his wife, not himself."

She couldn't see the problem. "Then he need only refuse the invitation. I'm quite certain my uncles won't be offended."

She thought Drogo gritted his teeth as he looked away and glared at the fire. For a man who prided himself on never losing his temper, he certainly simmered a lot.

"His wife would never forgive him if he refused the

invitation. She is insisting on an entire London wardrobe so she might act the role of countess-apparent." He grimaced as he glanced back at her. "If you're wrong and the child you carry is a boy, Celia will no doubt murder us all in our beds."

She might not understand the man's moods, but she was beginning to understand the path of his thoughts. Perhaps if Ceridwen had taken the time to understand her husband's needs rather than acting on her own immature impulses...

She would study that lesson later. The look of thinly disguised heat in Drogo's eyes stirred other, more primitive desires.

"We can surround the house with rowan and place grandmother's protective amulets under our pillows," she offered brightly.

"Not to deride your skills, my dear," he answered, "but I would prefer to err on the side of caution and avert Celia's pretensions entirely."

She tilted her head and tried to fathom the next quirk in this path. "You are saying you would prefer to have an heir rather than a girl? My talents aren't quite that developed."

He looked a bit thunderstruck at the possibility she might even think she had such a talent, then a smile reluctantly tugged the corner of his mouth. "You enjoy teasing me, don't you? Am I so easy a mark?"

"Sometimes." It wasn't just physical desire she felt when he looked at her like that. Something warm and shiny like the summer sun burned in her breast at his approval and understanding. She craved the full force of his attention and intellect as much as she craved his touch. She wished she knew how to gain both, but it didn't seem likely. "If you do not mind that our child won't be a boy, what are you asking of me?"

"I'm not convinced the child is a girl," he reminded her. "I would save Dunstan the pain of disappointment and the family of his wife's reckless expenditures, if I could. Let them be as they were and not encourage what they are not."

Ninian's eyes widened. "You wish to discourage their social aspirations for the sake of the family budget? That's not your decision to make, my lord. Dunstan is a grown man, well beyond any need for your protection."

"Devil take it, Ninian!" he shouted, before calming himself and resorting to a mere glare. "It would just be simpler if we kept our various and assorted relations apart. Let's leave it at that."

"'Ne'er shall Ives and Malcolm meet...'" she quoted from one of the legends. "Are you superstitious, my lord?"

"No, I am not, and I wish you would call me by name. We've been married well over a month and should be acquainted enough for that much familiarity."

She rose and straightened the lace of his jabot because she could not resist his proximity any more than the tides could resist the moon. "Acquainted, perhaps, but no more familiar than before. You will not listen if I tell you that Dunstan's wife is spoiled, immature, and too selfish to think of anything but her own pleasure. Deny her this invitation, and she will seek other entertainment. She is not your concern, Drogo." She looked up at him expectantly, hoping against hope that he would listen to her this time.

His curled eyebrows drew down in a frown. "She is young and beautiful, and Dunstan adores her to the point of spoiling her. I will not see him ruined because of it."

"You cannot stop him, Drogo." Disappointed, she released his lace and stepped back. She saw the fire in his eyes, knew she had the power to relieve both of them of this tension, but she would not. He must *listen* before he could hear. "You can offer choices, but you cannot control his decisions."

She would have walked away but Drogo caught her arm and held her back. His touches were so rare, she leaned into him anyway, resting her head against the strength of his shoulder as his free hand gently traced the slope of her belly. "You will ask your aunts not to invite them again?"

"No," she murmured. "I will ask them to be cautious with her. I will talk to her and explain that Dunstan is more important than my aunts. But I will not tell another adult how they can or cannot live their lives. We each must make our own choices."

He didn't fling her away in anger. She thought she heard disappointment in his voice, but he covered it with the cool concern he did so well.

"I will not force you to my way of thinking, then. How are you feeling? You look pale, and Sarah says your cough is not improving."

Reluctant to disturb him more, she debated the wisdom of mentioning her fear of remaining in London. Her mother had coughed like this, and she'd lost all her babes. Out of the isolated world she knew and into Drogo's broader one, she was bombarded with new knowledge and opinions, and she was no longer as certain as she once was of her grandmother's teachings. But she worried. Constantly.

As if hearing her thoughts, he stroked a straying curl from her face. "I cannot leave London just yet, my dear. Twane has embroiled me in a bit of trouble, and I must stay to deal with it."

That was the first he'd mentioned the suit to her. She supposed she could count that as a victory of sorts, though she did not feel triumphant. "Lady Twane and her sister are on the way to Paris as we speak. He cannot have her back." She twisted to search his face and caught his surprise before he hid it. "Sarah says he must bribe witnesses to lie. My grandmother had a potion that she swore would make anyone tell the truth…"

Drogo grinned, shook his head, and pressed a kiss to her brow. "Unleash a truth serum in London? Society would crumble, and civilization as we know it would be lost. Just keep our bun warm," he patted her tummy, "and let me deal with Twane, although I thank you for your offer."

Ninian had a sudden ripping understanding of the Ives' penchant for violence. A roar in her head demanded she plow her fist into his complacent smirk and kick his shins until he cried for mercy. The big oaf really truly thought she was a helpless, harmless twit of a female. Had he absolutely no notion of what she was, of what she could do?

He did not. He was much too practical to understand. Resignedly, she pulled from his grasp, turned, and met his gaze directly. The challenge had been thrown, and she could scarce back down now. "I have already removed Lady Twane from harm. If I can persuade Lord Twane to drop his ridiculous suit, will you let me return to Wystan?"

"I don't want you anywhere near the man," Drogo warned. "He's violent."

"If I don't go anywhere near Lord Twane and he drops the suit, will you take me to Wystan then?" she amended.

"Wystan is too far and the roads too unpredictable this time of year. We'll visit Dunstan at Ives if Twane drops his suit," he promised. "We always gather there for the holidays."

That wasn't what she wanted to hear. She had never learned defiance. She had, however, learned to go her own way. Deliberately dimpling and dropping a reassuring curtsy, she made her last offer. "Lord Twane shall not only drop his suit, he shall apologize in public, and I will be in *Wystan* for the holiday. You and your family are most welcome to join me."

She swept out, leaving Drogo openmouthed and staring. A lunatic, he told himself. She twisted logic willfully to her own devices. No woman could wish to jeopardize a child she so plainly wanted by taking the abominable roads of the north at this time of year. And she certainly couldn't manipulate a madman like Twane to her will.

She'd already heard about the suit and deftly removed Twane's goal in filing it, a small voice in his head warned, and she hadn't once consulted him.

Maybe, just maybe, she was a little more than the rural midwife she seemed.

But she was still a woman, with all the weaknesses of her sex.

He'd fight his own battles, thank you very much.

Twenty-four

SHOVING HIS HANDS IN HIS BREECHES POCKETS, DROGO WATCHED the activities in the kitchen garden from an upper-story window. Four strong men were carrying a potted tree into his backyard. An oak, if he was not mistaken.

Rowan bushes had appeared on his front step just yesterday.

He hadn't complained when his dilapidated hall table disappeared and a housekeeper took his hat instead. He'd growled slightly over the bills for new parlor furniture, but he had to admit the sunny yellow and blue silks of the new upholstery and draperies were a vast improvement over the funereal dark woods and torn leather of earlier. He'd even become resigned to ferns tickling his nose in every window and secretly enjoyed the herbal scents arising from various and assorted pots on his windowsills.

But he had good reason to be wary of potted oaks and rowans.

He watched as his nicely rounded wife dimpled and charmed the workmen into placing the container where she directed. Even well into her sixth month of pregnancy, she could make grown men stutter and fawn at her feet. He had thought he'd taken a biddable, quiet country bride to wife, not a temptress who could charm the devil out of hell.

That was unfair and spoken through his raging lust to have her in his bed again. Ninian deliberately charmed no man, not even him. She had his brothers running circles to do her bidding, but they each treated her with the respect due an unattainable goddess.

Drogo glanced up as Joseph joined him. Somehow, Ninian had persuaded Paul and David back to school, but Joseph had diligently applied himself to his apprenticeship. He had his own room near the courts, but he seemed to be here as much as there, drawn like a moth to Ninian's flame, Drogo suspected.

"She's creating a circle," Joseph nonchalantly pointed out, stuffing his hands in his pockets as Drogo did and nodding toward the window.

"She doesn't have enough trees." Drogo returned to gazing at the scene below. The lawn did seem to have taken on a circular shape. Bushes and flowers cascaded over each other in all four corners, leaving a round patch of grass in the center.

"The tree represents power." Joseph shrugged diffidently at Drogo's sharp look. "That's what Lucinda says." At his brother's uplifted eyebrows, he looked resigned. "We correspond. She knows a lot about drawing, and I want to learn."

Drogo uttered a colorful expletive and glared at the garden again. "They'll have you believing in witches too."

"Not witches," Joseph replied thoughtfully. "But there's a great deal we don't know about the earth's power. We don't know what causes lightning or how the stars are made or why it rains. Perhaps Ninian's family knows things we should learn more about."

"They believe they're witches and we're devils. They believe in talking to ghosts. They worship trees, for pity's sake! What can they possibly teach us?"

Joseph remained silent for several minutes before formulating a reply. "How to live peacefully with each other and with our surroundings?"

Drogo wanted to laugh, but he couldn't scoff aloud at this most gentle of his brothers. Besides, Joseph had a point. A small one, perhaps, but not one deserving derision. "I'll never understand how women think," he finally offered.

"Why bother when we can enjoy the results?" Joseph answered cheerfully. "You've given her a house and a family, and she's feathering her nest. Each to his own."

That was all very well and good, Drogo thought, if he didn't know Sarah was the one feathering the nest while Ninian…

Ninian stirred the air like a fresh spring breeze. She smiled, and grown men fell to their knees. She whispered sweet words over a child's fevered brow, and they healed. She laughed at his cantankerous brothers, and they metamorphosed into tame pets. She swept him a sidelong glance, and he drooled.

Ninian need only exist, and the world rearranged itself around her. If he didn't bed her soon, she really would have him believing her a witch. He just needed some release from this constant state of arousal to clear his head.

He didn't know if it was safe to make love to a woman heavy with child. He should ask one of his brothers what they did when their mistresses swelled with their brats.

Ninian would know.

"The duchess asked me to design a folly for their estate in Kent. I thought I'd take advantage of the break in sessions to visit the site."

Drogo felt his grip slipping. This was Ninian's fault.

"I thought your mother was returning for the holidays." He tried to remain impassive. Joseph had just turned twenty-one. He had no power over him.

"She does not object if we consort with dukes." Cynicism marred Joseph's cool response.

"She knows you are at a social disadvantage and doesn't wish to stand in your way." Drogo could blame his stepmother for many things, but he had always understood Ann's need to protect her children. He just thought her methods a trifle cruel and more than a little shallow. "You are welcome to join us at the estate, you know that."

With the tree centered in the circle, the workmen departed. As they watched, Ninian waved to the children who had gathered on the lawn. Laughing, they circled the tree with her, skipping and singing and clumsily holding hands.

Children? Where the devil had she found that many children?

"You know Dunstan's wife wishes us to the devil," Joseph replied to his invitation to the Ives estate. "If you do not mind, I would prefer Kent and Lucinda's drawing lessons."

Ninian had usurped his control, undermined his authority, and now everything was falling apart right before his eyes.

He had to put a stop to this before the family he'd fought so hard to keep together blew apart like so much dust in the wind.

❧

The autumn equinox had passed, and Samhain, or All Hallow's Eve, was almost upon them. She could ask the spirits for aid. She'd never been successful at summoning spirits, but Aunt Stella had promised to help. Ninian hoped that what she could not do with her own weak gift, a concerted effort of Malcolms could accomplish. Her marriage might depend on it.

She smiled as Drogo stormed out to join them.

Whispering to the nearest child, she sent them tumbling and laughing into the house for cake and milk. The nursery should be ready for the birthday party Sarah was preparing for her youngest. Happily occupied with her children, Sarah had lost some of her propensity for mischief.

Ninian tried her blandest smile as Drogo sidestepped the running children as if they were dangerous serpents. If he disliked her tree so much, he would really be in a pet at the stones her great-aunt in Ireland had shipped to London.

"Joseph won't be joining us for the holidays," he announced flatly, glaring at her. "I suppose you've made other arrangements for David and Paul as well?"

"I've invited them to Wystan," she said complacently, folding her hands over her distended belly and admiring the canopy of bare branches over her head. "I think they should like it very much. We sometimes get snow."

"Don't be ridiculous! Wystan is entirely too far. They can't travel those roads in winter, any more than we can. Ninian, I am not being stubborn about this, merely practical. I'm protecting…"

"…the world, I know, dear." Ninian smiled sunnily up at him, read the bafflement replacing his anger, and patted his arm. A coughing bout struck her before she could finish the argument. The cough was worsening. She had to return to Wystan soon.

"You shouldn't be out here dancing like a lunatic," he grumbled, catching her in his arms and leading her back to the house. "Why don't I have Dunstan come fetch you and take you to Ives early? You'll feel better there, out of the city."

Undoubtedly she would, but Ives wasn't Wystan, and she clung steadfastly to her grandmother's teachings. Without them, she would be nothing and no one, and she would not be reduced to the helplessness of a child again. She had to believe what she was doing was right, at whatever cost, or she would turn into her mother.

She let Drogo assist her to a couch in the parlor overlooking the garden. He summoned a maid to fetch the tea she'd taught Cook to brew. She could soothe the coughing with herbs. She wished she could gain confidence the same way. Each day in Drogo's more refined and cultured world sapped a little more of her belief in herself.

"I will send for a physician," Drogo said worriedly, pacing the carpet.

Ninian leaned against the pillows on the couch and concentrated on catching her breath. She shook her head at the suggestion. "No," she gasped.

"I cannot bear to see you ill like this!" He clenched his hands into fists and glared down at her as if he could scare the cough away.

Ninian smiled at the fierceness of his scowl. Drogo in a rage would be a fearsome sight indeed. Just his scowl brought his black brows down to meet his nose, and his dark eyes snapped with the unbridled passion he hid elsewise. Tension drew his jaw muscles taut, and his mouth into a dangerously flat line. Only the sensual fullness of his upper lip betrayed his true nature. She longed to taste his kisses again.

He must have caught the direction of her stare. His fists unclenched, and he drew a shaky hand over his hair, tugging it back in place. "You'll drive me mad," he complained, drawing up a chair to sit beside her.

"Sorry," she apologized between coughs.

The maid hurried in with the tea, and Drogo cut and squeezed the lemon he'd ordered delivered from a friend's orangerie. He'd learned to mix the lemon and tea the way she liked it, and Ninian sipped it gratefully.

"There is a purpose to the tree?" he asked conversationally as she sipped.

She knew what he was doing. An excess of emotion aggravated her coughing spells. He was attempting to calm her. Drogo was very, very good at settling her emotional weather vane, even amid London's turmoil.

She smiled and closed her eyes as the tea soothed her throat. She could almost sense her husband's presence now, although not in the same way as she did others. He didn't roil with cacophonic emotion or emit furious vibrations as his brothers often did. Drogo's was a mental and physical presence, soothing in some ways, disturbing in others. He stirred a restlessness in her that she thought pregnancy should have diminished.

"The oak represents strength and power," she answered his question as her cough calmed. "It's not witchcraft," she assured him. "We merely call on the power the earth provides. There is no magic to it."

"Of course not," he said dryly. "Everyone calls power from trees."

"Put like that…" She wrinkled her nose. "We're Malcolms. We can't change who we are. Perhaps at one time everyone had the power to summon the earth's strength, but the knowledge has been lost in time. Malcolms, on the other hand, carefully pass along their knowledge to each succeeding generation. Therein lies our strength."

"You will forgive me if I do not believe trees and rituals provide anything more than a form of entertainment?"

He wore his impassive face again. A man as strong as her husband had no need to call on powers other than his own. No wonder it was women who held the secrets of the earth. If she had shoulders as broad as Drogo's, she'd heave Lord Twane off the Tower.

She smiled forgivingly in the face of his disbelief. "We all find strength in what we can. I believe your daughter likes this tea. She is kicking quite enthusiastically."

That was dreadfully manipulative of her, worthy of Granny at her best. Drogo's gaze immediately swung with fascination to the slope of her abdomen. She loved the curiosity lighting his eyes. Unlike many men, he seemed utterly enthralled with every aspect of childbearing.

He pressed his palm to the place where their child kicked. "He doesn't kick like a girl," he teased. "We shall name him Hercules."

Ninian laughed. He made her so furious sometimes, she could smack him. Other times, he stirred her to a passion deeper than any ocean. Always, he made her feel alive, as she never had been before. Even knowing he stubbornly refused to accept her as she was, she could love him.

But she wouldn't. She had to go against everything he represented if she wanted their daughter to survive.

"We will name her Alana," she countered. "I think it only appropriate she be named after another saint."

"Alan, then, for that saint was a man."

"How is it you know so much of religious history? You are not a Malcolm."

The endearing grin he so seldom used twisted a corner of his lips as he pressed a kiss against her brow. "I am an Ives, madam, with all the education and books of the world open before me. At least some of us availed ourselves of the opportunity."

"That's true," Ninian said, caught by surprise at the thought. "As women, we've had to learn by trial and error and pass our knowledge on by word of mouth. But men can go to school and travel the world and learn from a vast array of sources. Isolated, women are not presented with the conflicting beliefs of others. I'm not certain which is better."

"Keeping an open mind is best," he assured her. "You will soon see I am right, and that you will be quite healthy and happy at Ives."

Ninian narrowed her eyes and wished she could put a hex on him. Obstinate man.

"Lord Twane is suffering the gout," she replied demurely instead. "Aunt Stella says his witnesses have already met with his barristers. His case should be crumbling as we speak. The apology will be a little more difficult to contrive. That's why I needed the tree." She was being manipulative again. She knew nothing other than that the witnesses and barristers met. She just imbued the meeting with the positive spirit she needed.

Drogo sighed, patted her hand, and rose from his seat. "The Lords have called a meeting on the morrow. I will deal with it. Why don't you help Sarah choose Christmas gifts for the family?"

"Make a list of recipients for me," she said sweetly, with her best smile. "I wouldn't wish to forget all of Dunstan and Ewen's by-blows. I'm just now learning all your father's."

"My brothers can play Lord Bountiful with their get," he answered dismissively. "I have enough to do with just my brothers. William will be there, and if I have anything to say about it, so will the rest. Resign yourself, madam, we are going to Ives."

He stalked out, lord of all he surveyed, commanding his troops with a finger snap.

She knew he was a busy man with many connections. She'd seen solicitors and men of business and powerful lords come and go through his study portals. He managed his numerous estates and controlled the strings of every family member as well. He attended to his duties in Parliament, wrote thoughtful speeches, and pored over financial records. He did what he thought best for everyone concerned, from the world at large to the least member of his family.

And she'd thought Granny with her amulets and potions was a manipulative old witch!

But honest men did not win against men who twisted evil to their own devices. Whether he knew it or not, Drogo needed her help.

No longer smiling, Ninian knew the conflict to come could very well be as explosive as thunder and lightning. No wonder Wystan had flooded. When heaven and hell met, earth was their battleground.

Twenty-five

"THE SERVANTS LIE. I AM A PEER OF THE REALM. WHOSE WORD will the Lords take? Twane will have to do better than that, I tell you." Restlessly, Drogo paced the worn carpet of his study. Neither Ninian nor Sarah had dared replace any of the relics in here.

His lawyer didn't look up but continued consulting his notes. "I beg your pardon for mentioning this, my lord, but you are an Ives. Your family has not made a favorable impression upon its peers. Your personal record may be pristine, as you say, but it will not diminish the scandals of generations.

Drogo cursed under his breath. He didn't have the patience for this nonsense. He'd rather be tracing a missing shilling on the account books than endure this type of public scrutiny. Damn Sarah for involving him with her lost souls.

Sarah had brought him Ninian. He couldn't damn her any more than he could blame her. He could only blame himself for letting Twane go this far. He should have shot the bastard.

"If they would let Lady Twane or my wife testify…"

"You know they will not, my lord. It's already been established that you and Lady Twane occupied the same household in Northumberland. You may bring in your servants to testify that you kept separate rooms, but if Twane's servants testify that you had sexual congress here in London before you left, there is naught you can do. Adultery is adultery, no matter the location."

He could lose everything. Twane would demand more money than he could raise if he mortgaged every property. His brothers would be penniless. He would have to start all over again. And Ninian... Who would she believe? Would he lose her too?

As if his anxious thoughts had drawn her, Ninian drifted into the room. She nodded at the barrister as he rose, but her loving attention did not divert from him. Drogo swallowed hard as his gaze swept over her soft and wholly desirable figure. How had she known he needed the reassurance of her trust and presence when even he would have denied it if asked?

"It's All Hallow's Eve, my lord," she murmured, brushing an invisible thread from his coat as she was wont to do.

Drogo didn't know if this was her way of being wifely, or if she needed to touch him as much as he needed her touch. He hoped it was the latter. "And...?" he prompted. Sometimes, she inhabited another world and needed reminding of this one.

The look in her angelic blue eyes was anything but angelic as she held his gaze. "My family has a... tradition... of gathering on this date. We will try not to disturb you, but quite a few of us are present."

He sensed that beneath that mischievous expression she was telling him something, if only he could interpret it. But he definitely did not want to hear what it was after seeing that unholy light in her eyes. Let them have their silly rituals. All that mattered to him was Ninian and the child she carried. He glanced at her worriedly. "How are you feeling? Are you sure you are up to company?"

The message in her eyes disappeared behind that bland smile he might learn to hate. "I am quite well, thank you, my lord. I'm sorry to have disturbed you."

He didn't want it to be this way between them. He wanted to take her in his arms and promise her the moon was blue and fairies would dance at her feet, if that was her heart's desire. But he not only didn't know how to go about it, he wasn't certain if she would appreciate it. Courtship after marriage was a damned confusing business.

He caught her before she could drift away again. When she looked at him questioningly, he traced a finger along the delicate curve of her cheek. "Your family is welcome here, my love. Give them my greetings, will you?"

A genuine smile lit her eyes. "I shall. I didn't know how much I missed them before. I thank you for bringing me here."

Stunned by that admission, Drogo let her float away. Had she finally grasped the advantages of London? Did that mean she might forgive him for keeping her here and allow him in her bed again?

The barrister coughed politely, drawing Drogo back to the moment. "My lord, if your wife's family shows its support…"

Hell. Now he'd be reduced to groveling at the feet of Ninian's uncles. "I have not asked them," he said curtly. "I would not embarrass them more than necessary."

"Of course, my lord." The barrister returned to taking notes.

Drogo had the sudden nervous urge to check on his kitchen garden.

❧

"Of course you may join us, Sarah," the duchess declared regally. "The more positive energy we generate, the stronger we will be."

Sarah glanced down at her fashionable gown with the dashing blue bows and striped ruching, then back at the simple white garb of Ninian's guests. "I'm not dressed properly."

"It's your energy we need, dear, not your material possessions. Come, take this place." Stella guided her to a position behind Ninian, outside the circle of stones that had appeared overnight.

"Can we really stop Lord Twane this way?" Sarah asked eagerly.

"He generates a great deal of very negative energy we must overcome, but negative energy is not stable. Just stand here and think positive thoughts. Do you pray in church?"

Sarah nodded hesitantly. "Sometimes."

Stella patted her arm encouragingly. "Then concentrate on doing so now. This is just our way of grouping our separate prayers into one powerful, healing whole."

Ninian hid a smile at Sarah's obvious bewilderment. Like much of society, Sarah considered church a place to show off her newest gown, if she attended at all. The simple attire of Ninian's cousins did not quite suit Sarah's image of church.

"Will we see spirits?" Sarah whispered as Stella swept away to position her troops.

"I've not participated in a long time, but I don't believe so," Ninian whispered back. "We're just uniting our power, as my aunt said."

"And that works?" Sarah asked in obvious disbelief.

Ninian didn't know. Her grandmother had taught her that Malcolms possessed strengths they must use wisely, but her grandmother had mostly used her greater intelligence to trick the less educated into doing as she bid. Her grandmother was a healer who dabbled more in manipulating people than illnesses. Ninian possessed the odd ability to occasionally know how people felt, but she considered that more weakness than strength, and her herbs were more practical than magical. Lucinda could draw mysteriously beautiful or evil portraits, but that accomplished nothing at all. Christina claimed to see colors that told people's characters. Mostly, that just made Malcolms odd, not strong. Perhaps if she drenched the House of Lords in Aunt Hermie's perfumes… She shuddered at the thought. She didn't know if any Malcolm had the power to sway the House of Lords. She just knew she had to try—just to make Drogo believe.

And to give her the confidence to leave him if he did not. If her grandmother had been right in this, then she had been right about the necessity of Malcolms being born in Wystan. Saving Drogo might mean losing her husband forever.

She would not think of that. She must concentrate on what was best for her child. Taking the hand of the cousin beside her, Ninian lifted her gaze to the tree in the center of the circle and joined in the prayer that Aunt Stella chanted.

❧

"They're all mad," Drogo muttered as he watched the ceremony from Ninian's bedroom window. They'd potted a tree in the middle of smoky, foggy London, where even the stars didn't shine, and now they stood around it in the chilly damp wearing little more than muslin shifts, singing songs. Mad. Lunatic. Silly fools.

His gaze shifted to Ninian. In some trick of lamplight from the windows, he could see her features as clearly as if the moon shone on them. As on the night he'd first seen her, she radiated loveliness and innocence. Tonight, however, he didn't see the loneliness he'd sensed that first time. She'd finally found the companionship she lacked.

She didn't need him.

That knowledge gnawed at his innards. If she didn't need him, he had no purpose in her life. It didn't matter if he lost the suit and his fortune. Ninian had her own wealth and a family to keep her. He was expendable.

He'd once thought it would be very convenient if he could escape all the ties binding him and have naught else to do but study the stars. He still thought that, but now Ninian at his side had become part of the picture.

He was the lonely, needy one. Not her.

Not liking that image, he scowled at the ceremony below. Since when did he need the company of lunatics?

He turned away from the window. Fetching a snifter of brandy from his room, he doffed his heavy coat and vest. Comfortable in shirt sleeves, he wandered back to Ninian's room and, picking up the Malcolm diary on her bedside table, settled into the over-size chair she'd provided for his use.

❧

"My lord? Drogo?"

Opening his eyes, Drogo watched as his wraith of a wife wafted into the room, wrapped in white, her fair tresses tumbling in abandon to her waist. She smelled of fresh air and thyme, with the underlying fragrance of very delicate roses. Entirely wholesome, her eyes glowing with blue fires, she exuded everything fresh and lovely that existed in this world. He had no understanding at all of what went on in her bewildering mind, but he could no more resist her than he could resist water when he thirsted.

"Your Ceridwen did not fare any better at the hands of her Ives husband than any other female has over the centuries." He set the book aside and rose as she approached.

"Legends do not come of nothing," she said wryly, coming to stand before him. Or perhaps she just sought the fire.

Drogo added more coals and stirred the blaze to warm her. "Unlike Ceridwen's husband, I won't doubt the child if it's a girl." Perhaps that was why she had quit reading the book to him. He wanted to reassure her that even though he had reason to doubt every woman who crossed his path, he did not doubt her at all. That probably made him as mad as she, but he had a deep need to trust her, so he did. He would disprove her superstitious legends.

She stood with her back to him and held her hands to the fire. "I thank you for that. I understand how difficult it is for you to believe."

"Do you?" He wrapped his arms under her beautiful breasts and pulled her back against him. She didn't resist. She bent into his embrace like a willow wand, always accessible. Why then, were they so far apart? Perhaps it was his own foolishness. If he kissed her now…

"Lord Twane should apologize on the morrow," she said serenely. "I'm certain you could have won without our help, but I needed to do this, Drogo."

He ignored her addlepated chatter. Somehow, he had to plant her firmly at his side. He knew no other way to do it. He pressed a kiss along her cheek and gently cupped her breast through the thin muslin. Satisfaction swelled in him at her sharp intake of breath. "Have we courted enough to suit you, moonchild?" he whispered in her ear.

She stiffened, but her nipple rose taut and needy beneath his caress.

"Do you believe in me yet?" she asked breathlessly, leaning into him and offering full access to his questing fingers.

"I believe you are the most enchanting woman in the world." He parted the ribbons of her gown, discovered a shift beneath, and loosened those ties too. She shivered as flesh brushed flesh, and he supported her softness in his palm. The fire's light illuminated skin as pure as the milk that would feed his child, topped by a ripe cherry he needed to nibble. He nibbled at her ear instead. He would take her slowly this time, as he had not in the past. He would worship her with his body, prove that their needs were the same.

"Drogo..." she whispered plaintively as he caressed her aroused nipple and lifted her waterfall of hair to kiss her nape.

"Let me love you," he murmured as she tried to turn within his embrace. "I will take care not to harm the child."

She knew she should be strong. For the sake of the child within her womb, she had to make him see...

But his mouth had found hers, and the lines between his world and hers blurred in a sweet haze. The fire heated one side of her, her husband's proximity burned the other. As his long fingers stroked her breasts, fire seemed to leap all around her. His mouth against hers plied his case tenderly, convincingly, until she opened and let him in, and she tasted his brandy and the hot rush of need.

She wrapped her fingers in his shirt and clung as her knees weakened. He surrounded her with strength, supported her with ease, and led her toward the bed as if she were weightless. She remembered how it felt to have the hard length of him pressed into her. The special scent of his maleness filled her senses. The scratch of his beard against her skin as he pulled down her bodice and blessed her shoulders with kisses revived the ecstasy she'd missed for so long.

He was an Ives, a man who needed women as much as she needed the affection he could not give. This was the pain behind the old tales then. Malcolm women required more than these physical caresses, more than an Ives could satisfy. Even as she loosened the buttons of his breeches and pulled his shirt free so she could stroke the muscled tautness of his flat abdomen and chest, she craved the emotion he could not offer.

"I'll make you happy, I swear it," he promised fervently as he drew her gown and shift over her head.

In the fire's light, she could see the pain and certainty of his vow in the darkness of his eyes, in the shadowed hollow of his jaw, in the determined line of his mouth. She stroked the sharpness of his jutting cheekbone and felt the muscle beneath tighten as he held still and let her explore. Perhaps it was better that she could not sense the source of his tension. She had a feeling the passion bottled up behind his controlled facade could explode and scorch if released.

"Will you let me love you?" she whispered in wonder, more to herself than to him. He wouldn't understand. She wasn't certain she did either. She just sensed his withdrawal at her words and wondered if anyone could reach him.

"I would give you anything you asked, if I could," he agreed grimly, pulling her tighter into his grasp.

Only his shirt sleeves separated his arms from her skin. Her belly held them farther apart than she liked, but she could feel his heavy arousal pressing into her. She had only this moment to think, to stop him, to force him to see... The instant he lowered his mouth to hers, she would be lost.

"Give me Wystan," she whispered back. "Let me go to Wystan to have this child."

He stiffened, and she knew she had lost.

"I cannot give you that," he answered in regret. "I cannot risk you and the child, Ninian. You must understand..."

"That you would protect what's yours," she finished sadly, drawing away, although every pore of her body screamed protest. "But some things are not yours to protect."

"Ninian!" he cried in anguish as she pulled away. "I will take you in May, when the roads are sound and the child is delivered."

"The Lords will be in session then," she mocked, widening the gap between them, rebuilding the wall one block at a time. She picked up her shift to cover her unwieldiness. She hadn't been conscious of her size before.

He grabbed her wrist and tore the cloth from her fingers, tossing it toward the fire. "Don't, Ninian," he warned. "Don't make a mockery of what is between us."

"There is nothing between us but this child, and there will not be that if you do not let me go." She jerked her arm from his hold, praying he would hear her.

"That is just one of your superstitious old wives' tales,

Ninian. Pregnant women imagine things. I cannot endanger your life over a superstition," he said in that logical, rational voice that made her sound foolish.

Coldly, she turned her back on him and drew the blanket from the bed to wrap around her shoulders. Ice formed in her veins when he did not approach her again. "Listen to me, Drogo. If I do not go to Wystan, *the child will die.*"

"Harm that child, and I'll see you burn in hell." He slammed out, leaving Ninian to see the vast emptiness of her future in the empty bed before her.

Twenty-six

COUGHING HARSHLY, NINIAN HUDDLED ON THE SETTEE BEFORE a roaring fire in the family parlor as Sarah fidgeted and squirmed and jumped up and down at every noise in the street.

"We will not have the news any faster if you wear yourself out waiting," Ninian remonstrated between coughs.

"It's all my fault." Sarah peered out the window for a glimpse of the street. "I never meant to ruin him. I just hoped I could make Drogo see that women are people too. That they're even more easily hurt than he..."

Ninian choked on a laugh, cleared her throat, and sipped her tea. "Sarah, you're a goose if you think he doesn't know that. Drogo's fault lies in protecting every person who stumbles behind his walls. He builds bigger and bigger walls, but he can't keep us out. Take away some of his responsibilities and mayhap he will relax and see what's around him."

Sarah didn't appreciate the philosophy. She threw Ninian a glare, then stretched to see farther down the street. "He has half a dozen brothers to share the responsibility," she said sharply. "Plus me and our mothers. He simply thinks none of us good enough."

"Well, admittedly, he has difficulty understanding people who don't think the same as he does, but he lets Dunstan run the main estate." Ninian watched anxiously as Sarah stood still, concentrating on something in the street below. Had the trial ended? Did Drogo send word? Would it make any difference at all? "And the rest of you haven't shown a great deal of responsibility," she finished lamely as Sarah cried out in excitement.

She clenched her fingers into her palms at the racket of doors and voices in the hall below. Sarah rushed out of the room, but Ninian remained where she was, praying frantically. It had been silly of her to risk everything on such an uncertain outcome, but she needed an impetus to force her to follow her instincts and not her wayward heart. She so craved Drogo's love and respect that she would forget everything she'd been taught to the contrary.

Lessons of the heart were hard to learn, but she'd finally grasped part of the message in the legends. If Malcolm women let their hearts rule, Ives men walked all over them.

Joseph bounded into the room, followed at a more sedate pace by Dunstan, Ewen, and Sarah. The younger boys were in school and hadn't been informed of the trial details.

"We won!" Joseph yelled ecstatically, flinging his lanky frame into a chair and grabbing for a cake from the tea tray.

Ninian breathed a deep sigh of relief. Her own fate still hung in the balance, but her fear that Drogo would suffer for his good deeds had outweighed her own concern. Now she could let terror creep through her veins as she waited for Drogo's reaction.

"What happened?" she demanded, needing to fill the minutes or hours until her husband arrived.

Ewen chortled. "Twane was hoisted by his own petard."

Dunstan glared at Ewen and accepted the hot coffee Ninian handed him. She had learned the older brothers preferred the bitter brew.

"Hoisted by something a little more vital to his anatomy than a petard," Dunstan corrected.

Impatiently, Joseph jumped in. "One of Twane's footmen turned on him, told the judges Twane had bribed and threatened the servants into lying."

Ninian's eyes widened, and she turned to the older men for confirmation.

Dunstan scowled. "Twane had them all fearing for their

lives until that lad broke down. Seems the boy's sister was one of the housemaids, and Twane had raped her repeatedly. He decided he'd rather die than let Twane profit from his crimes."

"After that, all the servants turned, probably figuring there was safety in numbers." Ewen smiled in satisfaction as he sipped his coffee.

"Thank heavens," Sarah whispered gratefully, sinking into a chair. "Where's Drogo? Did he challenge Twane?"

Dunstan snorted. "Big brother demanded a public apology. Twane will have to appear before all of Parliament this afternoon. There won't be a door open to him anywhere after this."

Joseph grinned. "That should teach them that all Ives aren't bastards."

Sarah giggled, and the men rolled their eyes, but Ninian had lost track of the conversation. Twane was publicly apologizing! Such a thing had seemed nearly impossible just yesterday. Their prayers had worked.

Now, Drogo had to believe.

No, he didn't. He would see nothing magical about right winning over might. She had proved nothing to anyone but herself.

That was all she really needed. She knew it was Malcolm power that had given the footman strength to tell the truth. She could not deny her heritage any longer. She must return to Wystan.

"Ewen, you have just come from the north." She broke into a lull in the conversation. "How were the roads?"

He twisted his handsome face into a grimace. "Horrible. It was icy, and a hay wagon turned over on one of the main bridges. Tore it right off the pilings. The weather was so bad that even the highwaymen stayed by the fire. I don't think I'll bother returning until spring. I can raise funds for my project over the winter."

Not reassuring, but she must believe what she was doing was right. Her cough was not improving, and memories of her mother's many miscarriages haunted her nightmares. Her mother had coughed often in London.

"Maybe we can celebrate the holidays in Wystan next year,"

Dunstan offered gruffly, apparently reading her dismay. "You will like it at Ives. My wife is eagerly awaiting your arrival."

Ninian sensed the falsity of that polite statement. Dunstan's wife thought her an interfering witch. At least one member of the family believed in her.

She smiled faintly in reply. "I shall have to time our next child for the summer months. If you'll excuse me, I think I shall rest now." She turned to Joseph. "My aunt says to tell you her invitation extends to all your family. Do not forget to tell them."

The men rose as she did, and Joseph smiled gratefully. "My mother will be in heaven. Thank you."

Sarah frowned and followed Ninian into the hall. "Drogo will not be happy to have his family separated," she whispered. "He's worked hard to bring us all together."

"Drogo needs to leave you all alone to make your own decisions." Ninian pushed past Sarah and continued down the hall, forcing Sarah to follow. "If Dunstan is to have Ives as his home, then he should be free to invite who he pleases, which obviously does not include your mother, since that would make his mother unhappy. Drogo does not take into account how people feel."

"But Drogo doesn't like choosing between his families," Sarah protested.

"Drogo needs to choose for himself, for a change." Ninian said sharply. "Let him go, Sarah. Give him the gift of freedom."

She entered her chamber and closed the door on Sarah's bewildered expression.

Heart pounding, Ninian prayed desperately that she was doing the right thing. She was manipulating events as surely as her grandmother ever had, but sometimes, people needed a fresh outlook to see beyond the boxes they'd confined themselves in. No one was ordering them to climb out of their boxes. They could make that decision on their own.

Instead of lying down on the welcoming bed, Ninian opened the wardrobe to choose what she would take with her.

❧

"Where is everybody?" Tiredly, Drogo entered the family parlor to find only Sarah sitting before the fire in the dark. He drew his hand over his hair and fought a sudden ripple of tension. "I thought you would have emptied the cellars of champagne by now and all be drunk as emperors."

Sarah emerged from deep thought to gaze at him in concern. "Where have you been? We waited for you."

Maybe Ninian had gone to bed early. He'd had some foolish hope she would wait for him to hear his side of events, but she had been up late last night with her foolish rituals. He hoped she hadn't made herself ill.

Foolish rituals. He glanced over his shoulder at the door, eager to seek out his wife. She almost had him believing in the power of prayer. Only a miracle had saved him today. He knew that, and it scared the hell out of him.

"I decided to follow some of Ninian's advice and stayed to speak with the judges and a few others. It doesn't hurt to have a few influential friends, I suppose."

"Ninian told you to go out with your friends instead of coming home?"

"Not exactly." He wasn't much of a hand at forging social ties, but Ninian had reminded him that his younger brothers needed powerful support to overcome their lack of legitimate name. "Dunstan and Ewen didn't take Joseph out celebrating with them, did they? He's too young—"

"He's older than you were when you made your first fortune. I think it's time you let us all grow up and move on with your own life."

A black hole yawned wide in Drogo's soul, and terror quickly filled it. He didn't examine the reason. "Where are they?" he demanded sharply.

"Looking for Ninian."

The emptiness gaped wider and swallowed him whole. He could feel himself sinking into oblivion. Desperately, he fought for a way out. "Ninian? Ninian seldom leaves the house. How could she get lost?"

"I don't think she's lost, Drogo," Sarah said gently. "She packed the baby linens and a few gowns and left. Joseph and

Ewen are searching coaching inns. Dunstan has taken the road to her aunts' estates in Kent."

Stunned, Drogo stood immobile. The dark room echoed as empty as his soul. She was gone. She'd left him. She hadn't even given him a chance...

She had. Last night. She'd asked him to believe in her, and he hadn't listened.

She was ill. The roads were too dangerous for someone in good health. She would destroy herself and the child returning to Wystan.

"She's gone home," he stated with certainty, striding for the door.

"To Wystan?" Sarah called after him, incredulously. "Why?"

"Because the fairies told her to," he cried out as he hurried for his room. He didn't know any better reason.

⇛

Icy rain lashed the carriage windows, and Ninian huddled deeper in the warm furs her aunts had provided. She hated to let the driver stay out in this weather, but if they did not go as far as they could before nightfall, the rain was likely to turn to snow. The driver had agreed with her.

They'd made good progress out of London yesterday afternoon. The weather had been fine and clear, giving her more confidence than she deserved. She really had no choice, though. Even her aunts had agreed the child must be born in Wystan. She carried their amulets and prayers with her for protection. She had to believe they would work.

That she had been able to defeat Twane proved that Malcolms really had powers and that her grandmother had been right about everything. The certainty overwhelmed her, and she couldn't explore this new knowledge just yet. Her child came first. From there, she must decide what she might do about the burn and her marriage.

She knew Drogo with his practical, logical mind could never understand an instinct he could not see or analyze. He scoffed at her legends, at her Gift, at the power of her family. If he could not believe in those, he could not believe in her.

She wished it could be otherwise. She had done all she could to make him believe. She had stayed longer than she ought in hopes of convincing him to listen. But he hadn't.

She coughed, a deep, racking cough that tugged at her insides, but her tea had grown cold, and she didn't reach for it. She'd bought the driver a flask of whiskey to keep him warm. She hoped he used it judiciously. It was almost as dark as night outside.

The carriage lurched in a muddy rut, and she could feel the rear wheel spinning. She held her breath, and the wheel caught on a rock, lurching out of the rut under the pull of the horses. The duke had fine, powerful animals. They would make it.

The icy rain turned to sleet pelting the windows. If muddy ruts froze, were they more or less dangerous? She hadn't traveled enough to know.

The driver's curses would have turned her ears blue if the cold already hadn't. She pulled her fur-lined hood tighter over her frozen nose and rubbed her hand over the uneasy tumbling in her belly. Her daughter didn't like this rough ride any more than she did.

The driver's frantic shouts and a horse's terrified squeal coincided with the carriage's dangerously jolting sway. Ninian grabbed the strap and tried to peer out the ice-sheeted window. She could see only the ghostly gray of ice and rain and fog and the dark shapes of trees beside the road.

They'd have to stop. They couldn't go farther in this weather. She didn't know how the driver could even see the road.

She unwrapped the furs to reach for the speaking hole when the carriage bumped again and she nearly struck her head on the far wall. She must be mad, just as Drogo said. How could they possibly travel to Wystan like this?

She didn't want to lose her baby.

Frantic, she cried out as the carriage shivered to a halt. They were in the middle of nowhere. They would freeze to death out here. What was wrong? Surely highwaymen wouldn't—

Something slammed against the carriage door. Ninian shot

back into the far corner of the seat and stared as the door shivered and shook. She heard no protest from her driver. Who
was out there in this storm? She heard a low curse as the ice
coating the door froze it shut. Perhaps they would go away?

A foot slammed into the vehicle's side, shattering ice from
the windows.

Ninian screamed as the door swung open and a drenched,
cloaked figure leaped in, spraying sleet and snow over the
velvet-padded interior. She swallowed her scream as soon
as the figure hurled his hat on the floor, uncovering familiar
dark brows, unpowdered queue, and a scowl that should have
petrified her.

As the door slammed, the carriage lurched into motion,
throwing them into separate seats.

Ninian hastily unwrapped one of her robes and threw it
over Drogo's soaked cloak. "I'm not going back."

"We'll freeze to death in a snowbank for your whimsy," he
informed her coldly, drying his face on the fur.

"I wanted to go home weeks ago," she pointed out.

He tossed the fur back to her, dropped his sodden cloak,
then swung over to sit beside her. Ninian offered him more
room on the seat to share her lap robe. Her heart pounded
frantically. Would he force the driver to turn around? He
would kill the child if he did. He would kill her. How could
she make him believe?

Without so much as a by-your-leave, he lifted her onto
his lap and wrapped both of them up to their noses in furs.
"Why?" he demanded. "Why must you go to the back of
beyond instead of staying with family?"

"Because Malcolm women cannot have their children
safely elsewhere. Because my mother lost all her babes in
London. Because I want this child, Drogo," she ended on a
pleading note.

He leaned back against the side of the coach, propped his
long legs on the seat, and arranged her on top of him so she
shared his heat from head to foot. "I could hire the best physicians," he insisted.

"*I'm* the best physician. You have to believe me in this,

Drogo. I know it doesn't make sense to you, but in just this one thing, for the sake of our child, believe in me."

He sat silent, holding her close until they both stopped shivering. Then reluctantly, he conceded. "You have driven me as mad as you, Wife. You ask the impossible, and for you, I'm almost ready to agree to it. Even should we arrive safely in Wystan, which I strongly doubt, we will be trapped there until spring. I must leave my family to their own devices, let my business fare without me, forfeit the rest of the session in Parliament, because of your strange whims."

Ninian buried her head against his shoulder. "I know. That is why I left without you. I'm sorry it has to be this way, Drogo, but I almost lost myself in London. I almost forgot who I was and what my grandmother taught me. It would have cost us this child. I must go back. You need not accompany me."

Divested of its wet glove, his hand wound deep in her hair and held her head against his shoulder as he stared somewhere into the space beyond them. Ninian could feel the power of his heart thumping next to hers, and she wanted it to be like this forever. She never wanted to be parted from him again, but for the child's sake, she had to be strong.

"I would not lose you," he finally sighed.

She could hear the air leave his lungs and the tension escape his hold as he admitted this to himself as much as to her. She was the one holding her breath. Could he mean…?

"If making babies is as easy as you say, then the child does not concern me as much as you do. If Wystan is the only way to make you well, then we will go to Wystan. If it's this important that you risk all to return there, I must believe you in this."

Breathing deeply of relief, Ninian curled into him as his strong arms held her tighter. She didn't entirely know what to make of his admission, but it moved her deeply, and she would cling to it in the dark hours that would inevitably follow. All that was important was that he had come after her, and he had not mocked her assertions. "Thank you, my lord. You will not regret this, I promise."

"I'm already regretting it," he said grimly. "And if I did not fear for the child's health, I would make you pay by riding you all the way from here to Wystan. I think it's damned well time to call this a marriage and move on with it."

Amused despite herself at his gruff surrender, Ninian peeked up at the square set of her husband's unshaven jaw and wriggled experimentally in his lap, confirming her understanding of the kind of "ride" he had in mind.

"Is that possible?" she inquired cautiously.

He squinted down at her. "You're the witch. You tell me."

Twenty-seven

THE VIOLENT LURCHING OF THE CARRIAGE INTO ANOTHER water-logged rut convinced Drogo that witch, physician, or lunatic, his wife would be safer at an inn. Even as she considered his insane proposition, he set Ninian away from him. His entire body screamed in complaint as cold swamped the places she'd snuggled, and he almost said to hell with it and snatched her back, but he'd spent over half his life protecting others. He couldn't kill the habit now.

"There's an inn not too far from here," he said gently as she looked at him in surprise. Had he ever really noticed her eyes before? He'd thought them a clear blue, but they reflected the mysterious silver light of the moon now. Something in his insides heaved unsteadily and resettled in a different place as he imagined hope behind that light. "I'll send the driver ahead on my horse to secure a room for us. The poor man's half frozen. I can drive us the last few miles."

"I would not see you made ill in my place," she said gravely. "I will concentrate on clearing the weather for you."

So, she was insane. It was a harmless insanity. Drogo kissed her nose and warmed his hands on her cheeks. "Concentrate on healing thyself, physician. I need a wife to warm my bed."

He pounded on the speaking door, halted the driver, and swept into the cold again.

He was definitely as mad as she. He suddenly felt freer than the hawk swooping overhead, and his heart did excited acrobatics at thought of the night to come. The damned ice would melt right off him, the way he felt now.

⁓

Ninian smiled at the frosted feather patterns glowing silver against the dark in the window of the inn's bed chamber. Tonight would be the wedding night she'd never had.

She glanced wryly at her unwieldy belly beneath the warm flannel of her bed gown. Unlike her more slender cousins, she wore her child low and full. There was no mistaking her condition, though she had three months to go. Not a fine sight for a new husband.

She glanced up as Drogo returned from the taproom with two steaming hot toddies. All the protective concern he usually extended to his brothers, he now lavished on her. Never having been the recipient of such cosseting, she was somewhat overwhelmed.

"You wish me drunk before we retire?" she asked in amusement.

"Warm and willing," he agreed with a leering lift of one curled eyebrow as he set the mugs down.

She'd never seen this side of her husband. He seemed almost lighthearted, despite the weather, despite leaving all his responsibilities behind.

She pressed her gown taut against the bulge of her belly. "Warm and willing perhaps, but a trifle ungainly. Even my aunts were not so large at this stage."

"That's because it's a boy," he whispered wickedly in her ear as he took her in his arms and stroked her roundness. "I tell you, Ives only produce males."

"Just what your family needs, my lord," she taunted, wrapping her arms around his where they rested at her waist, "more virile men to foist upon an unsuspecting world."

"More like what your family needs, my lady." He caught her by the knees and lifted her into the bed. "A rowdy male to disrupt all the family traditions."

"Oh my, I don't even want to think it." A male Malcolm. The idea spun her head in circles.

She sipped gratefully at the mug he handed her once she settled against the pillows and watched with interest as Drogo tugged off his clothes and folded them on a chair. They had but the one candle, and she could wish for more as his shirt joined his coat and waistcoat and she could admire the full expanse of his muscled back and shoulders. "Oh my," she repeated, for an entirely different reason.

He swung around and lifted a questioning eyebrow in her direction, giving her full view of the arrow of dark curls sculpting his breast bone and taut abdomen. She gulped and couldn't look away. She'd never really *seen* him.

Finally gauging the direction of her thoughts, Drogo reached for the buttons of his breeches. "If we've had our wedding night and the courtship is over, what do we call this, madam?" he asked tauntingly, slowly releasing the first button.

Shadows from the candlelight played against the hard ridge pushing his breeches flap outward. Ninian licked her suddenly dry lips. "Large," she answered mindlessly. She remembered another time and place she had thought that. Her husband was definitely not a small man.

Or a shy one. He grinned as he took her meaning, and the beauty of his chiseled features almost distracted Ninian from his breeches. Almost. As he shoved the fabric over his lean hips, she forgot about the white flash of his teeth against the sensuous fullness of his lips, or about anything at all beyond the evidence of Ives masculinity. Her aunt was definitely right about that. Ives men were very… *virile*.

He removed the mug from her limp fingers before she could spill the contents. "It's good to know there are still a few things I can teach my all-knowing wife." He snuffed the candle.

"I only know about herbs," she murmured as his heat and weight slipped beneath the covers beside her.

"Then let me teach you about men, my dear."

A very male hand covered her breast, and a hot, whiskey-flavored mouth parted her lips.

She thought surely she'd died and gone to heaven. Even the fairies couldn't offer such joy.

She was well and truly married then. To an Ives. So far, the only destruction was to her self-control.

She sighed in satisfaction as he guided her hand downward and taught her to touch him. She only needed her woman's power for this, and he held the key to that.

∾

"You needn't look so smug, Wife," Drogo complained jokingly the next day as they emerged from the inn into crystal clear sunshine. "We generated enough heat last night to burn off clouds for the rest of the winter."

Ninian demurely hid her smile in her muff as he handed her into the carriage.

Just her smile had the power to jolt his heart into a mindless clatter. That frightened Drogo as much as her smile filled him with pride. He knew better than to trust in women, marriage, or jolting hearts. He knew the best he could hope for was a warm bed and an uneasy truce until their next difference of opinion. But even in the bright light of day, he could remember with clarity the joy and hope she had wrung from him last night. She was definitely a witch of some sort.

He would do well to remember that she had twisted him to her will with this mad journey into nowhere. He'd dropped everything he held near and dear to see her safe. He couldn't remember anyone ever diverting him from the path he'd chosen—not since he was fourteen and his father died, leaving him with a mountain of debt. Even the estate solicitors had bowed to his authority.

Not Ninian.

Fortunately for him, she didn't even know what she had wrought. She simply smiled and snuggled close as he joined her, as if they were merely on a holiday excursion. He'd never taken a holiday excursion, and this wasn't one now. They were going back to a blighted land, a frozen nowhere, without friends or family to greet them, and she beamed as if he'd promised her paradise.

He glanced down at her warily. Pink had returned to her wan cheeks, and now that he thought about it, she had scarcely coughed at all since his arrival.

What if she really couldn't live outside of Wystan?

Panic coursed through him until he quelled it with logic. The rest of her family did quite well elsewhere. It was just a new bride's homesickness.

He could survive a winter in Wystan in return for the child she would give him.

"Have you heard from your steward? Has the burn recovered?"

On second thought… Drogo sighed and tucked her firmly under his arm. "The burn will be frozen. Concentrate on hatching that youngling and not what cannot be changed."

He didn't like the way she narrowed her eyes and crossed her arms in that stubborn manner he was beginning to recognize.

"Who says it cannot be changed?" she demanded.

She said no more, and Drogo let himself believe that was the end of it. Expectant mothers did not traipse about the frozen countryside exploring dead streams.

~❧~

Expectant mothers helped other expectant mothers deliver their babes, Drogo discovered some days later, much to his dismay as they finally arrived in Wystan.

"Thank goodness you're here!" Lydie exclaimed as she rushed into the great hall before the driver could carry in their luggage. "Cook's daughter has been in labor since yesterday, and I can do *nothing*!"

He'd almost forgotten Lady Lydie. He'd rather assumed Sarah had disposed of her somewhere, somehow. His mind instantly sought the legal ramifications of her presence here. Surely her father couldn't sue him…

"Where is she?" Ninian flung her fur muff to the table without a second look to the husband following her in.

"We brought her here last week since the roads are so bad. Hurry. She's growing weaker." Lydie rushed toward the corridor leading to the servants' wing.

"Ninian!" Drogo halted her before she could follow. When she turned to look at him questioningly, he could see her mind had already followed Lydie down the hall. "You've had a long journey," he said gruffly. "You need to rest."

She beamed that bewildering smile he couldn't fathom. "I love you, Drogo," she murmured, standing on tiptoe to kiss his cheek. "But I can take care of myself."

She was gone before he could even digest that "I love you" or rearrange his thinking to absorb it.

It was undoubtedly some wifely platitude meant to allay his fears, he decided, as he directed the servants to carry Ninian's things to his room.

But he was still in charge here. This was his home, and she would learn to live by his rules. After the lovemaking they had shared these last nights, she certainly couldn't object to sharing his bed on a regular basis. He'd be damned if he'd move into the haunted master suite.

As if in answer to his thoughts, a door slammed directly overhead and laughter rippled around him.

Ghosts didn't laugh, he told himself as he took the stairs two at a time. And he didn't hear ghosts. That was Ninian's bailiwick. Let her listen to them.

～

"You didn't bring that dreadful book with you, did you?" Drogo exclaimed as he came to his bed that night to discover his wife sitting up against the pillows, reading.

She flipped a brittle page and tilted the book to better catch the lamp light. "I keep hoping they will settle their differences and everything will turn out right. The castle was *hers*," she said indignantly, not looking up.

"*Was* hers," he corrected. "Her father gave it to her husband as dowry."

"He had no right. The castle belonged to her mother. It just isn't fair. And to not believe the child is his just because it's a girl…"

Drogo sighed and disposed of his coat and waistcoat. He obviously didn't have his wife's full attention tonight. "She married an Ives, my dear. We are not known for our trust in women or good fortune in marriage. I suppose he's sired a bastard or two by now?"

"Two," she said crossly, glaring at the pages. "Stupid man.

Both boys, thus proving his masculinity, I suppose, while his wife pines with loneliness and lets her love wither." She finally looked up at him. "I've not noticed stupidity as an Ives trait. Why would he do that?"

Drogo lowered himself to the mattress and removed the book from her hand. "It was a logical assumption," he explained patiently. "It's a known fact that we only sire boys. He'd been away on business and came home to find his wife with child. That would have stirred the suspicion of almost any man. The girl was all the proof he needed."

She punched her pillow into shape and slipped down between the covers. "It only takes one night," she muttered. "You know perfectly well that he would have taken her to bed the night before he left on an extended journey."

Drogo pried off his boots and flung them toward the wall. "If she was anything like you, love, he was mad not to have taken her with him."

"What's that supposed to mean?" she demanded as he blew out the light.

He slid between the covers and trapped her securely beneath his weight before answering. "It means the only time a man can be certain of a woman is when she's under him."

He caught her cry of outrage with his tongue and did his best to teach her that being under an Ives was no bad thing.

And perhaps, having a Malcolm woman under him wasn't half bad either.

Twenty-eight

"HOW DOES YOUR DAUGHTER FARE THIS MORNING, MRS. WHITE?" Ninian asked of the portly woman removing oatcakes from the oven.

The cook carefully shuffled the hot pan onto a cooling rack, then turned with a wide smile. "She and the bairn are well, thank you, my lady. It's grateful that we be to you and the good Lord above that you arrived in time."

"They say He works in mysterious ways." Ninian poked at the steaming cakes and decided to wait before burning her mouth on one. "Where is everyone? I thought Lady Lydie said she'd sent for the servants. I want to start cleaning out the master suite."

Cook blanched. "You no want to be doing that, my lady. It's a gloomy old place, it is. The chimney howls something fierce, and the panes rattle, and damp has set in. I'll air one of the newer chambers, shall I?"

Ninian dipped her finger in a bowl of cake batter and sucked her finger clean. This was Drogo's house. Sarah had been the lady here and in London. She'd never dealt with servants or been much use at ordering people about. But she sensed this simple woman's fear and sought to ease it, whatever the source.

"Feeding Lord Ives is a full-time chore," Ninian assured her. "You needn't air anything. Does this mean the others won't be returning?"

Mrs. White clasped her doughy hands in her apron. "They're afraid of their shadows, if you don't mind my saying so, my lady. They'll come when they're hungry, but not before."

Ninian sighed. She hadn't expected better. After all, even she'd believed the superstitions of Ives's devils and feared the legends when the village flooded. Living with Drogo had certainly widened her mind to look for new explanations.

She was beginning to understand why her grandmother had spent so much time telling people what they wanted to hear and giving them foolish amulets to conquer their fears. It wasn't easy being a witch.

But she couldn't pretend she was anything else anymore.

"All right, Mrs. White. You just take care of that daughter and new grandbaby of yours and see that we have meals, and Lady Lydie and I will take care of the household."

Selecting one of the cooler oatcakes, Ninian drifted out of the kitchen, her mind racing furiously despite her body's ungainly pace.

Her grandmother had said she was the Malcolm healer. Her grandmother had been wise in many, many ways that she was just now coming to understand. To be a healer, Ninian must be accepted by those she meant to heal. Otherwise, she was nothing but a breeding machine for an earl. Some women might aspire to that, but she wasn't one of them.

She had to be true to herself. Drogo wasn't going to like it.

❧

"Hello, Mary. Am I welcome here?" Ninian asked politely as the cottage door opened.

Mary's eyes widened. "Ninian!" Then remembering herself, she executed a clumsy curtsy. "I mean, Lady Ives. I…"

"I'm still Ninian, but Lord Ives really only has one wife, and I'm it." She couldn't resist the jest but bit back the ridiculous urge to smile. She didn't know where she stood in her own home, and she prayed frantically as her childhood friend looked uncertain.

Mary cast a nervous glance to Ninian's plain woolen skirt and the bulge only slightly concealed beneath it. "Aye, and he made short work of his duties, too. What is he thinking to let you wander about like this?"

She opened the door, and with a huge sigh of relief, Ninian followed her in. "Oh, we'll hear his shouts soon enough, I wager, but I could not wait for him to find time to bring me here. Walking is good for me."

"Walking in this damp and cold is not," Mary scolded. "Sit down, and let me fix you some tea."

The children crowded shyly into a corner as Ninian took a seat at the trestle table before the fire. Smiling, she reached in her pocket and produced a small sack of sweetmeats. She needed to go back to wearing the aprons she'd abandoned in London. She never had enough pockets.

At a nod from their mother, the eldest boldly crept up to inspect the offering.

"You have grown, Matt. I bet you're strong enough to carry water from the well." Ninian didn't need the child's shy smile to tell her of his pride at her recognition, but she liked it just the same. Drogo had taught her to read the way people expressed feelings physically, so she could better interpret the vague empathic vibrations she received. She thought that knowledge could be a useful tool when her patients were hurting and too confused for her to understand.

The children giggled happily over the treat and before long, the youngest had crawled into Ninian's lap. She felt good there, and Ninian smiled as she smoothed silken locks. "I have missed the little ones."

Mary still watched her warily as she prepared the tea. "You left them readily enough for the ballrooms of London. I'm surprised you came back."

"I did not leave them willingly," Ninian protested. "You didn't want me around. What was I supposed to do? Grow old and keep cats for company?"

"You never kept cats before *he* came along." Mary smacked the mug on the table. "The burn never flooded until Ives and Malcolm came together, just like the legend."

"The burn must have flooded if there was a legend about it," Ninian corrected. "And I never kept cats because

Grandmother wouldn't let me. I feared Lord Ives as much as you did, but he's only a man, like any other."

Mary smiled wickedly. "And he's proved his manliness. You'll not have time for the likes of us once the babe arrives."

"Don't be foolish. Of course I will." Ninian relaxed as they fell into the easy bantering of their childhood. "What else do countesses do? Tell me how everyone fares. Did Harry marry Gertrude?"

"After she got fat with child, he did. Beltane produced a fine crop this year. But it looks as if you'll have your own to deliver, and we'd best look to ourselves."

That was a problem Ninian had already considered. The alternatives weren't the best, but better than none at all. "I am teaching Lady Lydie what I know. She was quite adept at helping with Mrs. White's daughter. Perhaps she can act as my hands as I did for my grandmother."

"A lady delivering children? That'll be the day the sun doesn't rise."

"Well, let's not borrow trouble just yet. We have a few more months." A few months in which she hoped to teach Lydie the things she was eager to learn. The girl had been remarkably underestimated by everyone, but she'd survived out here on her own for months, raising her daughter without complaint, stalwartly resisting her family's plans to marry her to wealth. Ninian had learned a few things in London and understood now how much courage that had taken.

With Mary to lead the way and the knowledge that she had already saved Cook's daughter in childbirth to smooth the path, Ninian stopped to visit Gertrude and reassure her that she would help in her delivery. She stayed with the safe topics of local gossip and childbirth and didn't mention the burn. That was next on her list, but regaining the confidence of the village was of first importance. Apparently time and absence had proved to the villagers that she wasn't personally responsible for the burn's blight.

Worried about her ailing mother, Gertrude set aside her wariness to take her to her parents' house. Several of the older women were already there, and Ninian's arrival stimulated a discussion of ailments and remedies that took much longer than she'd anticipated. By the time she stepped outside the modest cottage, the sun had traveled well past noon, and weariness had set in, but triumphantly, she knew she had her foothold in the village again.

"Going somewhere?" a welcome voice asked dryly as she reached the square.

"Drogo!" She spun around to find him leaning against the tavern, apparently waiting for her to appear. He looked gloriously rugged in his country boots and old wool coat without the fripperies of London lace. He also appeared on the edge of fury. "You never lose your temper," she reminded him evenly.

"A man has to start sometime." He unfolded himself from the tavern wall so he towered over her. "Are you out of your mind, madam?"

"Not at all." She pulled her cloak more comfortably closed and met his glare without fear. "I am ready to return home, however."

"Whose home?" he demanded. "Perhaps you would prefer returning to your old one and pretending I was just a passing fancy."

She cocked her head and tried to interpret what went on beyond his inscrutable expression, but she could only see the anger. In Drogo's case, it seemed safest to be herself and watch what happened.

She tucked her hand around his arm and started down the street. "People don't seem to be angry at me anymore. The flood and superstition made them afraid, and maybe they're still wary, but at least they're listening now. How did you get here? Surely you did not walk."

Silence. She was comfortable with that. It took Drogo a while to work out hidden meanings, interpret, and decide on a reply. He was a very cautious man, and she smiled at him to show she didn't mind.

He appeared totally disconcerted by her smile. She smiled wider, and he scowled. Ninian's heart soared. He might not understand, but he was actually *seeing* her. That might not be as good a thing as she had hoped, but it was a more solid place to be than before, when she was just another cipher on his book of responsibilities.

"I can't turn you over my knee or cut your allowance or send you back to school or any of those things I do with my brothers. How in the world am I supposed to command your obedience?"

"You don't, no more than I command yours," she replied cheerfully. "Equality, remember? Is it so difficult to understand?"

"Equality," he repeated glumly. "You're carrying an impossible burden and can barely stand for weariness, and you expect me to treat you like a man?"

He halted before a gray palfrey with a small, nearly flat saddle. Without any further discussion, he swung her sideways on the saddle, then climbed on behind her. His legs dragged the ground as he gathered the reins in one hand and held her with the other.

"Not like a man." Ninian skeptically eyed the distance to the ground and granted his wisdom in choice of mounts. "I will freely admit that I cannot ride a horse as you do, although I should not mind learning on one this size. It is not *quite* so far to fall."

"And this one walks like a swaying bed." Drogo kicked the mare into a slow saunter. "Which is better for you than the farm cart, at least."

She watched the ground until certain she would not immediately slide off, then relaxed enough to appreciate the strength of her husband's arms around her. He pulled her closer as she leaned into him.

"Will you teach me to ride? It could be a very useful thing to know."

"You are six months gone with child!" he exclaimed in exasperation. "People fall off horses when they're learning. Accept it, Ninian. You cannot do anything but grow that child right now. The village is too far."

"I am not a melon ripe enough to burst." She concentrated on swaying with the horse. "Walking is good for me. Remember, I'm the midwife, not you."

"And you will tell me the cold and damp is good for you too?

And that growing so weary you can scarcely stand is healthy? I have six younger brothers who have tried every excuse known to mankind, Ninian. I know when I'm being gulled."

"I am a healer, Drogo," she said patiently. "I cannot heal if I cannot visit the sick. These people are my responsibility as much as your brothers are yours. Can you not accept that?"

Silence. Ninian thought she'd tear off his shirt and drive her fingernails into that thick skin to see if he was human, but she knew he was as human as she, and that was the problem.

"I've accepted that you carry my child, that you are a Malcolm, and that you know something of herbs. I accept that you're my responsibility now, and that I must protect you as well as the child from harm. Why can you not accept that protection?"

She patted his chest instead of shredding it. He really did not understand. "I'm not your responsibility, Drogo. I don't need your protection. I can very well take care of myself. Accept that, and we've found a starting place."

"If you don't need me for anything, then what the hell do you want me for?" he shouted, finally losing the temper he didn't have. "Am I to be your breeding stud and nothing more?"

Ninian laughed with a carefree joy that bounced off the icicles coating the trees. "Now we are getting somewhere, my lord," she said approvingly, snuggling into his warmth. "For in your eyes, I am no more than a brood mare. Just because I have the appropriate plumbing for that task does not mean that is who or what I am."

"You are an extremely annoying bit of baggage with far too much intelligence and freedom," he grumbled. "Your family was mad to let you grow up wild."

"My family accepted from my birth that I would grow up as I am. Their only choice was in whether to teach me to use my skills or abandon me to learn on my own. My mother preferred abandonment. I was lost and miserable not knowing who or what I was, only knowing I was different. My grandmother showed me how to make the most of my differences."

He rubbed his hand thoughtfully over the place where their

child grew. "And since I can teach you nothing, I have no purpose? What is it you want of me?"

"Acceptance, my lord." She closed her eyes and rested against him, hearing his heart beat. "I wish people to accept what I am and not ostracize me for my differences. That's all I've ever asked. Perhaps, someday, I could learn to help you with your responsibilities, and then we could work together."

"Right. I'll give you the mine books when we reach home, and you can find where we need to cut costs."

He still didn't understand, but he was listening and not rejecting her. That's all she could ask, for now. "Introduce me to your foreman, and I will tell you if he's cheating you," she answered dreamily, half asleep with the sway of the horse and the warmth of his arms. "I'll bring you children and teach you to laugh."

"And if I don't want to laugh?"

"Then I'll cure you of that too."

She nodded off in his arms, leaving Drogo with the terrified feeling that he walked a precipice whose edge he could not see and beyond which he had no idea if air, water, or rocky boulders awaited.

Marriage had been a mad idea. He should have stayed in London, where he knew where he stood and what was expected of him.

But sitting here with his wife and child in his arms brought him a joy he'd never known, even as his head spun with uncertainty.

Maybe he could solve the problem that was his wife while he was here.

Twenty-nine

DROGO CARRIED HIS SLEEPING WIFE INTO THE CASTLE. SHE WOKE enough to hug him groggily, but her sweet breath soon warmed his neck again as she returned to slumber.

He didn't know what he was doing with a woman like this. He'd once thought he might marry some graceful doe-eyed beauty who would drift through his life like a butterfly, going about whatever odd business women tended during the day, warming his bed occasionally at night. If he'd given it any thought at all, he'd imagined she would be content with a little flattery, a little jewelry, and whatever attention he could provide between his other pursuits. He was quite certain if his father had given his wife that much, his parents would have stayed together.

But no, he had to bed a moon-eyed country bride who thought London a bore and delivering children her task in life. Instead of inspecting his estate in Ives, roping his brothers into the holidays, and exploring the profitability of a new shipping venture, he was stranded in the back of nowhere, dancing to his wife's merry tune—all because she carried the child he'd thought never to have. This wasn't how he'd planned his life.

He supposed he could humor her for a few months. He could explore expanding his mining ventures and look into the canal some of the other owners wanted to build—if only he could be certain Ninian would stay where she belonged, the obstinate wench.

Today hadn't been a reassuring experience, but he thought he might have the answer to that.

Gently, he carried her through the winding corridors to the back wing of the castle. He hadn't comprehended Sarah's request to rebuild back here until Ninian had fully entered his life. After these last months of watching plants spring to life everywhere he turned, he had a better grasp of Ninian's talents.

With satisfaction, he lay his sleeping burden on the settee he'd carried down for her use. Not that she would ever use it, he acknowledged ruefully. Maybe he could tie her down so he wouldn't have to chase after her.

She woke again as he stepped away. Drogo watched with secret pleasure as her sleepy blue eyes widened with astonishment. He didn't think he had ever seen anything so innocently beautiful since his brothers were babes in the cradle.

"My word!" she whispered, pushing herself onto her elbows and staring.

He'd ordered all her potted plants carried in here, and after consulting with a few of London's noted naturalists, he'd had quite a few more delivered. He didn't understand their purpose or appeal, but Ninian's fascinated wonderment was satisfaction enough.

"I wasn't certain if the servants were keeping it warm enough," he admitted as she continued her wordless examination from the settee.

"Oh my." Ninian struggled to sit, accepting Drogo's hand as she drank in the sights and smells of moist earth and green leaves. She clung to that strong hand as she stood and touched a fern. It was sending out new fronds—in the midst of winter.

Tightening her grip on his hand, uncertain if she dreamed or not, she brushed her fingers against the fragrant leaves of a bay bush. The aroma filled the air.

"I never imagined…" She didn't even have the words as her gaze fell upon a rose bush with a single perfect pink bud. "My roses!"

"I told them to carry in the things you had at your grandmother's. I wasn't certain how they'd fare without you."

Ninian thought she would cry. All this time, she'd thought he hadn't *noticed*…

Blinking back tears, she gazed up through a watery film at this remarkable man who was her husband. His dark eyes held a hint of uncertainty, but otherwise, he maintained his usual stoic composure. She touched wondering fingers to his square jaw and caught a small smile curling the corner of his mouth.

"I didn't think you meant to return me to Wystan." She didn't understand anything about this man. She searched his face for understanding now. "Why would you do this?"

"I thought we would come here in the summer, and these things seemed important to you."

She didn't know what to say. No one had given her such an astonishing gift before. She gazed up at the panes of glass overhead. She could see blue sky and puffs of clouds. It was like being outdoors, except warmer. Her gaze fell downward and swept the tiled floor, finding the secret tiles of moon and sun and stars. Those tiles were older than Ceridwen. They traced back through generations of Malcolm women. She was home.

"I can't thank you enough," she whispered. "I don't even know how to begin to thank you."

He drew her into his arms and rested his hands above the child she carried. "You have given me a greater gift. The plants are small in comparison."

The bonds they had forged together tightened around her, frightening her more than a little. She was his as surely as this castle belonged to him. He'd bought her a pretty cage and fed her lovely treats and expected her to sing sweetly and remain loyally where he placed her. She had never asked for this.

"Perhaps I can grow some of the plants I lost in the blight." She tried to find the positive aspects and ignore the ones based on superstition. He could not hold her prisoner.

"Tell me what you need, and I will send for them," he agreed. "Perhaps you will be content to stay here and not wander the woods alone."

He'd said the words she dreaded. She tried not to imagine the silken bonds knotting tighter. She could not argue with him in the face of his generous gift. Perhaps she should have asked to be returned to her grandmother's house.

"I like wandering the woods," she said gently so as not to upset him. "But I shall like working here just as much."

"Good. Then I need not wonder where you are while I visit the mines." He kissed her cheek and released her. "I thought I would leave in the morning while the weather holds."

Oddly enough, she didn't want him to leave. The bonds he held her in were strange indeed.

Ninian forced a smile and turned to pat his cheek. "Do not be gone too long. It will be lonely here without you." And that, too, was the truth. Cupid's arrow had truly pierced her heart. She didn't want to be alone again. She had been alone far too long, and this man offered her understanding far beyond that of most others.

"It will be very strange without Joseph popping out of closets and watchmen dragging David home. I fancy we won't know what to do with ourselves." He kissed her again and then wandered off on his own pursuits.

Ninian didn't dare tell him that she had five expectant mothers, three feverish children, and an ailing old woman to tend to in the village. He'd surely chain her to the castle walls.

❦

Drogo's first suspicion that all was not as he planned occurred upon his return to the castle after a week at the mines. He hadn't intended to stay so long, but they'd shown him some exciting new possibilities, and he'd fallen in with some other mine owners to discuss the canal, and one thing had led to another. Perhaps he should have worried more about leaving his new wife alone for so long, but Ninian had wreaked havoc with all his theories about marriage. He actually trusted her.

Perhaps he had been a little hasty in placing that trust.

The new maid taking his hat and gloves at the door didn't disturb him. He had no objection to Ninian's hiring servants without his help. Sarah had done it all the time.

The tapestries hanging over the stair rail didn't bother him greatly either. He understood that women had nesting instincts he didn't possess, and he rather appreciated the results. If Ninian wanted to air the wall hangings, fine.

He didn't understand why there was a hustle and bustle in the moldering haunted master suite, however. He should have bolted the damned thing shut.

Taking the stairs two at a time, he discovered Lydie at the first landing, carrying her infant and an armful of linens. "What the devil are you doing?" he demanded crossly. "And where is Ninian?"

Lydie looked startled. "I don't know. Should I? She could be in the conservatory, I suppose."

"What's going on up there?" he repeated as a loud crash came from the suite.

"Oh." Lydie appeared vaguely guilty as she glanced over her shoulder. "They're cleaning. The chimney was a disgrace. I'm taking these down for washing. Here, would you hold Henrietta? I'll be right back."

Dazed, Drogo stared at the wide-eyed infant suddenly thrust into his arms. The infant blew a bubble and gurgled as he held it at arm's length and prayed it wouldn't break.

He'd only been fourteen the last time he'd held an infant. At the time, his stepmother had been wailing with grief, Joseph and David had frightened the nursemaid into hiding, and Paul had been howling as if his little heart would break. He'd tried picking him up, rocking him, patting him on the back as he'd seen the maids do, but none of those things had helped. The experience had terrified him. He'd disliked being helpless ever since.

Well, at least it wasn't howling. Holding the squirming bundle with both hands at arm's length, Drogo stalked up the stairs to see what the hell was happening in the haunted suite. He certainly hadn't authorized any repairs in there.

The first thing he noticed upon entering was the room's warmth. He raised his eyebrows in surprise at the roaring fire in the hearth. The damned thing was big enough to roast a pig.

He gazed at the newly replastered and painted walls. Someone had replaced the cracked and broken panes in the solar window, and sunshine streamed through the undraped expanse. It looked almost cheerful.

The child squirmed more forcefully, and terrified of dropping her, Drogo heaved her over his shoulder as he wandered into the next chamber where the bed had been. The men working on the walls tugged their forelocks in respect and returned to pounding. Apparently Ninian had worked some miracle of magic, and the servants were slowly returning. Women did have an uncanny knack of managing things like that.

If Ninian didn't mind this accursed chamber, he supposed he could endure it. The women were the ones who had complained of it before. He'd just thought the constant repairs a nuisance.

Thinking to locate Ninian in the conservatory, he started down the stairs, meeting Lydie as she hurried up.

"Oh, there you are!" she exclaimed breathlessly, not taking the infant he hastily shoved in her direction. "Your bailiff is in the study, and I can't find Nanny. I promised to take some of Ninian's arthritis remedy into town. Would you mind watching Henrietta until Nanny returns? And there's a letter from Ewen in the hall. Will he be here for the holiday?"

She didn't wait for an answer but grabbing up her skirt, flew back down the stairs.

Drogo noticed she wasn't wearing panniers or powder any more. Ninian probably kept her too busy for such frivolity. Realizing he still held the brat, he tucked it under his arm and stalked toward the conservatory. To hell with his bailiff. He wanted his wife.

"Oh, my lord, you're back, you are!" Cook exclaimed as she hurried from the kitchen. "I've none to stir the pudding, and my kettle is boiling. Come along, or it'll spoil."

No longer amazed by anything in the chaos his wife had apparently created in his absence, Drogo preceded Cook's shooing gesture into the kitchen. He didn't think he'd ever been in a kitchen before. He glanced around in curiosity but couldn't discern the purpose of the iron and wooden utensils upon the walls.

Cook shoved a wooden spoon at him, and he shifted the

babe to one shoulder to catch it. He stirred the contents of the bowl cautiously. It smelled like pudding all right. Why were they making pudding? There was enough here to feed a village.

The kitchen maid returned bearing firewood, which crashed to the floor upon sight of an earl in the kitchen stirring pudding and dandling a babe on his shoulder.

When the girl looked as if she would faint, Drogo decided he'd had quite enough. Shoving the bundle of flailing arms and legs into the girl's now empty hands, adding the spoon for good measure, he nodded curtly and all but ran out.

He didn't know how women managed it all, and he didn't want to find out. Where the hell was Ninian?

Not in the conservatory. He saw evidence of her presence in the apron draped over the settee and the partially planted seedlings on the potting bench. Already, a row of neatly labeled herbs had sprouted on the shelves. She'd been busy.

Feeling somewhat relieved at that, he headed for the tower. Perhaps she was actually napping through all this racket. Expectant mothers were supposed to sleep a lot, weren't they?

His bailiff caught him in the great hall before he had a chance to reach the stairs.

"My lord, a word with ye, if I might."

What was he doing hunting his wife in the middle of the day when there was work to do? The fresh air must be affecting his brain.

"Of course, Huntley. What is it?" Abandoning his chase, Drogo crossed the wide expanse of towering hall.

"It's the burn, my lord. Mr. Payton said as to tell you as soon as you arrived. Her ladyship insisted that he take her to the source of the blight. They've gone off over the hills, and it's been since early this morn."

Drogo thought he would kill her, if she did not kill herself before he got there.

Thirty

"THIS IS THE END OF THE EARL'S PROPERTY, MY LADY. YOU can see there is no sign of the source of the problem." Mr. Payton stood stiffly beside his placid mare as Ninian stared at the barren wasteland leading back to distant hills.

"The stream must come from somewhere," she insisted. "You have had all summer to explore. It's impossible to tell much of anything at this time of year."

"It could come from Crown land, for all I know. Or Scotland. There is naught we can do beyond this property."

"We could find the source and stop it," she said crossly, kicking at a dead limb lying in the brown leaves at her feet. She knew she couldn't walk farther this day, and the sight of the distant hills discouraged her. She would need a horse.

Mr. Payton had a horse. Mr. Payton was lying. She twisted the dying tip of an evergreen, and the needles fell off in her hand. "I can find my own way back. I want to look around some more. You may go about whatever it is you do." Furious, it took no effort to summon the imperious tones of her grandmother. It came as naturally as breathing, more naturally than the pleasant face she'd worn for so many years. If she was to be herself, she may as well begin practicing with this annoying insect.

"I cannot leave you here alone, my lady," the steward responded stiffly.

"Of course you can. I've walked these woods alone all

my life. I'm a witch, remember? Go away and leave me be."
Muttering under her breath, she set out along the stream
bank, taking more time to examine what she had missed
in her hurry to reach the source of the blight. The stupid
man should have told her he wouldn't go beyond Drogo's
boundaries. She would have to persuade Drogo to invent
more filters. It would be months before the child was born
and she could learn to ride. Perhaps they could experiment
with the water passing through different filters and determine which was most effective. Drogo would know how to
go about that.

Drogo would no doubt chain her to the wall for venturing out.

She heard Payton riding away as she scrambled down a
hillside he hadn't allowed her to traverse earlier. Men! They
must think her some breakable china ornament. How did they
think the human race had survived all these years? Certainly
not by women putting their feet up and doing nothing for
nine months out of every year.

At the bottom of the embankment, she crouched quietly,
listening to the burn's burble and the wind blowing through
barren tree branches. Sometimes, she could hear things in the
wind if she opened up her senses to her surroundings.

The crunch of dead leaves, the slipping of a hidden log, and
a loud curse weren't exactly the sounds she'd had in mind.
The resulting crash brought her to her feet.

"Who's there?" she called. She already knew whoever it
was had hurt himself and wasn't too happy about it.

"The bogeyman," a deep, irritated male voice called. "Are
you all right?"

"Of course I am." Brushing dead leaves from her woolen
skirt, she grasped a nearby sapling, tested it for sturdiness, and
pulled herself upward. The child inside her kicked gaily. Her
daughter liked adventure.

"Of course you are," the rough male voice mocked.
"You're a Malcolm. Why ever would I think elsewise?"

"Malcolms can be harmed, just the same as anyone else."
Puffing a little at the exertion of climbing the steep embankment in the direction of the voice, thankful her cough had

disappeared, Ninian steadied herself on an oak and glanced around. "You!"

The uninvited guest from their wedding lay sprawled in the dead leaves and debris in a washed-out gully beneath some rowan roots near the edge of the embankment. Massive arms crossed over his wide chest, he managed a magnificent, insouciant pose with one boot turned at an uncomfortable angle, his breeches torn on the bare rocks, while glaring at her from beneath brows more thunderous than Drogo's.

"My nose recovered," he said dryly. "My pride is still bruised."

"It looks as if more than your pride is bruised." She found a perch on the rocks where she could kneel beside him and tug at his boot.

"Leave it alone," he grumbled. "Just find me a sturdy stick, and I can go back to my horse."

"Ives men are occasionally stubborn but usually not stupid." Ninian tugged at the boot as gently as she could, but he still grimaced as it loosened. She noticed he didn't deny his family connection. "The foot will swell, and you will have to cut a perfectly good boot if you leave it too long."

"I'll steal another." He pulled his leg from her grasp and with a painful wince, hauled the stiff leather off his foot. "There, are you happy now? Find a stick, and go back where you belong."

"Since this is my husband's land, I am where I belong," Ninian said placidly, testing the bones of his sturdy ankle. "They're not broken, but the tendons are strained. I'll wrap it for now. You can soak it when we reach the castle."

"I am not going to the castle." Curtly, he jerked his leg from her hold. "I merely wanted to see that you were unharmed. Now go about your business, and I'll go about mine."

Ignoring his orders, Ninian worked at the material of her petticoat with a rock until she'd torn a gash in it. Without any particular sense of delicacy, she lifted her heavy skirt and ripped the hole wider until she had a strip the proper length. The blamed man couldn't even stand without help, so she didn't see much point in arguing with him.

"This is my business," she reminded him as she laid her

hands on his swelling ankle and concentrated. He radiated pain, and she worked to ease it. "I can give you willow bark once we are home, and it will feel better. There's not much I can do out here."

"I'm not going to the castle," he repeated wearily, leaning back on his elbows as she massaged away the pain. "You really are quite good. A Malcolm with a useful talent is rare."

Ninian understood more than the pain of his injury was talking. "People do not often appreciate our perceptiveness. Ives men in particular seem to have difficulty grasping things which they cannot see. Do you have a name?"

"Just call me Adonis and wrap the blasted ankle."

"Adonis?" She grinned at him, and he scowled in return. The resemblance to Drogo was quite remarkable. She'd judge him to be several years older and a stone heavier—all muscle and probably all between his ears. She sensed no evil in him, however.

"Greek gods are a rare breed in these woods. Why were you following me?"

"For lack of anything better to do." He grunted as she pulled the cloth tight.

"Do you live around here?"

"I don't live anywhere. Cease and desist, madam!" he howled as she pulled the cloth with all her strength.

"It will feel better when I'm done. If you don't live anywhere, then there is no reason you cannot come back to the castle. The ankle needs to be soaked."

"There is every reason in the world why I cannot go to yon blasted castle. Now find me a stick, madam, and be off with you. And if I were you, I'd not mention this encounter to your husband. In case you have not noticed, Ives tend to be jealous men."

"Now that really would be stupid." Knotting the bandage, Ninian stood and looked about. "Malcolm women cannot tolerate stupid men. It's no wonder the legends warn us against you."

"If you know that, why the hell did you marry the earl?" Cursing as he pushed himself to a sitting position on one of the rocks, he pointed toward a dead tree on his right. "One of those limbs should support me. Can you pull it loose?"

"Drogo is not a stupid man." She tested the limb, but it did not crack. She scuffled about in the leaves, looking for a better one. "He is an extremely considerate but very busy man who just has different goals than I do. That does not mean one or the other of us is right or wrong."

"Fool. You're in love with him. You don't have a chance. What in hell are you doing out here risking his precious heir anyway?"

Ninian spotted a stout limb on an outcropping and pulled herself toward it, ignoring the abrupt curses of the man behind her. "Looking for the source of the burn's blight. You wouldn't happen to know where it begins, would you?"

She slid back down, stick in hand, and handed it to the angry man who had pulled himself upright in his apparent haste to rescue her from the rocks. She offered him a dimpled smile, but he merely scowled more blackly.

"Don't give me that innocent look, my lady. I'm not so blind to Malcolm charms as my fool…" He didn't finish that statement but grabbed the stick from her outstretched hand and tested his weight against it. Satisfied it would hold, he met her gaze more calmly. "The blight begins at the mines to the north of here. Your husband's family does not teach their sons of the malignancies they perpetrate on the face of the earth in the name of progress. Perhaps Malcolms can point it out to them before it is too late and they destroy us all."

He heaved himself up the hill by brute force, using the stick as a brace. Fascinated despite herself, Ninian followed him up, carrying his boot. His shirt looked as if it had seen better days, and he wore no waistcoat. His long coat appeared tailored for a younger, smaller man. She thought the boots might be his only pair.

"Drogo's mines?" she inquired as they reached level ground. "Does he know this?"

"Probably not." The man—Adonis?—whistled loudly and waited. "He is only interested in productivity and profit and things that he can see and measure. His steward suspects though, and says nothing. It would cost too many people their jobs were the mines closed."

Ninian heard the sound of a horse galloping toward them. Shortly, he would ride away, and she would never know more. Curiosity wouldn't let her give up. "Please, you must come home with me. Drogo is away on business, if that's your fear. I think he would like to meet you, though."

"No, he wouldn't." The horse appeared around a copse of trees, and he whistled again. It slowed and obediently trotted in their direction. "I'll follow you part of the way to be certain you're safe, but I'll stay out of sight. If you know what's healthy, you'll not mention any of this to his noble lordship. I'm no hand at swords." He caught his mount's bridle and swung up.

Ninian handed him his boot. "Drogo isn't violent," she chastised him. "And I see no reason for violence. I'm quite certain he would listen to your theory about the mines."

"And I'm quite certain he would run a stake through my heart should we meet. It's late. You'll have to hurry to return to the castle before dark."

She wanted to tell him she would arrive much faster if she rode, but his horse was a large, restless stallion she had no desire to sit upon. Before she could formulate another argument, he trotted off into the woods, leaving her alone on the empty road.

"Dratted man," she muttered, searching the place where he'd disappeared but seeing nothing of him.

Who was he, and why was he following her about? Was it coincidence that no one had known of his existence until her wedding?

Very strange. Pondering his words about the mines, she abandoned her search of the burn and followed the more direct road home. She occasionally sensed his presence in the distance, but he didn't represent danger, and she could shut him out easily. She should have bound and gagged him while he was helpless and then gone to fetch aid.

Kicking up dust and simmering with resentment as well

as curiosity, Ninian didn't notice the rising cloud of dust on the horizon until she felt the stranger's alarm. Coming alert, she searched for some signal to identify the approaching rider. When she found none, she grinned. Drogo. Well, that was one way of identifying him.

Moses could have carved commandments in the granite monument of her husband's face as he caught sight of her and slowed his mount to a walk. He didn't bring the palfrey this time, she noted. He apparently hadn't thought he would find her.

"If you'll ride back into the woods, you'll find the missing Ives from our wedding," she informed him. "But he'll probably escape before you can catch up with him."

Apparently believing her comment as lamebrained as everything else she did, Drogo swung down from his horse. "What the devil do you think you are doing, madam?"

Ninian couldn't help it. He sounded so much like the surly stranger that she smiled. He always looked so startled when she did that. "You sound just like Adonis. The two of you must have been separated at birth." She looked up at his massive gelding with a frown. "I'll not ride that monster. I'm much safer down here."

Without reaching for her, Drogo pulled his horse around and walked beside her. He said nothing, and she figured he was grappling with the temper he didn't have. Her husband was very good at concealing anything resembling emotion. She thought he'd done it so long that he'd forgotten how to express any.

"I can make you lose your temper, you know," she said, scuffling the dust again. "But I'm rather afraid the result would be so explosive after all this time that you might blow us both up in the aftermath."

"You are not making sense, madam," he said stiffly. "I do not lose my temper. I do, however, worry when I cannot find my six-months pregnant *wife*."

The last words were forcefully strained through clenched teeth. Ninian cast him a sidelong look, but he stared straight ahead.

"You cannot keep a leash upon me, you know. Perhaps you would be more comfortable back in London where you do not know what I'm doing?"

"I don't think I'll ever be comfortable again." His voice sounded hollow and vaguely perplexed. "I'm not certain I've ever been comfortable, actually. You certainly do not aid the situation."

"I'm sorry. I truly did not mean to disturb you. You weren't home and the opportunity opened and I simply took advantage of it. Your steward wasn't very helpful," she said chidingly. "But Adonis—that's what he said to call him, although I'm certain it's not his name—Adonis says the blight begins far past the hills and into the mines, so there is naught I can do about it."

With a resigned expression, he finally looked down at her. "You really aren't crackbrained, are you?" He sounded as if he needed reassurance.

Ninian shrugged. "Not from my point of view."

He nodded and returned to watching the road. "Then this Adonis person really exists? He's not a fairy or something?"

She laughed at his bewildered expression. Logic was such a narrow-minded path to follow. "I bit his nose, if you'll remember. He's quite real."

"Why is it you're the only one who has ever talked to him?"

This was an odd tack for the conversation to take, but she assumed it was better than listening to Drogo explode with all that anger bottled up inside of him. "I don't know. I think he was following me today, but he fell and twisted his ankle and couldn't run away. He said not to tell you, and he refused to return with me to the castle. Do you think he might be another of your father's by-blows?"

Drogo thought about it. Ninian waited expectantly.

"I know little of my father's life before he married my mother. I don't like the idea of him following you, though. Will you stay in the castle from now on?"

He didn't sound very hopeful of receiving the reply he wanted.

Ninian took his arm and patted it consolingly. "I won't go farther than the village until after the babe is born, all right?"

His expression was bleak as he turned to her. "You, madam, will almost certainly drive me mad."

Ninian just smiled.

Thirty-one

"THERE'S SOMETHING WRONG, DROGO."

Reluctantly pulling himself back from his study of the stars, Drogo set aside his telescope and watched with concern as his very pregnant wife swayed into his tower study.

Almost into her eighth month of pregnancy and with the onset of severe weather, Ninian had finally given up her forays into the village, much to his relief. That hadn't stopped a steady trickle of villagers from traveling to his back door for Ninian's healing remedies. She thought he didn't know about the small infirmary—now containing one extremely pregnant young mother—in the servants' quarters. He didn't object as long as she took care of herself and the child.

Climbing the stairs was not taking care of herself. "Couldn't you have sent someone up here to me? You're not supposed to be on the stairs."

She collapsed on a cushioned window seat and caught her breath, protectively holding her belly. Her immense size worried him. He wanted to carry the burden for her. He should never have forced a child on her. He really didn't need a child. He needed Ninian. Life without Ninian lacked color. Life with Ninian meant flowers in unexpected corners, brothers who occasionally behaved with unexpected good sense, and nights filled with rapture.

Life with Ninian meant a constant stream of terror as she

escaped his protective nets. He ought to follow her advice and go back to London, so he didn't know about her escapades.

He didn't want to need her, any more than he wanted to need this child. Need did scary things to his insides that had him waking up in a sweat in the middle of the night.

But then Ninian would curl her warmth against his, and he'd fall asleep again.

Heaven and hell, all wrapped together in one bountiful bundle of golden curls.

The bundle of curls scowled at him. "You're supposed to ask me what's wrong, not scold me. I was in a hurry and didn't want to look for someone."

He'd given up any hope of logic from her months ago. She had a brain. She just didn't use it as he did. Moving to the window seat, he curled his arms around her and felt her relax against him. It was the only way he could share her burden.

"What is wrong?" he asked, hoping to pacifying her.

"I don't know."

Drogo smiled above her head. He'd almost expected that. "If something was wrong with the baby, you would know that, wouldn't you?"

"Yes, of course. It's not that. The ghost is trying to tell me something, but I cannot hear her. I can only sense her presence now, and she's anxious. She's pacing the room."

Drogo sighed. "I told you not to refurbish that dratted suite. It only upsets you. We'll use my old chamber tonight."

She dug her fingers into his arms. "No, she only means well. She was quite content once I carried your child. No one has complained of screaming or noises since, have they?"

"That's because I had the roof and chimney fixed. If she's whining again, it's just the north wind in those old panes."

"No, it's not that." She swung her head vehemently, batting him with soft curls. "For some reason, I sense it's Dunstan. Has he written to you lately?"

"No, but I hear from Ewen regularly. He would have told me if anything was wrong at the estate. They should all be visiting your aunts by now. It was gracious of them to extend the invitation to all of us."

"No, it wasn't," Ninian said irritably, rising from the cushioned seat and pacing. "They've been told to stay away from
Ives men all their lives, and now curiosity has beset them.
Your brothers will be sketched, perfumed, and examined as
thoroughly as you study your stars."

"Perfumed?" Amused by the idea of his rowdy brothers
succumbing to so many feminine wiles, Drogo didn't protest
her abrupt departure. Pregnancy exaggerated Ninian's mood
swings, he'd already noticed.

She waved her hand in dismissal of the question. "I told
them to leave Dunstan and his wife alone, as you asked, but
it's Christmas. They could not invite the others and not him.
It's Dunstan, I'm sure of it. This is terrible."

She clasped and unclasped her hands and paced as if she
could walk back to London. Drogo stood and caught her by
the shoulders. "What is terrible?"

She shook her head again. "I'm not a mind reader. I can
only empathize with someone close, preferably touching. I
must be empathizing with a *ghost*. That's insane."

Drogo smiled wider. "I've been telling you that. Now let
us go downstairs, and I'll tuck you into bed. You need your
sleep." He'd given up questioning her "empathy," deciding
she just noticed people more than most. Empathizing with a
ghost went beyond the realms of explanation into the fantasies
of a pregnant, hysterical female mind.

"He must be close," she asserted firmly as he led her to the
door. "The ghost surely could not be aware of him if he were
at Ives."

That worried him more than he wanted to admit. He
didn't believe in ghosts, but Dunstan usually sent him monthly
reports. He hadn't heard from him since London.

"There is nothing we can do." He tried to reassure her, as
well as himself. "You keep telling me my brothers are grown
men. Let them be."

"He's in pain, I know it," she insisted. "Send one of the
grooms to the nearest inn. There is no other explanation."

"The roads are pits of ice. No sane man would travel
them." He lifted her in his arms and carried her down the

stairs. "Dunstan is eminently sane, probably more so than the rest of us."

"Not tonight," she whispered. "Send a groom, Drogo, please. Bear with me on this."

And because it was Christmas, and she was far gone with his child, he did.

"They're here." Sleepily, Ninian nudged her snoring husband. Drogo didn't snore loudly, but he breathed deeply. Most mornings, she loved lying here listening to him, basking in the warmth of his muscled male body. Even though she had told him it was best to limit their relations until after the child's birth, he insisted she continue sleeping in his bed. She hadn't objected.

But this morning, she didn't have time to idle. "Hurry, Drogo. They're here and they're angry and they'll tear the walls down if we do not do something. Awkwardly, she eased her legs over the edge of the high bed. She would be quite happy when this child was in her arms instead of her belly. If she didn't know better, she'd think it a contrary Ives male who sat on her bladder well ahead of schedule. She didn't know if she could endure another month of this, much less two.

The cold of her departure apparently aroused Drogo from his torpor. He'd lit a candle and donned his breeches by the time she emerged from behind the dressing screen.

"What the devil are we doing up at this hour?" he demanded as he grabbed a shirt.

She dearly loved admiring the masculine contours of his chest and shoulders as he dressed, but she would have to forego the pleasure for now. She hastily donned the linen chemise she'd worn last night.

"Don't ask me why they would travel at night in weather like this. They're your brothers, after all. I suppose we could assume they wished to arrive before the snow."

"What the devil do my brothers have to do with anything?"

The pounding and shouts at the front portals answered that silly question. Ninian struggled into a loose wool dress and began hooking the bodice over her heavy breasts. She carried the child low, but the bodice was still a struggle.

Drogo tugged the top hook in place for her. "I don't think you've ever looked more radiant," he murmured, taking his time at the process.

"And you must be quite blind, my lord." But she blushed at the compliment anyway. She was learning to deal with the fact that he was an earl and an Ives. She was still having difficulty absorbing the physical intimacy of him as a man. She felt self-conscious and awkward next to his masculine grace.

"I daresay the noise is just one of your villagers with a wife about to give birth. We'll have to order the Beltane festivities spread throughout the year rather than on just one night."

She slapped his hand as it encroached upon a swelling breast. "They come to the back door, where they know they can rouse someone. It has to be your brothers."

She started for the door as soon as he released her, but Drogo caught her arm and held her back.

"No stairs, remember? I either carry you, or you wait here."

She hated this. She hated being helpless, coddled, and left out. But he was right. She pouted as he drew on stockings and shoes. He didn't have to be so damned *calm* about someone breaking in their door. If their visitors had an ax, she was quite certain they would have used it by now.

"Wait here," he ordered as he grabbed his coat and started out.

So, maybe he was more anxious than he showed, or he would have taken the time to carry her down. She was learning to read him, if she didn't go off on an emotional tangent of her own, like wanting to fling a knife between his shoulders for leaving her behind.

Barefoot, she wandered to the hall and stood at the top of the stairs, listening as Drogo hauled the bar from the doors. Oddly, the ghost wasn't making her presence known. Perhaps once she'd alerted someone, she figured her job was done. Or she hid from the Ives rage shimmering on the airwaves. Nothing ambiguous about that emotion.

She heard the argument as the door burst open. Dunstan.

And Ewen. Perhaps she was better off here, out of sight, until Drogo calmed them. She didn't think her child needed this kind of upset. Perhaps becoming too close to people was detrimental to her health. Maybe that was why her grandmother had advised her to stay in Wystan and live a solitary life. She'd never felt anything quite so sharply as this Ives fury. Her Gift had always been a weak one.

As angry male voices escalated, accompanied by the calmer tones of the groom Drogo had sent to the inn, and finally joined by the sleepy one of the housekeeper, Ninian sighed in exasperation and settled her bulk on the top step.

"If you do not all behave like civilized people and come up here to greet me, I shall roll down these steps to join you!"

She didn't think they would hear her, but angry exclamations ceased abruptly, as if Drogo had collared his brothers and cut off their windpipes. He would, too, if he'd heard her threat. Drogo might pretend impassivity, but he protected this child as ferociously as any wolf with his cubs.

She suspected Drogo loved his family so fiercely, he didn't dare express it for fear of being made too vulnerable to deal with them.

As she'd anticipated, Drogo appeared on the landing, Dunstan and Ewen's neckcloths in a firm grip as he shoved them upward.

"They're drunk," he announced with disgust from below. "Go on to bed, and Mrs. White and I will see them to their rooms."

Ninian tilted her head and concentrated. Usually, she did not seek out the pain of others unless called upon to heal them, but Dunstan would never ask for help. Beneath the drunken belligerency any fool could see, he registered a pain so deep, it physically hurt. She closed her eyes against the anguish of it.

"I think not," she said quietly, trying to arrange her scattered thoughts while Dunstan's pain bounced off all the walls of her mind. "Send Mrs. White for some coffee. Cook will have oatcakes shortly." She dared open her eyes to squint at Ewen. "Thank you for bringing Dunstan safely here, but you'd best follow Mrs. White to the kitchen."

All three men stared at her as if she were insane. Nothing new. But she was learning brawny Ives men bent easily beneath feminine breezes. With an exaggerated sigh, she tried to pull herself upright by grabbing a newel post.

Drogo instantly dropped his brothers and took the steps two at a time. Dunstan staggered at being left to his own power. Ewen caught the stair rail and stared at her with a slowly awakening grin.

"By all means, Countess," he agreed with only a slight slur and stagger as he attempted a bow. "Coffee and a roaring fire for me." He toddled back down the stairs.

Drogo helped her to her feet. "I'll handle Dunstan. You go back to bed."

Sometimes, even the brightest of men could be so obtuse. She stood on tiptoe and kissed his scratchy cheek. "Help Dunstan into the sitting room. I'll stir the coals."

Dunstan was already heading back down the stairs after Ewen. Torn, Drogo looked from one of them to the other, and giving up, chased after Dunstan.

The tinder Ninian added to the coals was burning merrily by the time Drogo steered his brother to a chair and flung him into it. Dunstan collapsed like a broken doll and buried his face in his hands.

"He's drunk," Drogo said unnecessarily. "He never used to drink."

The wind whistled through the chinks in the wall, and for the first time, Ninian couldn't distinguish between the wind and the ghost's vibrations. The distress level in here was much too high.

Behind Dunstan's back, she patted Drogo's arm. "Hurry Mrs. White and the coffee. He's frozen clear through," she whispered. Drogo would understand physical peril much better than if she told him his brother was dying of guilt.

Nodding reluctantly, acknowledging there was little he could do that Ninian couldn't do better, Drogo strode off in search of hot refreshment.

As soon as he was gone, Ninian pulled a second chair close to Dunstan's. He didn't look up or respond to her presence.

She'd seldom dealt with grown men in pain. They came to her for cuts and scrapes, but not with wounds so deep they weren't visible. She wasn't entirely certain how to proceed, except that she knew she must. This was Drogo's heir. She could not give him a son, so she must save the heir he had.

"Dunstan." Quietly, she reached for his hands, sliding her own between his callused palms and his face. The pain was almost unbearable, but this was something she knew how to control. She channeled it to a part of her mind that could deal with it while concentrating on her patient.

"Dunstan. It's just me. Tell me what is wrong."

His fists gripped hers so hard it hurt. His whole huge frame shook with the force of his anguish. Anger burned as deep as the pain, however, and anger won out.

He tore his hands away, sat up, and glared at her. All the mighty Ives rage wrote itself across his thunderous brow and stubbled jaw.

"I'm a murderer, madam. I have killed my wife."

Thirty-two

"MERRY CHRISTMAS, BIG BROTHER," EWEN SAID WEARILY, sipping at his black coffee and stretching his legs before the roaring kitchen fire. "Don't say I never gave you anything. Dunstan is a damned rough gift to deliver."

"I don't suppose you're capable of telling me *why* you delivered him?" Drogo accepted a cup of bitter brew from his brother while listening for any unexpected noises from above. He needed to return to Ninian, but he thought they might stand a better chance of reaching the bottom of this by dividing and conquering.

He was coming to rely on her warped logic far more than was good for him.

Ewen glared blearily in his direction, grimaced, and took another sip of coffee. "Not a pretty tale at this hour. Go back to your omniscient wife and ask her."

Stubbornly, Drogo dug in his heels, although the crack about his wife's "omniscience" rang alarms. How had Ninian known Dunstan was near? And in trouble? She'd never claimed to be a mind reader. But empathy? He shook his head. Perhaps she'd had a letter from Sarah and hadn't wanted to tell him about it.

"Ninian will be prying Dunstan's version of the tale from him. You'd better state your case here."

Ewen grunted something incomprehensible and managed another swallow of coffee. Finally emptying the cup, he held it out for another.

Mrs. White had already bustled upstairs to prepare rooms. Drogo had sent the cook away. With a sigh, he refilled Ewen's cup from the pot on the fire.

"He was going to kill himself." Ewen grimaced, whether at the coffee or his explanation, it was hard to tell.

Ninian would have known what to say. He needed Ninian here.

Drogo sank onto a bench and stared at his besotted brother. The usually dapper Ewen looked as if he'd been dragged through every mud puddle between here and London. A bruise scored one side of his jaw, dangerously near his eye. Ewen wasn't as strong or as quick with his fists as Dunstan. He'd taken a lot of punishment for what he obviously perceived as his good deed.

"Why?" was the only word that came to Drogo's bewildered mind. Why Dunstan, his heir, the brother he relied on most? Why was the sky blue? Nothing made sense.

Ewen shrugged out of his damp coat. "He thinks he killed Celia."

Drogo took a deep breath as screams ripped through his head. "Celia is dead?"

"Yup." Morosely, Ewen retrieved his cup from the table and sipped again. He looked at it with distaste. "Couldn't we add whiskey to this?"

Excellent idea. Shattered by the news of Celia's death, Drogo bumped around the kitchen searching for anything remotely alcoholic. Grabbing the cooking brandy, he returned and added a large dollop to both cups. He needed Ninian desperately now. He couldn't deal with this. He could deal with brawls and exploding carriages and the juvenile mischief his brothers dumped at his door—physical activities that had a beginning and an end and a solid reality he could handle.

He couldn't deal with suicide and death. He'd dealt with his father's death by controlling estate finances and his brothers with an iron hand. He couldn't control death.

Celia had been barely twenty, a mere child with her entire life ahead of her.

"How did she die?" he demanded.

Ewen shrugged and sipped generously of the liquored coffee. "That's a matter of some debate, apparently. You need to ask Dunstan. He claims he killed her. Personally, I think he had every right to."

Oh, God, this couldn't be happening. Drogo rubbed his brow and wondered how soon he could go to Ninian with this tale. Then he wondered why he should bother her with it. He was the one responsible for his brothers. Not her. Since when had she become such an indispensable part of him?

"Celia was a foolish little girl. What did she do to deserve to die?"

"Broke Dunstan's heart," Ewen answered grimly. "He loved the little twit. He believed her when she said she was visiting with your wife's family. He believed her when she said they gave her diamond bracelets. She wasn't foolish or a girl. She was a jade, first, last, and always."

Oh damn. Oh thrice-bedamned curse of the Ives. He should never have protected his brothers from the truth of their parents' marriage. He should have emphasized the dangers of ever linking themselves to any woman. Ives weren't meant to marry. Procreate, obviously, but not marry.

Then why the hell did he think Ninian was different?

Casting that irrelevant thought aside, he focused on the more immediate problem. "Celia found a lover?"

Ewen nodded wearily, resting his head on his hand. "Everyone knew it but Dunstan. They cavorted about London, attending the balls and soirees Dunstan scorned. He dressed her in the silk and jewels she craved."

"Who?" Drogo asked with deadly calm. He would kill the bastard.

Seeing the murder in his eyes, Ewen shook his head. "It doesn't matter. He died with Celia. If Dunstan killed him, I don't blame him in the least." Running his hand through his hair, Ewen looked uncertain. "I suppose there's one thing you ought to know."

Drogo waited. He was a patient man. He would have the whole story, and he would throttle whoever was responsible.

Dunstan was his heir. He would never do anything so insane as to murder his wife. If Dunstan had murdered his wife's lover, Drogo would defend his right to do so.

"Celia met the man while visiting with your wife's family. That's where Dunstan thought Celia was before she died."

He'd told Ninian no good could come of that connection. She'd ignored him. Controlling his rapidly disintegrating emotions, Drogo coldly continued his interrogation. "How did she die?"

"A broken neck. She was found at the bottom of a cliff between Ives and the duke's estate. Her lover had a pistol ball through his heart."

Dunstan was handy with his fists but not a sword. In a duel, he would have chosen pistols. Their accuracy was undependable, but a body wound almost always ended in death, sooner or later. Drogo kneaded his brow, wishing he could arrange his thoughts more coherently.

"The law?"

Ewen shrugged. "Don't know. I was at the duke's with everyone else when I heard about the discovery of a man's body. Dunstan had refused to attend the festivities, saying he had some beast birthing too early or some such. I rode out with the duke and a few others and was there when they discovered the abandoned carriage and horses, as well as Celia's body. There was no evidence pointing directly to Dunstan. It could have been highwaymen, except she still wore all her jewels."

Ewen closed his eyes and spoke carefully. "I told everyone I would ride to Ives to break the news to Dunstan. The duke very generously did not insist that someone accompany me. I rather think he sympathized with Dunstan and didn't wish to become involved in a marital dispute."

Drogo waited, knowing what would come. If Dunstan had done it, he would have taken the honorable way out. His heart curdled in his chest as he thought about it.

"I found Dunstan in his barn, cleaning his pistol. He was already six sheets to the wind, but he knew what he was doing. He tried to load the gun before I took it away, but I knocked him down. I had to have help to hog-tie him, and I didn't know what else to do, so I brought him here. As far as the servants are aware, he knew nothing of Celia until I arrived, so I thought it best to keep him from the magistrate."

Very carefully, Drogo set his cup down. Holding his shoulders back, trying not to breathe too deeply, he dragged himself up. "The housekeeper will have prepared a room for you. Get some rest."

Without thanking Ewen, without acknowledging the tale told, he stiffly strode from the kitchen. Every fiber of his body protested the tale. He relied on Dunstan's stability and sense. Dunstan would never have done something so patently useless. Dunstan would have thrown the lying slut out of the house—just as their father had their mother.

Oh, God, none of this made sense. They were cursed. It was only a matter of time until Ninian proved it. Why the hell was he so certain the child was his?

Because he desperately wanted it to be his. Foolish. He acknowledged the fear lurking in the pit of his belly. She was getting too close.

Distance. He needed distance. That worked best. Dunstan was innocent. Drogo knew that as well as he knew his own name. He would discover the truth of Dunstan's problem, take care of it as best he could, then return to work as he should have done instead of giving in to his wife's whimsy. Let her coddle plants and occupy herself as she would. He had business to take care of. With the appropriate distance, his life would suffer no disruption when the inevitable befell him.

Ninian looked up as her husband strode in like some iron automaton Ewen might have invented. With only a nod to her, Drogo grasped Dunstan's elbow and hauled him from the chair. She needed to talk with him. She needed to explain…

Drogo shook her off when she tried to halt him. Looking as if he stood beneath a hangman's noose, Dunstan straightened his shoulders and with only a cool nod in her direction, walked out of his own accord. Wordlessly, Drogo followed him, firmly shutting the door between them.

She didn't need to read Drogo to read that action. She had just lost her husband as surely as if he'd packed up and left.

The iciness of the ghost's presence did nothing to comfort her.

❧

"Tell me what you said to him!" Ninian demanded. She couldn't remember ever demanding anything of anyone at anytime, but she couldn't bear Drogo's return to the distant monster she'd first met in this damned castle. If it wasn't akin to moving a mountain, she'd shake him.

"I will have a door and a lock installed at the bottom of those stairs if you don't cease climbing them," he answered coldly, not looking up from the mathematical calculations on his desk.

"Dunstan is *dying* inside. He's killing himself! I can't help that kind of pain. He needs you, Drogo. You have to help him. Tell me what you said." How could she make him listen? What did she have to do to prove to him that she knew how Dunstan felt, knew what he was suffering?

"He was too drunk to talk sense. I'm handling it. You, madam, may go back to your plants and patients and leave me to deal with my family's problems."

He was doing it again, shutting her out, reducing her to the role of Wife and no more. She wouldn't have it. He'd listened to her and brought her here and they'd grown closer than ever these past months. She wouldn't let him deny that now.

"You, sir, are playing the obnoxious fool again, and I won't stand for it!" With a sweep of her lace-bedecked sleeve, Ninian sent all the papers on his desk flying into the air. The cold contempt in his expression as he turned to her was worse than fury.

"I am *not* a helpless nitwit to be patronized and treated as your brood mare! We are *equal* partners in this marriage. Dunstan is now my brother as much as he is yours, and if you will not help him, I will!"

Drogo stood, and catching her flailing arms, lifted her from the floor and carried her out the door and down the stairs. "You, madam, are more trouble than all my brothers put together. If you do not stay off these stairs, I will lock you in your room."

He deposited her, kicking and swinging, in the master suite, then stalked out, his granite face as immobile and inflexible as his mind.

Damn! If she were a real witch, she'd put a hex on him, turn him into a frog, and turn his damned tower into a lily pad where he could croak to himself all he liked. Stupid, stupid, *stupid* blind Ives men.

She hurled Ceridwen's diary at the door.

❧

"It's Christmas Eve. Shouldn't you be downstairs with the others, celebrating?"

Drogo adjusted the lens of his telescope and peered deeper into the night sky. "I don't see you and Dunstan down there."

"She has live hollies in the great hall. The whole town is bobbing for apples. She promised a flaming pudding and spiced cider. Lydie is playing the piano, and there will be dancing. Have you ever danced with Ninian?" Ewen balanced a compass between his fingers as he watched his eldest brother.

Drogo didn't turn around. At the moment, he wasn't even sleeping with Ninian. He'd left her to the suite and her haunts and returned to his old room. It was much saner this way, her with her pursuits, he with his. His theory on togetherness in marriage needed a few kinks worked out of it.

"I shouldn't think dancing possible for her at this stage."

"With Ninian, I expect anything is possible. Have you ever looked into that trumpery ritual her family performed at the wedding?"

Ewen asked that too casually for it not to be important. Grunting noncommittally, Drogo set aside his telescope to return to his desk and jot a few notes. According to his calculations, he should be able to see his planet again in a few weeks.

"They're all cork-brained. Peculiarities develop in families bred too closely, and Malcolms were isolated out here for eons. The royal family ought to look into that close breeding business." He made another note and checked an item off his list. Maybe that would satisfy Ewen sufficiently to return to the merrymaking.

"She gave Dunstan an amulet."

Drogo dropped his quill and glared at his brother. "An amulet?"

Ewen shrugged. "And a small pouch of herbs to wear around his neck. Told him the amulet would help him gather his grief and anger so he could deposit them in the pouch, that he can't be rational or make sense of anything until he rid himself of ill humors."

Drogo rolled his eyes and picked up the quill again. "Maggoty-brained females. Do yourself a favor and stay away from the lot of them. What did Dunstan do with the claptrap?"

"He's wearing them. He's helping her roll rocks into the stream too. She said you didn't have time to help her but had told her how to do it. Some kind of filter system?"

Drogo kneaded his forehead. He simply couldn't do it all. There were not enough hours in the day or days in the week, and he wasn't cut out for this nurturing, nest-building fool-ishness. He'd concentrated on investigating Celia's death and answering questions about Dunstan's whereabouts. He was almost grateful travel was nigh impossible this time of year. It prevented the magistrates from appearing at his door. The duke generously held them at bay while the servants swore Dunstan had never left home the day Celia died.

"I'll have Payton hire someone to move the rocks. Dunstan will be fine once he realizes he's wasting his grief on a tart like Celia. I have someone investigating the circumstances, and Mother has seen to the burial arrangements. There's nothing else we can do for now."

"Drogo, I don't think you understand," Ewen said a little more adamantly as his brother returned to his work.

Impatient, Drogo looked up again.

"Dunstan thinks she's a witch." Ewen set the compass down gently on the desk. "He believes that he must expiate his guilt before he can kill himself, and that Ninian is helping him to do that."

Drogo's thick brows formed into a thunderous cloud.

Ewen hurried on. "She's told him he can't die until you

have an heir—besides me, at least. I am apparently unsuitable
in the eyes of all. So Dunstan is attempting to work off his
debt to you while waiting to see if you have a boy, which
of course, we all know you will. Once that's settled, he's
assuming Ninian will help him die without causing the rest of
us too much distress."

Drogo wondered if the spiced cider his wife was serving
might contain a strong percentage of brandy. Or if he should
just lock the meddlesome creature behind closed doors and let
her spin her tales to her ghost. He couldn't believe his sane,
sensible brother believed that faradiddle.

He *could* believe that Ninian was thoroughly convinced the
child was a girl and that she was saving Dunstan's life.

Standing, he reached for his discarded coat while Ewen
watched him nervously.

Drogo shrugged and adjusted his neckcloth. "The woman's
a witch, but not the way you think. Come along, let's make
Dunstan grovel some more. Take it from me, earls in this
family need to learn humility."

Thirty-three

NINIAŃ WATCHED WITH MORE ANGER THAN TREPIDATION
as her husband descended the staircase with his dark brows
curled into thunderclouds. She'd thought Ewen's early
departure from the festivities ominous, and Drogo's stony face
proved her instincts intact.

She would have been happy to discuss all this with him if
he hadn't ignored her all week. She could have returned to
her grandmother's house and raised cats for all the good it did
to be married to a man like him.

She would have been better off at her grandmother's house,
actually. At least there she wouldn't have footmen stationed at
all the stairs, preventing her use of them.

Rebelliously, she decided she didn't want to live alone. She
wanted the love and acceptance she'd never known, the love
and acceptance Drogo wouldn't give her.

Tickling her cat's belly, she watched resentfully as Drogo
inspected the chair Ewen had attached to the banister with
pulleys and slides. If Drogo meant to waste servants on
guarding the stairs, at least now they were usefully pulling her
up and down in Ewen's contraption.

Laughter exploded around the mistletoe as the baker caught
Lydie with her hands filled with pastry and planted a kiss
on her cheek. Pies and scones flew everywhere, and a mad
scramble ensued as the children chased after them.

She wouldn't let Drogo spoil their holiday fun. The village

was bleakest at this time of year with summer's bounty far behind them and the worst months of winter still ahead. She wondered if it might be possible to find a curate who would settle this far from town. The village needed a church and a clergyman.

She wasn't certain if her aunts would approve the use of Malcolm money for a church unless the clergyman was a Malcolm.

"Am I invited to this gathering?"

Drogo's presence struck Ninian with such forcefulness that she could feel him deep inside her, where her heart should be. She no longer needed to seek his emotions to know where he was. She could sense him in ways she could sense no one else. She didn't bother turning to look at him. She continued petting her cat.

"It's your house. I can scarcely forbid your appearance."

"Immensely practical." He pulled up a chair beside hers and watched as two children scrambled to hide behind their mother's skirts. "Do they see me as an ogre?"

"They've not met you before, and anything new can be terrifying, even for adults." She adjusted her skirts so the cat could depart now that she'd had her required share of attention.

"Where is Dunstan?"

"Not that you've spent much time asking since his arrival, but he's in the kitchen, turning the spit."

"In the kitchen? Why the devil isn't he out here instead of doing the work of servants?"

"I doubt that you'll understand or believe me if I told you, so don't worry yourself. He's keeping busy, and I've hidden all the alcohol."

"I am capable of understanding grief," he replied stiffly.

"Perhaps, but you're not inclined to share it. The rest of us poor mortals will simply have to wallow in our weaknesses while you pursue your more toplofty interests."

"I do my best to provide for my family. That's all anyone can ask."

"Certainly." She dipped her head in polite agreement, then beckoned to a small boy clutching a new whistle. "Come here, Matthew, show me what you have won."

Warily skirting Drogo, Matthew clambered into Ninian's lap from her other side, proudly displaying his latest acquisition. She felt Drogo stiffen beside her, and instinctively, without any thought, she dropped the boy into her husband's lap. "Show Lord Ives how you can play, Matthew."

To Ninian's amazement, Drogo froze. He showed no evidence of knowing how to hold the child, how to show interest in the boy, how to even speak with him. Wide-eyed, child and man stared at each other in uncertainty.

Drogo had spent half his life providing for his brothers, but he'd never learned how to *love* them.

Startled, Ninian leaned reassuringly against his arm and placed the whistle at Matthew's lips. He tooted on it briefly, then scrambled from Drogo's lap and ran for his mother.

"You have six brothers!" she exclaimed impatiently. "Did you never once hold or play with them?"

"They had mothers and nursemaids to hold them," he answered coldly, not looking at her. "It wasn't as if I were their father. I was no more than a boy myself."

The picture was too painfully clear. Denied his own mother at an early age, denied the company of the brothers closest to him, then denied the company of his youngest brothers by duty and their grief-stricken mother, Drogo had never been taught the affection and understanding of a close, loving family. He'd never been held by warm, grubby hands or cuddled a tot in his arms. What a horrible, horrible way to grow up. At least she'd had the village children to hold, and her smaller cousins, when they visited.

Tears rimmed her eyes as she pulled away from him and felt him relax. Even *she* made him nervous. He didn't know how to deal with an emotional female who wailed and railed and expected understanding. He could bed her and protect her, but he would never know how to love her. Or even recognize love for what it was. How wrong she'd been to think he could change.

"I'm sorry," she whispered.

He looked at her with curiosity. "For what?"

"For asking far more than you can give." Sadly, she pressed

a kiss to his cheek and rose to pull Lydie's daughter from under the banquet table.

It scarcely mattered that he didn't ask her to dance when the fiddlers struck up their next tune.

≈∞

"You'd best hurry up and have that babe so you can climb between your husband's sheets again. He's near snapped the heads off all the servants. Ewen just left for the minefields rather than tarry here longer."

Lydie efficiently snapped a fresh sheet across an empty cot in the infirmary as Ninian returned from seeing off their last patient.

"I asked Ewen to check on the water in the mines to see if he could locate the source of the damage. I'm afraid many of these babies are being born too early because of that water. It's never happened like this before."

Ninian wearily settled into a chair and let Lydie do the physical labor. They really needed to hire more help.

"He did not even try to kiss me good-bye," Lydie complained. "I must have lost all my looks. I should have joined Claudia and her sister in Paris so we can all grow old and decrepit together."

Ninian smiled at this vanity. "You are all of seventeen. You have a few more years before decrepitude sets in. And I warned Ewen that I would have him shot if he played light and loose with you. Have some respect for yourself, and men will respect you."

"And what good does respect do me?" Lydie grumbled as she tucked in the sheet. "They nod politely and keep their distance and go off to play with their flirts and marry the chits their mothers choose. And their mothers never choose the likes of me. Maybe Frenchmen are different. Claudia seems content with their attentions."

"Men are the same all over, only in France, you wouldn't be able to understand their flattery." Ninian finished jotting down her notes on the treatment she'd used for the last infant's cough and pulled herself up again. "If you are tired of living here, we'll think of something else you can do once the roads are open. But I need you for a little while longer, if you do not mind."

Lydie dropped the sheet and rushed to hug her. "I do not mean to sound so spiteful! I love it here. I love the babies, and I want to help with yours. I'm just mad at Ewen, and I'm tired of Drogo looking through me."

Ninian hugged her back. "You must hit an Ives over the head with a large stick to gain his notice. Find someone who will love and adore you and worship at your feet instead. Large sticks are burdensome."

"And Ives men are lousy at choosing idiots to worship," a sarcastic drawl intruded from the doorway.

Covered in dirt from his toils at the burn, Dunstan leaned against the door frame, arms crossed, looking surly and disheveled but not angry. Ninian had known he was there, but he was so lifeless these days, she'd hoped to raise his temper. He merely looked bored and irritated, but she sensed a questioning restlessness just beneath his surface. He'd not shown that much life through the inevitable queries following Celia's death.

She narrowed her eyes. "Is there aught we can do for you?"

"Besides strangle your husband? Probably not. But there's someone in the woods who requests your presence."

"You would rather Drogo strangled *me*? I swear, he has eyes in the back of his head, and if he catches me roaming the woods, he'll clasp me in chains."

"Rightly so, I daresay, but he must be blind in half those eyes you claim he possesses if he hasn't seen your visitor before this. I think I must insist that I escort you." Suspicion wrote itself easily across his expression.

Ninian threw up her hands. "You're all madmen! Every last black one of you. Why does this visitor not come here like any decent..." Her eyes grew wide as she realized what she'd just said. "Adonis?"

"Is that what he calls himself?" Dunstan straightened and frowned even darker. "Bastard is more like it. If it's a measure of the man's desperation that he talked to me, you'd best see what he wants."

Ninian halted Lydie's protest with a pat. "I am fine. He won't be far. Ives men may all have heads of stone, but they take care of their own."

"I didn't," Dunstan muttered as he took her arm and helped her out the door.

"Even Ives men have limits," Ninian answered callously. "Next time, choose a woman who can take care of herself, and you won't have to worry."

"There will be no next time."

"There is always a next time, if not in this life, then in the next. God may forgive your mistakes, but He expects you to learn from them." She leaned heavily on his arm, forcing him to adapt his stride to hers rather than pacing angrily ahead of her.

"Then God must have sent you to make Drogo pay for his failings," Dunstan grumbled. "How in hell have you hidden yon Adonis from him?"

"I haven't. Like any Ives, this one does as he pleases. You would prefer I turn him into a toad?"

"I'd say he already is a toad." Drawing his lips grimly shut, Dunstan said no more.

Ninian had to smile as they reached a clearing not too far from the clump of birch she'd been eyeing with respect and wistful plans for a garden. "Adonis" sprawled his lengthy masculine frame upon some rocks and moss, much as a fairy king would oversee his kingdom while awaiting his attendants to present themselves.

"I see your boot shows no sign of disrepair," she said with amusement as this strange Ives casually rose to his full height—not out of respect for her, she suspected, but to intimidate Dunstan, who glared at him ferociously. As much as these men frustrated her, she didn't know how she had lived without their ever-changing entertainment. Men were so much more fascinating to study than women.

"My gratitude to you for that, my lady." He bowed perfectly while still keeping a wary eye on her escort.

"If you had the proper respect for the countess at all, you would not force her outside in this weather but would come to the door like any civilized person."

Ninian was quite certain Dunstan carried no weapon but his fists, but those were enough. She shot Adonis a warning look as she held Dunstan's arm tighter. "I'll turn both of you into toads if you do not behave. Now, what is it that you wish to tell me?"

"Besides the fact that you've married into a family of self-destructive Bedlamites?" Legs akimbo, arms crossed over massive chest, he appeared to guard the forest as he regarded Dunstan's distrustful demeanor with amusement.

"I assume the insult applies to yourself as well?" Dunstan countered.

"It does, else I would not be here."

"Stop it, both of you! I am weary of this posturing. You may insult your heritage after I leave. For now, tell me what it is I need to know so I may go back to my fire."

Reminded of her delicate condition, they instantly retreated from battle positions, although neither looked particularly abashed about their neglect. Ives men didn't know the meaning of embarrassment.

"I apologize, but I thought you might like to know that your husband's new canal and the foundry he and his brother are building will directly affect the burn's fate. They give no thought to the land they mutilate, nor to the effects of that mutilation."

"That's a damned lot of—" Dunstan raised clenched fists but halted immediately as Ninian grabbed his arm and moaned. A frown of pain creased her forehead as she tried to stand upright.

"Ninian?" Panicking, he grabbed her waist and held her up.

With a frown of concern, Adonis stepped forward, but Ninian waved him off. Panting, she let the pain roll away and straightened.

"I thank you for the warning, sir. I have asked both Ewen and Drogo to look into the problem. It would be most helpful if you could guide them, since they do not take me seriously." Seeing Adonis stiffen and back away at this command, she waved it away. "I understand if you cannot. I might be a trifle… indisposed… for a while, but I shall do what I can."

"My apologies, my lady, I should not have disturbed you." Glancing to Dunstan with deep concern, he asked, "Shall I help carry the countess to the house?"

Hesitating, studying the stranger, Dunstan shook his head. "Drogo is in the village. Send someone for him. I think the child is early."

Ninian would have smiled as the brawny stranger looked petrified, then recovered sufficiently to nod and run off, but the next contraction was swift and fierce, and she barely managed to hold back a cry of pain.

The child was not only too soon, but too quick. Malcolms generally weren't that impatient.

Thirty-four

"YOU'D BEST HAVE SOMEONE PREPARE A FEW GUEST ROOMS," Ninian said absently as Drogo dashed into the suite, nearly breaking his neck on a cat wrapping around his ankles.

"They told me..." he started to say, but his otherwise-occupied wife waved away his interruption.

"My family has a tendency to descend without warning. I'm sorry, I should have informed you of that."

Why the *hell* wasn't she in bed? Damned women...

He may have made a mistake thinking he could overcome the Ives curse, but that didn't mean he couldn't take care of his son—and she would have him dropping on his head at birth. He approached her cautiously, hoping to capture her without protest.

She paced in front of a roaring fire in the master suite, wearing naught but a white ruffled shift. He couldn't help staring at her huge belly, expecting his son to fall to the floor any minute.

"You need to be in bed," he said firmly, uncertain whether it was safe to grab her and haul her off to bed.

She slapped a portable writing desk in his hands. "Better make a list. I don't want to forget anything. Adonis says that the canal and foundry are causing problems—"

"Adonis?" Drogo roared. Or thought he roared. He'd never roared before. Flinging the desk aside, he grabbed his obviously addlebrained wife, intent on placing her firmly in bed where she belonged, before she addled his son's brains as badly as hers.

She slipped from his grasp, caught the back of a chair, and began breathing deeply and chanting under her breath.

Terror nearly blew the top off his head as he recognized the pain tightening her suddenly pale cheeks. His curses riddled the room, but he didn't dare touch her until she released the chair.

Finally, she breathed easily and straightened. "Five minutes apart. We have time. Do take note, Drogo. I can't do everything."

She couldn't do everything?

"You damned well can't do *anything*!" he exploded. "You're supposed to be having a child!"

"There's that temper you don't have," she reminded him, pulling a heavily worn, leather-bound book from the shelves she'd filled from her grandmother's library. "I've never done this for myself. I'm sorry this is happening so soon. I'd counted on my aunts…"

She flipped the book open to a marked page. "You'll have to recite the welcoming ceremony. Perhaps I can say it with you, if you speak slowly enough."

"Welcoming ceremony?" he shouted. Instead of grabbing his maniac wife, he sank both hands in his hair and pulled to make certain he wasn't dreaming. Or having nightmares. Was she or was she not having the child? And if she was, why in hell wasn't she lying in bed, surrounded by women?

"We always welcome new Malcolms," she answered with a diffident shrug. "It seems to ease labor. I don't seem to be dealing very well with the pain. I had no idea." She gasped and bent double.

His roar brought the rest of the household running.

By the time they arrived, Drogo had Ninian on the damned bed, where she belonged. She clung to her book as she gasped and chanted and curled up in agony. He thought her pain would rip the heart and lungs out of his chest if it did not cease soon. Sweat poured down her brow by the time she straightened and handed him the book again.

"I've marked the place. You may start anytime. Your daughter is in a hurry."

"My *son*, madam, doesn't need any superstitious nonsense chanted over his head." Drogo turned and glared at Lydie, who stood in the doorway bearing a bowl of steaming water. "Help her!" he commanded.

"There is nothing I can do yet," Lydie said simply, setting the bowl down.

Ninian's face looked small and exceedingly fragile against the pillows. The enormous lump of her stomach seemed to fill the bed as Lydie covered her with a sheet. Drogo swallowed hard. Ninian was too small. Even he could see that. He had thought her healthy peasant material, but she was like a transparent wraith who would shatter at the merest loud noise. Bearing his son would kill her.

"Ninian," he whispered as she closed blue-veined lids over the lovely pools of her eyes. Her skin was like the finest glass as he brushed it with his fingers—and just as cool.

Her lids snapped open, and she smiled vaguely. "I'm afraid I won't be of much use for a while. Dunstan must tend the filter, if you would be so kind as to see it's done properly. The rains will start soon, and the legends say they will ruin the fields. Perhaps, if you send for Ewen—" She bit her lip and breathed deeply, her hand instinctively covering her lower abdomen.

"Damn the burn and Dunstan and all else. Just tell these confounded women what to do to deliver the child safely." Drogo was aware of several of the village women lingering in the shadows behind him. Dunstan was back there somewhere too. He couldn't concentrate on any of them.

She smiled faintly. "They can do nothing but wait, my lord, just like you. You would fare much better if you listened to me."

"Fine, I'll listen." Firmly, he drew up a chair and gestured for someone to bring him the abandoned writing desk. This was something physical he could handle.

He obediently jotted down careful notes as Ninian rambled. He had no idea what he was writing or what she was saying, but just the exercise of applying quill to paper was sufficient to calm them both, until she whimpered and arched and clenched the bedsheets. Then the quill and desk flew into the air as he grabbed for her.

Drogo moved to the bed and held her awkwardly, not knowing how to offer comfort but giving what he could as Ninian bit back screams and clutched his coat sleeves. Her agony seared through him, and he could not imagine how much worse it must be for her. His son was tearing her apart. He was killing her.

He would surely die if she did. That would leave Dunstan.

Frantically, Drogo sought his brother as the contraction subsided, and Lydie hurried forward to wipe Ninian's brow. He wasn't any good at this comforting business. He needed something solid to sink his teeth into.

Without a word, he rose from the bed and elbowed his way through the crowd of onlookers until he located Dunstan pacing in front of the fire in the sitting room.

"If the child dies, and Ninian with it, I'll have none other," he announced as Dunstan swirled to look at him.

Eyes empty, Dunstan said nothing.

Drogo wanted to shake him. "Someone has to look after our mothers, the estates, the younger ones. I'm counting on you. Don't let me down!" he ordered.

"You'll live to be a hundred," Dunstan replied bitterly. "Don't look at me."

"I'm killing her more surely than you ever killed Celia!" He didn't shout. He was certain he hadn't shouted. He paced, not daring to face his brother with his fear, not daring to meet the matching guilt in Dunstan's eyes.

The wind howled down the chimney, shooting embers across the hearth. Drogo grabbed the poker and shoved the coals deeper into the grate. "Dammit, I thought I had this thing fixed."

"Women have children all the time. She'll live," Dunstan answered crudely. "You'll have your heir, and someday, a spare. You won't need me."

Drogo ignored him, lost in his own discovery. "We don't

give a damn what we do to the women as long as we plant our seed. That's the curse of Ives. We plow and plant and walk away, content we've done our duty, when they're the ones who toil and strain and dutifully produce our offspring until the soil grows barren and wasted from the effort. We *kill* them," he announced vehemently. *If not in body, then in soul*, he added silently.

"We should rotate crops?" Dunstan asked. "Or fields? That's what our father did."

A scream echoed through the darkening chambers, bouncing off the walls. Terror pounding in his veins, Drogo swung on his heel and stormed back to the bed chamber.

Ninian lay serenely, eyes closed, apparently asleep.

Wildly, Drogo glanced around, but the scream still shattered the calm. No one seemed aware of it but him.

A movement from the bed drew his frantic gaze. She still breathed. She was alive.

The scream still pounded in his skull. Warily, he relaxed as Ninian opened her eyes and smiled, but she didn't seem to be looking at him. She seemed to be hearing a voice beyond his range, and terror took root in his heart. He didn't want her listening to voices from the grave. He wanted her *here*, with him. To his horror, Ninian suddenly gasped, drew up her legs, and grabbed her belly in agony. Her scream joined the one in his head.

Or in the walls. Someone was in the walls, tormenting her! The scene in front of him dwindled to a distance. He watched the women surround the bed, saw the golden waterfall of curls across the stack of pillows, knew it was his wife bearing down in agony to produce his child, but he was no longer with them. He stood apart, watching from afar.

The wind howled, the draperies blew inward in the draft, the fire in the grate leaped and danced, and the screams grew more insistent. Ninian writhed in pain, and he could do nothing.

Why didn't the screams stop? Why did they torment her like that? Couldn't they see she needed peace? She needed strength and calm, not hysterical shrieks.

Furious, Drogo strode past the bed and ripped the billowing draperies from their rod. If some prankster hid in here... Nothing but the black glass of nightfall. The reflection of candle flame flickered back at him.

Not here then. The chimney. Determinedly, he wielded the poker still in his hand. A solid wallop to the stone shook loose centuries of dried mortar. He slammed it again. Beat it from the outside in, from the inside out, beat it until the poker bent and broke and the shrieks screamed through every particle of his body.

A cloud of soot smashed into the burning grate, wafting outward into the room, coating everything in a film of black. Women shrieked and scolded and chattered like magpies. The ghost still wailed. He could *hear* it.

Dunstan grabbed his arm and tried to lead him away, but Drogo shook him off. Grabbing the kindling ax, he stalked the room, searching for the source of the haunting screams. Sarah had done this. She must have planted whistles in the walls.

Locating a knot in the paneling, he swung his ax and splintered the wood. No ghost would torment his wife. No legends would haunt his son's birth. He was master here. He took care of all that was his.

"He's gone mad," one of the maids whispered as Drogo swung the ax into the paneling until it popped and peeled from the wall.

"It's the ghost," another whispered. "She haunts this place still. They say she drives Ives men mad."

Behind her, in the shadows, Dunstan paled and looked grim. He watched as his eminently logical, sensible brother tore apart the suite of rooms in pursuit of something none could see or hear but him. All because of a woman. A Malcolm woman.

The frail figure in the bed seemed oblivious of the destruction. Overcoming another contraction, she reached for the book her husband had abandoned.

Even Dunstan heard the wind's howl in the chimney.

Frantically, Drogo swung around, searching for another target.

"Drogo," Ninian called softly. "Hurry, please. I need the words."

Words. Drogo blinked. He glanced blankly at the ax in his hands, then up at the havoc he had wreaked of the room. He absorbed Dunstan's expression of horror and confusion. Puzzled, he set aside the ax and turned in the direction of the voice calling him.

"The words, please," she whispered between pants, handing him the book as he returned to the bedside.

Words had no power. They were just... words. Drogo gazed blankly at the ancient page.

From memory, Ninian began to recite the first line.

Seeing the agony creasing her forehead once more, Drogo hurriedly offered her the next line, reading slowly so she could follow between breaths. She smiled and seemed to relax, even as she writhed with the pressure contracting and bearing down on her insides.

Together, they chanted the whole silly ritual of flowers and trees and birth and life. Drogo ignored it when she removed a pouch of herbs from her bodice and sprinkled the dust across the covers. He kept the pace of the chant for as long as it seemed to ease her.

Sitting on the bed facing her, his back to the women, he read and chanted in the flickering lamplight, blocking out the whistling wind and howling chimney and the screams echoing in his mind. Ninian reached out her hand, and he held it, and the screams dropped into the distance. Squeezing soft fingers in his, he read louder.

"Thank you," she murmured, blue eyes opening and focusing steadily on his face—just before she raised her knees and groaned so deep, he swore the sound tore from the bowels of the earth.

"Here it comes," Lydie shouted excitedly. "Gently now. Bear harder, Ninian."

Hair matted and wet with perspiration, straining into the pain, Ninian didn't tear her gaze from Drogo's.

Heart in his mouth, he clasped her hand with both of his and willed her his strength, pouring everything in his power into her slender fingers. He could swear she smiled broader through her tears.

"I love you, Drogo."

The words whispered through him even as Ninian's face crumpled with pain and her scream split the air.

She'd said them once before, but he'd not listened. He'd not believed. He couldn't believe she'd said them again, not after all he'd done to her.

Distance. He was supposed to maintain his distance. He should be downstairs, getting drunk, waiting for the women to bring him the announcement of his child's birth. What the hell was he doing here, hearing words he'd never wanted?

An infant's weak cry filled the silence following Ninian's collapse.

She lay so still. Worriedly, Drogo watched for the blink of an eyelash, the restless rise of her breast.

Ninian, please, he pleaded inside his head, where none could hear but himself. He couldn't show his weakness, but it was there, growing wider and deeper and clawing with terror at his rib cage. *Ninian, don't leave me alone.*

Her eyelids moved, and he wept, great heaving sobs that shook his whole body.

He laid his head down on her breasts and cried like the babe she'd just borne as her hand squeezed his.

"Alana," she breathed in satisfaction next to his ear.

Light poured through him. The screams subsided and serenity filled him with a strength he'd never known, not physical strength, but something far different as he lifted his head and looked into shining blue eyes. "Alan," he declared firmly, grasping the invisible connection between them and holding on for all he was worth. "No mere slip of a girl could make that roar."

She studied him for a moment, then turned her gaze wonderingly to the babe Lydie held out. The roars emanating from the bundle certainly had a masculine edge to them.

"Your son, my lady," Lydie announced proudly, laying the squalling, kicking infant in Ninian's arms.

Obviously stunned but smiling with astonished pride, Ninian offered up the black-haired babe for Drogo's admiration.

As he daringly reached to push back a blanket edge for a better look, she murmured tauntingly, "He doesn't have a temper either, my lord."

Drogo's grin nearly split his face.

Thirty-five

"YOU HAVE YOUR HEIR, DROGO," DUNSTAN PRONOUNCED glumly, inspecting the babe in Ninian's arms the next day. "With that hair, there's no doubt he's an Ives."

"Had he been a girl, there would have been no doubt," Drogo replied stoutly, experimentally brushing a black curl.

Ninian rolled her eyes at this exercise in competition. "You should be glad he's not a Malcolm for all Malcolms are…" She blinked, bit back the word "witch," and stared at her son in curiosity. "…are fair," she amended.

Surely…? She had no way of knowing. A Malcolm had never carried a son. Of course, within living memory, no Malcolm had married an Ives. Was this the true foundation of the tales? If a Malcolm bore an Ives male, was there some danger he had Malcolm gifts?

An Ives witch? Or did one call them warlocks?

Oh my. Ninian studied rosebud lips sucking hungrily at a chubby fist, his puckered up face and closed eyes. Could he read emotions as she did? Was he sensitive to auras, like Christina? How would she tell?

She'd felt the ghost's gratitude and relief the night of Alan's birth, but what did that tell her?

She glanced up at Drogo, who had not stopped smiling since the child's birth. *He* had no doubts about his son, that was certain. He had what he thought he wanted. Let him deal with it.

She held their son out for him to take. "I'm tired," she said with her best dimpled smile. "You hold him."

She saw the panic in his eyes, the reluctance as he looked down at the helpless infant squirming in the blankets. Other women might assume that men had only one part to play in the creating and raising of a child, but she had no such compunctions. He wanted a child, he could care for it as well as she.

"Just put your arms out," she ordered. "Put a hand under his head."

With Dunstan as amused audience, Drogo could do no less. Awkwardly, he tried to wrap his arms around the bundle and manage his son's floppy head at the same time. Startled by the change in position, Alan whimpered in protest.

Frantically, Drogo tried to press the babe back in Ninian's arms. "He wants you."

"He doesn't know what he wants." Impatiently, she adjusted the blankets but refused to take him back. "We must teach him to want you as well. He's an *Ives*, remember?" she asked maliciously.

The infant kicked the blanket from his feet, and Drogo hastily attempted to adjust it. Instead, tiny pink toes emerged from a long linen gown, thrashing in freedom.

"I can't do this," Drogo muttered, balancing a head of dark curls and tugging at gown and blanket while juggling the whole awkward bundle without dropping it. "I have to take care of..."

"Your son," Dunstan intruded, watching over his brother's shoulder with a hint of amusement. "He's big. He'll be climbing the castle ramparts in no time. You can't ask Ninian to follow him."

Dunstan turned to Ninian. "You have done a fine job, Countess. I congratulate you. Now, I must be on my way."

"No!" she said sharply, catching him by surprise. "Not until the village's water is safe. None of you have given Drogo time to live his own life. You *owe* him."

Startled, both brothers stared. She glared right back. She might be half their size and nowhere as formidable, but by the goddess, she would have her way in this.

Drogo succeeded in balancing his son's head in the crook of his elbow while tugging the blanket to cover his tiny feet. He raised questioning eyebrows at brother and wife but opted to leave the argument to them. He had his hands full already.

"Ewen is already at the mine. I'm working the filter. Once we save the water—providing such a thing is possible—I suppose there is still another task I must perform to fill this never-ending debt?" Dunstan asked dryly.

"If it's punishment you want, then I think I'm best able to mete it out," she agreed. "Why should you be allowed to end your suffering when Celia's family must live with their grief for the rest of their lives? And what of her lover's family? Did he leave children or siblings who will go hungry without his support? Have you even thought to find out?"

Dunstan appeared too stunned to answer. In another instant, he would be too angry. Ninian pressed on. "Your debt is so enormous you cannot begin to fill it should you live a hundred years. An *honorable* man would attempt to pay his debts."

Fury blazed in Dunstan's dark eyes. The pain and guilt still swamped him, but plain black Ives fury inundated his soul. "I thought you meant to *help* me, my lady." He dragged the charm bag from his neck and flung it at her. "That's the last time I'll believe any woman." He stormed out, slamming the door.

Alan wailed. Drogo hurriedly attempted to return him to Ninian.

Stubbornly, she crossed her arms over her breasts. "Dunstan is a grown man and will do as he wishes, no matter how much you interfere. He is beyond your help. Your *son*, however, needs you. It's your choice."

Dumfounded, Drogo looked from her, to the door, to the helpless infant whimpering in his arms. Defeat rose in his eyes as he hugged his son closer to his chest.

"We may both regret this," he warned.

"I doubt any of us lead lives without regret." Wearily, Ninian rested her head against the pillow and prayed.

Drogo sat before the fire, rocking his son and watching his wife sleep. *His* son. *His* wife.

He wanted to find that distance again, that undisturbed plane where he could look down on his possessions and responsibilities and manipulate them like men on a chess board. The child in his arms prevented it.

He studied Alan's sleeping features. The babe had already found his thumb and sucked on it dreamily. Round baby cheeks gave no evidence of the square man's jaw he would someday possess, but the pugnacious chin hinted of a strong streak of Ives temperament.

Somehow, he had to lead this child into adulthood, teach him responsibility and duty, steer him clear of life's perils and pitfalls, as he had not his brother.

He'd not had the raising of Dunstan. He couldn't shoulder the blame for that, as much as he would have, if he could. He should have done something...

Ninian stirred against the pillows, drawing his gaze eagerly to her and away from his morbid thoughts. Since he'd torn the draperies from the window, moonlight streamed across the bed, catching in golden curls and illuminating translucent features. He no longer knew what to make of her—not that he ever really had.

He'd tried to analyze her as he'd tried to analyze the problem with the burn, with equally dismal results. He'd tried to think of her as a mathematical calculation where two plus two gave him four every time, but that hadn't worked either. Ninian's moods guided her behavior as erratically as the winds blew.

How could he remain distant from a son who needed his constant guidance and a wife who demanded attention with just her presence?

He couldn't, not and keep them by his side, leastways.

And he didn't want them out of his sight.

At least he recognized the impossibility of tying them to him. Ninian had accused him of controlling his family, and she was right. He felt much less helpless when he could control their behavior with the scratch of a pen quill on a banknote.

He couldn't control Ninian that way, or his son. They would do as they willed, with no thought to him.

Helplessness ate at his soul. He couldn't bear it. He didn't want to leave Ninian here, but he couldn't carry out his responsibilities unless he was in London. How could he tie her to him so she would follow?

As if she heard the panic of his thoughts, Ninian opened her eyes and smiled sleepily at him, striking a blow to his heart from which he would never recover.

He couldn't leave her. He was doomed.

❧

"You look as if you've swallowed a lemon, my lord," Ninian teased as Drogo appeared beside the bed, carrying their whimpering son.

"The brat has loaded his napkin and none of your nursemaids have appeared to take care of it," he grumbled, handing her the soggy bundle.

"I could teach you," she offered. He'd been the kindest, most considerate man in the world this past month, but he'd categorically refused to change dirty nappies.

He handed her a dry cloth and poured warm water into a bowl but stepped back in disgust at her offer. "Not a chance, madam. I'll drag someone up here by the hair of their head first."

She'd forgive him this one weakness. Alan kicked and squalled and doused everyone in sight when displeased, and hunger and dirty nappies displeased him. Skillfully, she caught flailing legs and rearranged his clothing to her satisfaction.

"Master Alan needs to learn patience," she observed once the infant was clean and dry and sucking greedily at her breast.

"Lord Alan," Drogo corrected. At her questioning look, he explained. "The eldest son of an earl bears the courtesy title of 'lord.' If my title included a viscountcy, then he would be Lord Wystan, but I have two earldoms instead."

Ninian sniffed. "He has as much chance of lordliness as your brothers. Crackbrained rogues, the lot of you." She glanced anxiously at the window. "Is it still snowing?"

Tearing his gaze from the sight of her bared breast, Drogo walked restlessly to the window. "No, it's stopped, but none will come in or out for a while, I wager."

She recognized his male restlessness. He'd managed to submerge it in his work, but she'd caught him looking at her with hunger more than once these past weeks. She was grateful he had not taken another woman to his bed as many men did, but they still had more than a few problems to sort out. She would have to be a little more cautious before surrendering herself this time, or she would end up like Drogo's mother—perpetually burdened with children and no husband to show for it.

"Dunstan?" she inquired softly.

"He can't leave any more than your family can arrive. He's sleeping it off with the horses right now. It seems he's found a drinking partner somewhere." He shrugged and returned to the bed.

Drogo's unabashed stare heated her flesh, and Ninian suspected he knew it. The makings of a smile curled his mouth as she tried to adjust her bodice more modestly.

"You cannot hide what nature gave you," he noted with satisfaction as he sprawled in the chair beside the bed.

"It did not need to give me quite so much," Ninian muttered.

He was in shirtsleeves and waistcoat, with his shirt unfastened to reveal the strong column of his throat. Ninian let her gaze drift to the flap of his breeches and swallowed at the sight of the bulge there. His gaze mocked hers as she hastily returned it to his face.

"Should I say the same?" he asked with a straight face. "I can scarce hide that I miss sharing your bed."

"You are the one who moved out of it," she said tartly, switching Alan to her other breast despite his sleepy protest. "Perhaps it's best left that way. I would not burden you with any further *responsibility*."

The mocking light left his eyes. "And I would not use you for my convenience and kill you with the agonies of childbirth. I can keep my breeches fastened."

Oh dear. When he said things like that, it reminded her

of how much she loved him, no matter how exasperating, calculating, or plain old muleheaded he could be. She loved the man behind the cold demeanor, the vulnerable man who must be taught to hold the child he adored.

"Fastened for another month, at least," she agreed with a smile intended to hold him captive. She couldn't deny him. Perhaps he couldn't love her in the same body-and-soul manner she loved him, but in his own way, he cared for her. Perhaps it was a Malcolm gift to love this deeply and thoroughly, and she shouldn't expect others to return it. She just didn't think he would ever—all evidence to the contrary— believe she had abilities beyond the natural. It simply wasn't within the limits of his scientific mind, and he hadn't love enough to believe what he couldn't see.

He took a deep breath and tore his gaze away from her to studiously watch the fire. "A month. By then, you'll be well enough to travel?"

She should have seen that coming. "It will be March. The roads will be swamps."

He lifted one curled eyebrow in her direction. "If you can clear the weather to travel to Wystan, you can clear it to go the other way."

He had her there, even though he mocked her. Had the earlier fair weather been coincidence, or had she really caused it? And could she do it again, for his sake and not her own? How could she expect him to believe in her if she continued doubting herself?

Grandmother had said she belonged in Wystan, that the people needed her here. She needed to be needed. The lonely child within her still craved acceptance.

Of course, if Drogo needed her...

His tears at Alan's birth had given her hope, opened her heart in eagerness—although what she hoped of an Ives, she didn't know. They were immensely self-sufficient men who prided themselves more on conquest and accomplishment than anything so ephemeral as love. She only had love to offer. Could he accept that?

As she eased Alan from her breast and buttoned her bodice,

she eyed her husband's broad shoulders casually slouched against the chair back, the long, muscled limbs sprawled across the carpet, and doubted the likelihood of Drogo ever needing anything. His noble lordship already had it all—including her.

Thirty-six

"SOMETHING'S NOT RIGHT." NINIAN SAT UP IN BED AND STARED worriedly at the fire crackling in the grate.

"Dunstan is drunk in his room," Drogo replied calmly, trying to focus his telescope in the direction of his planet from the window of the master suite. He didn't like leaving Ninian and his son alone long enough to go to his tower.

"Not Dunstan. It's the ghost; I'm sure of it. She can no longer speak to me, but I *hear* her."

He'd heard her once, too. Uncomfortable with that thought, Drogo relinquished his telescope to turn his attention to his easily excitable wife. "When did she stop speaking?" he asked, humoring her.

She looked embarrassed. "The only time she spoke was before we…" She gestured helplessly. "Before we made love the first time."

He grinned at her embarrassment and rose to check on their sleeping son in his cradle. "You mean, before we threw ourselves at each other in an excess of lust?"

"That, too," she answered huffily, tilting her head to listen to the wind. "Is it still raining?"

He used to look at her in profound befuddlement when she disappeared into that strange world inside her head, but now it was with as much amusement as confusion when he recognized the signs. "It is. The snow is almost melted. We are sitting on a great bog."

Ewen had rode in from the mine with the snow melt, before the rains began. He was in the library, busy drawing grand plans for improvements in the mine, while Dunstan continued to drink himself into a stupor every night. Drogo needed to set changes in motion, then return for the opening of Parliament.

And all he could think was... It was late March. How much longer before he could share his wife's bed? He admired the glint of firelight on Ninian's fair skin. Alan slept through the night now, abandoning those lovely breasts for a purpose, Drogo was certain. Surely, it was his turn.

She didn't seem ready to fall on him in a fit of lust but continued listening to the wind. "The rains don't usually come this early. I know the legends said we'd cause a flood, but I've been very careful. I *know* I haven't done this."

Drogo smiled at this foolishness. "Of course you haven't. You may have a few instincts stronger than normal, but the wind and the clouds cause the rain."

"Actually, I think I can." She sat demurely with hands in her blanket-covered lap as she listened to the wail of the chimney.

Prepared to be patient with his wife's idiosyncrasies, Drogo smiled and started to say something witty, but even as he lifted his hand to stroke her hair, he realized she wasn't with him.

Damn! He glanced down at her unfocused gaze, waved a hand in front of her face, and shook his head when she didn't respond. He *knew* she wasn't insane. Slightly addled, maybe, but a powerful brain churned behind that innocent-miss expression of hers.

"Ninian, stop that this instant!" he ordered. He wouldn't let the little twit frighten him. He'd damned well stand between her and the rest of the world, if necessary, but he sure as hell wouldn't let her terrorize him in return. Someone around here had to have a little sense.

The chimney stopped whistling, and the fire crackled more warmly. The room actually heated to a comfortable temperature as the drafts died.

In a blink of an eye, she was back with him, smiling. "That's better."

"I thought you said something was wrong," he said with suspicion. He certainly wouldn't forget anytime soon the last time she'd told him that. The last he'd heard, the authorities had no evidence with which to charge Dunstan with his wife's death.

She turned solemn. "Something *is* wrong. The burn is rising from the melting snow, and we'll have a flood if the rain doesn't stop. I can talk to the wind, but the rain doesn't hear me. If only my aunts would arrive…"

He sighed in exasperation and leaned over to kiss her mouth closed. He'd do anything for her, except become as crazy as she was.

Her mouth warmed hungrily beneath his, but she still didn't invite him into her bed.

⁓

"Water's out of its banks," Dunstan declared blearily, staggering into the breakfast room where Drogo and Ninian dined.

"Oh, dear." Ninian dropped her spoon and hastened to stand up. "And it's still raining. We'll have to hurry. Dunstan, do you think you can hitch up the wagon? We need to carry out the elders first."

Drogo jumped up when she did. "Wait a minute…"

Dunstan shook his head. "Can't. There's sickness. The babe will catch it."

"Why didn't someone tell me?" Frantic, Ninian ran for the door.

Drogo caught her by the waist and hauled her back. "Because we didn't want the contagion to spread to you. You are Alan's only source of nourishment."

She hesitated, looking from one towering man to the other. She couldn't lose Alan or this fascinating male family who accepted her and needed her more than they knew. But the village… It was her job to protect it. Grandmother had said so.

"If I cannot go, you must," she whispered. What if they wouldn't? What if these Ives men laughed her off as most people would? She couldn't desert the village. She couldn't harm Alan. Torn, she watched them with a prayer in her heart.

Dunstan scowled. "What the hell can I do?"

That was a start. "Carry the sick ones to my grandmother's house. It's on high ground."

Drogo's arm tensed around her waist. "I won't let you go. I can't risk it."

She turned and looked into his stern-jawed face. She thought she saw fear flicker behind his eyes. "You must tell me their symptoms, observe them closely, *listen*."

She was asking the impossible of him. Whether he realized it or not, Drogo commanded from an ivory tower while she was the one who walked among his family and tenants, listening. He didn't know how to hear the pain and sorrow behind brave words. He merely saw problems and looked for solutions.

"You are to stay here," he half-ordered, half-questioned, watching her warily.

"If you will be my eyes and ears," she agreed.

"If there's contagion, no one else must leave the castle, or they cannot come back."

She nodded, biting her lip. "Someone must tell me what you've found so I know what cures to use."

"I will write down all that I find and pass it to you through a window."

This was insane. She knew it was. She needed to be with her people.

And she needed to be with Drogo's son. No wonder the ghost quit speaking to her.

Nodding at the inevitability, she agreed. "But if the water continues rising, the village will not be safe," she reminded them.

"One thing at a time, moonchild. Gather up your linens and bedding and whichever of the servants you trust to follow orders. We will do what we can."

❧

What they could do wasn't enough. The burn spilled over its banks under a steady fall of rain. Drogo reported her grandmother's house filled to overflowing with the sick. Ninian's potions, plasters, and prayers weren't enough.

When Drogo appeared to tell her all of Mary's children were sick, Ninian resolutely reached for her herb pouch and began choosing the contents.

Outside the conservatory windows, Drogo narrowed his eyes. "What do you think you are doing?"

"I thought the herbs healed," she yelled back. She didn't have time for the nicety of pen and paper. "But maybe it's not the herbs. Maybe they really need *me*."

"That's ridiculous." He flung open the door and barred the way. "All of London's physicians could not cure this."

"All of London's physicians are quacks." She reached for a pot on a high shelf. She wished she had the agrimony from the burn. It was so much better for fever.

"I've ordered up the carriage to take you and Alan back to London. You'll be safe there." Like a mountain, he would not be moved.

"Lydie is still nursing her daughter. She can nurse Alan too. We can wean him to cow's milk." She swung and glared at him. "Would you leave your brothers if they were ill?"

"They're not your brothers, dammit!" Drogo roared. "You're my wife, mother of my son, and I will not let you risk your life for people who turned their backs on you!"

They had at that. They'd pushed her to the outside, never accepted her, and turned their backs when she needed them. She hadn't accepted herself either. She certainly couldn't expect those less knowledgeable in Malcolm ways to understand what she hadn't. It no longer mattered if they accepted her. All she really needed was to accept herself.

Smiling, she stood on tiptoe and pressed a kiss to her husband's stubbly cheek. He was such a handsome man, even when he was scowling ferociously at her. She wanted back in his bed. It was time. She didn't dare tell him that now, though. "They did not have the power to help me as I have the power to help them. You cannot stop me, Drogo. This is who I am. If you cannot accept that, you are no better than they are."

Panic bubbled through Drogo's blood as he watched Ninian calmly packing her bags and pouches, sorting through bits of dead leaves and grass as if they were of as vast importance as the infant sleeping in his cradle.

She couldn't turn her back on family. She couldn't just walk away and leave him.

"What of Dunstan?" he demanded as the panic bubbled wilder. He hadn't realized until then that he'd relied on her wisdom to keep his brother alive.

"He's a grown man," she said unsympathetically, reaching for her cloak. "I cannot stop him any more than you can if he chooses to waste his life. Only he can make that decision. But if you would make him feel useful, have him find Adonis. I'm convinced the water in the burn is responsible for this illness."

She wrapped the cloak around her and waited for him to move from the door.

She was small and helpless, and he couldn't let her out in the mud and rain and subject her to the depredations of the fever terrorizing the town. He must protect her, as he protected all that was his.

The burden of that responsibility overwhelmed him. He would have to throw her over his shoulder and tie her up and heave her into a carriage, and she would never speak to him again.

"Please, Ninian," he asked desperately, appealing to the intelligence he knew she harbored behind her crackbrained notions. "Don't you see I can't let you risk yourself?"

Unexpectedly, she wrapped her arms around his waist and rested her head against his chest. "I love you for who you are, Drogo. I love you for wanting to take care of us all. But at some point, you have to love us enough to let us do what we think best. You cannot think and act for all of us forever."

He clutched her close and swore he would do that so long as he was surrounded by fools and lunatics.

But they weren't, he knew. Ninian could produce results he couldn't comprehend. Dunstan was as strong and intelligent and reliable as Drogo himself. Ewen might be careless with money, but he had a brilliant mind. None of them were fools or lunatics. None of them were children any longer.

"I don't want to lose you," he whispered into her hair,

offering her the one fear that terrified him most, praying she didn't hear his vulnerability.

"You may regret that someday when we have half a dozen Malcolm and Ives rearranging the parapets and blowing up the kitchen." She nestled closer into his arms. "Or I could always promise to come back and haunt you should I die. There are no guarantees, Drogo. We must do our best with what little knowledge we have."

"Why couldn't we do it quietly in some peaceful corner of the world where there are no brothers or sick villagers or flooding streams?" he asked mournfully.

She laughed. "Or witchy aunts and cousins. The roads are causing difficulty, but they're on their way, Drogo. Don't say I didn't warn you."

He wasn't about to consider the onset of another pestilence. "Is there nothing you can do to protect yourself from the contagion?"

She shrugged and released him. "Stay away from the water, I suspect. But if the burn is flooding, then the wells may be contaminated too. I don't know how such things work."

The water. He could very well do something about the damned water. With something factual he could grasp, Drogo swung his stubborn wife into his arms and carried her through the swamp of the yard to the waiting carriage.

"I will fix it," he promised. "If I have to blow up the whole damned mine, I will fix it."

By tomorrow night, he'd have her in his bed, and the planets would return to rotating around the sun again.

Thirty-seven

"WHERE'S NINIAN?" A YOUNG VOICE CRIED FROM THE FRONT entrance of the castle.

"Where's Alan?" an older one called no less eagerly as its owner swept into the great hall trailing an assortment of silks and scarves.

Lydie stared in amazement from the staircase as an entourage of fair and chattering Malcolms streamed across the threshold, followed by a collection of servants bearing trunks, carpetbags, and various and assorted oddments whose purpose Lydie could not immediately discern.

"Where's Drogo and those fascinating brothers of his?" another feminine voice purred as an enchantingly beautiful Malcolm in full powdered wig drifted into the room to admire a tapestry.

Lydie had accepted her place as nursemaid to the infants, understanding that Ninian's talents and knowledge were far greater than her own. She hadn't complained when all the servants, almost to a man, had followed either Ninian or Drogo to their assigned tasks. But she did rather object to playing the part of lowly housemaid to a swarm of chattering females.

She glanced ruefully at her woolen gown unadorned with panniers or petticoats and decided she'd followed Ninian too far down the path of rural dishabille.

"Hello, I'm Lady Elizabeth, Ninian's companion." That sounded innocuous enough. Using the poise with which she'd descended many a grand stairway, she glided down this one. "I'm so sorry that no one is here to greet you. You have come at just the wrong time. There is illness…"

The small, gray-haired lady trailing scarves hurried forward. "Yes, yes, we know. We have come at just the *right* time. But first, show us dear, darling Alan. An Ives! It is beyond imagining. We've never had a male before. Be a dear…"

As they swept her up the stairs again, Lydie glanced over her shoulder at a familiar greeting from below.

"Lead the way, Lydie," Sarah cried cheerfully from the back of the pack. "We're about to find out how it's *really* done!"

How *what* was really done? Lydie wondered, before she was forced into the current of chattering excitement and lost her ability to think of anything at all.

~

Ninian laughed as kegs of ale rolled off the farm cart and through the rose-covered gate of her granny's garden. Two milk cows mooed loudly from their tethers at the back of the cart. They must have emptied the castle cellars. Drogo had solved the water problem—for now.

"They'll all be drunk," Mary whispered in puzzlement from behind her.

"Better drunk than dead," Ninian answered cheerfully, hurrying back to the makeshift hospital. "No one drinks water until Drogo has found the solution."

"But it's been a year and no one has found a solution," Mary protested, hurrying after her. "We haven't even figured out the *problem* yet."

"But that's what Ives are good for." Cheered by this evidence that Drogo finally understood that he wasn't an island all alone, Ninian returned to mixing the elixir that seemed to work best on the children. "They're not devils. They're geniuses. One cannot expect geniuses to think the way others do."

"No, I suppose not," Mary said doubtfully, reaching for the pot Ninian indicated. "But why haven't these geniuses done something sooner?"

"Because they're idiots." Still smiling, Ninian added a squeeze of lemon, sniffed the result, and nodded approval. At Mary's puzzled expression, she dimpled. "Men cannot be smart about everything. Ives are idiots about people and geniuses about things. Adonis will explain it. Tell me when he arrives."

She swept off, not hearing Mary's weak "Adonis?"

❧

"The water pumped from the mine must run off into that stream down there." Dunstan gestured to a valley farther down the hill where a stream lapped over the banks.

As another load of coal rumbled from the mine's black hole, Dunstan, Drogo, and Ewen stood on a hill opposite, watching the operation as the rain drizzled around them.

"I suppose closing the mine isn't an option?" Ewen asked.

"It would bankrupt half the countryside, put men out of work, and leave their families to starve," Drogo replied absently, studying the distance from mines to stream.

His particular talent was math and finance, talents he'd developed to save his family from ruin. He might waste a few spare hours on the impractical study of the stars, but he knew nothing of mechanical operations. He couldn't see how a mine miles distant from a village could cause disease.

"A holding pool," Ewen suggested. "An earth barrier to hold the mine runoff, prevent it from reaching the stream…"

"That could take months," Dunstan objected, showing some sign of interest for the first time since the holidays. "You would need men, shovels…"

The terrain here was barren—bald hill after hill, giving the feeling of looking into forever. The dark figure traipsing along the distant stream could easily be seen from any rise. Drogo watched the confident stride with growing suspicion.

Abruptly leaving his brothers to argue the mechanics of the problem, Drogo strode downhill in the direction of the stream. He had a right to know.

The other man had to have seen him coming, but he stuck to his intended path. With cold gray rain obscuring the landscape and a fog rising off the water, Drogo strode determinedly in a path intersecting with the stranger's.

The newcomer evinced no surprise as Drogo appeared in front of him. Shoving his rough, ungloved hands into his coat pockets, slouching his tricorn hat so the water ran away from his face, he waited for Drogo to speak.

"Adonis, I presume?" he asked dryly.

The other man bent his head in what could have been agreement. "The Earl of Ives and Wystan?" he countered.

"The same. My wife claims you can tell us the origin of the burn's problem."

"Ives' machinations and Malcolm foolishness," he replied without hesitation. "Your wife's family has arrived. Make no mistake, they can cause as much chaos as yon mine has wreaked."

"Shall we go somewhere drier to discuss this?" Drogo didn't want to hear more superstitious fancy, but he damned well wanted to know more about this man who looked so much like himself.

The larger man regarded him warily. "You haven't much time for discussion. The flood will reach the castle walls soon. And the witches are brewing a storm. They have yet to learn that just the diversion of a whisper of wind can disturb nature's balance. The loss of one small butterfly can start a chain of events reducing a village to sticks."

The castle. And Alan. Panic licked along Drogo's veins, but he was growing accustomed to it now. He panicked when he could not control events, but as Ninian had warned, he could only control so much. He must learn just how much was his to control.

"How do you know so much about Malcolms?" It wasn't an idle question. He could see the stamp of Ives on the man's features, but no Ives he knew of had ever consorted with Malcolms in recent memory. Until him.

The other man looked as if he would refuse to answer, then shrugged. "My mother is one. Are you in this with me, or not?"

Another Malcolm and Ives offspring, one who had evidently survived his unusual childhood, and in *this* generation, not a past one. Why didn't the Malcolm women know of this anomaly? For Alan's sake, he needed to know more.

He needed to save Ninian and his son first.

Drogo studied the stranger's open expression carefully, then nodded, accepting what he didn't have time to thoroughly investigate. He needed help, and this man offered it. "Come meet my brothers. We're in this together."

✧

"We've driven the sheep to the highest shelters we can find, but the wind is picking up. They hate wind. And if it starts to thunder..."

Nate's father didn't have to finish the sentence. This was a farming community. Everyone knew the erratic temperament of sheep. They'd dive off the nearest cliff if frightened enough.

Ninian peeked out the window. Water ran down the road in front of the rose gate. Wind tossed and turned the leafless limbs of the trees. This was even worse than the night she and Drogo had first made love. But Drogo wasn't here, so it couldn't be their fault. It was just some fluke of nature.

"My lady, your family has arrived," a soaked messenger shouted, emerging from the kitchen but unable to navigate the crowded parlor of pallets, children, and parents.

Every head in the room turned. Embarrassed, the messenger made a show of doffing his dripping slicker and hat. Silence suddenly reigned, and Ninian knew all eyes had turned to her.

The wind howled, the rain increased, the flood waters rose higher, and her family had arrived. The villagers needed no more than two and two to reach four, and she couldn't be certain that they weren't right, though it wasn't as if her aunts *intended* harm.

She had no way of knowing how the illness spread, if she could carry it to the castle or if the water or something else beyond her knowledge caused it. She dearly wished to speak with whichever of her aunts had arrived, but she didn't dare risk Alan or her family.

"Why couldn't God have made me a mind reader?" she grumbled. "At least that would have been useful."

"Healing is useful," Mary pointed out. "The children are much better now that you are here."

They did seem better, but Ninian saw no proof that her gifts were responsible. She was better organized, more knowledgeable, and simply noticed symptoms better than most. If she could but teach Lydie the same, she would do as well.

That's what she preferred to believe, just as she preferred believing her family really did not affect the weather, that her meager prayers to the wind did no more than make her feel better. Perhaps she would never truly know, but so long as people *believed* she could help, they needed her. Perhaps faith counted most.

Giving up any hope of seeing her family soon, Ninian knelt beside the next child in line, lifted the toddler into her arms for a hug, and persuaded a mug of sweetened willow water into her. Her breasts ached with milk, but she had a potion for that too. She just hated the idea of giving up Alan's feeding so soon.

"The water's across the road!" someone shouted several hours later as the wind continued to howl and the rain poured.

"My chicken coop!" Alice wailed as she watched the river of water rising below.

What the devil was her family doing? If they couldn't stop the rain, then they needed to help her with the sick and leave the weather alone.

Not that she'd noticed any of them with a talent for healing. Reading auras and painting portraits was just as useless as recognizing the fears and anxieties mounting around her as swiftly as the flood water.

❦

"What do you mean, we can stop the flow with gunpowder!" Drogo shouted.

"Well, he's right." Ewen scribbled a quick calculation and sketch on the battered flyleaf he'd torn from a book in his pocket. "A keg or two, at just the right angle, and we can bring a good part of that hillside down. We'd have to pump—"

"A keg or two? Where the devil would we get a keg or

two, providing we're insane enough to attempt it?" From the door of the cramped mine foreman's cabin, Drogo glared at the misty gray rain covering the countryside. He needed to go back to Ninian. And Alan. He'd take them to London and safety, out of this world of lunacy that seemed to have infected even his brothers.

"I can find it," Adonis declared without inflection.

"He's Scots," Dunstan commented, with seeming irrelevancy.

Ewen and Drogo turned to stare at their taciturn brother. The stranger merely tipped his chair back and produced a pipe from his pocket, tapping it on the table to clean it before reaching for the tobacco in his other pocket.

Ever curious, Ewen asked the less obvious question. "How do you know?"

Dunstan shrugged and took a gulp of ale. "Accent. English tutor, apparently, but definitely Scots underneath the polish. One of the tenants has a Scots wife."

"What the devil has that got to do with the way the world turns?" Drogo asked acidly. He didn't even know who the damned stranger *was*. His national origins were of small concern.

"If you want to trust a Scot with gunpowder, you're more a bedlamite than your wife. What do we know of him, anyway?"

The stranger crossed his arms over his chest and raised a questioning eyebrow, as if he, too, were interested in the answer.

"Ninian trusts him. She said he had the answers." Even as he said it, Drogo knew how insane that sounded.

Dunstan was quick to point out the flaw in his logic. "She's a Malcolm. For all you know, the lot of them want us out of Wystan. When was the last time an Ives could trust his wife?"

There the question stood in all its stark cold logic, asked by the latest victim of an entire string of failed Ives marriages dating back generations.

Why would any sane Ives trust a wife with a history like that to draw on?

The stranger raised eyebrows remarkably like his own, and Drogo scowled at his look of expectation. One more question to be solved—who the devil was this damned Adonis? As far as he was aware, his father was the only son of the earl who had survived adolescence. He supposed there were uncles and cousins elsewhere. Ives weren't precisely a close-knit family, given their tendency to lose wives and children on a regular basis. And the earls had only been gone from these parts for fifty years or so. The features could have carried through several generations.

His mind had wandered from the crux of the matter. Why would an Ives trust his wife?

The crushing weight of that question nearly killed him. Could he believe Ninian's dimpled look of innocent abstraction? Or should he believe the night she'd come to his tower had been a ploy? Would she have forced him to suffer the torment of the damned while he watched her bearing his son for some obscure revenge of her own? She'd told him often enough Malcolm and Ives don't mix. That damned diary proved it.

He thought of Ninian casually scooping up a village child and kissing his cheek, of Ninian scolding his younger brothers back to school, of her surprised and pleased expression when she'd thought she'd conquered the weather just for him.

If he had been fooled by those performances, then he deserved to play the part of fool now. Trusting Ninian and her instincts meant risking the mine, the village, his brothers, and everyone around them. He had to do it, or just give up and die.

He fixed his gaze on the stranger Ninian trusted, the stranger who looked like a slightly older version of himself. Adonis met his gaze squarely, defiantly. Could he trust this man with dynamite and his mine? Ninian would. He would trust her, and keep the man under close watch at all times. He had little choice. Ninian would never leave Wystan while the flood threatened, and saving her and his family held priority.

"Ewen, have the men start digging the holes to plant the charges. Adonis, make up a better name than that of a damned Greek god and take Dunstan with you to fetch the gunpowder."

Adonis dropped his chair to the ground and nodded. Dunstan and Ewen looked at Drogo as if he'd lost his mind.

Drogo ignored them all as he strode for the door. It was damned well time for them to shoulder a few of the responsibilities around here. "If the charge goes off wrong, it could blow up the whole mine and send the river down the valley with it. I'm clearing everyone out of the mine, and then I'm warning the village."

Adonis puffed thoughtfully on his pipe as Drogo slammed into the rain. "Well, hell," he muttered when no one else said a word. "Call me Hades, then."

Thirty-eight

LIGHTNING STRUCK THE OAK IN THE CORNER OF THE GARDEN. Thunder rolled, and children screamed in fright.

Glancing into the growing twilight, Ninian watched someone's rooster float by on a broken cart. The sense of wrongness had grown to overpowering this past hour. She could scarcely think for the fear clouding her mind.

She had to go home.

If she were to have faith in her instincts as Granny said, she had to listen to this one, whatever the risk involved.

She glanced around as mothers settled their small ones down. Whether it was her herbs or her touch or the ale and milk Drogo had sent, the fever seemed to be diminishing. There were no new cases. And almost the entire village had migrated here during the day. The house was packed to over-flowing with both healthy and ill.

Mary had acted as her right hand all day. She knew who needed what. Without giving another thought to the impossibility of what she had to do, Ninian removed her apron and set it on the kitchen table. "I'm going home," she announced.

Everyone within hearing panicked, as she'd known they would. It made no difference. The sense of wrongness con-stricted her chest too badly for logic. Carts couldn't traverse the flooded road. She couldn't ride a horse. But she had two legs. They would carry her.

Mary's husband and Harry, the shoemaker, accompanied her. She didn't know what they thought they would protect her from, but she didn't have time for argument. She cloaked herself as best as she could, hitched up her skirt and petticoat to hold them out of the mud, and set out down the straightest, highest path through the woods.

The men objected. They feared the growing dark and the fairies and whatever haunts they thought inhabited this unexplored territory. Ninian didn't fear anything but fear itself. And she had more than plenty of that to spare.

Ignoring their objections, she hurried on, splashing through puddles larger than those she'd encountered last May. The storm still howled overhead, but she concentrated on chanting it away. Let the men think her mad as well as a witch. It didn't matter. What mattered was in the castle ahead.

The closer she came, the more she felt the panic. It wasn't her panic. Her aunts? The ghost? Drogo? She couldn't tell.

As they reached the once babbling burn at the edge of the cleared portion of the castle yard, Ninian stared at it in bewilderment. Everywhere else the burn had become a raging river. Here, it pushed at the banks, but did not flow over. How could that be?

"Look, look there!" Harry pointed upward, toward the castle.

In the gloom, candles and lamps had been lit. They sparkled through the drizzle from the mullioned windows of the great hall. Most of the bed chambers overlooked the garden in the rear and couldn't be seen. But light gleamed from Drogo's tower—not from the windows at top, but from a crack half way down and widening as it reached the ground.

"The whole thing will fall," Mary's husband predicted, shoving his hands in his pockets and leaning forward as if that would give him a better view.

"We'd better get everyone out of there," Harry suggested, looking toward Ninian for agreement.

Persuade her pampered, light-minded, chattering family out of the warmth and comfort of a castle into the gloom and rain of a storm? Not in this lifetime. Never inclined to logic, they would merely look for the appropriate ritual to repair cracking towers—not that she could remember any ritual as practical as that.

She was beginning to develop some understanding of Drogo's frustration with her.

"The hall will be safe." She hoped. She really didn't know which way towers tumbled when they fell, but it looked like the hall was a safe distance. "We'll have everyone go to the hall."

Giving her doubtful looks but not arguing, the two men assisted her over the rushing water and plodded diligently toward the endangered castle.

❧

"Drogo-o-o!"

The scream exploded in his head as clearly as if the speaker stood beside him.

Startled, Drogo jerked on the reins, and his horse nearly lost its footing in the mud. He stared around the dark woods, but he knew he would see nothing but rain and trees.

Ninian. He was certain he had heard Ninian.

That wasn't possible. Ninian was safe and warm in her grandmother's house, fussing over her village patients. Ninian never screamed.

"Drogo-o-o!"

She was screaming now.

All the panic bubbling and building in his blood these last hours spilled over and erupted, leaving him oddly calm as he kicked his mount into a dangerous gallop. Mud and water flew beneath the horse's hooves, but he was oblivious to the filth coating his breeches and boots. Ninian wouldn't call for him if she didn't need him.

How could Ninian call for him if she wasn't here?

It didn't matter. He gave into instincts he didn't possess, pressing his horse to dangerous paces, leaping streams he would never have crossed had he given it thought. Ninian pounded in his blood. She lived inside his skin as surely as the person he thought he was. She was the soul he'd never had.

He approached the castle from the rear and saw no lights. Perhaps Adonis had been wrong. Perhaps Ninian's family hadn't arrived. He should continue on to the village, but he needed to check on Alan...

He needed to check on Ninian. She was here. He could feel it.

Abandoning all logic, he smacked the animal into the stable and rushed for the side door. He'd send someone else to the village to be certain everyone was on high ground. He had to see to the safety of his wife and son.

He heard the low murmur of chanting voices as soon as he entered.

Cursing the darkness, cursing his stupidity in panicking, Drogo threw off his soaked cloak and hat and strode swiftly toward the great hall. He hadn't the patience for the social niceties of greeting Ninian's family. He just needed to see that everything was all right, warn the villagers, and send Ninian packing. Somehow.

Ninian exploded through the doorway into his arms before he reached the hall.

"Drogo, the tower! It's cracking. The stones are falling out. It's crumbling to the ground. I don't know what to do. I'm so glad you're here!"

She flung herself into his arms, and he wrapped her close, relieved beyond bearing that she was safe and whole and his. The screams in his head were just that—screams. He'd panicked. He knew better than to panic.

"It's all right," he soothed. "Is everyone safe and dry? Where is Alan?"

"We're all in the hall. Water is seeping down the tower stairs. I was afraid the tower would topple on the roof. Aunt Hermione is chanting the storm away, but it doesn't seem to be working. And the ghost is screaming inside my head."

He held her steady just to steady himself. "That tower has stood for hundreds of years. It's not going anywhere. Is Alan well?" Even as he reassured her, he remembered the explosion his brothers planned. How far would the quake travel? Would they stop the water's flow or worsen it? How would that affect the tower? It stood nearer the burn than the rest of the castle.

"Alan is fine. My cousins are keeping him entertained, but he's fussy and crying. I need to go back to him. Please, Drogo, look at the tower. Something just isn't right."

He knew better now than to argue with Ninian's instincts. Disregarding his muddy clothing, he caught her close and pressed a kiss to her willing lips. They molded eagerly to his, and he drank deeply. Tonight, he would have her. She was ready, and he no longer doubted anything about her. He didn't know how it was possible, but they were one and inseparable and he trusted her as he trusted himself.

"I'll check the tower," he promised as he reluctantly pulled back. "Ewen is planning to explode gunpowder to dam the mine water. Warn the others they might feel vibrations. I must send someone to the village to be certain everyone is on high ground."

"They're all at my grandmother's. There is no higher." She watched him with worry. "Are you sure that's safe? If the ground vibrates…"

He didn't know the answer. He pressed a kiss to her forehead. "Tell your aunts to chant for safety instead of annoying Mother Nature."

"I will. Harry and Mary's husband are here. Shall I send them to you?"

"With lanterns, if you will."

She hesitated a moment longer, searching his face. "Drogo, I understand why you do not always believe me. I know I do not always behave as you think I ought…"

Impatient to check the tower, he almost didn't listen, but something in her voice halted him. She had told him he didn't *listen*, but he wanted to learn. Perhaps his impatience stemmed from dealing with people who didn't have the same level of intelligence as he, but while Ninian may not understand many things he said, she understood much more than he did about some things.

"And I do not behave as you think I ought," he reminded her. "Is there something bothering you?"

Her face lit with relief. "Yes, yes, and I know you won't like it, but the cries in my head are warnings. It's as if the ghost is trying to reach me, but…" She shrugged helplessly. "She doesn't know the words. I see a dark hole and water and the crack in the tower but I cannot understand it. They're pictures, not words. I have never had this happen before. It's a very odd feeling."

He wanted to dismiss this silliness. He wanted to tell her she was hysterical, but it was patently obvious she was not. She was worried, maybe frightened, but she was trying to explain something she did not understand herself. And she had been right one too many times before. Fear gripped his stomach.

"Keep everyone in one place. Keep the lantern well-trimmed. Stay near the door. If the hall begins to shake, if you sense any danger, leave. Go to the stable. That should be solid enough."

She nodded and gripped his coat sleeve with relief. "I'm so glad you're here. I was afraid you wouldn't hear me call."

With that enigmatic comment, she ran back to warn the others.

She'd called him? And he'd heard?

Perhaps there was more to being one inseparable soul after all.

Drogo was already studying the widening crack at the base of the tower by the time Harry and Mary's husband arrived bearing lanterns. The light revealed what he already feared—the underlying foundation was bulging outward. He wasn't a mechanical genius like Ewen, but it didn't take much to understand that some pressure was building against the inside wall. It didn't take much more logic to combine Ninian's warnings with his own knowledge and common sense: water was flooding beneath the castle.

"Did this place have a dungeon?" he asked while trying to visualize the schematics of the castle's lowest floor.

"Don't know, but most of these old towers did," Harry answered, poking at the crumbling mortar and watching the water stream through from the rain outside.

"The conservatory!" Ninian rushed down the dark hall toward them. "The conservatory bars the old entrance! I can see it. They filled in the moat and built on top of it. There was a door."

Drogo couldn't doubt her now. Dashing out in the mud and rain to knock holes in walls because his wife believed a ghost's warning proved that his brain was as cracked as hers, but he had no better solution. The whole damned tower would topple on to the roof if he did nothing, and he couldn't swear the roof would hold beneath the weight.

Only Ninian could drive him to this insanity.

"The water must have found a way into an old tunnel, but there's no way for it to escape. We'll have to find the weakest spot in the foundation and dig it out."

"Somewhere near the conservatory. Between it and the kitchen. There used to be a garden." Ninian looked pained and confused as she said it.

Drogo took her in his arms and squeezed her. "We'll take care of it, moonchild. Just tell your family to chant for safety and leave the weather alone. It's not the weather that's at fault. Your very strange Adonis told me to tell you that."

"*My* Adonis? He's an Ives if ever there was one."

"Claims to be half Malcolm, my dear. Go entertain your cousins with that."

He loved the incredulous light in her eyes as she looked up at him. He loved her. With every fiber of his being. He didn't even know what the damn hell love was, but he recognized it, through her.

"Go," he whispered. "Trust in me."

She smiled. "I do." And she was gone.

Thirty-nine

THEY HAD DUG A HOLE TO THE FOUNDATION AND WERE IN MUD
up to their ears when the explosion rocked the very ground
they stood on.

In the rain and gloom, they could hear the ghastly creak of
the cracking mortar as the ground shook and water pounded
against stone.

"Out!" Drogo shouted, shoving the nearest man from the
hole while his other helper scrambled out the back.

Before Drogo could follow, a flood of water crashed
through the hole, tumbling him backward in a surging tide,
carrying him helplessly toward the raging burn.

"*Drogo!*" Ninian screamed as the two men carried the inert
figure of her husband through the front doors.

She thought her heart would tear from her throat with her
sob as she ran toward them. He was so pale… Drogo was
never pale.

Behind her, the chanting deteriorated to a murmur of questioning voices, but she had no mind for her family. Even the
ghost had quit screaming in her head. Her only thought was
of the man they lay upon the hearth, where the fire's warmth
could dry him.

Except he looked as if no fire would ever warm him again.

"We're sorry, my lady," Harry whispered, removing his hat

as Ninian fell to her knees beside her husband's still form. "He saved us first, and 'twere too late for him. We pulled him from the burn down by the road."

"Drogo," Ninian whispered, testing for a heartbeat, breathing, anything...

He was nearly blue with cold, and she couldn't find any sign of life. Panic welled, but she refused to give into it. The physical presence that flowed between them pounded through her blood where she touched him. Blocking out the grief and consternation of the people hovering around her, blocking out all but the man who held her heart in his, she sought deep within her where instinct dwelled and let the healing power guide her.

Her fist crashed into his chest. Solid bone and muscle hurt her hand, but she pounded again, and again, forcing his heart to acknowledge her presence. If she could find Drogo anywhere, it was through his heart. He hid it from others, but she knew it was a large one, that he loved and loved deeply but simply didn't know how to express it. She would wake up his heart if it killed her.

Faintly, the beat thrummed beneath her fingers, and she instantly fell on his mouth. She would breathe life into his lungs now, breathe in the air his heart needed to expand.

Someone tried to pull her away, thinking her gone mad with grief, but she shook them off. She was strong. They couldn't take her where she didn't wish to go.

Hermione started a new chant, a chant of birth and life, and Ninian breathed with relief, pouring the air she gulped between the lips of the man in her arms, pushing on his chest, forcing his heart to pump and his lungs to take what she offered. Tears streamed down her cheeks as she breathed and pumped and her arms trembled. She could do this. God had given her more Gifts than she'd ever accepted. She could feel Drogo's heart, his lungs, his soul. He was here with her. She knew it. She just needed to reach him.

A surge of warmth and love flooded up her fingers, seeping from all the places she touched him, swamping her with a giddy ecstasy that had tears streaming down her cheeks as she realized they emanated from the man beneath her.

He gasped and choked on a breath, and cheers resounded among the non-Malcolms at this sign of life. The women continued chanting, adding their spirit to Ninian's, warming her, returning her strength, holding her in this moment so she didn't disappear entirely into that place inside her where she'd found the knowledge and healing she needed. She wept and collapsed against Drogo's chest as it heaved up and down.

Instinctively, his arms circled and held her close.

Her aunts and cousins crowed in triumph and crowded around.

Sarah ran up with blankets and dry clothes. "I don't think I can do what they do," she whispered to Ninian as she lay the garments beside her. "But I do know when a man is wet and cold. Drogo hates being cold."

Ninian's smile wavered only slightly as she nodded, and Sarah backed away. Sarah was confused about many things, but her heart was in the right place.

Drogo coughed again, and she debated whether she should push on his chest some more. When she tried to stir from his arms, he pulled her closer.

"Don't move," he croaked. "Don't you dare move."

Laughing, crying, she buried her face against his chest and let him dig his fingers into her hair. He was alive, and he was the same odiously demanding man he'd always been, and she loved him dearly. And he loved her. She could feel it, at last. She thought she would drown in the flood of emotion pouring from him. It was a good thing he normally dammed it up.

"You're soaked, my lord. You will catch your death if we do not dry you out." She was soaked, too, from lying upon him, but the heat flooding through his body was so welcome, she didn't mind the damp.

"I have a distinct feeling I have already caught my death and you called me back." His eyes popped open, and he lifted her chin to study her face. "You *are* a witch."

She watched him silently, to see how he accepted that knowledge. She was just beginning to understand some of the enormity of it herself, although she still didn't believe in magic. This hadn't been magic. This had been some deep, underlying knowledge she'd called upon in time of need. A Gift. Not magic.

Drogo stared into the innocent blue that mirrored his own amazement and knew the wall about his heart had cracked as wide as the tower foundation, and love spilled as free as the burn's water. She was the part of him that was missing, the soul he'd never known, the love he'd never expressed. Her breath breathed inside of him now.

"Consider me bewitched," he added as a small frown of worry began to crease her brow. "I'll love you until the stars stop shining and beyond. Now tell all those women to go away and get me out of these damned clothes."

She grinned and swallowed the tears she'd been holding back. He could see the tracks of them down her shiny cheeks. His little witch was here with him completely, not in some world of her own making. It shook him to know how much she cared.

"Perhaps we should go to our room, my lord," she suggested with a wicked smile.

That was the best idea he'd heard in a long time.

∽

Stripping off their mud-soaked clothes, they stood naked, warming themselves before the fire, clasped in each other's arms, flesh to flesh.

"I haven't changed," Drogo warned. "I'm still the man you've berated and accused of stubbornness and lack of understanding."

"I love that man," she murmured contentedly from within his embrace. "And I'll still yell at you for your denseness. And prick your arrogance until you're forced to see the world around you. Just tell me you love me again, and I'll accept your obtuseness."

He smiled against her hair and drew his hand down over a well-rounded posterior, snuggling her closer to where he needed her. "I'll tell you every morning when we wake, and every night before we go to sleep. But I'll never admit such foolishness in public."

She chuckled, and he could feel the vibrations deep in his chest.

"I will. I'll yell it at the top of my lungs and embarrass you daily. Every time you do something stupid, I will yell my love at you."

"That should cure me," he admitted dryly. "My brothers will laugh me into an early grave."

"Your brothers," Ninian whispered, sliding upward so their bodies brushed against each other as she kissed his jaw, "need to stay in school where they belong. Then we would need not visit London so often."

Thoughtfully, he played a devastating tune upon her breast. "Sarah may have the London house, and they may run to her. You and I will visit Ives and your families when we must travel. Will that be far enough from the city for you?"

"You shield me from the city," she murmured, exploring his chest as he explored hers. "You just must accept my responsibilities are here. I can train Lydie—"

He covered her mouth with his, and she nearly drowned again in the heat and love he offered. For this, she would do anything.

He released her mouth, and their gazes met. She stumbled down the deep tunnel he opened into his soul.

"Our responsibilities are one and the same, equal. We will work it out, moonchild."

And she believed him.

He kissed her forehead, then seared a trail along her throat, drawing closer to the tempting pout of full nipples. "Tell me the time is right, that the moon is in its proper phase, and that you want what I want."

She caught his hair and tugged until he lifted his head and looked down at her.

As she met his gaze and struck him with the full brunt of her adoration, Drogo nearly staggered beneath the enormity of it. The woman breathed love, bathed him in it, and eased all the nagging doubts always simmering beneath his surface. If he just let himself *feel* instead of inquiring into the logic of it, he would never question their marriage again. The bane of Ives marriages was too much logic and not enough trust.

"For you, the moon is always in its proper phase. I want your children, Drogo. I want you. Take me to your stars."

He didn't require further reassurance. Carrying her to the downy warmth of the bed, he covered her with his body and pulled the feather-stuffed covers over them.

"Is the tower safe?" she inquired as he nibbled her ear and tried to absorb all the nuances of her giving curves beneath him.

"The pressure is gone. It shouldn't tumble just yet." With a moan of delight, he cupped her breasts and felt her swift intake of breath as he caressed the tips.

"It stopped raining," she whispered against his ear.

Just the brush of her breath aroused him to the point of driving need. But he wanted to savor this moment. His wife, his love, the mate of his soul… He'd never thought such a thing possible. "The stars are out," he agreed, stroking lower, bringing her hips closer to his. "We're safe, and I want to lose myself in you and not discuss the weather."

She quivered as he touched her where she was wet. "In that case," she murmured with a groan as she arched into him, "we didn't cause the flood this time."

With that utterly inexplicable, illogical statement, she stroked him, and incapable of anything else, Drogo drove deep inside her, where they understood one another on levels beyond the ken of mankind.

❧

In the hall below, Alan slept contentedly for the first time all evening. Hermione rocked him in her arms and watched without surprise as the massive front doors flung open and two thoroughly soaked Ives men stumbled through.

Her eldest daughter, Leila, lifted her swanlike neck and watched the newcomers through provocatively lowered lashes. "The murderer and the inventor," she murmured in a suggestive voice, "but not the Malcolm. Interesting. Shall I see if an Ives suits me?"

Hermione looked to the sleeping babe in her arms, glanced

to the brawny Ives men dripping across the floor, and decided not to issue the usual warning to her daughter. Ninian had never finished reading Ceridwen's diary, but Hermione had read the ending first. Driven mad with grief, Ceridwen had sworn to lock herself in her husband's tower until he loved her again. In a notation in a very male hand, the diary claimed she'd died there, and her husband had sealed off the room so no other could ever suffer the same fate.

Ceridwen's ghost was free at last.

Perhaps the legends of Malcolms and Ives needed a few more stories told.

Epilogue

BLAZING SPARKS LEAPED HIGH INTO THE NIGHT SKY AS THE Beltane fire roared heavenward and the fiddle struck up a dance. Laughing figures rushed to throw their branches on the flames, then danced off in each other's arms.

On the outskirts of the clearing, in the twilight between fire and forest, Ninian smiled at the merriment.

"I heard Nate married a miner's daughter." Gertrude lifted her fussy babe to her shoulder and watched as a new crop of maids and bachelors wove a spell of seduction in the fire's light. "Seems the miners don't take well to men who won't accept responsibility, and they were a little harsh with him."

"He has twins." Ninian tried to muffle her laughter at Nate's fate. "Imagine how many wee ones he'll have at his feet in a few years time."

Gertrude glanced at the teething babe on her shoulder. "One is enough for a while. You're a lifesaver."

Tapping her toe to the music, Ninian merely shrugged, then slowly smiled as a tall, dark figure emerged from the forest's edge. Even after all these months, her heart pattered faster at his approach.

He'd been off inspecting the new dam at the mines, ensuring that the dangerous runoff never harmed the burn again. She'd missed him.

Drogo didn't ask, didn't speak at all as he reached for her hand, drawing her toward the music and the dancing. He merely watched her face with that studious expression she loved so well, and finding what he sought, smiled and guided her into the steps.

They twirled and laughed and let the rhythms of the night sweep through them, knowing with the confidence of lovers how the night would end, with no need to hasten the thrill of excitement coursing through them.

An earl was too lofty a personage for his tenants and the villagers to approach, but on a night like this, with a keg of good ale to share and the music to blend them, even an earl wasn't a stranger. Ninian laughed as she danced off with Harry, leaving Drogo to discuss sheep breeding with Nate's father. Drogo knew nothing about sheep breeding, but he would learn, she had no doubt.

As the moon slipped down the far side of the sky, he returned to claim her, dancing her into the shadows outside the fire's light where the murmurs of other couples blended with the cries of night birds and the rustle of other nocturnal creatures, and the pounding thrill of their blood matched the thrum of the earth.

"Now," Drogo commanded, flinging his cloak over a bed of pine needles and drawing her into his embrace. "I'll not wait another minute."

"It's Beltane," she teased, slipping the buttons of his waistcoat from their holes and seeking the heat of his chest. "A night of power. Can you not feel it?" The vibration thrummed through her fingertips as she rubbed against him and his grip tightened. "A child conceived tonight—"

"Don't tell me," he groaned, attempting to unfasten her fingers from his clothing. "The moon is in its proper phase, and unless I wish to spend next winter in Wystan, I'd better keep my breeches buttoned."

"Well, I did agree to spend winters in the south with you," she murmured demurely, deftly avoiding his hands and reaching for the breeches buttons he'd just deflected. "And the moon is definitely in its proper phase. We would make lovely babies tonight."

"No." Firmly, he caught her wandering hands and held

them back. "I want you healed and healthy and well recovered before we even think about it. And then if you insist on having our babes here, I want them in the summer so I can summon physicians and midwives and your damned family can arrive on time to help you. You are more important to me and Alan than this moment's pleasure."

"I do so adore you, Drogo." She stood on tiptoe and kissed his jaw, then moved to cover his mouth with her own. While so engaged, she drew her wrists from his grip and reached for his buttons again.

"Ninian," he moaned in protest against her mouth, trying to hold her and catch her hands while not releasing her lips.

"It's all right," she murmured, finally parting the ties of his shirt and neckcloth and running her hands through the crinkle of curls on his chest. "This is sheep country. I have a present for you. I even wove a ribbon around it. If you're very, very good, we will not have to worry about the phases of the moon tonight."

"You *are* a witch," he muttered as he parted her bodice and slipped his hands beneath. "And you'd best be talking about what I think you are talking about."

"I've shown *all* the women how to make them," she replied after gasping for breath from his thorough kiss. She blinked in amazement at the night sky overhead. How had she come to be lying down already?

"Excellent. I'll have Ewen establish a manufactory just to supply all my brothers," Drogo replied with a hint of grimness as he kneeled between her legs and his hand slid up her thigh. "Why didn't you think of this sooner? Joseph has just written me for an increase in his allowance to cover his new dolly bird."

She sighed as he touched her where she needed to be touched. "I made certain they all have samples." She cried out as he suddenly withdrew and glared down at her. She smiled back. "Dunstan delivered them. Surely you did not think I—"

He caught her mouth with his and drowned any further protest.

When he finally surged into her, ribbons and sheath and all,

Ninian was already halfway to the moon and ready to fly to the stars. He took her there and back, showed her the heavens from his perspective, then held her gently as they tumbled back to earth again, where she reigned.

"Has the Society verified your finding of a new planet yet?" she whispered, still spinning among the stars although Drogo's heavy weight pressed her into the earth.

"Our equipment needs refining. I would ask Ewen, but it is a full-time task to keep him focused on the foundry. We can wait." With care, Drogo rolled on his back, carrying her with him. Now he could see the stars while holding heaven in his arms. "He has decided the chemicals in the runoff from the mine might be useful in some foolish notion or another, and I have had to persuade him that he must spend his days on something that can provide him with a living and use his spare hours on his less profitable ideas."

"He'll learn. You have taught your brothers well. They're almost all on their own now. Have you heard from Dunstan?"

Reluctantly, Drogo adjusted her wool skirt to cover her more warmly. "The lack of all that frippery women wear is a definite advantage to this place," he murmured.

Ninian propped her elbows on his chest and lifting her eyebrows in the same manner as he did.

He grinned at the result. "I could keep you in nothing but shifts in London. It's warmer there."

"Not that warm. Now what have you heard from Dunstan?" she demanded sternly.

Drogo sighed and rested his gaze on the beauty revealed by her open bodice. "He is working as steward on one of your uncle's estates and sending his earnings to Celia's mother and younger sister. You didn't have to send him away from Ives," he grumbled. "They have no evidence against him."

Drogo had men searching high and low for Celia's murderer. Dunstan might carry the weight of guilt, but he could no more have murdered his silly wife than Drogo could murder Ninian. He would prove that, someday. Drogo couldn't change the fact that his son would now inherit the estate and title that Dunstan had once thought his.

"He didn't murder Celia, trust me," Ninian murmured, reaffirming her beliefs. "And I didn't send him anywhere. He chose not to take any more of your earnings. I will never understand the workings of a male mind." Tauntingly, she leaned forward so her breasts brushed against his chest.

"You understand this part too damned well." He lifted her so he could taste the ripe fruit she offered and almost forgot where they were until he heard her cries echoed elsewhere. Deciding this was not a respectable thing for an earl to do twice, he reluctantly pulled back.

She punished him by rolling off and buttoning her bodice. "This part has nothing to do with minds," she said firmly, although Drogo noticed with interest that her hands shook and her nipples definitely appeared ready for plucking.

He stopped her progress by sliding his hand beneath the cloth and giving her what she wanted. "It's all of one piece. This—" He pressed a kiss to the place his hand fondled. "—eases the mind so it can function properly. We'll need to test that theory."

She laughed and slapped him away. "If your mind functioned any better than it does now, we would never get anything done. I found agrimony near the burn today."

"Did you?" Some other time, he might have cared, but she was escaping him now, and he wasn't done. Hastily, he fastened a few buttons so he could leap up after her.

Her back toward him, she shook her skirt out. "Life is returning all along the bank. Adonis was right. It had to be the runoff from the mines. But just in case, I shall gather seeds as they appear and try to start them in the conservatory."

"We're going to London, remember?" He pulled her back against him and rested his chin on her hair. "Have you seen Adonis and squeezed some answers out of him?"

"He'll tell us in his own time. I haven't seen him since the explosion. I think he went off with Dunstan. And I'm teaching Lydie about herbs. She learns quickly, and she's teaching Mary's sister. I don't see why it must be just Malcolm women who learn these things. All women can be educated."

Uh-oh, they were moving swiftly into one of her latest crackbrained notions. Knowing better than to argue, Drogo cupped her breast, regretting that she had already covered it. "Sarah is still disappointed that we never uncovered any treasure, even after digging out the tower foundation and replacing it. It must have been the hole in the foundation that caused the shrieks."

Ninian laughed, a crystal clear chime that rang through the night as she snuggled closer into his arms.

"The ghost spoke, and we have found the treasure," she informed him as Drogo wrapped his arms about her waist and she dropped her head against his shoulder to smile up at him. "It is just not the gold and jewels that Sarah wants."

He lifted his brows and waited.

Her lips bowed into that enigmatic curve he loved so dearly as she replied, "The only curse on Malcolm and Ives is our inability to learn from our differences."

"I'm learning," he declared, staring down at her innocent expression in bewilderment. "What has that to do with the ghost's predictions?"

"Everything." Her laughter lit the sky as she turned and wrapped her arms around his neck and obliterated all thought with her kiss.

༺ྀ

And so, a new legend appeared in the *Tales of Malcolm and Ives*.

About the Author

Patricia Rice was born in New York but learned to love the warmer Southeast. She is now California dreaming and working her way West by way of St. Louis. Improving houses and then moving is apparently her hobby. She is married with two grown children who also have settled in warmer climes. She would love you to stop by www.patriciarice.com to see what she's doing now or join her at Facebook at http://www.facebook.com/PatriciaRiceBooks and on Twitter at https://twitter.com/Patricia_Rice.

Watch for the NEW title in the Magic series
by Patricia Rice

The Lure of Song and Magic

Coming from Sourcebooks Casablanca in January 2012